The Aurora Aura

The Aurora Aura

Mark Joseph Good

Photos provided by the author
Book Design by Nancy R. Koucky, NRK Designs

Aurora Aura is published by Okos Owl Publishing

Printed and manufactured
in the United States of America

This book is dedicated to the life and memory of my friend,
Mitzi Campbell Babb.
Mitzi was a believer in paranormal activity.
She was a lover of animals, nature and life.
She was a follower of the Wiccan Faith.

Sadly, she was murdered by an individual that lived in darkness.
The attached image was drawn by me as a gift to her, over 6 years ago.
It is my rendition of Mitzi as a Woodland Sprite but designed after the
attached photograph of her. It is currently worn by a friend of hers as a
tattoo. That individual is a friend that I have yet to meet,
but feel that I know her through Mitzi.

RIP little sprite.
Yes, I love you too.
Mark

About the Author

Mark Joseph Good was born and raised in Baltimore, Maryland. His adventurous life took him to Colorado where he worked in the logging industry and to Florida where he became a scuba divemaster, a jeweler, and a master falconer. He spent a career as a highly decorated wildland firefighter with the Florida Forest Service. After retiring in 2018, he had time to focus on his creative pursuits: music, art, and writing. His first book, *Come Fly With Me: Tales from a Master Falconer,* is a collection of stories about the sport of falconry and Mark's bond with his birds of prey. The Aurora Aura weaves a story that includes his Hungarian/Jewish heritage, the paranormal, and a love story. When Mark isn't writing he can be found spending time with his Eurasian Eagle Owl, Thorin Oakenshield, and his loyal bloodhound, Remi, tending his orchid collection or driving in the country in his classic Corvette.

Acknowledgments

I would like to thank everyone who has supported my writings thus far. *The Aurora Aura* is my second attempt at putting pen to paper. My first handwritten attempt was *Come Fly With Me: Tales From A Master Falconer.*

I would like to thank a distant relative for his gift to us all. László Joseph Biro. In 1938, he invented the ballpoint pen and sold the rights for $16,000. As I handwrite all of my books, I have used many of the pens that he invented. Thank you.

Why do I handwrite my manuscripts you might ask?

The answer is that I am partially handicapped in my left hand and arm due to multiple injuries that damaged that part of my body. I simply cannot use a keypad as my wrist does not turn. It forces me to handwrite all documents.

Enter a dear friend since 1987. Juanice Shelton Christian and I met and worked together for the Forest Service. Many years passed but we stayed in touch. She volunteered to be my typist, a first draft editor, and a sounding board of sorts as I would bounce ideas off of her almost daily as I created both books. When I decided to create my own publishing company, she was there for that too.

Trying to create a name was difficult and I learned quickly that most of my thoughts were not original. They were already taken. I wanted the name to represent intelligence. Being bright or smart. Like Smart Owl Publishing. It sounded more like Smart Ass Owl Publishing, so I declined. It was Juanice who asked me if the use of a

Hungarian word would please me. (my mother's side of the family is Hungarian)."Okos." Okos means clever in Hungarian. "Okos Owl Publishing". Clever Owl. Yes, that was it! Thank you, Juanice! For everything.

Thank you to Nancy Koucky, owner of NRK Designs for cover designs and book layout on both of my books. Nancy also assisted me with many other aspects of the publishing world including getting my books registered and displayed on social media and in stores. This was not exactly in her job description so I offer a special thank you. It's been a semi-rough road. Thanks again, Nancy.

Lastly, thanks to Janos Jozef Fonod in St. Louis. Four years ago he gave me a black and tan bloodhound, Remi. She is the best dog that I have ever owned and is my constant companion as I write. Thanks, man. Much appreciated.

They say that "it takes a village to raise a child." My books are my children.

Table of Contents

Prologue

Lazlo Joseph Somogyi, MD was the son of Jewish/Hungarian immigrants who were displaced from their homeland during World War II. He was born in the United States of America in a small coal mining town outside of Ward, West Virginia. Calling it a town is an overstatement, as Ward was barely a village at that time. His family resided in little more than a coal mining encampment of makeshift cabins, or shacks, that were erected by "the company", as most people referred to it in the area. The company owned everything. They constructed their makeshift villages for employees, which were little more than derelict "slave" communities, where once there, very few ever managed to leave unless flat on their backs in a box.

The company owned the local store. A facility that allowed families to purchase essential items in order to survive. The store allowed a credit line to each employee, which, because wages were so low, kept them in debt to the company. Over time, songs would be written about owing one's soul to the company store.

Many of Lazlo's family back in Europe never managed to escape the gas chambers of Nazi Germany. They perished there in misery, alone and afraid. But the Somogyi family made it to America and so they were given a chance at freedom. Even if that freedom sometimes felt like a kind of slavery, it still tasted sweet. It also promised a life that had no limitations, if you were willing to work hard for it. Even as a boy, Lazlo knew that he was capable of working hard.

Lazlo's father was named Julius. He had no middle name.

Simply Julius Somogyi. It was common in Hungary that names were chosen this way. Lazlo's mother was named Eztar. Eztar Biro originally, until she married Julius. Then, of course, she proudly became Eztar Somogyi.

Julius and Eztar had dreamt of coming to the United States and starting a family while living in the land of freedom. They had achieved their goals thus far, but their dreams were far greater than anyone in the coal mines ever knew.

Eztar was known by many as a healer and a sort of midwife. She wanted her firstborn to be an American doctor. It was because of this desire that Julius and Eztar decided to give their son a full name. He would have a middle name to honor their family. A name for which he could be proud: Doctor Lazlo Joseph Somogyi, MD.

Eztar knew in her heart that somehow, just somehow, they could make this happen. Eztar's personal family bloodline was one of gypsy ancestry. They were known as soothsayers. Some even called them "white witches". Eztar didn't care for that at all. She was born some twenty-five years earlier "under the veil", which meant as a newborn child, she had a thin membrane covering her face that needed to be removed immediately after birth. This was a spiritual sign that she would grow to have special abilities and an understanding about life that others would not have.

This included the power of premonition and psychic ability. These were common traits that were attached to being born in this manner. There were others born this way in her family line. Eztar's grandmother Mary shared this trait and taught Eztar a lot as her daughter grew from child to woman.

Eztar also knew that she had a great responsibility to educate her son. So, she did all that she could, but somehow her heart was heavy, as she knew that certain sacrifices would need to be made for him to succeed.

Lazlo was a smart child who would soon grow into an intelligent twelve year old. He was creative and resourceful, never failing to impress his mother with his ability to achieve. Oddly, he was good in the kitchen and loved assisting his mother with her recipes. He understood that the slightest change in ingredients could make a meal either wonderful or a catastrophic failure. Food was far too rare to risk failure, so Lazlo was careful to do it correctly. Eztar knew that his time in the kitchen was very much like a chemistry lab that would assist him in becoming a doctor.

Every chance that he could get, Lazlo would hang out with all the men socializing together after a long, hard day underground in the mines. This was their chance to drink and smoke while the miners told stories of their plans in America. Many also shared experiences from back in Hungary, telling tall tales that kept Lazlo intrigued with every word. He often wondered where the alcohol came from, considering the limited money available here in the camps.

Over time, and after much alcohol consumption, a few of the men began to trust him and shared a secret that only the men shared between themselves. They made their own moonshine, white lightning, or corn liquor.

Eventually, the men showed Lazlo how, and more importantly, where it was done. Corn could be purchased on credit at the company store and if each man contributed his part, nobody would be the wiser that it was being made into booze.

One of the much older men, a fellow named Steven, took Lazlo to his still and told him that he had decided to quit making the elixir that was desired by so many. He would give it all to this young boy so the product would continue under new management. Lazlo saw this arrangement as a way to make money to help pay for his education one day.

Piece by piece, Lazlo moved the still to the crawlspace under his family shack and attempted his first batch of moonshine. His dog, Blackie, curiously watched his every move wondering exactly what his human was trying to do. Blackie hated the smell. Lazlo made sure that no one was home on that particular day, and this was probably a good thing.

After starting the fire under the still, he and Blackie crawled out to solid ground just in time to witness the still explode! It blew the entire back corner off the home.

Lazlo knew that he couldn't hide from his mistake and he certainly couldn't lie and blame someone else. He was raised to stand behind his shortcomings or accidents. But he knew there would be hell to pay when his father returned home from the mines. He expected less of a reaction from his mother. She would be disappointed in him and say something simple but true, that would make him feel the guilt of a thousand sins committed by his ancestors.

Mothers could do that to their sons. It was a highly developed and treasured skill, especially with Hungarian women. Lazlo would rather face the belt from his father. It would be painful for a time, but the injury would heal much faster than his heart.

When his mother returned home to finish cooking dinner for the family, she completed a fine Hungarian stew called *Pörkölt* that she had left simmering on the stove. The stove was an old wood burner, so low heat was achieved by the use of coals from the heating fire of the night before. In the United States, the name *Pörkölt* was called *Goulash,* written as *Gulyás* in Hungarian. These things happen over time and traditions are easily lost. Either way, Lazlo loved his mother's cooking and he hoped that he wouldn't miss out tonight as a punishment for his accidental behavior.

Eztar didn't notice the missing back corner of her home until after she entered the front door. Her mouth dropped open in shock, her knees buckled, and she fell to the floor.

Lazlo tried to catch her, with little success, and she began sobbing. She could see daylight straight through the house. The rear walls and floor were completely shattered, and gone.

The remains of the still lay in pieces, charred, surrounded by the crater caused by the explosion. Eztar regained her composure and stood up for a closer look. Before a word could be said, Lazlo started to explain exactly what happened, and how the still exploded. He was crying now too, the guilt washing over him in waves.

"I'm sorry Momma! I'm so sorry! It was an accident…I got the recipe wrong!" His innocence touched her deeply as she gazed into the swollen eyes of her young man. This was her son and she believed every word he said. The two of them crumpled together as Lazlo dropped to the floor.

"I believe you my son…every breath that you speak. It was a terrible mistake and I thank Jesus that you were not killed."

Eztar held his face in her hands while kissing the tears from his cheeks and uttered a simple but profound statement, that at the moment he did not understand.

"Lazlo…you my son, are a *White Lighter, … Fehér öngyújtó*. I saw it in you the day that you were born, and I see it in you today. You are pure of heart and close to your God. There is no deceit here. I will speak to your father when he returns home. You have nothing to fear. Now let's get this mess cleaned up."

When Julius arrived home hours later, Lazlo had worked hard to clean things up as best he could. He covered the giant hole with a wagon tarp until woodwork could be completed the next day. Eztar stopped Julius at the front door. He sensed something was out of the ordinary.

"Julius my love…we need to talk. There was an accident here today that damaged the back of our home. Lazlo caused it, but I don't want him punished. He's a special boy." She explained what happened while keeping her husband calm because many more important things needed to be said.

"Julius *szerelmem…Újra gyerekkel vagyunk*"

"Julius my love…we are once again with child."

So much in one day: The shock of the explosion, the happiness of a new child. Julius was overwhelmed and he too began to cry, but these were tears of joy!

Lazlo joined his parents on the front porch, not knowing why they cried over a simple *moonshine still* explosion. He continued to be afraid that his father would take a belt to him as punishment. He was shocked when Julius pulled him in close to his chest, hugging Eztar and him at the same time while kissing their faces repeatedly. Blackie sensed the positive atmosphere and jumped onto the happy group while wagging his tail, barking, and licking them all in their faces.

"*Le a kutya… kérlek, szállj le*"

"Down dog…please get down."

But it was said in a happy way, between laughs and tears. This was another moment to make this family stronger. Relatives had been killed in Germany, but God was giving them another child and they were thankful.

Any pregnancy can be dangerous. Millions of children are born around the world, and nothing goes wrong for the most part. Sadly, many are not successful, so a woman worries. Eztar, being a midwife, knew these risks. She also knew that she was the only woman living in these mines who possessed such skills. She prayed to her God every day to help her and provide the strength she needed to get through this mother's ordeal.

The months went by quickly, and she watched her belly grow. She knew, without doubt, that this baby was another boy. He was the unborn baby brother for Lazlo. Life was good. Premonitions were coming true. Eztar was happy. However, deep in her heart, she knew of the sacrifice that was coming to test her in the near future. She kept reminding herself that God sacrificed his son, to save mankind. Who was she to challenge her destiny?

The owner of the coal mine knew of the pregnancy for some time. He also knew how financially difficult it was to survive here, even without children. His heart ached for this family and had concerns for their safety and survival. Almost a year ago, he personally paid to have the damages from the explosion repaired. No one requested it. The community was going to pitch in, but he intervened and took care of it himself. He even paid the local men extra to complete the project. He liked Julius and Eztar…Lazlo too. He wasn't sure why, just a very strange feeling of obligation, like saving a lost puppy on the side of the road. But he followed his heart, and his heart said to help.

"My God…they don't even know my name?" His name was Laird Conner. He too, was an immigrant. He, too, understood the need to survive here in this new world. On this thought, he swore to himself to assist this family in any way that he could. "Tomorrow, I will tell them my name."

"Meanwhile, Eztar will need a real doctor. I will take care of that too." With these thoughts in mind, he walked off into the night to travel home to his wife and three children. They needed to know his plans, too.

Mr. Laird Conner was successful. He owned a large home with property. He owned a car, a wagon and several horses. The bank owned the coal mine, but the arrangement was financially a good one. He loved his wife and children, but something about the housing conditions, and the manner in which these kinds of companies functioned, troubled him. He wanted to do better. The Somogyi family would be a start.

Conner also had a family doctor that made house calls. He would ask him to visit Eztar soon.

Dr. Steven Joseph Sherlous, MD visited the Somogyi home with Mr. Conner on Monday morning. Eztar was surprised, but Laird quickly explained the arrangement to her and had already made sure that Julius would be present for this meeting. He even paid him for his time, a thing unheard of in this industry.

Eztar and Julius were confused, but Eztar sensed this was an ordained moment and that she should not question God. She convinced Julius that it was good and agreed to an exam. She was almost nine months pregnant. Eztar was feeling much better knowing that a real doctor was there, in her home.

Dr. Sherlous performed a routine exam on Eztar as Julius held her hand. Everything was good. Lucas would be born in a week.

The name Lucas just came to her the night before in a dream. She even saw a birthmark on his shoulder in the shape of a star. She felt the strong presence of God with her growing family and knew that she was being guided. The paths of her children were being set in stone before them. Praise the Lord!

Before he left them that day, Dr. Sherlous casually mentioned that his wife, Martha, could not have children and how she longed for a family of her own. She loved hearing about him delivering children when he would come home. Martha would hang onto every word as he described the births. Eztar told him that her firstborn, Lazlo, always thought he should be a doctor. Dr. Sherlous smiled, nodded, and quietly left the family to their thoughts.

As he left the home, Julius looked at his wife and said, "Such a kind man…I really like him."

Several days passed and Eztar knew that the time was getting near. She asked for Dr. Sherlous to be called. Within an hour or so he arrived with a calm demeanor and a smile on his face.

"Relax, Eztar… everything is going to be fine." And it was. Lucas was born in three hours and twenty minutes without issue. He did, however, have a star-shaped birthmark on his left shoulder. Eztar said it was a mark from God. No one dared to challenge her.

Everyone was gathered for this event. Family, friends, doctor, and Laird Conner were inside, while most of the community waited outside, receiving minute-by-minute updates from Julius.

Eztar called everyone to gather around her bed. In particular, she wanted to touch both sons at the same time after introducing them to one another. She had already discussed her plans privately with Julius, but no one else knew what she had on her mind.

Eztar looked lovingly at her sons as she spoke to Lazlo. "How badly do you think that you want to be a doctor?"

Lazlo responded, "Momma…I want it more than anything in the world!" She proceeded to explain that another premonition had come to her that showed her the path that needed to be taken. She had already shared it with Julius and he too, agreed. They were ready to make a huge sacrifice if everything fell into place. Lazlo looked puzzled.

"Dr. Sherlous…my first-born son is still young, still a boy with much to learn about life. He needs more than can be provided for him here. He needs guidance, direction, and focus. You need a family and a son. If you accept this, you could provide the means to allow him to follow the path that God set for him. You can be the driving force to make him become a doctor. If he chooses this, we will watch from afar…but he will not only be our son…he will be yours too."

Dr. Steven Joseph Sherlous started to cry. He gazed lovingly at Lazlo and said, "If he will have me, and of course, my wife who I know would be thrilled to take him in."

"So, Lazlo? You can even keep your name. What's it going to be?"

Eztar added a thought…Lazlo my son, Jesus was a *White Lighter* too.

First Encounters

CHAPTER 1

"Laaazzz! What the hell, man! Where are you anyway? You could have stopped that goal if you were in a wheelchair!"

The crowd was going crazy, screaming and cheering…but this was an away game at a rival school. A championship game, nonetheless. Lazlo was simply disconnected emotionally, thinking about his birth mother, being recently hospitalized.

The Maryland Terrapins were now up by two points, three-to-one over Johns Hopkins University. This rivalry was as old as the history of the schools themselves. The first meeting between these teams was reportedly in 1924. The honor of both schools was at stake. Lacrosse was taken very seriously in the state of Maryland. Oddly, the state sport is 'jousting'…yes, riding a horse with a long lance, like a medieval knight. But to these college students, Lacrosse reigned supreme!

Lazlo was a Midfielder. His position was considered one of the most difficult in the sport. A Midfielder covers both offensive duties and defensive duties too. Physical and mental conditioning is critical for success. They cover the entire field. Today, Lazlo quite literally 'dropped the ball'.

Time out! The official blew the whistle to stop further play as Lazlo's teammate Bruno came charging over. Bruno was a Defender. His position was full-time defense, and to protect the goal area at all costs. He took it personally when a "Middie" like Lazlo fell back into his area and made a mistake…especially one that could cost them the championship. Bruno was a large young man, roughly six feet, eight inches or so tall at a lean 225 pounds! He carried a very imposing lacrosse stick that added to his intimidating appearance. The defender stick was longer than the other positions on the field. They were friends, but right now, in this time and space, Lazlo feared him!

"What the fuck, Laz?"

Lazlo thought that Bruno might really strike him. The potential was real.

"I'm sorry bro…my mother is in the hospital, and I just can't shake it. I'm sorry…"

Bruno exhaled to regain his composure and forced himself to calm down. His adrenaline was off the charts.

"Look Laz…if you don't get your shit together, the coach is going to bench you. You'll be done! The last game of your senior year! You cannot, I repeat, cannot afford this. Don't let it happen! He's watching now, and if he calls you in, you better beg, plead, and kiss his ass to convince him you still have something to offer. Kapeesh? Now go pucker-up damn it!"

Lazlo knew that Bruno was right. Everything was riding on this game. Everything!

"Laz…remember that crazy play we pulled off against Loyola Maryland's Team? We beat those dogs! (referring to the Loyola Greyhounds). Let's do it again…these guys will never see it coming!"

The two of them quickly convinced their skeptical coach. He knew they needed a miracle and maybe these two could bring on the second coming! "Do it!" Game on! (The whistle blows to resume play) The "Terps" were feeling a win in sight and kicked things into high gear! With this aggression, games can be won, or mistakes can be made. The line is very fine. Lazlo and Bruno hoped for the latter. The play that they used once on Loyola was an unexpected, field-length, two-man drive that resulted in a goal by Lazlo, the mid-fieldman. It needed a great deal of luck or a guardian angel. Lazlo prayed for both.

The Maryland Terrapins' offense attacked! Their striker was

charging the defensive line like a wild banshee, but Bruno was waiting, ready to strike with his long stick! In perfect synchronization, Lazlo broke into a sprint for the opposite side of the field! *Do not go offside, do not go offside, his brain kept repeating to him.*

The striker, #10, was in full sprint to take his shot and secure the game when WHAM! Bruno hit him with a check that sent his teeth flying, making an awful bone-crunching sound that could be heard in the stands! He dropped like a rock, but 'game was on' as Bruno scooped up the ball and sent it 100 mph downfield to Lazlo in a full sprint towards the opponent's goal. The move was like a ballet, as Lazlo viciously attacked the enemy goal. SCORE! The Johns Hopkins fans went crazy. Three to two was announced over the loudspeaker system…seven minutes remaining in the game.

Lazlo was also the "face-off" midfielder. After a goal, two players battle at center field to regain possession of the ball. Extra skill is needed by these individuals to do this successfully. Games can be turned quickly.

Now, Lazlo was mentally playing for his mother. He turned his grief and fear into assertive aggression. He needed to win, for her. They were close to tying this game! The whistle blew, and Lazlo charged the ball and his opponent, literally running him down as he collected the ball, pivoted, and sprinted toward the goal. He needed another miracle and felt directed somehow, to take a crazy longshot that no one would expect. He intentionally bounced his high-speed missile at the goalkeeper, with hopes it would take an unpredictable angle at over 100 mph! Once again, SCORE! GOAL! Tie game! Three to three! With five minutes left on the clock. The fans roared! *This* was a championship game!

The clock continued ticking as the game moved forward. Those five minutes felt like an eternity. Bruno and his other defenders did a great job at holding the Terps at bay. But you can't win with a tie.

Lazlo signaled the coach for a time-out. Only ninety seconds were left on the clock. The whistle blew, stopping time progression. Johns Hopkins needed a meeting of the minds. Lazlo called in another "middie" who played the left side. His name was Clayton Middleton,

#12. Clayton was a southpaw. He carried his stick left-handed. Lazlo wanted to add this seemingly unimportant aspect to the equation. It could be a recipe for success.

"Bruno…pretend that we're going to repeat our second goal. Talk to me out there…tell me something like "Let's do it again man! Make them hear it! Clayton…you're going to take the shot! They'll be expecting me or a striker, but we'll slide you in unexpectedly. And Bruno? Be ready to play dentist again and knock someone else's teeth out!"

Bruno grinned, showing one or two of his own were already gone. "Will do my friend…will do…"

Once again the Maryland Terrapins attacked the defensive line and again Bruno was waiting. Lazlo started his sprint towards the other goal! But Clayton started running too…all the way over on the left side boundary line, almost unnoticed as all eyes expected Lazlo to once again, attempt a score to win the game.

The striker attacked but Bruno was faster and more aggressive. WHAM! Again, you could hear bone break at 50 yards away…this time a jaw. He went down hard as Bruno grabbed the ball and shot it downfield to Lazlo! Clayton was just over his left side as they quickly gained ground on the goal!

The goalie was watching Lazlo, expecting a repeat attempt to score when Lazlo passed the ball left to Clayton. The goalie was blocking to his own left, expecting Lazlo to shoot, but this opened his right side and allowed Clayton a solid, clean shot on goal that was never touched! SCORE! GOAL! Cheers rang out through the stands! Even Terps fans knew that they witnessed something fantastic! Johns Hopkins – 4 Maryland – 3 Final Score. The facility erupted as fans flooded the field. What a game!

Lazlo's first thoughts were that his mother would be proud. His father too…and his father and mother figures, Steven and Martha Sherlous. Without them, he would never have made it this far. He was about to graduate with a degree in medicine from Johns Hopkins University! Life was beyond good! Life was near to perfect…except Momma was ill.

Dr. Sherlous decided not to make it to the game. Even though he, too, had once attended Johns Hopkins. He visited Eztar and Julius at the hospital in West Virginia. He knew that he would hear the results of the game in good time and share it with the Somogyi family.

Lazlo was mobbed by the fans! They considered him the game hero, even though Clayton scored the final goal. Lazlo was voted Most Valuable Player for all his effort, but he felt guilty accepting the award because he had cost the team one point, by allowing them the score when his mind wandered. Fans can be funny that way, and Lazlo was not egotistical in any way.

The field was alive with energy! Lazlo could feel it! To him, it was like electricity filled the air. In his mind, he imagined the likes of a Tesla coil, created in the late 1800s. He had never felt anything like it in his life, and it made him smile like he had never smiled before.

"Lazlo my friend! I knew that you had it in you!" beamed Bruno. "You saved the day!" But Lazlo kept thinking that it was Clayton who scored the winning point. Friends could sense his genuine modesty and it fueled them on. People wanted to shake his hand, girls hugged him and planted kisses on his face. Several even secretly passed him their phone numbers and dormitory information. He was amazed.

Clayton then entered the fray and hugged Lazlo like a brother! "Thank you, my friend…thank you! I cannot wait until next year! (Clayton was a junior classman) I'm sure to make the team now, next year…because of you. Come now…someone is waiting to meet you. Come and meet my cousin from Spain. She is here on vacation between classes and took notice of you today on the field. Please come!"

Lazlo turned his gaze ahead of Clayton and witnessed the most beautiful girl in the world. She was absolutely stunning in every way! Clayton took over again smiling as he noted Lazlo's approval and said, "Lazlo my friend…this is my favorite cousin, Maria. She is from Spain and is attending the University of Granada. She is a junior there in a medical program. Sort of like you."

Lazlo's eyes met Maria's as they both reached forward for a formal handshake that was instantly charged with a light electric shock, causing them both to slightly flinch. Lazlo pulled his hand away, but Maria reached forward and took his hand again, making sure the connection wasn't broken the second time. It happened again only with more intensity. They both smiled, but her gaze was deep…even intense.

"I'm sorry if the odd static electricity hurts you," Lazlo exclaimed.

Maria replied, "I'd expect nothing else from a true *White Lighter*."

The Girl in Green

CHAPTER 2

"Okay, now you have my attention, Maria. Only my Momma, I mean my mother, has ever used that term to describe me. She only said it once and I didn't really understand what she meant. She also told me when I was a child that Jesus Christ was a *White Lighter*. What does it mean? And just how did you come up with such a conclusion after just meeting me?"

Maria smiled and Clayton laughed a little. Not a laugh to make fun, but a laugh as if to say, Brother, you have so much yet to learn and Maria has much to share. "Maria studies Experimental Psychology at the University of Granada in Spain. It's the real deal man. She's what they call a *synesthete*. I think that your mother is one too."

Lazlo was extremely skeptical but pondered on the information.

"You tell him, Maria. It's your field. It scares the shit out of me personally. It's gypsy crap, hocus pocus, and crystal balls in my opinion. But she and her associates swear it's real."

"Well, thank you for that supportive translation of my studies, Clayton," Maria laughed. "So, to answer your question and to plant the proverbial seeds that will grow many more…let me ask you a question first. Do you believe in the human aura? You know, the energy field that surrounds all living things? Before you answer, what is your take on religion? I don't care which one…just religion in general? Are you a believer? I think that your Momma, if I may call her that, is a believer.

Her comment about Jesus Christ being a *White Lighter* proved that to me. But it is not just Christianity. Christ wore a halo. So did Buddha. As did many other religious figures. They were *White Lighters*. You, Lazlo Somogyi, are also a *White Lighter*. Your Momma saw it in you. I see it in you too…even as we speak. So, I ask you again…Do you believe in this energy field that we call an aura?"

Lazlo hesitated. He was confused, yet curious. After having the game of his life, and studying medicine for six years, this girl…this woman, simply took the wind out of his sails with serious questions about the supernatural. Or so it seemed.

"I have been watching you for hours, Lazlo. I see your white aura. So do you believe it?"

"Because of my Momma, I want to believe… but I cannot see them. Tell me more, please."

Maria responded by inviting Lazlo to a small café where they could speak more privately in a hopefully quiet atmosphere. A cup of coffee would be nice, they both agreed. She invited Clayton and Bruno, but they politely refused, sensing a connection growing between Lazlo and Maria. Finding a fan-based bar and a few beers was much more appealing than hearing someone compare their star "middie" to Jesus Christ. So, Lazlo and Maria went to a place called Java Jennifer's, and the team members gravitated to a local Irish pub called Tommy's.

Java Jennifer's was also known by the locals as JJ's. It was a quaint hole-in-the-wall establishment that simply made you feel good being there. College memorabilia filled the room and covered the walls. They placed their orders and settled in when Lazlo felt a strange sensation that they were being watched. It wasn't game-related. It was something else.

Almost immediately, an older woman he had never seen before, approached their table. She looked kindly into Maria's eyes and said, "I can see how much you love him. It's a special love that one rarely experiences. Whatever you do, don't let go of it!" Then she walked out of the building quietly. Maria blushed, as Lazlo looked at her, almost stunned.

"What the hell was that?" Both of them felt a strange connection after the mild electric charge when they shook hands. There was admittedly an attraction… But true love? They were both taken aback by the encounter. For some minutes they sat quietly waiting for their order. After all, they had really just met.

Maria spoke first, "So, where were we?" She was still trying to cover up some of what the old woman exposed of her new feelings. Maria then went into lecture mode, just to get some basic facts out on the table, and to cover her embarrassment.

"All living things have an aura. It is a life force, an energy, that is all our own. Some of us are fortunate to be able to see it with the naked eye. Your Momma for instance… and me. This condition, or gift, is called *Neuropsychological Synesthesia*. We are referred to as being *synesthetes*. It would appear that our brains are wired a bit differently than most people. Scientifically, we have more synaptic connections than 'normal' folks."

"We are also considered to be empathic. Having high levels of empathy for all living things around us. I don't mean the jokers who like to pretend and claim these traits. They're out there. But they're not real. There are things to look for that aid you in being sure. A true empath can read a room. They see the fakes. The lies. People hate them for it. It's kind of like if you have a bad teacher or boss that lies to everyone all the time and gets away with it. The true empath sees it. They can read the intentions, feelings, or moods of others. It can be a curse. Many true artists are empathic. The great ones for sure! Musicians…creative people. It's a full package."

Lazlo was entranced listening to her speak.

"Professor Pilan at the university is the current expert in this field. I take as many of his classes as I can."

She then addressed Lazlo's mother by asking him a question about her. "Would you say that many people view your Momma as being connected somehow to the paranormal?"

Lazlo knew this to be true. Momma could predict the future! His answer was yes. Momma even predicted the star-shaped birthmark on his brother Lucas before he was born. *This is getting weird, he thought.*

Maria slightly changed the subject back to the scientific aspects of this condition.

"You didn't ask why you and others are called *White Lighters*…"

Lazlo said that he was afraid to really ask, it's all kind of spooky.

"Once again, think about religious figures in history. Christ is a very well-known one. His halo is usually portrayed as white, or maybe an off-yellow golden glow. He was a *White Lighter*. That was his aura. The aura is defined as a luminous radiation surrounding a person. It can be at the head, or the entire body. Scientific and religious studies have determined that each color has a definite meaning. White being the rarest. White is considered pure, and spiritually connected. It doesn't mean religion. It means spiritual. There's a difference. *White Lighters* are intelligent. Very quick of the mind. They also have a tendency for perfectionism."

Lazlo was tapping his fingers on the dish under his coffee cup.

And, she added, "Nervous energy." Then she smiled as it was his turn to blush.

"My aura is green, Maria added with a smile. I have been read by a fellow *synesthetes* and they had no doubts. One day soon I hope to have my aura photographed with a special camera. That would be proof by having it on film. I look forward to it. A green aura means you are loving and faithful to true love. We too experience empathic abilities, but not like the white aura. Green is good!" And she smiled again. Lazlo was starting to love her smile already. Green was also his favorite color.

"Every color has a different meaning. Some overlap and the color of your aura can change. The worst color aura is black. It is dark and reflects a life that is unhappy. Even evil, depending on the individual. Adolf Hitler comes to mind."

Lazlo knew that name all too well. Yes, he was an evil man.

Lazlo then jumped in with a question. "You mentioned taking a picture? How?"

Maria responded…

"In 1939, a Russian technician was working in a government facility that dealt with extremely high voltage. His name was Simon

Kirlian. Comrade Kirlian noticed light radiating from his fingertips while working one day. Further studies had him inventing what is known as 'The Kirlian Camera'. Lazlo…it is *all* real!"

"Kirlian's research prompted other scientists to start their own research on the subject. Dr. Konstantan Korotkov, also Russian, created the GDV, gas discharge visualization. His camera photographs the bio-photons (light) emanating from a human's fingertips. It is said that he also observed patients in certain hospitals glowing, while under medical treatments. It is quite possible that he too, was a *synesthete*."

Lazlo felt the almost uncontrolled urge to stop her from speaking… mid-sentence. He was amazed and highly impressed with her knowledge, but most of all the enthusiasm with which she delivered the information. She was real, and she wholeheartedly believed in every aspect of this subject. To say he was impressed was an understatement. Lazlo simply loved her energy!

"Maria… Maria…" She continued to talk without hardly noticing his attempts to interrupt her. Lazlo was trying to be polite, but he had a very serious question to ask of her.

"Yes, Lazlo… What is it?"

"What is your full name? You didn't get to tell me who you really are and I want to know."

"*Mi nombre completo es Maria Cordova Valdez…* Maria Cordova Valdez," and she smiled that smile of hers that completely lit up the room, and Lazlo's heart.

Like everything else about this young woman so far, Lazlo loved her name too. "It sounds so aristocratic. I love it!" He tried to sound confident, but slightly stumbled over his attempt. He started to laugh at himself and couldn't look her in the eyes. Maria laughed too, trying to offer that feminine support that most women can offer to their men when the guy does something stupid.

"You're cute," she threw in his direction, knowing the simple flattery would bring him around. And it did…

Truth be told, Lazlo had no idea that his comment about Maria being an aristocrat had hit much closer to home than she might have wanted. This was not the time or the place for her to disclose personal family information that could attract a man for the wrong reasons. Now Maria wondered…Was my response a bit too formal when I gave Lazlo my full name? Maria was comfortable in high society crowds. She grew up with it, and spent most of her life thus far, being a member of a well-known political family in Spain. In her homeland it was common for her to travel in government sedans with bodyguards… but not here… thank God.

In Granada, Spain, the government is considered a Parliamentary Monarchy. Technically speaking, it is a Social Representative, Democratic Constitutional Monarchy. The monarch is the head of state, while the Prime Minister is officially the "president of the government." The parliament is called the "Parliament of Andalusia." It has 265 senators and Maria's father was one of them. Yes, she was almost considered royalty. This gave her the ability to go to any university in the world and to take vacations in the same manner. Money was no object, although Maria had a natural distaste for anyone that flaunted their wealth. She preferred, when she could, to socialize with more common and down-to-earth people, doing common things. She was sincere about this in her heart, but certainly would not refuse the gifts that came with being born into a wealthy family.

Lazlo still gazed at her like a love-struck puppy, waiting for her next words. He was falling quickly for this dark-haired beauty.

Maria realized that she had allowed her mind to wander slightly and hoped that Lazlo didn't notice.

She tried to change the subject but found herself now being the one stumbling over her words and thoughts. "So, not to be too forward or anything but I heard that your Momma was in the hospital. Is she okay? And where is she right now? If you don't mind me asking…"

Lazlo was flattered that she seemed to care. After all, they had just met a few hours earlier. And no, he didn't mind.

He hesitated to collect his thoughts. "I was told that she was taken to Lexington for now, pending some tests. They need to determine if that facility is suitable to treat whatever the problem really is. The message that I received from Dr. Sherlous said that they suspected some kind of stroke. He said that she was comfortable and that it wasn't life-threatening, but he was heading there tomorrow anyway. He's a wonderful person. I was partially raised by him and his wife. It's a long story, but without them, I would have never had the chance to attend medical school." Lazlo stopped talking, thinking about his mother now. "I need to go see her, too."

"Then you should," Maria quickly added.

Lazlo smiled as she lightly touched his hand. Oddly, he felt another light electric shock when she touched him. Not like the first time, he thought... But it was there. Maria felt it too. They both wondered exactly what this sensation was that they seemed to share... Hopefully, time would tell.

Maria was very family-oriented, and the fact that this young man obviously loved his mother as much as he did, impressed her a great deal. She didn't want to jump to conclusions, but she had felt emotions with Lazlo that she had never shared with any other man even after many dates. Love at first sight, she pondered...could it be real?

"So, Lazlo... graduation isn't very far in the future. I came here to see my cousin Clayton play in the championship Lacrosse game while enjoying a vacation. I have had hopes that he might move back to Spain to be near the family when he graduates, but who knows? Clayton was sort of a military brat and moved around a lot following his father's career. My aunt fell in love with an American in uniform and as they say...the rest is history. That's why people are surprised to learn that he and I are related, as our last names are not the same. Aunt Lucia gave up the Valdez moniker to become a Middleton. The things we do for love."

Lazlo was learning many personal bits of information very quickly from Maria as she openly shared her life with him. He liked it. The connection that they felt with one another was growing rapidly. While in some ways it was intimidating, overall, it was exciting...and a good thing.

Maria gazed at Lazlo making direct eye contact with him. She didn't think about her next move, or where it might take her. This was a moment of acting from the heart, not the head. It was simply a trait of the Spanish blood running through her veins.

"Lazlo. When are we going to go visit your Momma in the hospital?"

Love in Lexington

CHAPTER 3

For a moment, Lazlo was slightly taken aback that this new person in his life had simply invited herself to not only meet his family under unusual circumstances but to travel with him to do it. Strangely, it suddenly seemed not so out of the ordinary. He found himself welcoming the thought of it.

"I plan to leave sometime tomorrow if I can get a bus ticket soon enough. Dr. Sherlous set up a small bank account for me to use for college expenses. It's limited, but I have enough for something important like this. Can you afford a ticket? I wouldn't want to see you put out because of my family issues."

Maria smiled. "Yes, I think that I can make it happen. I've never been to Lexington, and I've never ridden on a bus before. It'll be fun!" Maria didn't think the time was right to let Lazlo know about her Porsche 356A parked in a garage near the campus. She didn't want to lie to him, but things were moving quickly, and exposing her financial condition didn't seem like the right thing to do. Not yet, anyway…

Maria and Lazlo parted ways that evening just after 10. They wanted to get an early start in the morning to purchase bus tickets for their trip to Lexington. Neither of them knew what to do as they said goodbye. Was it too early in the relationship for a quick kiss? Lazlo wondered if a friendly parting handshake would cause yet another static shock between them. Interestingly, Maria was thinking the exact same thing.

So she decided to take the initiative, and leaned over to Lazlo, giving him an ever-so-brief kiss on the left cheek. Maria did it fast because she feared the static charge happening again. And it did! She felt it on her lips and caught a light blue flash jump between them. It was minor, but it was there! What is it that keeps causing this, they both wondered… and they decided to call it a night.

They headed in opposite directions, with both of them in their own trancelike states of mind, wondering what was going on between them. Fate has a way of working strange miracles.

Maria met up with a girl that was going to school at the University and got a ride to her car. After which, she drove to her hotel, took a shower, and fell into bed.

Lazlo went back to his dorm to settle in but was interrupted by Clayton Middleton, who was very drunk.

Clayton slurred his words badly, "Lazlo and Maria, sitting in a tree, K I S S I N G…" and he fell face first into the bed.

Lazlo shook his head looking down on his pathetic-looking friend. "Jesus, that is some real grade school shit," he said with a laugh.

Clayton raised his head just enough to mumble, "I love you man… we're gonna be family."

"What are you talking about, man? What do you mean, *family?*"

Clayton still mumbled in a manner almost impossible to translate… "Maria neber getz clooose tos peoples…neber eber…shes lubs Lazlo!"

Clayton then giggled and fell sound asleep.

Lazlo was stunned. Clayton's message just didn't seem to fit the woman with whom he had just shared an evening and now had plans to travel with to see his mother in the hospital.

Morning seemed to take forever because Lazlo just couldn't get Clayton's words out of his head. While there was some truth in Clayton's words, the likelihood was that he had exaggerated everything. Lazlo had never been in love before so the emotions that flooded his heart and mind were overwhelming. He decided maybe it was best to do nothing at all. This might be much harder than he imagined.

Maria had suggested they meet at JJ's for coffee, and then walk to the bus terminal, which was one-half mile up the road. She was waiting when Lazlo arrived.

Lazlo guessed that she was as nervous as he was, and most likely didn't sleep very well either. They both wanted to get their "adventure" started. After a quick cup of coffee, they paid their bill, Lazlo left a tip, and off they went towards the Greyhound bus terminal.

When they arrived at the bus station, Lazlo had already decided that he was going to treat Maria to a ticket. It was the manly thing to do. At least he thought so. His coal miner elders had taught him old-fashioned Hungarian manners.

"Two tickets to Lexington, please." Lazlo proudly attempted to take control of the morning's events. Maria just watched, amused while her new friend took over. She smiled to herself and was actually flattered that he would go this far. Maria knew that he couldn't afford it, but told herself that she would share the truth with him as soon as possible. She didn't like being dishonest about her financial position, but she had to be sure that Lazlo was as genuine as he seemed. She hoped that he was.

After a brief wait in the boarding area, they heard the call over the loudspeaker, "Bus number 205 to Lexington, boarding at Gate Seven."

Lazlo was raised as a traditional Hungarian boy, learning the ways handed down for centuries. The times were changing, and women's equality issues could be confusing. In a Hungarian household, for instance, the man enters the house before the woman. This includes male children too. The mother and daughters enter last. Doing this simple act out of order was considered very bad luck. Lazlo wondered to himself if this included boarding a bus or airplane. He really did not know, so he'd need to act quickly if he acted at all.

He could feel his palms starting to sweat under the pressure of this new scenario. Lazlo believed that communication was key in situations like this. "Maria…this might sound odd, but my heritage, being Hungarian, has some strange beliefs that affect our family functions. Simple enough superstitions that our elders seem to treasure. One of them is based on a bad luck belief regarding which gender should enter the home first. My family has practiced this all my life and way before it. Do you have anything like this in Spain?"

Lazlo intentionally didn't mention which gender that actually was. He was learning how to play this new game as he went along.

Maria mentioned her own background. "Oh yes, Spanish men are gentlemen. They always treat women with respect, carrying their luggage for them, opening doors, pulling out the chair at a dining table…things like these. It is considered proper etiquette and a sign of respect."

"I'm sorry Maria… Can I take your carry-on bag for you? My apologies that I didn't ask sooner." Maria smiled. Lazlo was trying so hard to do everything right, and it showed. Maria was flattered at his efforts and handed him her bag. When they entered the bus, Lazlo made sure to step to the side, slightly bowed his head, and said, "After you, my lady." He did it in a light jest, but his action was sincere, and based on her reaction Lazlo knew that he might have just scored yet another goal.

Another goal by midfielder Lazlo Somogyi! And the game was on!

The Greyhound bus was oddly shaped compared to other buses. The seating was elevated in a manner that required a small staircase of sorts to get to your seat. Once seated, you were elevated higher than one might be in a typical bus. It gave you a better view of the highway and the countryside around you as you traveled. Lazlo liked it. Somehow though, he couldn't shake the odd competitive feeling that this bus represented a rival Lacrosse team, Loyola Maryland. Greyhounds. He laughed at himself as to just how stupid that thought even was. Damn dogs!

Lazlo looked at Maria with admiration. "Getting comfortable? It's not a terribly long ride. I expect to sleep a bit if I can. I was up late last night with Clayton." Maria smiled and briefly questioned if Clayton was okay. Lazlo said that he feared Clayton would have one hell of a hangover when he woke up later this morning. Maria frowned ever so slightly, but to Lazlo, she still looked radiant. She knew her cousin well and wondered if, in an inebriated state, he might've said something foolish to Lazlo about her or their family. For now, not to worry. Today was a new day and she was enjoying Lazlo Somogyi's company.

Maria slipped her arm through Lazlo's and took his hand. In one simple movement, she rested her head on his shoulder and quickly fell asleep. Lazlo was surprised yet thrilled at this contact. And at the moment, there was no static shock. He was afraid to move as he didn't want to disturb her. So, eventually, he too, fell asleep.

It was over a two-hour trip to Lexington. Lazlo's mother had been transported from Ward, West Virginia, to the Roanoke Memorial Hospital in Lexington, Virginia, because it was one of the closest established hospitals within a reasonable distance of Ward. Dr. Sherlous was also connected to several other doctors on staff there. He felt that this would keep him better connected to the Somogyi family. Roanoke was also closer to Maryland than the "other Lexington", to the west of Ward by possibly another twenty miles or so. Lazlo was happy they hadn't transported his Momma to Kentucky.

Maria woke up first, quickly ate a breath mint that she carried in her pocket, and then stopped to gaze at her new friend Lazlo. He most certainly appeared to be an original item… the real deal. He was honest and sweet. Obviously loving and intelligent and family-oriented. And yes, Maria found herself being very attracted to him. He was a good-looking young man in great physical condition. What more could a girl ask for? He was also going to become a doctor of some kind…a noble profession. Maria pondered her own guilt of not being 100% honest with him. She needed to remedy that situation. The longer that she waited, she could jeopardize everything trying to protect her own family interests. That could be a terrible end, to a wonderful beginning.

Lazlo snored softly as he slowly began to wake up. He coughed slightly and wiped his chin with his sleeve as he felt a slight bit of drool rolling down his chin from the corner of his mouth. He was immediately embarrassed when he realized where he was and what was happening. He sat up quickly to regain his composure.

"I'm sorry Maria…wow, I must have been out like a light."

Maria smiled while giving Lazlo's hand a squeeze, "I liked watching you sleep. You were so at peace, and comfortable in yourself. I witnessed a completely and totally honest side of you. If you want to know, your aura is still most definitely white. I really look forward to meeting your parents, but I admit mostly your Momma because she too, is a "seer." Her knowing that you were a *White Lighter* as a child is very special. I want to talk with her when she is well enough to do so."

The bus was just arriving at the Lexington terminal as their conversation was coming to an end when Maria added a thought.

"So…what was it that was expected of Hungarian men that you so obviously tried to keep from me?" With that, she grabbed her carry-on bag and headed for the bus exit with a big smile on her face.

Exiting the bus, with Lazlo trailing behind her, Maria hailed a cab. Maria made it obvious that she was paying for the cab and gave instructions to the driver to take them directly to the Roanoke Memorial Hospital. He acknowledged that he was very familiar with its location. Lazlo was slightly taken aback by this, but deep down inside he knew that he simply could not afford to pay for everything for the both of them on a simple college allowance from Dr. Sherlous.

It was a short ride to the hospital and as they approached the entrance, Lazlo began to feel some apprehension about his visit. He wanted to see his Momma badly, but he was also afraid that her condition might have somehow changed her. He knew that having a stroke is serious and many people never return to normal. He worried that she just might not be the same. Maria sensed this and took his hand in hers as they walked to the information desk. Neither one of them let go as they navigated the hospital's front desk to Room 214. After exiting the elevator, they found the nurses' station and requested information on his Momma.

Lazlo was feeling overwhelmed. The closer he got to the room, the faster his heart was beating. Maria sensed this and spoke up quickly. He was relieved that she took control.

"We're here to visit Mrs Julius Somogyi, please. Her name is Eztar. We're family, and this is her son," she pointed to Lazlo. The nurse responded that they needed to sign in and that Eztar already had company, but it was okay for them to go in. She then directed them to the fifth door on the left, Room 214. She smiled and excused herself to complete her other duties. Maria and Lazlo turned to find Room 214.

As they approached the rooms numbered from 200 to 224, they both made a mental note as they walked. It was like a countdown to a nervous launch of a rocket, but the closer they progressed to their destination, Lazlo slowed. He was truly afraid of what he might find in Room 214.

Room 214. Both Maria and Lazlo allowed their eyes to scan the name and chart hanging on the wall outside of the door. Eztar Somogyi. Yes, this was the correct room. They could hear male voices coming from inside. Lazlo glanced at Maria and they entered the room. Before seeing his Momma in her bed, Lazlo noted his father, Julius, and Dr. Sherlous sitting in chairs near the foot of the hospital bed. The three of them made eye contact and smiles appeared on both of the older gentlemen's faces. Lazlo was still terrified at this point. Maria smiled at both men. Before introductions could be made, Eztar sat up in bed and called out to her son, "Lazlo, you made it!" She then crossed her head and chest with the typical father, son, and Holy Ghost hand gesture of the Catholic faith. Eztar smiled brightly at her son. Her eyes then turned to Maria before either one of them approached her bed.

"Maria *gyermekem. végre találkozunk. Gyönyörűen nézel ki zöldben*"

"Maria, my child. I finally meet you. You look lovely in green!"

Dr. Sherlous did not speak Hungarian, but obviously Julius did. As did Lazlo. Maria did not speak the language either, but she understood the unspoken connection between two women who felt their own love for the same man. And as *synesthetes*, they both understood more than most others. Even Lazlo and Julius were a bit shocked at what just took place. Maria went to Eztar's bedside, took her hand, and leaned over to kiss her on the cheek. Eztar's face beamed like a lighthouse. Lazlo started to relax somewhat as he too approached his Momma's bedside.

He greeted her from the opposite side of the bed, taking her other hand as he too kissed her cheek while saying, "Momma, I love you." Both he and Maria held onto Eztar, one on each side of her, and she could feel the spiritual connection that had formed between the two young people. Their auras were joining. This union was real.

"*A lányom. Üdv a családban.*"

"My daughter. Welcome to the family."

Lazlo translated this conversation to Maria, just to be sure that she understood. Julius did the same for Dr. Sherlous, who seemed shocked by the events.

Maria said that she understood everything just fine. Dr. Sherlous was quickly learning that there was much for him to understand about the culture of these Hungarian friends and family. He actually questioned Julius' translation of Maria wearing green, when in fact, she wore a predominantly red and gray outfit with limited colors.

Julius explained that much like Eztar seeing Lazlo as a *White Lighter*, having a white aura, she immediately identified Maria as having a green one. "This is a good match," he reported. "White and green share compatible traits. Did we tell you that Jesus, the Christ, was also a *White Lighter?*"

Dr. Stephen Joseph Sherlous realized he had much to learn.

The group continued the visit together. Lazlo went to his father and his surrogate father, hugging them both, and thanking them for supporting him and for being there now for his Momma. He then asked Dr. Sherlous for the medical translation of what was happening to Eztar. They spoke in front of Maria and Eztar, but their conversation was pretty much just between the men.

Keeping in mind that Lazlo had just all but completed medical school, he was versed in diagnoses of medical maladies. Upon entering the room, he caught a quick glance at Eztar's chart and knew the situation. Out of respect for his surrogate father/doctor, he wanted to allow Dr. Sherlous to explain the medical situation. It would be the respectful thing to do.

Dr. Sherlous said, "Your mother had a minor stroke. This is caused by a lack of oxygen to the brain. She has been put on a blood thinner to prevent it from happening again. At times, these things do cause various levels of brain damage. It is actually quite amazing that so far, this does not appear to have happened to her. So, I think from a medical standpoint, she seems fine."

Lazlo was thrilled and hugged his doctor-father again. This was the best news he had heard in days.

"Did you hear that, Maria? She's going to be fine!"

Eztar then spoke to Maria and Lazlo.

"So, when did you two kids fall in love anyway? I have felt her presence recently in your life, but nothing as strong emotionally as what I feel today."

Lazlo looked from his Momma to Maria and replied, "I think that it is happening as we speak." Maria's smile lit up the room…

The Talk

CHAPTER 4

"Lazlo…we need to talk," Maria said softly. She smiled at him in a way that melted his heart, but there was a concern in her voice that he had never heard before. Lazlo found himself feeling a little uneasy. Was his family too pushy? He imagined they were a little surprised with their sudden relationship.

"What is it, Maria? Did my family somehow offend you?" He waited for her response. "They can get quite forward at times, I know. Their beliefs probably seem strange to others, but their hearts are pure."

Maria shook her head saying, no. Lazlo was still confused. "Then what? What else could it be? You look so troubled and it's scaring me. Have I done something wrong?" Once again Maria said no.

Lazlo contemplated the chain of events that brought them to this point. He was so happy to learn that his Momma was going to be well, that all of the talk of Maria being a daughter to the Somogyi family and her loving Lazlo just sort of washed over him. He was happy. But now he was confused.

"Let us find a place to sit, perhaps a small park area here at the hospital." She took his hand and they went to find a map of the property. Maria noted to herself just how well their hands fit together. Like a glove, as they say. Their touch was perfect. Maria located a map on the wall near a waiting room and found a food court area with picnic tables. This would be a good place to talk.

Lazlo's palms were already starting to sweat. What on earth could this be, he wondered? Maria purchased two cups of coffee, and they sat down at a table away from other people. Maria took both of Lazlo's hands in hers and squeezed.

"Lazlo… things are moving so fast. The time we've spent has been very special to me. I feel things with you that I have never felt before. I see things in you that take my breath away. And I admire things in you that make my heart stand still. It is easy for me to dream of a future with you. I already love your family after just sharing an afternoon with them. Your Momma made me feel so welcome; she is a very special lady and you are a *very* special son. I have dated very little in my life so far. My education has always come first. My family, too. We are all quite close. As a young girl, my dreams were always about a white knight on a white stallion sweeping me off of my feet and taking me to some far away land. The knight would be my true love and we would live happily ever after. Is that a foolish little girl's dream or do you think it could be the premonition of a future reality? No need to answer. Just listen now to my words."

And Lazlo did, as Maria continued…

"My family is of an old bloodline. In my country, it can be traced back centuries. The name Cordova Valdez is and has always been highly respected and many of my ancestors were people of great political power. Even today, many of the men work in government positions. Politicians, military officers, and others of importance. …My uncle is a senator. My Papa also serves the people of Spain. In Granada, at the University, one of my other uncles is a well-respected professor. He is a leader in my field of study, experimental psychology. I am a junior there, studying neuropsychological psychology. My Uncle Diego oversees the department. Diego Pilan, PhD."

Lazlo stopped her mid-breath before she started her next sentence. "Maria…what does this have to do with anything? Why are you suddenly so upset this afternoon? I don't understand."

Maria continued, "Today was my very first bus ride. You are the first boy that I've ever felt attracted to. Your Momma is the second true *synesthete* that I have ever met, other than myself. And I believe that you might be one too. Lazlo, I'm almost 21 years old and have never been kissed! Can you believe it? And now I'm falling for a young man that I barely know, and I feel terribly guilty. You are a wonderful boy from a poor coal mining family of immigrants and I don't deserve you." Maria started to cry…

"Maria…I still don't understand…what troubles you and why do you say these things?"

"Lazlo… I'm rich! My family's wealthy! I'm sorry if I've deceived you while I tried to figure out if you were true and real. And now I know that you are. I feel so ashamed of myself. Can you ever forgive me?"

Lazlo was stunned. He didn't truly understand what he was feeling. He needed to breathe… alone… he needed to think.

"Maria, please stay here. I promise to return shortly. I need to speak with my Momma and Papa on this matter. I really do not know what to think right now. You have confused me, and I don't understand why. I have very little experience in the ways of the heart, but I do know that I want to understand *your* heart. Please stay here… Please…" Maria nodded. Lazlo left the food court to return to Room 214.

When Lazlo entered his Momma's room, he noted that Dr. Sherlous was already gone. Julius was asleep in a chair, but Eztar was very much awake. She wasn't surprised that he was by himself. Lazlo started to explain why Maria was not with him on this return visit but Eztar stopped him by saying, "There is no need to explain my son, I know."

"Momma…what's happening?"

Eztar took her son by the hand and pulled him to the side of her bed. "Please sit Lazlo." The mood of the room was serious, and quiet… except for the light sound of Julius snoring in his chair.

"Please hear my words, and listen carefully. People often search a lifetime looking for their perfect match. Sometimes they actually find it, but they don't even know it. Pride and ego cause differences that lead to them moving on, in hopes of finding another. Life can be cruel." Lazlo was intently holding onto every word. Eztar continued, "Careers can tear relationships apart, family disputes, religion, educational levels, my God, we humans have excuses for everything instead of just following our hearts when it counts. Remember how as a child, you were told stories of how our long-lost relatives had their spouses chosen for them?"

Lazlo said, "Yes, even as children. They knew that they were betrothed to another." Eztar then explained the process behind a true Hungarian/gypsy betrothal.

"If done correctly, the match is selected by a seer, like me. It's not really all that complicated. I have watched you since your birth. I have taken notice of the girls you have met in school, as you grew up. Classmates. Children at church, etc. I haven't seen one who seems right for you. Until now. As a *White Lighter,* your match is a difficult one. People misunderstand it but Jesus had Mary. History can be misleading. Why do you think you have not yet dated at age 23? You have the ability to *see.* But until recently not one female has caught your inner-eye. Once again, until now."

Eztar continued, "A white aura is indeed compatible with a green. They feed off of one another, sharing energies that most cannot see or understand. Maria is your match. I knew it before I even met her, but when she entered my room today, I simply knew. She has a very light green aura, almost white, so close to being a *White Lighter* herself it is amazing. Like you my son, she is pure. Maria would make a wonderful wife for you at some point in time."

Lazlo spoke without looking at his Momma. "But she lied to me..."

Eztar squeezed her son's hands to get his attention eye to eye. She wanted to make a strong point to him that he would not question or doubt.

"Lazlo...she did *not* lie. She protected herself and in doing so protected you too. The two of you haven't even known each other for a week. Much has happened in that time. Emotions have been strong, have they not? You brought her to me for approval because in your heart you already know that you love her...and she loves you. This is a very special thing. For most people, it never happens in a lifetime. God has made this gift to you and to her. Treasure it. Nurture it. And treasure her. We are entitled to keep secrets in our hearts. I could sense that Maria hides the secret of having had an aristocratic upbringing which causes her great concern. You can see it in the way she walks or maintains her posture, and her manners in addressing those around her. Yes, I picked up on all these things as you did too. Even her name that you privately whispered to me… Cordova Valdez? Come, my son, there is much to be learned about this woman. And she too, wants to learn from you…and from our ways. Share your hearts and grow together. There is no rush… but please do not let her slip away. I love her already."

Eztar smiled at her son. "Now what was it you wanted to tell me?"

Lazlo glanced over at Julius, who was still sleeping soundly and yes, still snoring lightly.

"Thank you, Momma,…thank you for opening my eyes. I do love her. I feel it in my soul. I hope that my leaving her downstairs hasn't destroyed my chances with her. I need to return to her as quickly as possible and amend any damage that my own insecurities may have created. I love you, Momma!"

Lazlo ran out of the room to go and find Maria. After descending the stairs rapidly, two to three steps at a time, Lazlo reached the first floor. He could have taken the elevator but honestly thought that it would be far too slow. He rounded a corner at breakneck speed and collided with Dr. Sherlous.

"Whoa, Lazlo…slow down! What could possibly be so important to you that you risk injury to yourself and your family?"

Lazlo was short of breath… "Maria," he said. "Have you seen Maria?"

"Why yes, I have. She's in the food court by herself, having a cup of coffee."

Thanks, Dad," shouted Lazlo as he resumed his run. Dr. Sherlous hesitated to regain his composure. Lazlo had never called him Dad before. This truly touched the old doctor.

Lazlo rounded the final turn leading into the food court and saw Maria exactly where he had left her. Close to an hour had passed. The dining area was all but empty. Maria was sitting by herself until Lazlo arrived. It was obvious to him that she had been crying. Her eyes were red, her makeup smeared, and she held a tissue to her nose, also slightly red. Lazlo gazed at her and thought to himself that she was the most beautiful woman that he had ever seen. He started to smile but regained his composure out of fear that she might think he was laughing at her. This could not have been farther from the truth.

"Maria, forgive me. My reaction was that of a total jackass. I have no idea what I was thinking, and I overreacted. I'm so sorry. I think that it was perhaps more the fear of the unknown and things moving so fast. I'm new to this and I have a lot to learn. I hope that you might give me the opportunity to learn these things with you. I ran to my Momma in my confusion, and she guided me to the right path. That path is to you. In the future, I want to run to you for my rescue, and I want you to run to me too when you need your 'knight in shining armor'. I know that this is all happening so fast. I hope we can learn with one another."

Maria was stunned at this chain of events. Lazlo stood in front of her table, with hopes of an answer that would make things normal again between them. She slowly stood up and gradually walked in his direction. The last few steps were covered rapidly as she quite literally ran to him, throwing her arms around him while burying her face in his neck. Lazlo loved the sensation, the feeling of another human so close to him, holding him tightly. He breathed in her scent and tasted her skin as he lightly kissed her neck. He didn't think about it at all. It was just the natural thing to do.

"Maria, I don't care where you came from. I don't care if you are rich or poor. I don't care about your history or that of your family. We can make history on our own. I know it has only been days, but I find myself loving you and I think that you feel the same. I just need to hear from you, that you *do* feel the same. My Momma has chosen you…and said that we should be betrothed…like in the old country. How do you feel about this?"

"Oh Lazlo, you couldn't have made me any happier. Thank you. I trust your Momma as a seer. Everything seems to be steering us together."

They were both standing together now, facing each other. Lazlo's hands were on her shoulders and hers on his hips. Their bodies touched as they gazed deeply into each other's eyes.

"Maria…may I kiss you?" She knew that this would be the first kiss for each of them. She had dreamed of it for years since becoming a teenager. Many ideas flashed through her thoughts from stories she had read in teen magazines over the years. She knew that her answer was yes.

"Yes, Lazlo, you may… I welcome it as my first."

Lazlo gently moved his face toward hers. She moved closer to him. Lazlo saw the light green glow emanating from her skin! It was her aura. I can see it, Lazlo thought to himself. But he closed his eyes and allowed their lips to meet.

The kiss was one of innocence. It was gentle and soft. The sensation was ecstatic for each of them. Lazlo inhaled her sweet fragrance. They held one another so close that each could feel the other's heartbeat as they tightened their embrace.

Maria made the first attempt to take this experience to another level. She slightly opened her mouth which encouraged Lazlo to do the same. They had both heard of the French kiss, but until this moment had no idea what it truly was. The exchange happened naturally between them as they pulled each other closer. This intimate moment would change their lives forever.

As they released their embrace, Lazlo ended their encounter with a hug as he whispered, "I love you."

Maria had found her knight and her life now felt in balance. She smiled. "I love you too, Lazlo."

Learning More
CHAPTER 5

Maria paid for a hotel room just down the road from the hospital. She offered a room to Lazlo too, but he had already decided he wanted to stay in Room 214 with his Momma. Dr. Sherlous made arrangements for a cot to make things somewhat more comfortable. She gave him a slightly questioning look that said, "Does this have anything to do with my money?" Lazlo laughed and assured her that it did not. He had accepted the fact that they come from vastly different social backgrounds. He honestly didn't see it as a problem. Hopefully, his feelings were correct, and nothing would change between them.

As they stood together, after walking her to the hotel, Lazlo once again started to notice the light green glow that seemed to hover around her. It reminded him of the pictures in the Bible of Christ and the angels. He was surprised that he could now see her aura so clearly.

"Maria…how old were you, when you knew that you could see an aura?" She hesitated, at first, and then she answered quickly. "I was twenty-one." Lazlo was amazed. "Does this surprise you, my love?" Lazlo calmly replied that he simply thought it had been longer, but he really didn't know why.

"You were my first, Lazlo," she smiled. "The first time I saw you on the field last week, I saw your aura right away. That's when I knew."

"So, I was your first, and you were my first earlier today. Maria, I saw yours when we kissed in the food court. It is a beautiful green. Like a Northern Light…a Borealis. We also shared our first kiss together. I feel there are many firsts that we are to experience together. I am looking forward to them very much. I can still see yours now. You are absolutely glowing."

They stood together for a moment just sharing their newfound emotions. Lazlo leaned over gently to give Maria an innocent good night kiss and as their lips lightly touched, they both experienced a shared static electric shock that made them flinch. Each one of them was quite literally shocked by this happening yet a third time since meeting. Lazlo kissed the back of Maria's hand and added, "We need to get to the bottom of this." They both smiled as he departed for his walk back to the hospital.

Lazlo couldn't help remembering a conversation between Maria and himself before boarding the bus hours earlier. There were questions left unanswered regarding the roles of men and women in different countries. Maria had seemed to conceal something that perhaps she either didn't want to share, or maybe just not at that time. Lazlo was curious. After a few steps, Lazlo stopped to look back at Maria as she stood there watching him. He called to her, "You knew what?"

Maria laughed and said, "I'll tell you tomorrow." This still didn't give him his answer, but he now knew that this was simply a coy game to play with his emotions. Lazlo sighed and continued his walk back to his family.

Maria retired to her suite with a smile. She felt like she was walking on a cloud! She shut the door to her room and like a giddy schoolgirl, she jumped onto her bed, back first, like a child might create a snow angel. She rolled around laughing out loud, overcome with all of these crazy emotions caused by this Lazlo Somogyi.

Maria decided to relax after a shower and watch some television. To her pleasure, she found a late-night movie on one of the three available channels, "Breakfast at Tiffany's." She had never seen it but heard it was a wonderful tale about young love and social status while living in the city. Maria fell fast asleep within the first half hour.

Lazlo settled in with his Momma in Room 214 and knew immediately that this was going to be one of those long nights. He could tell by the look that she gave him that she already knew much of what he had to share. But she wanted to hear it from her son's mouth, in his own voice. Eztar patiently waited until he was ready to talk.

"Momma, I had no idea what it would be like to love someone that isn't family. I've heard about it and read about it, but I just never found a girl that I thought would interest me in that special way. Meeting Maria changed all of that overnight. The sensation is mind-boggling! So far, I love everything about her. She is amazing!"

"We kissed today…after I ran out of your room to apologize to her…it was unexpected, but it was nice. I liked it a lot. I could tell that she did too. We were nervous but quite comfortable. When she hugged me it was more of an embrace. It was very emotional, in a good way."

Eztar responded that she thought this was all a very wonderful start to something special.

Lazlo continued, "Momma, something else happened when we kissed. Something totally unexpected. I saw her aura. I *really* did. It was a beautiful green, like the Northern Lights."

"Yes, it is Lazlo… I have seen it too, as I told you yesterday. A beautiful aura for a very beautiful girl. Are you surprised? I've told you all your life that you are a *White Lighter*, like Jesus. You too, are empathic…truly. It is a part of your being. Why would you think anything else? Accept it, my son, it is your gift. Few can say that they truly possess such a thing."

"It's all happening so fast. It's just overwhelming." Lazlo sighed and shook his head.

Eztar could sense that there was more on his mind than he had addressed so far. There was something else troubling him. "What troubles you, my son?"

Lazlo looked at his Momma, truly wanting to hear an answer to his next question.

He began with, "Momma, when I was first introduced to Maria, we shook hands. Oddly, there was an intense static electric shock that discharged between us. We both felt it, but even more strange to me, we each saw the flash of electricity where our hands touched. I've experienced static shock before, but not anything like this. It actually hurt a little bit and we both pulled away at the same time."

Eztar encouraged him to continue.

"Well…it happened again with our first kiss, but not as intense… a light shock as I saw her aura, but it was there, nonetheless. And then a third time tonight after I walked her to her hotel room. It stopped our kiss, so I just kissed her hand and walked here to talk with you."

"Oh, Lazlo… Did you know that you were going to be such a hopeless romantic?" Eztar was smiling. "This is yet another trait that will make you an exceptional man as you grow. These are wonderful words to hear."

"But Momma…the shock…what is it? I know that it isn't typical static electricity."

Eztar hesitated with her answer, as she knew some truths, but also knew her son was entering an area that very few ever experienced. This was the world of spiritual mysticism and the paranormal. Even a skilled seer doesn't get to witness every aspect of these in a single lifetime.

Eztar tried to explain her thoughts. Much of this she knew, much of it she presumed, but a lot of it was new, even to her. She needed to put all the pieces together. Her empathic skills would assist in achieving this task for her son.

"Lazlo…all living things have an aura. Even decaying matter, like a log. While we identify a person's aura by a color, like you being a *White Lighter*, our colors can change to reflect our moods or mindsets. It can be a temporary change, or a person can completely change due to a life event. You might not be white every minute, of every day. At times, your aura might have a tint of blue or another color. But overall, I know you to be white…pure of heart. I have watched you for 23 years. Your Maria is green. Her aura looks like the Northern Lights as you noted. But her aura is a light green. That light phase of color makes her soul lean towards the white side. Either color is good, and both are a positive match. However, a true white aura, like yours, is very, very rare. Religious deities are usually said to be white in almost all forms of religions. Your aura is indeed a special one."

"Maria too, has a very special aura. The lighter Borealis color green pushes her closer to the white side. It is why she was immediately attracted to you. Remember that I mentioned the aura in a person can change every day, even minute to minute if the situation encourages it. Now it is rare that anyone is a true *White Lighter* like yourself, but even more rare that you would meet another one…and *extremely* rare that your souls would connect in a romantic manner such as you've done. My belief is that when the two of you have experienced this electrical discharge, it happened when you were at your normal white aura phase, but Maria was drifting from her green aura, toward the white. Are you following me, Lazlo?"

"Yes, Momma, I think I understand."

"Good. When both white auras are at their highest point of energy, the amount of electrical charge created needs to be discharged from their bodies. In the cases of Maria and yourself, it creates a spark, or a shock, as it leaves the bodies. The intensity will vary as will the frequency of occurrences."

Eztar sighed. "The truth is, your relationship is almost too perfect. So, your extremes will be extreme. Emotionally, you match. Physically, it will be a challenge at times. I imagine that your love life together will be something very, very special indeed. Something that most people only dream of. But be aware, once this really gets started, as her partner you will have much responsibility to keep her satisfied. But by doing so, she will dedicate herself to you and no other for eternity. You are both very fortunate, but with great fortune comes great responsibility. Do you understand?"

"Yes, Momma…thank you."

"Now go to sleep, Lazlo. Get some rest."

Lazlo was restless and had trouble getting to sleep. There was simply so much to think about, so much to absorb. He wanted to be with Maria, but he needed to spend time with his Momma. She needed him too. Lazlo began to feel a tug at his heart that most young men experience as they become adults. Only one mother can birth you into this world. They are attached to you, wholly, but even *they* know that the day will come when their man-child chooses another woman to share his life. Many mothers fight this natural transition.

Lazlo was happy that it seemed Eztar understood, and was willing to share. Maria would be a fine choice if she indeed felt the same way about him.

Once again, he noted to himself how quickly things seemed to be developing. Lazlo watched his Momma sleeping, breathing comfortably. He couldn't help but notice that even in her sleep, there was a smile on her face. He hoped that it was for Maria and him in their upcoming life together. Lazlo dozed off himself moments later and felt his own smile leading him down a path to pleasant dreams.

Hours passed and morning arrived with light from a beautiful sunrise entering the room. It was going to be a wonderful day.

Lazlo looked over at his Momma as she woke up and they exchanged a smile. He also took note that Julius had re-entered the room sometime through the night and was again asleep in a chair near Eztar's side.

"Good morning my son," Eztar said softly to Lazlo.

"Good morning, Momma…did you sleep well?"

Eztar smiled and nodded, "I had a dream last night. It was about my own father. Who, as you know, died during the war. His name was Lazlo, too. László Joseph Biro. Papa was a very unique man. He was a machinist by trade, but he practiced the art of gem cutting, and he was also an inventor as a hobby of sorts. In 1938, he invented the ballpoint pen. Sadly, he would never escape Europe during the madness of Adolph Hitler. He was destined to die in the gas chambers in Poland. He sacrificed much for his family. You were named after him and I want you to carry his name proudly. Never forget his accomplishments."

Lazlo had heard the stories of his grandfather throughout his childhood, but it had been some time since Momma mentioned him. The dream had a meaning buried deep within it and Lazlo felt sure that Momma was going to allow it to resurface shortly. And she did…

Eztar continued. She spoke of her childhood and Hungary. "I adored my Papa. He was proud to be a Magyar. 84% of the Hungarian population carried that bloodline, but he still believed his family heritage to be special. Royal gypsies! He'd joke about it openly, all the time. He desperately wanted to escape to the New World… America… Land of the free. But he never made it. His family, however, did. Now, his grandson is about to become a doctor! I am so proud," Eztar said.

Eztar looked over at her son as he intently listened to her voice. Her speaking had a way of mesmerizing him. It was relaxing, like becoming a young child again hearing a bedtime story.

"Yes Momma, what do you need from me today? It seems like there is something special on your mind." Julius started to stir, gradually waking up, and took note of the conversation already in progress. He knew what was coming next.

"Lazlo, I need you to make a trip to Ward. I need you to return to our home and retrieve an item for me from our house. It is extremely important to me. You should also take Maria. It would be good for her to see where you were raised, and to possibly even meet some friends. Will you do this?" Eztar waited for his answer.

A trip to the coal mines would be an eye-opener for Maria. "Yes Momma, I will go. I'll speak to Maria shortly. We agreed to meet for breakfast at a little café here in town. We can discuss the details there."

"What will we be collecting for you Momma? And where is this treasure?" Lazlo snickered.

Eztar became quite serious and stressed to Lazlo, "The item is a small leather bag, no larger than a wallet. It has a cord attached to it that acts as a drawstring. The contents are priceless to me. You must promise that once collected, neither you nor Maria will view the contents. Do you promise?" That would come later Lazlo thought to himself.

Lazlo knew that she was serious and that he should doubt nothing about this *quest*. He readily agreed and swore to do what she asked. He wondered what it could be.

"One last thing my son…you will need to know how to find it. I did not leave it out in the open. This treasure, like all others, is hidden."

Lazlo knew of stories where Hungarian relatives buried coins in mason jars around their properties. He imagined it to be done this way. He waited for Eztar to continue.

"You will recall the layout of the kitchen area in our home in

Ward. Go to the old pot-bellied wood stove there. Underneath the stove is a cast iron black kettle pot for boiling coffee or tea. It is old and rusted, not used in years. Look inside the pot and remove the contents. Your quest will begin there. Now go to Maria and explain the need for your trip. Make it an adventure of sorts and have some fun."

Lazlo acknowledged that he understood. He checked with hospital doctors in reference to how long it was expected that his mother should remain in the hospital. It appeared that she would stay for another two days at most. He then left for the café to meet Maria.

Lazlo saw from outside the café that Maria was already there. She was obviously in good spirits and smiled brightly as Lazlo approached the table. Maria stood up to greet him with a hug and gently kissed him on the lips as a friendly but loving hello. There was no static shock. They were both quite surprised but looked at one another with a shrug, as if to say, "Well… I guess it won't happen every time. Maybe that's a good thing?" Lazlo pondered his Momma's thoughts on the subject. White Light energy. He wanted to know more.

The two of them sat down together and ordered breakfast. Lazlo began to explain the strange turn of events and the request made by his Momma. Little did he know, her motives were slightly more than what she explained. Eztar was still a mother. Mothers protect their sons. While she in fact already felt great affection for Maria, she didn't want to see Lazlo get hurt by his first love, especially if this relationship was just a rich girl's fancy. She doubted this to be true but needed to be sure. Maria had most likely never seen a coal mine or surrounding villages. The level of poverty was quite extreme. These humble beginnings would make Lazlo a better man. Eztar felt that his future wife should witness this environment firsthand, in person. If Maria was indeed as special as Eztar imagined, it would be good for them both. If not, the truth would be told. Eztar prayed that her spiritual reading of Maria was accurate. If she was correct, these two would be married one day.

Maria and Lazlo were finishing their breakfast and had discussed the trip to Ward while eating. Lazlo mentioned taking a bus and walking to his home in the hills of Ward. He was about to stand up, but Maria stopped him.

"Lazlo…I have a car." Maria waited for his response. The information had caught him a bit off guard.

"Oh," was all that he could say at that moment.

"I'm sorry, Maria. That just seemed to come from nowhere and I was very surprised. So where is it?"

"Well…that's the problem…it's back in Maryland near the campus. I left it in a parking garage. It would be a lot of extra travel, but I thought we might take the bus back to the college, pick up my car, and then travel to Ward. It would give us the freedom of being on our own time and you could show me the countryside of West Virginia. I have heard that the mountains there are beautiful. What do you think?"

Lazlo was still trying to absorb the thought that Maria owned a car and that it was here, in America. The more he thought about it, he realized that he wasn't sure why he was surprised. A road trip in a car could be quite an adventure.

"Sure, why not? Let's do it!"

Off they went to the Greyhound Bus Terminal…again. This time Maria approached the ticket window. "Two tickets to Baltimore, Maryland please…" They boarded their motor coach within the hour and started their journey together, back to Baltimore. After some more talk about why they were going to Ward and some of Maria's expectations of their trip, the drone of the big engine and the tires humming on the asphalt made them both a little sleepy. Lazlo nodded off first. His sleep recently was in bits and pieces anyway. He didn't have the luxury of a hotel room and Maria knew it. She would make that up to him soon. He deserved some special treatment.

After they exited the bus, it was a short walk to the parking garage near the Greyhound terminal. They strolled hand-in-hand toward their destination, oblivious to the time. Love has a way of doing that.

Upon arrival, Maria showed the attendant a receipt and he retrieved the keys from the lockbox. It appeared that she had paid in advance as no money was exchanged. Lazlo just watched.

Lazlo then asked Maria what kind of car she owned, "What is it Maria, an old Ford truck?" he said, jokingly.

Maria didn't seem amused, and she usually laughed at all his jokes, mostly to just be polite. Lazlo sensed a strong mood change in Maria. "Well at least here in Baltimore, it should be American-made, and that's reliable transportation!" Lazlo had always heard his father and his uncles talk this way, so he assumed it to be true.

Maria turned her back on him and looked off into the large garage. It seemed that the temperature dropped to at least forty degrees. Her Spanish temper was starting to reveal itself.

Lazlo decided to leave well enough alone, but it was already too late. The damage was done, but it was about to get far worse. He just didn't know it yet.

They both heard an engine start in the garage. A low, throaty rumble. Lazlo had never heard anything like it. The sound caught his attention. What could it be? Maria's car?

The sound grew louder as the attendant accelerated the car through the turns in the garage, making the tires squeal just a little. Maria smiled as she knew the little car well. Around the turn came a pristine, 1957 Porsche 356A, a classic in any timeframe. It was glacier white. Maria knew that meant Porsche color #5713. She knew her little sports car inside and out. It was the perfect color for a would-be-*White Lighter*. She had missed her little car and was happy to get it back. She looked forward to sharing it with Lazlo. But he was not smiling.

"What's wrong Lazlo? This is my little car…my Papa gifted it to me last year after I finished my first year at the University. He had it shipped here for my vacation with my cousin." Lazlo responded from the heart as any *White Lighter* would, but he quickly regretted it before he even finished his grouping of sentences.

"This is a Porsche, correct?"

Maria immediately said yes, with great enthusiasm. Lazlo interrupted her before she had the chance to say more. Her smile disappeared.

"It's an Adolf Hitler car!"

Lazlo calmed himself and while looking at the ground spoke

out loud, "Hitler killed my grandfather. He had him gassed in Poland. Many of my other relatives were also murdered in the concentration camps. My parents were fortunate enough to survive the holocaust. They fled Europe and settled in West Virginia. I have hated everything that represents that man for close to two decades."

Maria didn't know the history of her Porsche. For her, a car was just that. Something to drive for transportation, and in this case fun. She loved her little toy. She slowly meandered over to Lazlo with hopes of somehow offering an olive branch. She prayed to herself that he wouldn't pull away, emotionally or physically.

"I had no idea, my love… I'm so sorry that you carry this pain. We all grow up with insecurities others can't see. We hide them with the hope of not finding them again. Sorry that my excitement over sharing something that I love has caused your pain to surface. I'm sorry about your family. I'm sorry about your grandfather. I hope that you will forgive me for causing you pain, even though I had no idea my actions, as simple as they were, would do such a thing."

Maria held his hand and gave it a light squeeze. "I call my car Lola. You'll see that she too, is a *White Lighter*, although she's been known to run a few red lights without my permission. She has a mind of her own." Maria laughed lightly. Lazlo gazed at this wonderful woman who was trying to lift his spirits. Her efforts were working.

"Please allow me to put a thought in your head." Maria went on to say, "A car is just a car. Adolf Hitler didn't invent the Volkswagen or the Porsche. He just took credit for it. Do you feel that buying an Italian sports car means that you support Benito Mussolini? Or perhaps the new Japanese cars? Are purchasers supporting the emperor of Japan? I find it hard to think that way. The world has enough hate in it. There is no need for me to be part of that. My heart is filled with love."

She looked into his eyes and said, "I'll make you a deal. I want you to drive my Lola to Ward. My little car aims to please. The time on the road with her should change your mind, hopefully. But I'll make you a promise… if we arrive in Ward later tonight, and you still feel the same way, I will either immediately sell her or gift her to my cousin Clayton. He adores her! Deal?"

Lazlo was moved beyond words and started to softly cry, not knowing if it was still sorrow for his grandfather and other relatives, or happiness over his love towards Maria.

"I'm sorry too, Maria. I think I overreacted and now I feel like a fool."

She threw her arms around him and gave him a big hug.

"You know, in the movies, they say that love means never having to say that you're sorry. I disagree…love means not taking sides and knowing that being sorry for something is most often a two-way street. We hit a moment where I unknowingly hurt you, and then your reaction hurt me. Thank you for being the man that you are. I love you, you know?"

Maria smiled. "Isn't that the most important thing?"

Lazlo nodded. "That's always the most important thing."

"Now, Lola…meet Lazlo…and Lazlo…meet Lola. Let's go to West Virginia."

Lola, Lazlo and Maria

CHAPTER 6

Lazlo had never seen a car this small before. Ford made the two-seater T-Bird, but this was much smaller. Lazlo walked to the front of little Lola and excused himself as he fumbled around for the hood latch. "Excuse me, my lady, not to get personal but I'd like to see what you've got under your bonnet. Isn't that what they call a hood in Europe?"

Maria laughed out loud. At first, he thought that she was laughing at his bonnet joke, but he quickly realized it was something else and perhaps the joke was somehow on him.

"You're at the wrong end," laughed Maria. "If you want to get personal with my Lola, you need to be at her rear end…maybe slide up under her bottom." Maria continued to laugh. "Lazlo, her engine is in the rear!"

Lazlo quickly figured out that he was messing with the trunk. "My Lord, what else have they done with these cars overseas?" He walked to the rear where Maria was standing. Looking at Maria he asked, "So what's under that hood? Our smallest American V–8 is a 289 Ford or a 283 Chevy. What's she got?"

Maria opened the engine cover to reveal a little four-cylinder, air-cooled engine with two big carburetors, one mounted on each side of the engine. In the center was a generator to provide electricity. There was no radiator.

"Well, ain't that a thing," said Lazlo, as he got closer for a better look. "She's sporty, but I can't believe that engine could have much power. What size is it again?"

Maria happily wanted to share her knowledge. She simply loved cars! "Well…she's measured in cc's, cubic centimeters instead of cubic inches like here in America. She's got a 1300cc motor, technically 1290 cc's. We call it a 1.3 liter. It really means that compared to the 289 V-8 you mentioned, she's somewhere around 90 cubic inches. Lola can get up to around 85 mph fairly fast."

Lazlo frowned and shrugged. "This is going to be interesting," Lazlo said.

Maria smiled as if she knew a secret that had never been told. "I think that we better get moving. You can drive a clutch, can't you? Lola has four on the floor."

Lazlo went to the passenger side and opened the door for Maria. "Yes, I know how to drive a clutch but this will be the first time I've driven a convertible. There's a first time for everything."

"My love, many of our first times will be experienced together," Maria smiled as she got into the car.

"My goodness she sits so low! I mean, crap, our butts will be sitting on the road!" Lazlo said.

Just getting inside to drive took some special effort. Maria guided him through the best technique. Once inside, Lazlo played with the stick shift to get the feel of it and adjusted the seat, so his long legs reached the pedals comfortably. He put in the clutch, located neutral, and turned the key. Lola immediately came to life with a roar! She didn't sound like only 90 cubic inches! Lazlo looked at Maria and smiled. "Let's go!"

"Should we practice a bit before we hit the road?" Maria suggested.

After 5 or 10 minutes of driving in a nearby parking lot, Lazlo felt more confident. It was time to hit the highway. They had an approximate 6-hour drive to Ward, at over 385 miles. Lazlo headed west on I-68 knowing that only one other highway was needed just north of Ward, I–79 S. It would be an easy drive.

Lazlo looked ahead to the entrance ramp on the interstate. The speed limit was 70 mph. He wondered to himself if Lola could perform in this environment. Lazlo pressed the gas pedal to the floor in 2nd gear and was surprised at just how quickly Lola redlined her motor for a 3rd gear shift. It seemed almost effortless. He repeated the process from 3rd to 4th gear and was happy to see the 70 mph speed limit was met rather quickly. He looked over at Maria and saw she was beaming! She was enjoying this a great deal.

It wasn't long before Lazlo approached an 18-wheeler semi-tractor trailer and didn't want to get buffeted by the wind coming off of the big box, so he downshifted to 3rd gear, accelerated to 4th, and quickly passed the big truck. He glanced at the speedometer and was surprised to see 85 mph under the needle.

Lazlo looked at Maria and yelled over the noise of the wind, "Hard to believe she's under 90 HP!"

"I told you so! She's fast and she knows it! She really does great on country roads."

The interstate highway was uneventful once they settled in, but Lazlo decided that he needed to experience Lola on some twisty roads. As he got closer to Ward, he started to think which ones might work. At the I-79 S junction, north of Ward, Lazlo stopped for dinner at a local truck shop and got his chance to give a man's opinion on her little car.

He did note that 75 mph on an interstate with the top down created a ringing in his ears and a slightly sore throat from yelling back and forth to Maria. We need sweet tea. Maria laughed and pointed to the cotton balls that she had shoved in her ears earlier without Lazlo noticing. "I never drive highway speeds without them. Sorry that I didn't bring extra." When Lazlo tried to exit the car, he was once again surprised by the low stance of the vehicle. He had some trouble getting out. "She sure is low…but I guess that's why she handles so well." They walked around for a few minutes to stretch their legs before taking a booth inside the restaurant. Lazlo immediately ordered iced tea. Maria ordered a coffee.

When the waitress arrived, she ordered a salad and a lemonade. He was famished and ordered the "Trucker's Special", which was also called the "Belly Buster." It was a half-pound burger, made of prime Angus beef, loaded with two kinds of cheese, both Swiss and cheddar, fried onions and mushrooms, sliced tomato, lettuce, mayo, and ketchup. All on an oversized sesame seed bun! It came with a side of french fries and a slice of homemade pie, your choice of apple, blueberry, cherry, or pecan. Lazlo ordered the blueberry. Before the waitress left with the order, Lazlo politely added… "Ma'am, could you please have them spread some peanut butter on the bottom part of the bun? Under the burger. I love it when it melts like that." She smiled and disappeared into the kitchen. As a waitress of some 20+ years, she had seen it all. One trucker ordered the rainbow trout topped with strawberries a few years back. Peanut butter on beef was nothing.

Maria, on the other hand, was amazed.

"Is this some kind of high-protein training diet that your team endorses?" Then she smiled. Lazlo laughed and suggested that she try it when the waitress served it later. They settled in talking about the last leg of their journey.

Lazlo had developed some slight concerns for Maria's comfort in the coal mining village. They would be arriving after dark. Lazlo's childhood home had no electricity to speak of, just an old generator. Cooking and heating were handled by woodstoves and yes, plumbing was outdoors in a typical "outhouse". Water was supplied by a well. If they did spend the night after a late arrival, lighting would be small portable kerosene lanterns. The generator would make too much noise at that late hour.

On the other hand, the truck stop also had a small motel attached, and rooms could be rented for a reasonable rate, with breakfast waiting in the morning before their trip south. There would be no food at the home now but the Company Store wasn't far away. He would tell all of this to Maria and let her make the choice. Either way, home was not too much farther now. Lazlo hoped to stay at the truck stop location.

The waitress delivered their meals and Lazlo quickly attacked his burger. Between bites, he remembered offering her a taste. "It really is great," he exclaimed. Maria was hesitant but decided to give this monstrosity of meat a try. To her surprise she liked it! No, she *really* liked it! "Another first for us babe… and I believe it's a good one," he said.

Maria smiled but added, "If you intend to feed me like this, I will become fat in no time at all!" Lazlo took her hand and assured her that it wouldn't make any difference to him. They continued eating, and Maria helped herself to a few of Lazlo's french fries every now and then. She tried his pie too, having never tasted blueberries before. It was yet another first and she quickly determined his Trucker's Special was an excellent choice.

As they finished their meals, paid their bill, and left a tip, Lazlo decided to share his proposal regarding the overnight stay and the last leg of the trip. He offered Maria the possible choices, without revealing his opinion. He really wanted to do what she chose. Lazlo didn't care if they didn't stay there tonight. It didn't matter.

It didn't take Maria long to make a choice. "Let's go to Ward tonight!" She seemed excited. Lazlo not so much. But he tried to hide it. Maria wanted to experience his origin…where he grew into a young man. This would be an honest representation of his very being. She smiled at the thought of it.

"So, let's hit the road! But before we go, please show me how to put Lola's top up. I don't want to be eating bugs on top of my pie, and I fear if Lola rolls into Ward 'topless' she might draw some unnecessary attention." Lazlo smiled, as Maria laughed. She liked his stupid jokes. Most of them anyway.

Lazlo had gotten quite comfortable with Lola after spending over 300 miles behind her wheel between Baltimore and the truckstop. With the top securely in place and the windows installed, Lazlo eased her out onto I-79 south to Ward. He was feeling confident and floorboarded Lola in 1st gear causing the tires to really screech and throw some burned rubber smoke. Maria laughed and commented that she thought Lola was really smitten by Lazlo. He looked back at Maria and replied, "I think that I'm smitten by her too." They both knew what his remark really meant. Maria took his right hand in hers and south they went to Ward, West Virginia.

The night sky was beautiful with lots of stars. Traveling at night left little chance of really seeing the area, but there would still be tomorrow. For now, the evening offered time with Lazlo, and the chance to actually see where he was born, played as a boy, and partially grew up as a young man until he moved away with the Sherlous family. This would be an adventure not to be forgotten.

After roughly an hour, Lazlo turned onto one of those country backroads that she mentioned wanting to see. He had to slow Lola to almost a crawl because the dirt roads were so bad. Most were blackened with soot from the coal industry all around them. Village dogs chased them as Lazlo navigated the area.

It was quite surreal. Maria thought in her life thus far, she had witnessed poverty. As Lola's headlamps shone on the derelict homes throughout the neighborhood, Maria quickly determined that she had never seen such poverty before. Lazlo had been born into a world of destitution. Now he was about to graduate from a major medical university, Johns Hopkins. This was a miracle in itself. And here he was, driving home in a Porsche with a young Spanish aristocrat, holding his hand.

Maria realized that this was a kind of test. Eztar wanted to be sure that this young love was real. If it wasn't, the chances of the adventure ending suddenly could happen. Maria looked at Lazlo, squeezed his hand again, and was overwhelmed with the recurrent feeling of love and pride. Jesus was born in a manger and said to be the 'King of Kings'. Wealth and possessions really meant little. Maria knew this, even if she did come from a family with money.

Soon they arrived at a structure that Maria presumed was Lazlo's childhood home. It was dark except for the light from the car headlamps. A large rat scurried into the bushes near the structure.

Lazlo explained that these kinds of *kit* homes were commonly ordered through a magazine, either Sears or Montgomery Wards, and were only 500 or 600 square feet. There were no walls, so most families stretched clotheslines from front to back and side to side. Then they would hang blankets to create a form of privacy. He explained further that his Father had some carpentry skills, so he built rooms. Nothing special mind you, but functional.

Lazlo exited the car but left the engine running so the lights wouldn't drain the battery. He ran over to the passenger door and opened it to let Maria out. He then asked her to wait while he went inside for a hand-held lantern. They had several inside.

Maria watched as Lazlo opened the front door and brought out a kerosene lantern. Then he offered her an old chair to sit on while he turned off the car. Lazlo was back in a flash and then lit lanterns in every room. The dim lighting allowed Maria to focus more on just how sparse the furnishings were in the home. Basically, there were just three rooms: the front area where she sat, and what appeared to be two bedrooms. The main living area consisted of a kitchen, dining area, and a makeshift sitting room. There was a wood stove for heating and cooking in that area. An old sink had been installed, but it drained to the outside through a pipe that went out a hole in the wall. Water had to be carried in by bucket.

There was no indoor plumbing. Lazlo had mentioned the outhouse earlier.

Maria now understood why a mother like Eztar would have agreed to let the Sherlous family take her son away from this environment. Being pregnant, and then having another child would be an additional challenge, as space, food, and money were scarce.

"Well…this is it!" Lazlo opened his arms wide as if to hug the entire room. "Let me show you the bedrooms. My old room belongs to my brother now, he's staying with friends while Momma recovers." He took Maria by the hand and led her to his old room first. It wasn't much to see really. Just an old single bed, four walls, and a small table and chair where he could do his homework. Maria glanced around, almost nervously.

"Come see my parent's room, it's a bit larger." Lazlo pulled her by the hand to give her a better look.

Maria took this room in too, but it had a different emotional effect on her. This is most likely the place where Lazlo was conceived. Where he was fed and raised by his Momma. Much of his life had been spent between the confines of this room nestled inside of a minimal shack. This saddened Maria, but it also made her proud to think about how far Lazlo had come in his life.

Lazlo looked at Maria and lovingly spoke to her, "If you want us to drive back to the motel, I understand.… just say so, and we will go as soon as we look for Momma's treasure."

Maria was overwhelmed with emotions that she simply did not expect. Her respect and admiration for Lazlo seemed to grow in leaps and bounds. She felt such empathy for him, knowing that he had survived here, and thrived to become the man that she loved. Maria thought to herself, if this wasn't so right, if it wasn't destined to be, then I wouldn't be here.

"Lazlo, of course, I want to stay here with you tonight. Are you okay with that?" But before he could answer Maria threw her arms around his shoulders and neck while kissing him passionately. Lazlo carried Maria to his parents bed and gently lowered her to a comfortable location. He joined her there and they kissed each other long and deep. Maria allowed her mind to wander and she remembered the old woman in the coffee shop. How could she have known?

Maria lay on her back and Lazlo lay next to her. She slowly unbuttoned her blouse, exposing her breasts to her lover. Lazlo had never been with a naked woman. Maria was the most beautiful woman in the world! And she was here with him in his childhood home, ready to give herself willingly.

Lazlo looked at her, no, he admired her, as a thing of beauty. He was so thoroughly smitten that his hands began to shake.

"You're trembling, my love," said Maria. "Are you okay?"

"Yes," he said. "I'll be fine. You are overwhelming me. I love you more than I ever imagined."

"I love it, and I love you too," sighed Maria. "Show me more."

Lazlo lightly massaged her starting at her shoulders, tracing the lines of her body with his fingertips to her hips. He placed his hand on her stomach and tickled her navel. He was exploring and she loved it. Lazlo continued to kiss her while dragging his wet tongue down her neck to her breasts. He gently suckled her and she softly vocalized a slight whimper at his touch. Her reactions aroused him greatly and this aroused her too. Now it was her turn to disrobe him teasingly and to expose his manhood to her, here in this sacred place. The two of them were lost in time together. They forgot where they were, and why they were here. All that mattered was that they were together. After what seemed like minutes, but was closer to an hour, Maria offered herself to him and they made love to one another in a way neither had ever imagined! Their climax was also one of complete togetherness but at that moment they both witnessed something extraordinary. Their intensity was electrically charged beyond belief. Lazlo noticed that Maria was glowing in a solid white light! A white aura! Is this what his Momma, Eztar, said that she knew? Maria gazed at Lazlo in disbelief, "I see your white aura, my love! I see it strongly!"

Lazlo responded to Maria, exhausted, "I see yours too…and you're a *White Lighter*." He smiled as he gazed into her eyes.

They laid back down together and fell into a deep and wonderful sleep with Maria's head on his chest.

They had located their own special treasure in each other's arms.

Search and Recovery

CHAPTER 7

Maria woke to the sound of a rooster crowing. It really wasn't daybreak quite yet, but the organic alarm clock seemed to know his job. She looked over at Lazlo who was still sound asleep and watched him breathe, slowly and rhythmically. It was somehow soothing to her. As she watched him it made her think of the events last night and she relived them in her memory. It made her smile. Luckily it wasn't cold outside this time of year, so the temperature in the house was comfortable. Maria decided to get dressed and have a look around. Perhaps take a look outside. Lazlo won't even know that I am gone, she thought to herself.

Maria got dressed and headed to the front door. She was greeted by an old black dog with a gray muzzle as she walked onto the makeshift porch. He had seen his better days but was extremely friendly and wanted her attention. "Could you be Blackie?" Maria exclaimed. It had to be. She had heard stories of Lazlo's childhood pet. It was possible that Blackie was young when Lazlo moved to the Sherlous property. He could now be a 12 or 13-year-old dog. He started pawing at the door to go inside. "Well, I hope that you really live here," she said as she opened the door. The would-be Blackie ran straightaway into the home, tail wagging, looking for his old friend.

Maria left the door slightly ajar as she went looking for the outdoor plumbing. This would be yet another first…and she laughed.

After a successful new experience, Maria returned to the house after getting some breath mints from Lola's glove box. She brought them inside, guessing that Lazlo might appreciate one too.

Now Blackie greeted her all over again. He was a happy dog! Lazlo appeared behind him with a big smile on his face. "I see that you two already know one another?" And he hugged Maria good morning. She passed him a mint and they both laughed.

"Who's taking care of him?" Maria asked.

Lazlo explained that the local people around the village camp were like family and most of the dogs just sort of lived among them. He was getting food and water and sleeping where he wanted. But Blackie obviously missed Lazlo. He was his boy!

"So did you sleep well?" Lazlo asked.

Maria said that she actually slept very well. And again, she flashed her wonderful smile. "I will treasure last night for the rest of my life," and she hugged him again. This time they kissed, but she still longed for a toothbrush and some water.

Reading her mind, Lazlo said they could get water from the well. "I'll come with you," said Maria. She wanted to experience this too and grabbed onto his arm while escorting him to this well, wherever it might be.

He carried a bucket to a strange-looking hand pump just a few feet out of the ground. There was a trough there with water already in it, but it didn't look really clean. Maria frowned.

"Don't worry, that's just for priming the pump, to get the water flowing." He demonstrated by pouring a few cups of this water into the top of the pump handle. After manually pumping the handle, like you might jack up a car with a flat tire, the water began to flow. Lazlo filled their bucket as Blackie drank from the well.

Maria laughed. "This is so much fun!" Lazlo just shook his head, grinning from ear to ear. This was the first time that he ever thought priming a well was fun.

They went back to the house where Lazlo had several toothbrushes, soap, and other necessities. He showed Maria how to use the sink. He could see it was all an adventure to her. Lazlo took his turn with the outdoor plumbing and returned to find Maria on the floor playing with Blackie. "If my dog likes you, I like you… If not? Well… look out! But it looks like Blackie has good taste."

"If you would like a cup of coal miner's coffee I'll make some," said Lazlo as Maria and Blackie continued playing. Blackie barked repeatedly. He liked this new human. "I'll fire up the wood stove. We have coffee and sugar here, I'm sure."

"Sounds great to me," said Maria.

Julius kept a small amount of split oak wood inside the kitchen, and it wasn't long before Lazlo had a fire roaring. He located a bag of coffee beans in a cabinet with a jar of sugar beside it and showed Maria how the old coffee grinder worked. Another hand crank tool of many years past. Again, Maria was thrilled to try it herself and walked around pretending it was an organ grinder and little Blackie was her monkey. She was having a ball! Her innocent acceptance of everything made him love her even more.

"So, Maria, we need to think about breakfast and there isn't much here. We have several choices but each one has its…" Suddenly, there was a loud knock on the door that interrupted him. Blackie barked aggressively at the door!

"Shut up, ya mutt!" Came the shout from a voice outside. It was a voice that Lazlo knew all too well from years gone by. He opened the door. "Janos! You old coal dog! Look at you!" The two men embraced in a hug. "Maria, this is my cousin and old friend Janos Vestourgome!" Janos shook hands with Maria and said "You can call me John. Most can't remember Janos. It's okay." Now he petted Blackie lovingly.

"So, what the hell brings you back to this shit hole, you big lug? I thought you'd be a big-shot doctor by now?" Janos was waiting for a reply when there was a light knock on the door by a woman carrying a picnic basket. "Lazlo, you remember my wife, Eleanor?" Lazlo looked at Janos and said, of course, I do, asshole, I was at your wedding. Lazlo mumbled under his breath, *"te hülye bunkó"* meaning, "You dumb jackass." Eleanor shook hands with Maria and shared a light embrace while explaining that she fixed them breakfast after realizing it had to be Lazlo here when they saw the lights last night. Janos saw the car and figured Lazlo must be a successful doctor now living in the big city, to own such a ride. Lazlo quickly explained to them that the car belonged to Maria. They were surprised.

"Please…eat. It's still hot from my oven and grill," instructed Eleanor. "I knew there was no food here to speak of. Eat. Then we can catch up."

You didn't have to tell Lazlo twice. He grabbed the basket to check out the contents. He stopped abruptly though, and apologized to Maria, handing her the basket. "Ladies first,"…and he smiled. Maria blushed.

Janos chimed in, "They're not married yet!" And he laughed. "We were wondering what was what and who was who… that's okay. Maria, you are family now if you want us. Now eat!"

Maria was pleased to see fresh biscuits with a jar of honey, crispy bacon, several pieces of fruit, and a chunk of cheese with a knife. Everyone dug in like it was the first meal they had in days. Eleanor slapped Janos on the hand and said, "Darling, you already ate one breakfast today," and they laughed. Maria told Eleanor that it was the best breakfast she had ever had…and she meant every word. Lazlo's coal miner coffee was the icing on the cake.

Breakfast turned into a conversation about recent events. The family knew of Eztar being ill but didn't have details since they didn't own a phone. Word traveled slowly around these parts.

Lazlo told them about Eztar and her illness. Then he spoke about how he had met Maria at a Lacrosse game at Johns Hopkins. He also explained that he had not yet graduated, but would soon and that there was a possibility for further education. He was still considering it. Hopefully, his family would be at the graduation. He invited Janos and Eleanor too, although he doubted that they would make the trip.

"More college," Janos exclaimed. "This guy always was the smart one in the family. Except when he blew up the still."

"I just got the recipe wrong," muttered Lazlo…but he laughed it off.

Janos changed the subject, not wishing to offend his favorite cousin in the world. "So, what brings you back to 'black-lung' territory?" Eleanor looked on, wondering this herself.

Lazlo said, "We are on a treasure hunt! Momma asked that I retrieve something of great family value. I have no idea what it is, but it means a lot to her. I also promised that when we locate it, we do not look at the contents until we're back at the hospital with her. Do you want to help?"

Eleanor and Janos exchanged glances but the looks on their faces said more.

"What gives Janos?"

Eleanor urged her husband to speak.

"Well…it's all a rumor mind you…more family bullshit if you ask me, but the treasure talk has been in the family for decades. I'm surprised that you aren't familiar with it."

"Go on," urged Lazlo.

"Well, our grandfather, from which you inherited your name, worked closely with the Nazi machine. He hated them mind you, but he had many skills that paid the bills before they gassed him in one of the camps. The rumor was, he took something of value from them and was caught. It ended in his death. Our family was devastated and over time stories were created that made him a hero, saying that he took steps to secure the future of his bloodline. He sold his ballpoint pen invention to a fellow named BIC, in 1938, but it was sold for only $16,000. That sounds like a great deal of money, but it ended there. No royalties. He got screwed. Do you think your Momma knows something?"

Lazlo was shocked. He knew nothing of this. But that might make sense that the daughter of this man was assigned the task of protecting his treasure.

"So let's get started!" Lazlo stood up and headed for the wood-stove. Everyone watched, looking confused. He reached for the old rusty tea kettle on the floor that never seemed to serve a purpose. Lazlo lifted it, removed the lid, and looked inside. There was a small metal tin in the bottom, the size of a credit card. He frowned. When he opened the tin, it revealed a handwritten note from his Momma. He knew her handwriting. Lazlo read the note out loud to his family.

Good job. If you find this, your life is soon to change.
Congratulations! Get a shovel and go to the outhouse
for a dig. Ten paces due south marks the spot.

Everyone stood up quickly. Janos was the first one out the door.

Several shovels were leaning against the back of the house waiting to be used. Janos grabbed the first, and Lazlo took the second one. Off they went to the outhouse. Janos was looking around frantically trying to figure out due south. Lazlo knew but wondered exactly where Eztar started her pacing. Was her back against the southern wall of the structure, perfectly centered? This could make a critical difference in locating *the spot*, as she called it. He also realized that her shorter height meant shorter paces. His longer strides would overshoot the mark. He decided to let Maria do it. Eztar and Maria were similar in size. She would start dead center against the south wall and pace from there. They all counted out loud with her as she slowly walked. "One, two, three, four, five, six, seven, eight, nine, and ten."

The location was just flat earth, and dirt with no visual qualities, but this is where Eztar said to dig, so they would. Janos led the attack. Lazlo laughed and watched. Maria was beaming with enthusiasm, "This is so much fun!" Lazlo loved seeing her girl-like innocence. It was refreshing.

Janos continued to dig, somewhat carefully, as he knew the history of his family members putting valued items in mason jars for safekeeping. He didn't want to break a jar if indeed, there was one here. They all heard a light "clinking sound" as his shovel struck something in the soil below ground level.

He was right. A sealed mason jar appeared as he carefully continued his dig. Lazlo reached down and lifted the jar out of the ground, He brushed off the dirt. The lid was removed with minimal resistance. Lazlo reached inside, finding another note, written in Eztar's hand. He looked at everyone before he opened the folded piece of paper.

Once again, good job! But you're not there yet! A
very special person died for this treasure, and it can't

> *be given up to just anyone. It is destined for the*
> *namesake of László Joseph Biro.*

Lazlo stopped reading and looked at the others. "I wonder how long ago she put this clue in the ground?"

Janos was excited. "Read more, man, what else does it say?"

Lazlo read …

> *What comes from the Earth, black as dark night, but*
> *like a boy turns to man, it transforms to white light?*

Everyone stared at Lazlo holding the clue in his hand. He repeated it several times out loud. Janos was frowning. "What the hell is that supposed to mean?" Lazlo started to smile as he thought that he might know the answer. It could be so simple, but still so challenging. "Coal." Lazlo stopped. "Coal. I think that's the answer."

Janos was losing his patience. "What the hell, Lazlo! We live in a coal mine! That's just plain stupid, man!" He kicked at the dirt to relieve some frustration.

Lazlo took control of the search again. They needed to get back on track.

"Janos, I need you now more than ever. Yes, we are in a coal mine. Everything is blackened, even my dog." Janos asked how Blackie could possibly know where the treasure is. Lazlo laughed. "No, not Blackie…Black coal."

Lazlo thought quietly to himself for a minute.

"Now think…as a boy, I remember my Papa using coal in our stove. He quit because he became concerned when miners were coming down with the 'black lung' and dying from it. We changed over to wood, mostly oak. Julius had a coal bin. It was somewhere here on the property. I remember an old truck driving through the village delivering coal to families for heating and cooking. Do you remember?"

Janos tried to recall the location of the bin, as did Lazlo. It was so long ago, and the wood had rotted away, for sure. Rain and snow would have washed away much of the coal. Where was that old coal bin?

Lazlo recalled being in his bedroom when the truck delivered.

Once in a while, he'd even look outside to watch it dump the coal. He remembered seeing it from his window. The window was a starting point. Everyone followed Lazlo to that spot.

Standing outside of the window Lazlo tried to remember how the truck arrived. Where did it dump? He looked to an area overgrown with vegetation and weeds and decided that's where it was. Janos too, said that he remembered seeing it there as a child. The brush would need to be cleared.

Their project continued after they located a few farm tools that would aid them in cutting back the vegetation. It was hard work, but they soon began to see the dark stain on the soil from the black coal.

"Now, we carefully dig," directed Lazlo.

After a time that seemed an eternity, Janos was once again first to hear the 'clink' of his shovel on yet another mason jar. He exposed it and gave it to Lazlo. "You are his namesake," Janos said with a smile.

This jar contained another note from Eztar and an old leather satchel on a decaying leather cord. It fit the description shared with him by his Momma. The note read as follows:

> *To my son Lazlo. This belonged to your grandfather*
> *from which you received your name. He died for it.*
> *He died for all of us. When we ran from our home-*
> *land, because of the German Scourge, I sewed this*
> *little pouch that belonged to my Papa into the hem*
> *of my skirt for protection. I wore it onto Ellis Island*
> *in New York, and I carried it here to West Virginia.*
> *It is meant for you and anyone that you love. At this*
> *writing, you are but two years old. I have protected it*
> *for you. If you are reading this, I am either dead or*
> *sick in some way and felt something else wonderful*
> *was happening in your life. If I live, I will have*
> *asked you to swear to not open our treasure until*
> *you are back with me. Please honor my wishes. You*
> *are a smart boy. I think that you know what it is. I*
> *love you, my son, Momma.*

Lazlo started to cry and Maria hugged him. Janos and Eleanor quietly looked on. After Lazlo regained his composure, he continued.

"Janos, Eleanor, Maria, and Blackie," Lazlo laughed at Blackie. "You are part of my family. You are part of Eztar's treasure. I will honor her wishes and go to her tomorrow, maybe even today. I will not open the satchel. I promise you though, a part of the contents belong to you too. Bide your time…tell no one…and you will receive a gift from our grandfather. Please bear with me… Agreed?"

Once again, Janos was driving himself crazy with what might be in the little wallet-sized bag.

Lazlo continued… "Keep our secret to protect it. Remember the clue. Black as dark night, transformed to white light? GrandPapa was many things. But one of his skills that served the Germans was his ability to cut gemstones."

Lazlo rolled his fingers on the leather, feeling the contents of the satchel. There were at least a dozen hard items inside, none smaller than a grape. He believed that they were cut diamonds, and the value could be priceless to their family.

"I think that our grandfather cut the stones and stole them from Nazi Germany. They suspected him and he did die for it, but not before he gave them to Momma. She felt that they needed to come to me. Maybe it was a promise to him to give the future to an unborn child. I will try to learn how it happened. Again, I promise part of this is now yours too. Please take care of Blackie. And please tell no one. Our lives are about to change if I am correct."

They all hugged each other, Lazlo kissed Blackie, and after collecting their travel gear, they headed for Lola.

Eleanor and Janos walked them to the car for a parting look. Janos admired Lola. Lazlo smiled at his cousin and added, "Maybe you'll own one like her someday." And off they went, heading back towards the hospital to visit his Momma.

A Mother's Gift

CHAPTER 8

Lazlo wanted to drive so Maria gave in with a smile that said, "I told you so!" It was true, he was really falling for Lola. Lazlo was surprised that these two European ladies could both capture his heart at the same time and so very quickly. He simply loved being behind the wheel of this hot-blooded little exotic.

Maria and Lazlo discussed the possibility of delaying their trip to the hospital by grabbing a room at the truck stop for the night. It would be an early check-in, but a clean room and a shower would be nice before really hitting the road. Lazlo was thinking about one of those trucker meals that he had enjoyed before. Some private time with Maria would be nice too. Lazlo smiled at the thought of it.

"What are you grinning at mister?" Maria was giving him a look.

Lazlo laughed, "Well, I was thinking about that burger from the truck stop. It was good! Maybe we could stop there again?"

Maria smiled seductively. "Is that all you want there?" she asked. "I was thinking about getting a room with a shower. We could start back in the early morning feeling fresh."

"Great minds think alike," laughed Lazlo…so the plan was quickly made. The trucker's paradise it would be.

They arrived at the motel and decided that one room would be fine. It was a nice room, with two double beds, air-conditioning, a

TV, and a bathroom with a full shower and bath. Lazlo volunteered to allow Maria to shower first. He would wait and watch some television. He really didn't do that very often. Lazlo flipped through the three available channels and saw an episode of the western, *Bonanza*. After a few minutes, he fell asleep on the bed. Eventually, Maria came out of the bathroom wearing only a towel wrapped around her body. She obviously had hopes for some personal time with Lazlo, but he needed his rest, and she knew it. For now, she snuggled in beside him, kissed him on the cheek, and fell asleep herself. She would dream of their night before.

Roughly an hour passed before Lazlo stirred. He woke with Maria tucked in beside him like a glove. She was simply perfection in his eyes. He didn't want to wake her and decided to go get cleaned up while she slept.

The hot shower felt invigorating. Lazlo could feel his muscles relaxing and his concerns for the day melting away. But he was getting hungry, and lunch was starting to sound good.

He got dressed, quietly at first, but then realized he needed to wake Maria if he intended to feast at the truck stop. He started whistling *Satisfaction* by the Rolling Stones. Maria didn't stir, so he whistled louder. Still no response. Okay, Lazlo thought to himself, I need to ramp it up and sing. He jumped into the chorus with, *I can't get no – oh, satisfaction… I can't get no – oh, satisfaction because I tried, and I tried, and I tried and I tried… I can't get no…* Then he went into a fake guitar run while pretending that he was Mick and Keith combined. Maria was watching while pretending that she was asleep. Lazlo attempted to imitate Jagger's dance moves, shaking his hips in as provocative of a way he could manage. By now he was lost in his little rock 'n' roll fantasy and had forgotten what the purpose of this song even was. As he turned his back on Maria, she stood up on the bed dancing to his rhythm with him while screaming, "Take me, Mick!" And like a wild, young groupie she pulled off her towel, swinging it over her head and then tossing it in his face yelling again, "Take me, bad boy!"

They both started laughing hysterically and fell to the bed, side-by-side. I didn't know that you were a rockstar, Maria chortled between breaths!

Lazlo said, "Neither did I." They both continued laughing, Lazlo fully clothed, and Maria totally naked, before they both realized the absurdity of their situation. Lazlo gazed at her lovingly, "You are so beautiful, you know?" He gently kissed her on the lips…

"But damn I am so hungry!" Lazlo covered her with the towel as he got up from the bed and asked her to get dressed and come with him to eat. "There'll be plenty of time for this later on and I look forward to it, but seriously, I am starved!"

Maria loved his unpredictable boyish charm. Without thinking, she stood up, got dressed, and said, "I'm hungry too…let's go eat like truckers!"

After arriving at the restaurant, Lazlo scanned the dining area for the same waitress that they had several days ago. He didn't really know why, but he liked her. It only took a few moments, and there she was, in section C.

Lazlo nudged Maria to show that he had located her, and that's where he wanted to sit. Maria shrugged her shoulders in agreement and they went to section C. As they got closer, Lazlo strained to see the name tag on their server, and it was Marge. He wanted her to believe that he had remembered her name.

"Marge!" Lazlo called to her as they approached her area. She turned and looked in the direction of the big idiot calling her name. "Remember us? You're our favorite waitress!" Maria just rolled her eyes in astonishment at Lazlo's antics. Marge responded with a brusk hello and pointed to table number eleven a few feet away. Lazlo smiled and escorted Maria to their seats while telling Maria that he thought Marge really liked him. Lazlo grabbed two menus, gave one to Maria, and began to look things over while remembering his feast here several days ago. Maria was still looking at him and shaking her head in disbelief. Why do men feel the need to impress, even when their actions at the time aren't really impressive? She laughed to herself guessing that this was simply one of the boyish moments that the young girl in her somehow found attractive. She knew that it was all on her behalf. Yes, he loved her. There was little doubt of that.

Maria perused her menu looking for something tasty, but light. She simply couldn't afford to eat like Lazlo and allow her figure to disappear.

She noticed a special mahi-mahi steak with a side salad garnished with fresh pineapple. Let's go Hawaiian, she decided. A nice cup of coffee on the side would be wonderful. Lazlo looked like he was still searching for his Momma's treasure as he intently searched the three pages of the menu. "It all looks so good," he exclaimed.

Maria suddenly realized that because of Lazlo's upbringing, these restaurant visits were really something special to him. As a child, he had never experienced it. Dr. Sherlous was a busy man, so even after moving in with their family, these outings were somewhat rare for Lazlo. She needed to remember that and never take it for granted.

"So lover boy… What's it going to be?" The voice did not come from Maria. It was Marge.

Lazlo was caught off guard and slightly embarrassed. He lightly stuttered, "I'm not sure yet…"

Maria jumped in and ordered her cup of coffee and two ice waters with lemon while asking Marge for a few more minutes. Marge looked at Lazlo before leaving and said, "Take your time sweetheart, my shift really just got started." And off she went.

Lazlo looked at Maria and revealed to her, even though she already knew, "She called me sweetheart!"

Maria began to laugh out loud as she absorbed the total sincerity of her newfound love. This is a very intelligent man that lives life simplistically. She found Lazlo and his personal mannerisms to be quite refreshing.

"So, what's it going to be, big guy?" This time the voice belonged to Maria.

Lazlo looked up from his menu and smiled. "I think I'll have a large, sweet tea, no lemon. And I want my blueberry pie again, but this time a la mode, with strawberry ice cream." Maria frowned just a bit but quickly remembered the melted peanut butter on the burger. It was pretty good. Lazlo went on…

"I've never eaten real Mexican food before. No kidding. I know it's hard to believe but I want to try a Mexican burrito. It looks good." Maria warned him that they could be spicy hot, and the food might burn your mouth. Maybe we'll ask Marge how they prepare it here. Stomach upset can also be a common reaction hours later. Lazlo agreed that they would ask Marge.

Marge returned with the coffee and water, Maria placed her order quickly, and all eyes turned to Lazlo.

"Miss Marge… I have never tasted a burrito. No kidding. I just said that to Maria here." Marge smiled. "I don't want a spicy one that burns my mouth or makes me sick. But the pictures really look good! What would you suggest?"

Marge explained that she understood and that Mexican/American food in the 60s was more American than Mexican. "Stay away from the ones labeled as 'green' and you should be fine." She suggested the burrito supreme, chicken, with sides of yellow rice and refried beans. Marge then explained how it would be covered in cheese, sour cream, and its own salad…all on top. "It's a large meal sweetie, but you look hungry." They finished the rest of their order and settled in to wait for their culinary adventure. Lazlo and Maria were both grinning from ear to ear. Their love was rapidly becoming infectious.

It wasn't long before Marge returned with their plates. Maria's food looked delightful, a lighter side meal of healthy fish and vegetables. No reason to feel guilty eating this. She watched Marge place Lazlo's huge buffet in front of him with a smile. "Here you go, sweetheart… It looks *muy bueno* to me. Enjoy!" And off she went. Lazlo took it all in, digging into his pie first. After all, the ice cream was already starting to melt. He didn't want any of it to be wasted. He tasted the beans and rice which caused him to smile. Lazlo then nodded to Maria that so far, this was very good.

It was time to attack this close to foot-long massive tube of meat and veggies. He didn't know what to expect. Maria told him to just cut it in half and work his way to the ends, half at a time. "Some people mix the rice and beans together and eat them with the toppings," coached Maria. Lazlo took a small bite at first, but then quickly forked up another when he realized just how much he savored the taste.

"Oh, my God! This is sooo good! Maybe we should move to Mexico!" This was yet another first with the two of them, at least for him anyway. It was his first Mexican meal, and he loved it!

They finished their food and sat for a while talking and drinking coffee before paying their bill and getting up to take a short walk to burn some calories.

Lazlo joked by reciting a commercial from television, "I can't believe I ate the whole thing!" Maria wasn't familiar with the connection and really didn't understand his joke. *Alka-Seltzer* wasn't a product yet in Spain. She laughed anyway, just to make him happy.

They browsed the truck stop gift store for a while and then headed to their room. It was late afternoon, and they hadn't really planned when they'd leave in the morning.

When they got to their room, Lazlo was still raving about his burrito. This was another discovery for his limited palate. He recalled having never tasted real butter until living with the Sherlous family. It was a real treat! Eztar and Julius simply couldn't afford the butter churn or the ingredients, so they did without…like so many other things.

Maria just smiled that smile of hers and put on her somewhat 'wifely air' of simply tolerating her partner's little idiosyncrasies. She meant no disrespect, she just thought some of his explorations into his new world were funny. But Maria always reminded herself of Lazlo's humble upbringing. Wait until we visit Spain one day, she thought. But quickly erased it from her mind.

They briefly discussed their itinerary for the next day and decided that a very early start was preferable for them both. Lola would need *petro*, as Maria called it, and the fueling area for trucks was open 24/7. This would allow them to address it early and decide if Lola was to travel topless or not. Weather reports were good so far.

Lazlo looked at Maria longingly and said, "Speaking of topless…"

Maria smiled and started to disrobe for her lover.

After a very restful night's sleep, Lazlo and Maria woke early, knowing that the day ahead of them was to be a full one. They gathered their belongings and headed outside to greet Lola and ready her for their trip. Her top was up, so the pair decided to leave it that way, at least for now. Maria wanted to get her little car fueled up and oil checked before a quick stop in the diner. She preferred higher octane fuel because she believed that Lola performed better on it. Lazlo didn't really have an opinion as Maria was paying the higher price per gallon for this minor luxury. Today, he was simply pumping the fuel as there was no attendant on duty yet. "As you wish," Lazlo said to Maria with a smile. Maria smiled back at him affectionately.

Maria then commented that she really wasn't hungry, but a cup of coffee would be a nice start before hitting the highway. Lazlo agreed but thought he might grab a Danish or some similar sweet morning confection. And so, they did.

It wasn't long before they were once again on I–68 E heading back to Lexington. Lazlo reached into his pocket making sure that his Momma's treasure was secure. Feeling the objects moving inside the leather satchel relaxed him, temporarily putting his mind at ease. On this trip, they took turns driving but it was Lazlo that started the first leg of the journey. He was really starting to love this little car and surprisingly admitted it to himself. Some good things did actually come from Germany.

They safely arrived in Lexington in the afternoon. This time they decided to just grab a simple lunch at a hamburger joint that was becoming quite popular at the time. The big sign even told you how many burgers they were selling nationally. Lazlo had never seen that done before and thought it strange. No matter…the food was pretty good.

Maria suggested that they should get a room together at the same motel where she stayed the last time they were in town. There was no reason for Lazlo to sleep in the hospital again. Eztar might even be being released today, she thought to herself. So, they checked into the motel after their meal, grabbed a bagged burger and fries combination for Julius, and headed over to Roanoke Memorial Hospital.

Entering the hospital felt different this time for Lazlo… Much more relaxed. The stress of his first visit there had him feeling more like the young boy, Lazlo, than the adult man, the up-and-coming Dr.

Lazlo Somogyi. Today, he felt like the doctor again and was simply visiting his Momma who was a patient in the hospital.

Maria and Lazlo both remembered Room 214 and after a brief check-in, headed for the room. They were almost immediately greeted by Julius, and after hellos and hugs, Maria handed him the unexpected bagged lunch from the yellow burger place. They didn't have these in Spain, so the name escaped her. Julius was thrilled! He had never eaten at one of those places before. The family simply couldn't afford it.

Julius sat down and hungrily attacked his meal as Maria and Lazlo approached Eztar's bedside. "Momma, so good to see you!" Maria also said hello but with a bit more controlled emotion. They each took one of her hands with a squeeze as they asked how she was feeling.

"Oh, I'm fine… They could have released me yesterday, but Dr. Sherlous felt I needed more rest. He'll be here later. We've been expecting you. By the way Maria, you look radiant! So, tell me about your visit to Ward, and the house. What happened over the past few days?" Eztar knew without asking, but she wanted to hear it from both of them.

Maria did most of the talking as she explained how much fun the visit was for her. She told of how she met Blackie, and the cousins, Eleanor and Janos. Eztar could sense Maria's sincerity about even the simple things, like heating up the wood stove for coffee. Yes, she knew in her heart that Maria was indeed the one. With that thought she decided to allow her to stay and see the contents of the leather bag that they had retrieved.

"Lazlo, could you please close the door for me? We all need to talk."

Lazlo did as he was asked and returned to his Momma's bedside. Julius had already finished his lunch with a smile and stated how much he really enjoyed it, thanking them both. Eztar gazed at her son and this new love in his life…Maria. She approved and felt wonderful things were on their horizons. She also felt a strong bond already growing between them. This made her very happy.

"So…did you recover our treasure? And even more importantly, did you have fun?" Eztar waited for their responses which came quickly,

"Yes, and yes!" Maria explained that she loved the treasure hunt and how wonderful it was to work together, getting to know Janos and Eleanor. She already felt a bond with them in that short time. This is what Eztar had wanted to hear. Family was more important than treasure. Wealth was a secondary part of life. Love was the primary point. Eztar knew this and now knew that Maria felt it too.

"Did you keep your promise?" Eztar inquired.

"Yes Momma, absolutely!" Lazlo beamed. "Janos wanted to peek in the bag but Maria and I said no."

"Very good…so give it to your Momma."

Lazlo reached for the old weather-worn satchel and handed it to Eztar. She smiled. "Now get comfortable…there's a story I wish to tell …."

Family Treasure

CHAPTER 9

Eztar began, "My Papa…your grandfather, was many things. He was a brilliant man. László Joseph Biro. He was an inventor. He was a scholar in his own right. And he was one of the best gem cutters perhaps in all of Europe. These traits attracted the likes of Adolf Hitler. Hitler was a thief. He used his army to steal anything of value. Land, art, gems, gold, and silver…nothing was sacred. Hitler forced people to work for the Nazi machine under threat to their families or to themselves. Punishment was death if you failed to comply. After stealing many inventions from my Papa, Hitler decided that the gem-cutting skills of your grandfather would best serve him and his Nazi monsters. Besides cutting stolen raw diamonds from his African exploits, he had cutters re-cut existing works of art to hide their original identities."

Eztar stopped and carefully emptied the contents of her father's treasure on her lap. 12 beautiful blue diamonds appeared in the light coming in from her window. They were breathtaking! She started to cry softly, remembering her Papa's sacrifice. Her family tried to comfort her, but she gently protested and continued to speak. Her next words were spoken softly, almost under her breath. "Reuben, Simeon, Levi, Judah, Dan, Naphtali, Gad, Asher, Issachar, Zebulun, Joseph and Benjamin." Each stone had a name. These were the names of the original 12 sons, the basis of the 12 tribes of Israel. These were not storybook characters, but real people who were a part of the origin of the Hebrew faith. Her father shared one of those names. Joseph. He carried it proudly to his death, knowing that he had created something of almost eternal worth, in this world of God and man.

Eztar sighed, and continued…

"In 1669, King Louis XIV of France purchased some rather unique and beautiful diamonds found in India. These were very large stones and near perfect. He was a collector and kept a selection of his favorite priceless works of art in his palace. King Louis fell in love with one large stone that would be the centerpiece of his collection. He commissioned a young gem cutter for the job that took years to complete. This French king had visions of a gold scepter, specially made for him. He selected a beautiful blue diamond that weighed an astounding 115-carats! Some called this stone *The French Blue*. Others lovingly referred to it as the *King Louis Blue*. This gem became a national treasure and one of the King's most prized possessions. After the King's death, the jewels were sold multiple times to different countries over several centuries. They could be viewed by visitors from all over the world. However, in the passage of time, *The French Blue* was stolen."

Lazlo and Maria recalled the story from history class. Listening to Eztar's tale was much more dramatic.

Eztar continued… "In 1901, Lord Francis Hope inherited a beautiful blue diamond from his grandfather. It weighed 45.52-carats. He and his family were in debt and he sold the stone to pay their bills. According to legend, the original 115-carat *French Blue* was never mined in India. It was stolen from a Hindu temple and the priests placed a curse on anyone that violated their sacred shrine."

"The stone, sold by Lord Hope, was said to be the exact color and composition as the *Blue* and many believed both then, and now, that they were both cut from the King's original stone."

"*The French Blue* disappeared for decades never to be seen again… but the one from Lord Hope was another story. When it was sold, it was then named *The Hope Diamond*." Eztar explained further that the two diamonds both carried the curse. It was said that because of the bad happenings that seemed to follow ownership of the *Hope*

Diamond, it was finally donated in 1958 to the Smithsonian Institution in Washington, DC."

Everyone was listening intently. There was no sound in the room except for that of the medical monitors and Eztar's voice.

"My Papa told me as a young girl that the Germans commissioned him to a special project of re-cutting several large blue diamonds in the very early 1940s. He was sworn to secrecy with a constant threat of death in the camps if he violated this. He was to reduce the size of the large stones in hopes to hide their identity and possible origins."

"Hitler, who was very intrigued with any paranormal activity, believed these stones had a direct connection to a mystical world. He wished to use the stones to influence supernatural events that he himself would control. My Papa told me of studies that were conducted on the stones before they were cut. Hitler believed that King Louis used the original stone to rule France. No one knows for sure. What we do know is that my Papa and other scientists decided to run a special test on the stones, and the results were astounding!"

Eztar went on. "The test the Nazis performed was called a short wave, ultraviolet, electromagnetic radiation test, or scan. It was done several times to each stone. Today we know this to be UV light. Ultraviolet. When the stones were tested, the diamonds immediately radiated a deep red color. The transition of blue to red was a sight to behold. This process was not new. The technique was over 100 years old. Testing gemstones, however, was a bit different."

Eztar continued her story, that she had kept to herself for so many years.

"After the *Hope Diamond* was donated to the Smithsonian, scientists there had read about Papa's testing in Germany and duplicated the test. The diamond glowed a deep red! Papa believed that all the stones came from one large diamond from India. These are pieces of the cursed *King Louis Blue*! Do you understand what this means?"

Eztar took a minute to get a drink of water, catch her breath, and regain her composure. She was getting quite excited sharing this information that she had secreted away for much of a lifetime.

"Lazlo… I started getting my abilities as a seer after my Papa entrusted me with his stones. Somehow Hitler knew more about the stone's power than anyone else. If the stories are true, the stones had great paranormal power."

Eztar then explained how Papa tricked the Germans during the re-cutting process. "He secretly cut similar-looking blue stones. Topaz, if I remember right. Papa brought the original stones home one at a time for me to hide them."

"Initially, the Nazis searched our home and didn't find anything. But they kept coming back."

"I had sewn the real stones into the hem of my skirt. Even after a search of our home one day they found nothing. But they took Papa to the camps and I never saw him again." Eztar began to cry.

"We fled Hungary as a family, sadly, without Papa. When we came to the United States of America, I wore that same skirt onto Ellis Island with the stones hidden in the secret seam. No one knew."

It was a lot to share in one sitting, a very emotional road. Eztar felt the weight lift from her shoulders. She said to Lazlo, "The stones are yours. I have protected them for decades, and I knew the time would come, one day, to give you the stones.

"Your graduation, my stroke, and the arrival of Maria in our lives convinced me that the time was right. I feel in my heart that this is the right thing."

Lazlo didn't know what to say. "Thank you, Momma," was all that he could manage. He was in shock.

Julius obviously knew all this history, having lived most of it himself. He sat quietly opposite Eztar and smiled whenever anyone looked in his direction. Now he looked at Lazlo and said, "I laid out the treasure map and buried the clues. I even chose the coal bin because, while working in the mines, I was always told that coal could turn into diamonds. I never found any though." He laughed.

Eztar said, "There is something else that you need to know, Lazlo. Dr. Sherlous is friends with a gemologist here in town. This man did work in New York City, but he said the diamond industry was dishonest. He felt that relocation was in order, and so moved here. He is honest and quite knowledgeable. A few years back, we allowed Dr.

Sherlous to transport one of the stones to his shop for examination. His name is Benjamin Goldsmith… a fitting name for his profession. What we found was quite interesting and supports what Papa shared with me years ago. As best he could tell, the stone perfectly matched the color of the *Hope Diamond* in Washington, DC. It was also graded as VS1, which is a good grade. After doing some research on the *Hope*, at the National Library in DC, Mr. Goldsmith arranged for an ultraviolet test to be done. Our stone glowed red like fire! This is rare! We shared more of our story as we knew it, and he too, now, believes that our 12 stones were cut from *the French Blue*, or *King Louis Blue*. Everything matches perfectly! It's quite amazing…but Papa died for it. I believe that his death was also a part of the curse that follows the original stone. I can see it no other way. Mr. Goldsmith was shocked when he learned the entire story. He feels that these diamonds are priceless! I cannot even imagine what that really means. When we asked him to be more specific, he laughed and said, What more do you really need, priceless is priceless. You name your own price and it could be millions of dollars!"

The room was silent, and Lazlo asked his Momma if he could hold the stones. "Of course, my son, they're yours," she said.

Lazlo reached for one stone. He didn't know why he selected it but he questioned Momma: Is this one Joseph? She smiled and answered, "If you want it to be"…

What happened next was only seen by Lazlo and Maria. They didn't understand why it concealed itself from Eztar, but it did. When Lazlo picked up the *Joseph Stone*, it ever so briefly flashed a vivid red, as if a light was hidden inside it. Lazlo dropped it on the bed in surprise. He looked at Maria to see if she had seen it too. Her face told him that she did. But Eztar and Julius did not. Now we have a new mystery, Lazlo thought to himself. And he scooped all 12 stones back into the satchel.

"For now," Lazlo said as he stood up with the bag of diamonds, "I think these need to be locked up somewhere safe. Maybe in a bank safety deposit box. I'll keep one with me when we go back to Baltimore. I can put it in the bank box there too. Better safe than sorry." And he tucked the bag into the top pocket of his trousers. He hugged and kissed his Momma and Papa, and motioned Maria to the door. "This secret must be protected at all costs," Lazlo promised a fast return as it was believed Eztar's check-out from the hospital would be today.

Lazlo wanted to treat his parents to a nice hotel room as a gift. He knew Maria would pay for it. The two of them were getting comfortable with that arrangement. Maria really didn't care about the money.

Lazlo confirmed that his Momma was to be released today, but like most hospitals, they couldn't say when. He asked that Maria go back to their hotel and rent a room for his parents. Something nice… something elegant, if possible. He imagined a suite with a giant bed, like for honeymooners. Eztar and Julius deserved it. Maria agreed but before leaving, Lazlo advised her that the banks were still open, and he wanted to secure the stones. He removed his *Joseph Stone* and tucked it away safely in his pocket. He took the other stones to the local National Bank.

The bank staff was friendly and helpful. It took very little time to acquire a safety deposit box, where, after paying the fee, Lazlo was given a key. He was left alone in a rather plush, private room, with a metal box to hide his personal fortune.

Once Lazlo's treasure was secure, the bank manager carried the box to a room with an impressive number of compartments and keyholes. He allowed Lazlo to witness him securing the box and locking it. And then he smiled and thanked Lazlo for his business. They shook hands and Lazlo left the bank.

Now it's time to find Benjamin Goldsmith, Lazlo thought to himself.

The Good Goldsmith

CHAPTER 10

Lazlo noticed a meter-maid writing tickets and figured that she would know the town business owners.

"Excuse me…ma'am? I'm trying to find a jeweler named Goldsmith. Do you know the name of his shop and its location?"

The young woman responded, "Oh, you mean 'Old Ben'…sure, he's right around the corner," as she pointed in the direction of the street. "He calls his shop *The Good Goldsmith*. I like the name, he's a knowledgeable old fellow."

Lazlo thanked her and moved on. Finding the shop was easy as a large sign was hanging out in front displaying the name. Lazlo opened the door and little bells jingled. Upon entering the shop Lazlo was greeted by an old gentleman who was clearly of Jewish heritage. He had a white beard and wire-rimmed glasses and a black felt hat. Before Lazlo could say a word, the man extended his hand to Lazlo. "Welcome to *The Good Goldsmith* I am the owner, Benjamin."

It happened quickly, but when 'Old Ben' extended his hand, the sleeve of his shirt moved slightly upward revealing a numerical tattoo on his forearm. Lazlo saw it immediately and knew that Ben had survived the Holocaust.

Lazlo did not react, but instead took the hand of this fine gentleman with friendly enthusiasm. "My name is Lazlo Somogyi and I believe you know my parents."

Benjamin stopped in his tracks with a look of surprise on his face. "My boy, not only do I know your parents, I knew your grandfather! We have much to discuss." Now it was Lazlo who looked shocked.

Benjamin went to the front door and locked it while hanging the closed sign to prevent interruptions. He then pulled the window shades to block the view from outside. "Come, my boy…into the back. Come."

Benjamin took Lazlo to the rear of the shop, an area not open to the public. The jeweler's workbench was covered in gold and silver scraps from previous repairs. A large safe was bolted to the floor in a corner of the room. This was a room for artistic creativity. It made Lazlo imagine his grandfather cutting the 12 stones in a similar location.

"Mr. Lazlo… I knew what László Biro did in Germany. I was there! He and I were friends, but I was much younger than him. We both knew Hitler's plans for the *French Blue*. I was sorry to hear of your grandfather's passing, but before it happened, we discussed everything! I promised him that if I could, I would offer my help to his daughter, your mother, and her family. I came to this area of the United States so that I could be of help. And doing this, I have not been 100% honest with your mother or the kind Dr. Sherlous. Mostly for their own protection. The curse on the original stone is real. Only a very special person can contact this phenomenon and not be affected by its power. These are rare individuals. Some of our elders in Hungary referred to them as *White Lighters*. Are you familiar with the term?"

Lazlo quietly replied that he was…but did not yet elaborate on the details…he needed to hear more.

Old Ben shared everything that he knew with Lazlo. He knew that Eztar planned to give all 12 of the stones to her son. Benjamin was perhaps the only living soul who knew the entire story. He knew of the connection to the *Hope*, locked away in Washington, DC. Yes, Ben *was* the only one.

Lazlo asked his newfound friend if he had witnessed the ultra-violet testing done on the stones in Germany. The answer was, "Yes. And I personally tested one of them here, in this room. I have only seen one. It was the smallest of the 12, I was told."

"So can you do it again, here today?" asked Lazlo.

Benjamin looked shocked. "You have them here with you?" He was whispering at this point. Lazlo responded that he had the largest one and that he was calling it the *Joseph Stone*. The old jeweler smiled and commented to himself, "László would have liked that."

"Might I see it?" Benjamin was truly interested in reuniting with the stone. When Lazlo said yes, he immediately put on a pair of white cotton gloves, to prevent skin contact with the diamond.

Lazlo had decided earlier to keep the *Joseph Stone* in the original satchel but secured the others in the locked drawer at the bank. He removed it from his pocket. He then poured the diamond onto Ben's workbench while closely watching his reaction. Benjamin turned on the high-powered jeweler's lights and this stone came alive with color! The old man kept muttering repeatedly, "exquisite…simply priceless… exquisite…" Lazlo was beginning to understand just how valuable this family treasure really was.

Benjamin Goldsmith then set up all his gear for photographing jewels. He could look deep inside of a stone, searching for imperfections, flaws, carbon spots, things that lower the value. The *Hope* was said to be a VS1 and these other stones appear to be the same. Basically, speaking, that is far from perfect. It means that under magnification of up to 10 times, no real flaws can be seen, with a jeweler's eye. However, there was much more to these stones to make them quite special. Benjamin knew the stories. He set up the diamond to receive its dose of ultraviolet light. When he turned on the power, the *Joseph Stone* immediately turned almost blood red. This was indeed one of Biro's works of art! Ben was grinning from ear to ear. Lazlo just watched, taking it all in. The stone quickly returned to normal color.

Lazlo's next move was not planned. It was an unpredictable hunch, and he really had no idea what would, or would not, take place in the next two minutes. But something told him that he was doing the right thing.

Without warning Lazlo reached for the mounted stone with his bare hands. Benjamin shouted, "No! Not with your bare hands!" But it was too late. Lazlo held the diamond in his fingertips as they both watched a pulsating red color take over the *Joseph Stone.* It flashed like a strobe!

Benjamin Goldsmith stared at Lazlo in awe. "My God! You are a *White Lighter!* Never in my life did I ever hope to witness such a thing. And I saw it too! Without the camera, but how?"

Lazlo dropped the diamond in the bag. "I have no idea, my friend… I have no idea."

Promising to return, Lazlo left Old Ben and *The Good Goldsmith* to think about what had just occurred.

Home Away from Home
CHAPTER 11

Lazlo went straight away to Maria to tell her about his morning meeting with Old Ben. She told him she thought their talk sounded wonderful. Maria had been busy too. She got a room for Eztar and Julius for two days, not just the one. And yes, she rented the honeymoon suite for them. Her smile was infectious and it made Lazlo smile too. Maria advised him that she paid in advance for their meals and room service too. She had thought of everything. There was more.

Maria had contacted a local cab company and requested a car and driver. Should Eztar and Julius want to go to a restaurant, the driver would take them and after dinner pick them up as well. It was all paid for in advance. Lastly, the cab was their transportation back to Ward. No stone was left unturned.

Lazlo was stunned. He hugged Maria and told her that she was the most wonderful woman in the world. He then kissed her and made her feel that his compliment might be true…at least in his eyes. Maria felt a wave of satisfaction flow over her, adding to her already wonderful morning helping Eztar and Julius. Good things were happening.

Lazlo remembered that Dr. Sherlous had mentioned being at the hospital on the day of Eztar's discharge. This would be perfect if he could coordinate it and then get them to their room at the hotel. Lazlo needed to speak to Dr. Sherlous anyway before leaving town again. He needed to get back home to his dorm room and his friends at Johns Hopkins.

Graduation was right around the corner in a few weeks. Lazlo wanted to speak to Dr. Sherlous about the '12 brothers' and to let him know that he met Benjamin Goldsmith. Also, the 11 brothers were in a safe in a local bank. Finally, the *Joseph Stone* would soon be safe in a bank in Baltimore. Lazlo smiled at the thought of his progress since finding the satchel on their treasure hunt. Life was still moving quickly in many ways that he never imagined.

Maria and Lazlo returned to the hospital to find his Momma dressed and ready to go. Upon seeing the two of them, Eztar's face lit up. Dr. Sherlous was already there, which was good. Once again, Lazlo closed the door of Room 214 and asked everyone to please have a seat. He explained his meeting with Benjamin and their conversation. He discussed retesting one of the diamonds and the results. He also explained that Old Ben personally knew László Biro and had worked with him in Germany, and the promise that he made.

Then he went on to explain Maria's gift of the hotel suite. Eztar and Julius were already amazed, but when their food and travel arrangements were confirmed, Eztar openly cried. She went to Maria and hugged her while kissing her on the cheek. "You wonderful child. Thank you!" This was all that Eztar could manage in her current state of joy.

Lazlo then went to Stephen Sherlous, who also proudly carried the middle name of Joseph. "Father, Lazlo softly said…life is changing quickly now, and I owe so much of it to you and Mother Martha. I simply cannot ever truly repay you, but I want you to know…if you ever come to need or desire payment in any way, I intend to do it. You only need to ask."

Steven Joseph Sherlous hugged Lazlo and became emotional. "There will be no need, my boy…your success and happiness will be enough payment. Thank you."

"My graduation is in two weeks. I hope everyone will be there. Even Janos and Eleanor, if possible. Let us know if any special arrangements need to be made. I was considering a limo. I hear that they are pretty nice." Lazlo looked at Maria and she shrugged… "Why not? It's just a big car," …and everyone laughed. Truth be told, in Maria's family, all of the money recently spent wouldn't even be noticed. But Lazlo still didn't really understand the magnitude of her family's wealth. Maria hoped in her heart that somehow his family treasure would enable Lazlo, her love, to be comfortable in his own status, to never doubt their love or any dependence on her family inheritance. Everything seemed to be working wonderfully, and Maria was happy.

The Somogyi family said their farewells as Maria and Lazlo left the hospital to get reacquainted with Lola. It wasn't a terribly long ride back to Baltimore, but it could be somewhat tiring making the trip repeatedly. Lazlo even suggested that Maria drive the first leg of their adventure. During the trip, he noted that they should visit one of the main banks in the downtown area of the city. It only made good sense to secure their new friend, *Joseph*. Lazlo remembered a bank on the east side of town on Eastern Avenue. It would be as good as any.

Maria drove the entire trip and Lazlo fell in and out of sleep several times throughout the journey. He woke up as Maria navigated Lola into a gas station. Lazlo got out of the car to pump the gas. Once again, there didn't appear to be a station attendant on duty. It seemed that the oil companies were starting to do away with that friendly service to save them money on a national level. Kind of sad, Lazlo thought to himself. Maria excused herself as she went towards the building to locate a bathroom. After grabbing a few drinks, Lazlo decided to drive and remembered the M&T Bank on Eastern Avenue, in Highlandtown. He decided that would be the one and went in that direction. Crab cake sandwiches were in order and crab houses were everywhere on the east side. But this would need to wait until *Joseph* was safely in the bank.

Locating the M&T Bank on the East side was easy. Lazlo and Maria secured the *Joseph Stone* successfully in another new safety deposit box. Lazlo was feeling comfortable with their progress and was becoming hungrier by the minute thinking about crab cakes. No one had introduced Maria yet to this Maryland delicacy. She couldn't help but wonder what the big deal was about crab cakes. She decided to accept that everyone from Maryland was just a little bit crazy. They decided to take a walk along the storefronts of Eastern Avenue until they located a crab house. It is jokingly said among locals that in Baltimore, there's a crab house on every corner, so they took their chances. They came upon a place just off Eastern Avenue, on Lombard Street. It was called *Bud's Beer Garden and Crab House. Bud's* was a very distinct hole-in-the-wall crab house loved by the locals. Maria and Lazlo went into *Bud's*. Lazlo made sure that he opened the door for her and allowed her to enter first. Maria smiled… "You are such a gentleman," she said with a wink. Lazlo was in heaven. After being seated by their hostess, a waitress took their orders of identical crab cake sandwich platters served with french fries and coleslaw. They didn't know that the sandwiches were quite large. "We'll have *Natty Boh* beers for both of us," said Lazlo. National Bohemian was the local favorite brewed in Baltimore. He enjoyed the distinct flavor. Maria thought it bitter. No matter…it was a part of the experience.

When the food was delivered to the table even Lazlo was amazed at the portion sizes. This looked like it was going to be his kind of place. The crab cakes were huge, served on oversized burger-style buns. Each sandwich had a slice of tomato and a piece of lettuce on top of the very thick crab cake. Yellow mustard and mayonnaise were served on the side in plastic containers. The side of fries filled the platter, leaving little space for the mound of coleslaw. Everything was sprinkled with 'Old Bay Seasoning', a Maryland special taste. It also was cooked into the crab. Never challenge a Marylander's Old Bay. They just might fight you to defend it.

Lazlo explained that one of the key ingredients in making a true Maryland Cake is no filler. They are made of 100% quality meat from the crab body and sometimes claw. Crab-style cakes made in other parts of the country simply do not follow this standard.

Lazlo waited for Maria to take the first bite. He watched her with great anticipation. With some apprehension, Maria nibbled on the side of the crab cake and her face lit up with approval. "You see," beamed Lazlo. "It's really good!" Lazlo then took a huge bite of his own sandwich, rolled his eyes in pleasure, and savored this special treat.

Between bites, he asked Maria what she thought of her sandwich. "I really do like it! It's a bit spicier than I imagined…but in a good way…the crab just melts in your mouth. Old Bay, huh? It would be good on chicken or tuna fish too!" And she was right, of course. It is.

They finished their meal and walked off a few calories in Patterson Park, not far from the beer garden. Then they went back for Lola to drive home to Lazlo's dorm at Johns Hopkins. Lazlo drove.

Maria called ahead to reserve a room at the same hotel that she had rented earlier in the week. This time she openly invited Lazlo to stay with her. He accepted. It would sure be better than sleeping in the dorm with Maria's drunken cousin, Clayton. Yes, Clayton Middleton would most likely become family one day to Lazlo Somogyi. Lazlo laughed at the thought of it.

In a short time, Lazlo and Maria arrived at their hotel near the campus. They checked in and put their belongings in the room. Even though it was a rental for only a short time, the two lovebirds had a feeling that they had returned home. Lazlo recalled the old expression "a home away from home." Maybe this is what it means, he thought to himself.

Maria picked up the room phone and placed a call to Cousin Clayton. He picked up on the 3rd ring. "Hello…this is Clayton… who the hell is this?" Clayton had an odd way of answering the phone.

"It's me, you big lug! What other woman would waste her time calling you in your dorm room?" Maria laughed.

"Oh, hey sis…when did you guys get back into town?"

Maria advised her favorite cousin that they had just arrived and would be sharing a room at the hotel down the road from the campus. She remembered growing up with Clayton as kids. They were constantly together and most people thought of them as siblings. Maria laughed to herself remembering those special times.

Clayton said teasingly that things were sure moving fast between her and Lazlo but added that he saw it as a good thing. "You picked a great guy Maria. Lazlo is top-notch!"

"Thanks, Clayton…it's good hearing that from you. Now…on to other things…we need details on the graduation plans and activities.

Lazlo's family is to travel here from Ward. I want everything to be perfect and I want them to be as comfortable as possible. I'll pay for everything…even a limo for their transportation."

"Wow! You really did fall for my roommate! I had a feeling that he was the one… That's cool. What can I do to help?"

Maria and Clayton continued their conversation for another ten minutes and Clayton promised to assist in the arrangements that were discussed. It will be a great weekend. As they ended the call, Clayton left Maria with the final thought… "You did good sis… I'm happy for you… I'm happy for you both…" and he hung up. Maria thought about Clayton's words, and she smiled. Lazlo had fallen asleep on their bed and was softly snoring. Maria laughed to herself. Yes, it must really be true love…

Graduation and New Birth

CHAPTER 12

The two weeks passed quickly. It was graduation day before Lazlo knew it. It was still hard to believe that he was about to become a doctor. This was something that he had wanted most of his life, and now it was just a few hours away from becoming reality. The funny thing, he thought, was after attending college for what seemed like an eternity, Lazlo was having second thoughts about practicing as a medical doctor.

Lazlo was seated on the side of the bed in their hotel when Maria entered the room excitedly telling him that the limo had arrived with his family. She directed them to their assigned rooms and provided information with details about the actual commencement ceremonies. Eztar and Julius, Janos and Eleanor, Martha and Steven Sherlous traveled together in what Maria continued to call 'the big car'. Other members of the family were also arriving from nearby cities and towns in the northeast parts of the country. Most would be staying at the same hotel. Maria had a list of names. Vestourgome, Somogyi, Bohacik, Biro, they were all there. Maria was thrilled to see how they all came in support of Lazlo and his education. This was going to be a wonderful day, she thought… But even as Maria reveled at the possibilities of the day, Lazlo seemed distracted and not enthusiastic over his soon-to-be reward for all of the hard work.

"What troubles you, my love? I can sense that your heart is

stressed." Maria waited for his reply. After several moments She asked again, "What is it, my love?"

"Maria… I'm not sure if I really want to be a medical doctor anymore. I find myself becoming very intrigued by your own studies. You know…paranormal psychology. I want to learn more about the human aura. I want to study the scientific facts about being a *White Lighter*. Why did the *Joseph Stone* turn red when I touched it? And what really makes us share static discharges when we touch? These are the things that currently tug at my heart. I really need to know more. And I fear that most of my family will be disappointed if I change my destiny." Lazlo sighed heavily… But Maria understood.

"Try to clear your mind my darling. You will do what you feel is best for you. Enjoy this day as it will soon be behind us. Love your family and friends. They will understand. In the meantime, I will contact my uncle in Spain and discuss getting you enrolled there at the University. You can continue your studies and learn the things that call to you now." Maria held him by the hand and smiled her smile that stole his heart. "Rest easy Lazlo…all will be well…"

Lazlo felt the weight of the world lift from his shoulders as he gazed into her eyes. Her words were magic and he realized that he was already thinking about Spain. His worries shortly disappeared…

"I love you, Maria! Let's get dressed for this little party and I'll graduate with honors!"

Maria knew that her work, for the moment, was done.

The graduation ceremonies were being held outside on the campus. It was quite elaborate and no expense was spared. After talking with Maria, Lazlo felt relaxed. He was no longer concerned about what others might think of his life choices. After all, it was his life.

Lazlo was dressed in his cap and gown, heading towards the graduation grounds when he noticed his family and friends looking for their seats in the visitors' area. Maria and Clayton were together, followed by Eztar and Julius, with the rest of the Hungarian clan and the two very special people that made this day possible, Martha and Stephen Sherlous. Lazlo greeted them all before the commencement started.

"Welcome…welcome…thank you all for making it to my very special day!" Lazlo beamed. He hugged and kissed each and every one, almost missing one very special friend. Lazlo heard a light whimper and looked down to see his dog, Blackie, on a leash at the feet of Cousin Janos! "Blackie! Come here, boy!" He lifted the dog to his face as Blackie licked him repeatedly. "I can't believe that you brought him here! And he rode in the limo?"

"He wanted to come so badly he chased us down the road!" Janos advised Lazlo. "We had little choice…he'll be fine." This was the icing on the cake, and it totally completed the day for Lazlo.

"I better get over to the graduate seating area, I'd hate to miss my own wedding," an expression that Eztar always used with Lazlo growing up, to keep him on time.

The ceremony started and was mostly a blur. Select alumni gave speeches and school faculty wished students well on their new journey in life. Clayton and Janos were both starting to fall asleep when they were awoken by a voice on the loudspeaker system announcing, 'Lazlo Joseph Somogyi, graduating with honors'… The crowd erupted…LAZLO! Voices could be heard from his friends and teammates, "Way to go man! Great job! Hate to see you go!" Eztar and Julius stood dumbfounded at this recognition for their son. And they both cried… Eztar sobbed, overwhelmed with joy. Eztar looked at Martha Sherlous and saw that she too was crying for their shared son.

Lazlo accepted his diploma, stopped mid-stage to face the audience while holding the parchment paper over his head, and yelled into the crowd, "We did it, Momma! We did it!" It took several minutes for the crowd to calm down, and it slightly delayed the proceedings, to the surprise of the faculty on stage. However, they knew that Lazlo was a special student, and they understood his popularity.

Lazlo made his way to Maria and the family while absorbing every second of his wonderful day.

Now it was time to make plans to really start his education. Plans needed to be made for Spain.

Lazlo abruptly stopped and looked around at the crowd. "Ben?"…

Maria heard him say. "Where is Benjamin?" Lazlo continued looking around. Maria looked away. Lazlo pushed on. "Maria, what happened to Benjamin? I feel something awful. Where is Old Ben?"

Maria slowly and softly told Lazlo that Benjamin Goldsmith had passed away late yesterday in his home. His family found him with a sealed envelope on his lap addressed to Lazlo Somogyi. It was supposed to arrive today by courier. It could have been read to Lazlo over the telephone, but Ben had stamped it *confidential* in red ink, so they thought it would be better to send it.

Lazlo was stunned. He had just recently met the old gentleman, but the connection to his grandfather created a rapid bond between them. Lazlo was happy that they shared what they did that day at Ben's shop with the *Joseph Stone*. Ben knew things that no one else knew until he shared them with Lazlo. He was now the rightful owner of the '12 brothers'. Lazlo wondered about the curse on the stones. Did this paranormal power somehow take Benjamin too, for his part in re-cutting or testing the stones? Did it cause his grandfather's death directly, or was this all just superstition? Lazlo shook it off and convinced himself that it was nothing, simply tall tales. He hugged Maria and stood silently with her in the crowd. The festivities went on, but Lazlo's heart was not in it. He mourned for Benjamin and for László Biro too. They both gave everything to protect their secret.

It was almost like mystical clockwork, but within minutes of his conversation, a courier arrived searching for Lazlo Somogyi. He was calling out into the crowd, "Envelope for Dr. Lazlo Somogyi… Envelope for Dr. Somogyi!" Lazlo heard the words but he couldn't quite wrap his head around being called a doctor.

Maria called out to the young courier. "Over here! He's over here!" Within seconds he was face-to-face with Lazlo and asking for his signature before giving up his delivery to its owner. Lazlo complied while Maria fished in her purse for a tip. It was a substantial one and the young courier beamed…

"Thank you, ma'am! Thank you very much!"

Lazlo stood there staring at the envelope in his hands, stamped confidential. Ben had addressed it to Dr. Lazlo Joseph Somogyi. Lazlo smiled… What the hell could this be? Lazlo opened the letter from Benjamin and read it out loud to Maria. It wasn't very long. It read…

> *Doctor Somogyi,*
>
> *I am not well, and I am old. I have lived through both horrible and wonderful times. Your grandfather and his work were the latter, even under bad conditions.*
>
> *I have a friend named James. He knows some of our stories. Please call him in Washington DC at 301-288-4189. He'll know what to do. His last name is Ledbetter.*

Lazlo would later learn from one of his college professors that Ben's friend was James Vernon Ledbetter, the eighth secretary of the Smithsonian Institution in DC. Prior to his appointment there in 1964, Dr. Ledbetter was a Yale University biology professor. He was also Director of the Peabody Museum of Natural History.

Old Ben had friends in high places.

Both Maria and Lazlo were quite surprised, but now they knew that they needed a telephone to call Ben's old friend. They excused themselves from the group and headed for their hotel room.

The Smithsonian offices would be closed on Sunday so if they reached Dr. Ledbetter today, they'd travel on Monday. This would give them 24 hours or so to visit with family and friends.

Hope

CHAPTER 13

The next 24 hours went by quickly. Lazlo placed his phone call to James Ledbetter and was fortunate to connect with him, although their conversation was brief. It was determined that they should meet in Washington DC on Monday, before lunch.

Dr. Ledbetter gave Lazlo the information that he needed to enter the facility as a fellow doctor, not a tourist. Lazlo was excited but quite nervous about this meeting. He had a hard time sleeping and it being a beautiful May evening, Lazlo suggested going for a country ride in Lola to get some fresh air.

After driving into the countryside, Lazlo noticed how beautiful the stars looked…they were breathtaking. Lola's radio was tuned to the Rolling Stones performance of *Time is on My Side* from 1964. Lazlo glanced over at Maria and noticed a faint shimmer of green light. It surrounded her like a fire!

Lazlo stopped the car on the side of the road. "Lazlo! You are radiant! Can you see your own skin? There is a beautiful white light surrounding you," Maria said. Both of them could sense the presence of their own auras as they admired the displays that were showing from the bodies of their partner. They were in complete unison. Lazlo reached for Maria's hand and when they touched, the intensity increased as her aura color transformed from green to white. Lazlo could feel the static charge.

The song on the radio began to sound a bit like static itself, making Mick Jagger's voice fade in and out. Eventually, they lost the station altogether. The airwaves went dead. Maria and Lazlo exchanged looks of confusion and awe. This was amazing, and it fueled Lazlo's desire to learn more.

Maria's gaze turned skyward and she said, "Lazlo… Look at the sky!"

Lazlo looked up in time to witness a beautiful green Aurora Borealis glowing above them. It seemed that the sky was somehow in tune with their own aura activities. Was this even possible?

Lazlo insisted that he and Maria kiss, to determine if there would be an electrical reaction under a solar storm.

The couple leaned into one another and kissed. Their lips shared a spark between them, but they didn't stop. Maria increased the intensity of her kiss. Would it increase the intensity of their auras? They both peeked through closed eyes to witness a white glow radiating from both of them. The white glow circled them like a halo and became so bright, they couldn't open their eyes. When they released their embrace, the strength of the bright light began to diminish into the night air.

The borealis lasted through the night. Lola's radio failed to recover until morning. Lazlo knew that something magnificent had happened. And both of them had experienced it. Lazlo yearned to know more.

Monday morning arrived quickly after a day of socializing and celebrating with friends and relatives. Everyone wanted to know the details of Lazlo's trip to Washington DC, but he felt sharing that information would be premature, as he really didn't know exactly what Dr. Ledbetter had in mind.

They loaded Lola up for a day trip to the capital.

"Maria, I'm so excited to see Washington DC and the Smithsonian Institute. There are dinosaur displays, tropical gardens, airplanes, spaceships, educational displays, and special collections. It's all there!"

What he didn't know was that Dr. Ledbetter had some pretty big plans for Dr. Lazlo Somogyi.

It wasn't a long ride from Baltimore, Maryland to Washington DC, but the traffic was always bad. The roads were not the best and traffic congestion was quite common. Lola performed well but quickly learned that stop-and-go traffic made her European drivetrain run a little bit hot. She preferred the open road highway speeds of over 70 mph. Lazlo found himself getting bored in traffic. Maria just smiled.

Before long they were in downtown Washington DC. The Washington Monument stood tall and proud. Lazlo had directions to the Mall and a code to a parking lot for staff at the Smithsonian. Surprisingly, it was not difficult to locate.

The couple shared the driving on this trip, but at the moment, Maria was at the helm. She approached the main gate and was greeted by a uniformed guard, wearing a gun. The weapon surprised her a bit. It surprised Lazlo too. "I guess they need to protect some really valuable stuff here," Lazlo said

"Code number please," requested the guard. "Who are you here to see?"

Lazlo had memorized the number and quickly responded, "712357, Dr. James Ledbetter. My name is Dr. Lazlo Somogyi." He still thought that the title sounded a little odd.

The guard signaled another officer and the gate opened automatically. As Maria pulled Lola past him, he called out to Maria, "Parking space 32." He pointed to the spot. After parking Lola, the two of them made their way to the ground-floor employee entrance of the Smithsonian. They were looking for the Museum of Natural History and they had arrived.

Once inside, Maria saw a guard and asked for Dr. James Ledbetter's office. The officer gave them instructions on how to get there.

Traveling to the third floor, Lazlo and Maria entered a hallway with expensive paintings and leather-covered antique furniture that lined the walls. Potted tropical plants were everywhere. It was quite beautiful.

Maria said, "Look, Lazlo, the name is Dr. James Vernon Ledbetter."

They entered the office and were greeted by a secretary who wore a name tag that said, Jill. Lazlo introduced himself as Dr. Lazlo Somogyi, and his friend Maria.

"Hello, I'm Jill, Dr. Ledbetter's secretary. Have a seat. He's expecting you." It didn't take long and Dr. James Ledbetter entered the room and enthusiastically shook hands with Lazlo while formally introducing himself to the couple.

"I have heard a great deal about you, Dr. Lazlo… A great deal indeed. I was close friends with Benjamin Goldsmith and was deeply saddened when I heard the terrible news. Ben was a wonderful human being, and his passing is a great loss to all of us."

"Roughly a week before his passing, Benjamin called me to discuss some things, well…specifically *You.* He was vague on some details but I already knew enough about his history in Germany working with the Biro fellow, and the secret project that cost László Biro his life. I am familiar with Hitler's acquisition of the Blue stone and of his beliefs and desires. I was quite surprised to learn that you are in fact a descendent of Mr. Biro."

Lazlo responded, "He was my grandfather…"

This seemed to strike him deeply. Ledbetter continued, "As I mentioned, Benjamin was vague on some aspects of why he thought we needed to meet, although I knew that if you were somehow connected to the project in Germany, even after all these years, we needed to meet. Ben did mention some paranormal activity followed you and your bloodline and I take great interest in this. There is something that I wish you to see. Walk with me and I will tell you more when we reach our destination."

"So tell me about yourselves, from where do you hail?" James was making small talk, but he really did want to know more.

Eventually, they arrived at the entrance to a room with several armed guards standing in front of obviously locked doors. The sign posted in front said *We are Closed Due to Renovation. Our Apologies.*

Dr. Ledbetter nodded to the guards as they moved out of the way allowing him to unlock the doors.

Once in the room, Lazlo noticed there was also a control panel on the inside by the door. James carried a small radio, similar to the one seen outside on the guards downstairs. He spoke to someone on his hand-held unit. "Base to S-1…shut down sector seven."

"10-4" responded a voice on the radio. The lights briefly flashed and other security lighting came on.

Maria and Lazlo were both intrigued by the events. The security, armed guards, locked doors, and special treatment.

What had Benjamin shared with this man?

"Please…come with me," James urged.

They entered a large room that served as a display area for a collection of gemstones. It was obviously a priceless collection from many countries over many centuries.

As they walked along, they passed more officers working in pairs…all armed. This is serious shit, thought Lazlo to himself. His eyes met Maria's and she squeezed his hand. They moved on, following Dr. Ledbetter to an interior room. He took them straight to a beautiful showcase, all alone in the center, with a sign labeled *THE HOPE DIAMOND*. "Please allow me to introduce *The Hope Diamond*!"

Maria's mouth dropped open. "Oh my God!"

Lazlo could feel his heart beating rapidly. He felt a strange attraction to this piece of history. Dr. Ledbetter was watching Lazlo's every reaction. What was going to happen next, had never happened before, and most likely would never happen again.

Another signal from James and several guards assisted in mechanically lifting the elaborate showcase glass off its base, revealing the magnificent diamond. "Benjamin told me that you have a way with diamonds, Dr. Somogyi. Please, show me."

"We only have a short window of time and the backup security system will re-arm." James mentioned, "Pick her up…we'll talk further afterward."

Lazlo could feel his hands starting to shake, Maria watched him, in awe of what was taking place.

"Pick her up," James quietly repeated.

Lazlo reached for *The Hope*, lifting her by the diamond chain that supported her weight. He admired her and thought of the history. But nothing happened. Nothing at all. Again James spoke, "Lazlo… touch *her*, directly. Touch the heart of the stone!"

Lazlo placed the tip of his index finger on the top facet of her crown and his hand began to glow! A white aura pulsed through his very being and radiated throughout his body. And the *Hope*? This beautiful blue gem flashed and then glowed a crimson red! Dr. Ledbetter couldn't help himself. "Jesus Christ Almighty!" he said in awe. The security system buzzed, and secondary lighting kicked in. James grabbed his radio to alert security to stand down. "All is well," he said. Maria's green aura started to reveal itself too. Even to the eyes of those present who had never seen an aura before. Lazlo placed the *Hope* on Maria's neck and her aura turned white! Everyone present was in a state of amazement.

The security staff, while trying to maintain their composures, were also surprised beyond belief. This was like something from a Buck Rogers comic book! Dr. Ledbetter noted their reactions and without hesitation called to all of them in earshot, "Enjoy the show, but say nothing to anyone, I mean it! You are sworn to secrecy and any violation of this clause in your contract will result in immediate termination."

Everyone responded with, "Yes sir!"

Lazlo looked back at the diamond, still glowing red on Maria's neck. They looked beautiful together! Lazlo stood trancelike gazing into the light created by this phenomenon. Lazlo knew that a solar storm had started two days ago and that it was still active at this moment. His mind was racing to figure out a possible connection.

James asked Lazlo to remove the necklace from Maria's neck and place it back in the showcase. It needed to be secured before the alarm system automatically reactivated. If they were a second late, alarms would sound in the facility and at every police station in the city. Lazlo responded swiftly and placed the *Hope* back in her resting place as the guards lowered the showcase.

Dr. Ledbetter once again spoke into his small radio. "S1 to the security base."

Again, the voice answered quickly. "Base to S1."

"Power up all security measures at this time, sector 7."

"10–04" responded the Base. Immediately the lighting returned. The guards at the door removed the *Closed for Renovations* signs and operations returned to normal in a matter of seconds.

Dr. Ledbetter looked at Lazlo and became quite serious. "So… Dr. Somogyi…what is it that you intend to do with your life?"

A Difficult Offer to Refuse
CHAPTER 14

Like most other things in Lazlo's life, this day was also moving very quickly. As a matter of fact, the entire time, since meeting Maria, life seemed to be in fast forward. Graduation was a blur, the weekend after was like the blink of an eye, and here he was now, talking to the scientist who runs the Smithsonian Institution. It would appear that Dr. Ledbetter was very interested in Lazlo's future, after being a witness to the interaction between him and the *Hope Diamond*.

After a minute of quiet thought, Lazlo responded to James's inquiry.

"Well… I plan to continue my education, but I want to change to the field of neuropsychological psychology. I am beginning to find it quite interesting. That is currently Maria's major." Lazlo hesitated and then continued, "Forgive me…our introductions were brief and I simply referred to her as Maria. Please allow me to introduce you to my girlfriend, Miss Maria Cordova Valdez." Maria offered her hand, which he lightly shook, but more like you might do with royalty.

Maria then added, "I'm on vacation here from Spain."

Dr. James Ledbetter then spoke softly under his breath, "Will wonders never cease?" He looked slightly embarrassed and added, "Forgive me… I am familiar with your family name…" Maria smiled that enchanted smile of hers and Lazlo jumped into the conversation to continue answering the question.

"Maria's uncle is in charge of that department at the University of Granada, in Spain. She feels that her connections there would offer me easy enrollment into the college, with my current background. We are actually just getting ready to contact him this week."

James looked at Maria and asked a question that he already knew the answer to. "So, your uncle is Professor Diego Pilan?"

Surprised, Maria answered with a simple, "Yes."

"Oh my… I have known Diego for almost 10 years! And I think that I might have met you once as a little girl, exercising a white stallion. I was there on government business in reference to jewels and other such things. Diego was very proud of your equestrian abilities. He escorted me to an arena where you practiced." Maria remembered and smiled.

"Such a small world," Maria said.

"Lazlo…back to business. Let us go to my office so we can speak privately. We have much to discuss."

In the halls of the Smithsonian, James was casual. His topics of conversation were general, mostly small talk about Johns Hopkins and Granada. Lazlo could tell that there was much more on his mind.

They reached his office and he directed them to an attached conference room. Coffee, tea, and water were already waiting. This kind of treatment felt strange to Lazlo, but he could see that Maria was accustomed to it.

"So, Dr. Somogyi … let's get down to brass tacks, shall we? Benjamin Goldsmith was a brilliant man, much more than a simple jeweler. I knew of his connections to Nazi Germany. And of course, I knew of László Joseph Biro. I did not, however, know about you. Somehow you stayed under my radar. That is a rare thing that I hope to investigate later. Benjamin refused to share details about you but absolutely insisted that I bring you here to meet the *Hope*. He also insisted that you touch her…as you did. Now why would he want to pass you to meet me at this time? How would he know that it would create a paranormal response, such that I have never even imagined? I'm sure that you alone have the answers that I seek. Trust me, I can make it very much worth your while. Care to share?"

Lazlo shifted his weight in the chair, out of nerves more than need for comfort.

Lazlo shared the basic story. "My mother is a person with paranormal abilities. She has been able to see auras and such. She explained that I also have these abilities and I am a *White Lighter*. Likewise, Maria is also a *White Lighter*. We are definitely connected somehow by it."

Dr. Ledbetter stopped him and questioned the 'how and why' that Benjamin knew that the *Hope* would turn red at your touch. Lazlo hesitated but shared, "he witnessed me do it before."

That got James's attention. "You did it before?" questioned the doctor. "How could that even be possible? You've never had access to the *Hope Diamond*…"

Lazlo was wondering to himself if it was safe to share any more information. He stopped and asked James, "It sounded like you had something in mind for me…. Is this somewhat true? Not to fret, I am also empathic," Lazlo laughed.

Once again Dr. James Vernon Ledbetter became serious. "If you are what I think you are, and can do what I think you can do, the Institution will offer you a title, a competitive salary, benefits, vacation, and travel expenses. We will also arrange for you to further your college education at our cost. Yes, even if you go to Granada. You will represent the Smithsonian Institution while attending, but your schedule will be split. Does this interest you?"

Lazlo replied, "When might I officially start?" and he smiled.

James smiled back while saying, "As soon as possible. Now tell me more…"

Lazlo trusted James. He was reading him every step of the way and felt confident that he was a man of his word. Lazlo extended his hand as a gesture of morally sealing the deal. James reached out and with a firm grip shook Lazlo's hand. "Then it's done," said James. "As long as I hear what I want to hear."

Without hesitation, Lazlo looked straight into Dr. Ledbetter's eyes and stated, "I own the '12 brothers'. They were a gift from my grandfather before he was murdered and before I was born. My Momma smuggled them out of Europe."

Ledbetter didn't know the name, '12 brothers'. He did know the history of László Biro's missing 12 diamonds, cut from the *French Blue*. Dear God, could they be the same stones? "Are these the stones that you demonstrated for Benjamin?" asked James.

"Yes, in a sense," replied Lazlo. "One of the stones that I shared was the *Joseph Stone*. Old Ben was able to observe my interactions with it. I simply touched it and it glowed red, like the *Hope* did today. I have no doubt that the *Hope*, and my 12 stones, are all from the *French Blue*. And I believe that King Louis also tapped into the powers of that original stone and curse. I believe that the curse killed my grandfather. And years later, killed Benjamin." The room went silent.

Dr. Ledbetter was completely familiar with the history of the *King Louis Blue*, or *French Blue* as it was once called. The Smithsonian owned the *Hope Diamond*, technically it was on loan, but never to be returned. James knew of the 12 missing diamonds that László Biro died for, but after all of these years, they were more legend than fact. But they were indeed fact, Benjamin Goldsmith had been living proof of this. And Benjamin was connected to *this* Lazlo…a relative of the original. It had to be true! If it wasn't a true story and Ben had not visually seen the so-called *Joseph Stone*, he would have never arranged for Lazlo to come to Washington DC. And Maria. What were the chances that this child of so long ago, blood to the Cordova Valdez fortune in Spain, would be connected to Lazlo Somogyi? These isolated pieces were starting to come together like a carefully designed puzzle. James Ledbetter didn't believe in chance, or coincidence. He was not a gambling man.

"No, this must all be real," he said out loud, but to himself.

"When can you start?" Dr. Ledbetter asked Lazlo.

Lazlo looked at Maria and she hesitated, just a bit.

"I wanted you to meet my Uncle Diego next week. I'd hate for us to not share that." She meant next week…not next month or later.

At this point, Dr. Ledbetter knew that this new information regarding the history of re-cutting *the French Blue* was groundbreaking. This was new history in the making. Scientifically, the potential for learning more about the paranormal aspects of the stone, and the pieces from it, were astronomical. He didn't want to do anything to jeopardize even a remote possibility of destroying a relationship with Lazlo Somogyi before it really even got off the ground. James knew that he needed Lazlo more than Lazlo Somogyi really needed him. It was time to cater to Dr. Somogyi's needs and desires.

"Lazlo…after what I witnessed here today, I am convinced that the Smithsonian needs you. It needs your special talents, your family history, and yes…access to the stones that you possess, for further examination. You need to further your education and gain more knowledge on your obvious connection to the paranormal. I am confident that we can work together to achieve all of our goals and more. Something tells me that we have only touched the tip of the iceberg on this subject. You and Maria start making your arrangements to visit her homeland and meet her family. I'm sure that Diego will find you very interesting. I will personally call him in advance. You will be traveling as an employee of the Institution. How does the title Associate Curator sound? We will discuss the details further, but does this sound suitable?"

Lazlo looked over at Maria and she was smiling. He knew that she approved. At this point, he approved too, and could only begin to imagine the possibilities of where this new business relationship could take them both. Life continued to move quickly for Lazlo, and so far, he was seriously beginning to enjoy the ride!

There was still a nagging thought in the back of his mind. It would resurface every now and then when he relaxed.

These stones are cursed. Countries have fallen. People have died, and others have been killed for these pieces of stone. László Biro perished because of them. Benjamin Goldsmith too. Lazlo still wondered if his Momma's illness was connected in some strange way to the stones. There was so much to consider if you indeed believed in the things that were not so normal in our world. Lazlo Somogyi believed… completely.

"You kids take your time. Do what you need to do regarding your travel plans. Stay in touch with me so that the Smithsonian can pay the expenses for our new Curator. Meanwhile, I'll have my secretary contact a realtor to assist you with lodging here in the district. We will also select an office for you here, in this building. I'll notify you when we need signatures on your employee package. Just formalities of course, but it needs to be done. If necessary, we can have them sent to you by courier if it's more convenient. Don't trouble yourself…we'll handle most of it. Any questions?" Dr. Ledbetter extended his hand once again to Lazlo while saying another goodbye.

Lazlo's head was spinning. "No, for now, I think that I am overwhelmed enough," he laughed.

Maria grabbed onto his arm and they left James Ledbetter alone in his office.

"My Lord there is so much to learn…so much to study," James muttered to himself. "Great things are about to happen in this field of science. Great and wonderful things!"

The Trip to Granada

CHAPTER 15

Both Maria and Lazlo thought that their trip to the Smithsonian was a huge success and a great start for a wonderful future.

Old Ben had taken steps to ensure that Lazlo moved in the right direction. This could complete the task of László Joseph Biro, back in Nazi Germany.

When László Biro was executed, Benjamin had no idea what really happened with the 12 stones that were stolen. He lived the rest of his life wondering, and dreaming of the day that might provide answers. The meeting with Lazlo Somogyi was that day.

Maria quickly placed the phone call to Granada, Spain. So much had happened in such a short period of time, and she wanted to share her story with her family. Specifically with her Uncle Diego. His personal interest, and his work at the University, would have him very intrigued with Lazlo. The paranormal abilities experienced by this entire Hungarian family were rare and exciting. Maria was sure that he would agree.

It took a few moments for the call to go through as it was channeled by an overseas operator, who finally got through to Diego Pilan. "*Hola*? Diego speaking…*Buenos días*."

Maria said, "*El Tío Diego, ¿cómo estás?* It 's Maria! How are you?"

"Maria, my love! So good to hear your voice! I have missed you my child very, very much." Before Maria could utter a word in response, Diego continued, "So, I have heard a great deal already about this young man in your life. "Yes, Lazlo sounds very special indeed."

Maria was somewhat surprised initially, but knowing her uncle, and all of his connections around the world, this wasn't unusual.

"So, how did you hear about Lazlo? And yes, he is very special. I believe that you will like him a lot. I hope to marry him one day. While I know it seems sudden, I truly love him, but we plan nothing in the immediate future. It will be somewhere down the road. For now, we want to study together and work together." Maria waited for his response.

Diego then explained that he had received a call from Dr. James Ledbetter at the Smithsonian. Dr. Ledbetter was very enthusiastic about working with Dr. Lazlo. James had explained that he believed Lazlo had paranormal abilities.

"Now Maria… If I had one peseta for every person who claimed to have paranormal abilities, I'd be twice as rich as I am now!"

They both laughed. Maria knew that Lazlo's abilities were very real. She also knew that Uncle Diego would come to believe it too. Diego realized that for James Ledbetter to be so enthused, something special was working on their behalf. He was looking forward to meeting Lazlo Somogyi.

"So, as I understand it, Lazlo will be working for the Smithsonian, while furthering his education in Granada.

As a foreign student, Lazlo's tuition would be dramatically reduced, but James notified me that any differences would be covered by the Smithsonian. Lazlo, as I understand it, would be given an upper-level title with many perks. This young fellow really must be someone special, as you say…and I am guessing that, for now, you may not be able to share exactly what that might be."

Maria smiled, and then shook her head. "All in good time, Tío, all in good time."

"Meanwhile, what do we need to do to get him officially registered before next semester? Maybe we can expedite things," Maria suggested.

Diego laughed. "It's already done, my dear. I took care of things yesterday. Dr. Ledbetter is quite serious about your young man and I intend to find out exactly why."

Maria answered softly, "And you will… Soon enough."

Maria continued to explain. "We intend to visit within the week. I am feeling more than a little homesick. I miss my family and Spain. The United States is pretty wonderful but it's not home. I want more than anything to introduce Lazlo to Papa and as many of the Cordova Valdez family as possible. I'm not sure how long Lazlo will stay on this trip, but most likely, I will stay. I have to ship Lola home. I have already purchased a new car for Lazlo. He doesn't know yet. It is a belated graduation gift to him. A new Chevy Corvette convertible… Pearl White. The only color for a *White Lighter*. I have even come up with a name for it. Baby Jane. We'll call her BJ for short.

They ended their call reluctantly, as it had been some time since their last conversation.

After ending her call with Diego, Maria almost immediately placed another call to the Friendship International Airport outside of Baltimore, Maryland. She secured two first-class tickets for Lazlo and herself to Spain. This was to be another first, as Lazlo had never flown before. They were scheduled to travel in four days. Maria's cousin Clayton, would handle shipping Lola as quickly as possible just before their departure.

Lazlo was currently in Washington DC. He was traveling with a real estate agent hired by Dr. Ledbetter. Living in the DC area was going to be costly, especially close to the Smithsonian, but it seemed that money might not be such an obstacle.

Maria and Lazlo were to have lunch together in the afternoon. Maria was also really looking forward to assisting with the decorating at his office, not to mention picking out a townhouse that would be his first personal home, as an adult. There was so much to do…

Lazlo instructed his real estate guide to have him back at the Smithsonian by 12:30. Maria was actually a guest there and she was allowed to use the telephones to arrange whatever she could for their trip. This also gave her access to Lazlo's office, where she could think about the ways that she could personalize things for her man. After lunch, she would join the house-searching pair, with hopes of finding a home. Waiting for his return, Maria explored the museum exhibits near Lazlo's office. She wandered to the *Hope Diamond* display and stood in front of it in deep admiration.

Maria softly spoke to the stone. "So exactly what is it, that you love so much about my Lazlo?" She gazed deeply into the center of the diamond and thought that she saw a golden sparkle, almost a flash that emanated from the heart of the diamond. It was gone as quickly as it had arrived, but it gave her a chill. She could feel her skin react to whatever it was. Goosebumps, she imagined. That was weird.

As Maria walked away, she found herself looking back at the display over her shoulder. Again, she saw a light sparkle, but it wasn't a reflection from the showcase lighting, it was from within the stone! She was sure of it!

Real Estate Follies

CHAPTER 16

"Maria Cordova Valdez, please report to the office of Dr. Ledbetter. Your appointment has arrived. Thank you." She actually thought this was pretty cool and headed in that direction. She was smiling again, and for now, forgot about her experience with the *Hope Diamond*. Maria needed to remember to tell Lazlo.

Lazlo was waiting for her in the hallway outside of Dr. Ledbetter's office. They greeted one another with hugs and quick kisses.

"Let's go outside and walk on the Mall, it's a beautiful day," exclaimed Lazlo. "There are plenty of places to grab lunch at an outdoor café. Let's find one together!"

The couple settled in at a little café fashioned after the current 'beatnik' lifestyle that started in the late 50s. Visitors drank espresso coffee concoctions while listening to live poetry readings. Sandwiches were the common fare. Maria thought it was a little like Europe. But this was a first for Lazlo.

Being on a tight schedule, they hurried back to Lazlo's office to find their real estate agent waiting. Lazlo quickly made the introductions.

"Maria, this is Debbie. Debbie, this is Maria. Let's get started" The three of them headed to Debbie's four-door sedan.

As the afternoon proceeded, the group toured several homes. The last one, however, caught Lazlo's attention from the outside, even before entering the front door.

It was a three-story brick townhouse. It was trimmed in white colonial woodwork with two pedestal columns outside of the front door. Lazlo looked at Maria. There was something special here. Maria noted the black ironwork on the short staircase leading up to the columns. Two horses stood on their hind legs in a fashion that reminded her of her stallion back in Granada. Amber lights were also near the horses. She liked it very much. So did Lazlo. "Let's go inside," prompted Debbie.

A large hand-carved wooden door welcomed them into the home. Upon entering, Lazlo was taken aback by an open-air foyer that was highlighted by a crystal chandelier that looked like diamonds. More important than the crystals, was the color. They were pale blue. Again, the couple exchanged glances. This could be no mere coincidence. Other mystical forces were at work today. Maria allowed her mind to wander back to the *Hope Diamond* display. She had felt the stone communicate with her. Maria shook off the strange sensations and allowed Debbie to continue her tour.

The home was exquisite in every way imaginable. The craftsmanship was near perfect and the overall design matched the efforts executed by the builder. Lazlo felt that this was meant to be their home in DC.

"How much?" Lazlo blurted out. Maria rolled her eyes, and Debbie laughed out loud before answering.

"The actual price hasn't been advertised by the owner yet. He is a friend of Dr. James Ledbetter and desires that it only go to a very select client, preferably connected to the Smithsonian. Oddly, when they contracted my services, they selected the price range in which we should shop. They seem to know what you can afford. My guess is that there will be no issue if the home interests you. Also, quite oddly, I was just given this listing after lunch today, moments before meeting you and Maria. It was also very much like someone hand-selected it… just for you."

Lazlo beamed. Maria's face showed signs of concern, but she didn't really understand why. "It's such a beautiful home," she said.

They left the house and went back to the Smithsonian where Maria and Lazlo went to his new office to consider decor. Debbie met with Dr. Ledbetter and advised him of their choices. James seemed quite satisfied and thanked Debbie for her efforts. He would now handle the rest.

James made a private phone call to an unnamed man who was somehow connected to the events that were unraveling before their eyes.

"Hello. This is Ledbetter. Yes, they want the house. We can deduct a portion of his pay to handle the basics of setting him up under our agency. Yes, sir, I expect no problems. Yes sir. I sincerely believe that Dr. Somogyi is in possession of the missing 12 diamonds that were stolen by his grandfather. It would complete the puzzle and answer so many questions, wouldn't it? Yes sir. I will handle all of it. You may consider it done." The mystery person disconnected from their end. James stood, holding the phone receiver in his hand, looking somewhat concerned. Lazlo was a nice guy, and he had no desire to hurt him. James hung up the phone.

Maria and Lazlo were sitting in his new office recalling the events of the day thus far. It was a whirlwind. Maria asked Lazlo if he had any thoughts on what he wanted his office to reflect. She hadn't really thought about it, but as a child growing up in the coal mines, he had few photos, almost none of himself or his family.

"Photos. I want lots of photos! Framed. I know that there is one of Blackie. I'd like it on the wall somewhere. I'm sure that there are others. Family. That is important to me. And photos of us together. Can you make that happen?"

Maria said. "Yes, my love, I will start looking into the details. Very soon."

Maria suddenly remembered her encounter earlier with the *Hope Diamond*. The thought of it still made her feel a bit uneasy. Lazlo noticed that Maria had become very serious. It was obvious that something was troubling her.

"What is it, Maria? I feel like someone just removed the sunshine from my sky."

Maria shifted her weight uncomfortably in her chair. "We need to talk… I have some concerns."

She explained, "I visited the gem display. There was no mistake… no imagining it. Something in the diamond was aware of my presence. Quite honestly, even with my knowledge of the paranormal, this encounter freaked me out a bit. It was like it somehow knew who I was!"

Lazlo approached Maria and hugged her, offering support.

"I believe you, Maria. I have experienced similar feelings with the *Joseph Stone*. Contact with the *Hope* was overwhelming. I can't even describe it. But I need to know more."

The telephone on Lazlo's desk rang. It surprised him, but he quickly answered it. The caller was James Ledbetter.

"Hello, my friend…we need to speak to one another…in person. Could you come to my office, please? There are things to discuss."

The two of them immediately left for Dr. Ledbetter's office, as they were overwhelmed with feelings that something very important either happened or was about to occur. They entered his office together, soon after.

James wasn't expecting Maria but did his best to hide any discontent. His conversation was for Lazlo alone.

"So, Maria…" James smiled patronizingly. "How is the office decoration progressing? Is this guy helping or hindering your creativity?" He laughed, but truthfully he was the only one who saw any humor in it. Before Maria could answer, Dr. Ledbetter quickly moved on. "You know…come to think of it, we have a large storage area that is filled with office furniture. Fake plants and trees, chairs, sofas, things to hang…even artwork that pertains to the work we do here. Maybe even photos of the *Hope Diamond*. Let me arrange for you to have a look while I talk to Lazlo."

He wrote down directions to the room and handed her a key. "Take your time. This could easily take an hour or more." James obviously wanted her gone. So off she went…but not at all happy about it. Lazlo's empathic senses were kicking in. Something didn't feel right. James was acting like a different person.

"So, Lazlo…let's get down to brass tacks… I know things about you and I'm learning more every day, but I really don't know what you want in life. Sure, you went to a great school and studied to be a doctor. You have a wonderful woman in your life who has enough old money in her family to support you in luxury for many lifetimes. You seem to have a very supportive family and lots of friends. People like you. You're in your early twenties with a lifetime ahead of you. But what do you really want? I mean, *really* want?"

Lazlo was surprised at the blunt nature that seemed to take over James's personality. It could easily be viewed that he spoke the words of another person. Someone with much greater authority. Lazlo noted that caution needed to be used in this new scenario. He needed to learn who was pulling the strings here.

Before he could answer, Dr. Ledbetter continued his quest for personal information. "That thing that you did with the *Hope Diamond* was extraordinary! I've been told that you also have a deep interest in the Northern Lights! Did you witness the displays recently?"

Lazlo briefly answered yes, before James caught a breath and then continued. James leaned in closer and motioned for Lazlo to do the same. It seemed that he had a secret to share.

"Lazlo, my friend… I have powerful friends in high places. I hope that you will get a chance to meet some of them someday. Do you have any idea that in the past week, the United States was almost pulled into a nuclear war? I'm not kidding!" Dr. Ledbetter stood up straight and adjusted his jacket to show his pride in being privy to this information.

He continued, "There was a strong solar storm that created high-voltage discharges in our northern hemisphere. The storm blew out our secret satellite system on our northwestern Canadian border. The military believed it was an attack by Russia. It took days for our President to be convinced otherwise. He nearly nuked the Soviet Union over an Aurora Borealis! No shit!" James gave a sarcastic laugh.

Lazlo failed to see the humor in this event, much like James' earlier joke that he told at Maria's expense. His jokes were just too forced.

"Lazlo… I want you to succeed in your endeavors. Help me, to help you…can you do that?"

Dr. James Ledbetter was waiting for a reply. He fully expected an answer to his question. James looked at Lazlo, almost guessing that his stare would somehow coax out a preferred response.

"So, I'm asking you, bottom line, what is it that you really want to do?"

Lazlo carefully chose his words as he addressed his supervisor.

"Right now, Dr. Ledbetter, I want to collect my girlfriend and some personal items from my office. I then want to spend my first night in my new home after just receiving the keys. Maria and I have some business to attend to. We need to pack. Then I plan to fly to Spain with Maria and start a new chapter in our lives."

James shook his head. He didn't quite know what to say. He wasn't expecting this kind of open defiance.

Lazlo added… "When I return, I promise to discuss solar storms, human auras, the Northern Lights, and cursed gemstones. I hope that my response is sufficient."

Lazlo walked out of the office.

The trip to Granada, Spain was looking very good indeed.

Agents, Boxes, and Landslide
CHAPTER 17

Maria and Lazlo boarded their first-class flight to Spain. Lazlo was still doing a mental checklist going over every detail of the trip. Clayton had taken care of getting Lola on board a freighter leaving Baltimore a day earlier.

Lazlo checked on his parents and other family members to make sure they had gotten home safely. Maria had driven Lazlo to the bank in East Baltimore, where he collected his *Joseph Stone*. But before going into the bank, he purchased a small leather pouch attached to a leather cord. This necklace would be his place of safekeeping for the diamond.

Maria noticed his distraction and grabbed his hand and squeezed it tightly. .. "Hey baby… are you OK? You seem so very far away."

Lazlo smiled and said, "I'm a little nervous about flying over the ocean. First time, remember?" Yes, Maria did remember. She remembered her first time too. When she was just a child. But somehow, she felt that there was much more on Lazlo's mind.

"Well, we better get comfortable. The flight will take over 24 hours…settle in, and sleep if you can." Before she knew it, Lazlo was asleep.

Back at the Smithsonian, Dr. James Ledbetter was greeting a new face in his office. The gentleman treated James as a superior and was reporting to him.

"So, what did you find? You followed Dr. Somogyi before he

went to the airport, yes? Where did he go? Did you follow him inside?"

The man shifted his weight nervously. "Yes…He visited a bank. I followed him inside and pretended that I wanted to open an account. I watched him closely until he went into the back behind locked doors."

James frowned, "And what was back there? Did you check? Was the area marked?"

"Yes, sir! Safety deposit box lock-up. He went inside with nothing and seemed to leave with nothing. It was a very short trip."

"Very well… Now speak of this to no one." James waited until the man was gone. He closed his door and reached for the telephone on his desk.

Dr. Ledbetter dialed the number. He wanted complete privacy.

Three rings and a voice responded. "Hello, Landslide." James didn't bother to identify himself. It was clearly understood who he was.

"We had the doctor followed to a bank in East Baltimore. He visited a safety deposit box there, privately. My source reported that he seemed to come out with nothing. Carrying 12 diamonds back to Europe would be foolish. I personally believe that they are still in that bank. What do you want to do? How do you wish to proceed?" James waited for a reply.

"We'll handle it, Ledbetter…my men are very good at what they do. I'll have them visit before the day's end. We shall see what our new doctor is concealing around Baltimore City."

Ledbetter thought to himself, Lazlo's got the 12 missing fucking diamonds! That's what he's got! And he slammed the receiver down on the phone.

Within the hour, two black four-door sedans parked in front of the M&T Bank on Eastern Ave in Baltimore. Eight men, dressed in dark suits entered the bank in military fashion. Two locked and guarded the front doors while the other six picked critical locations around the bank.

They were greeted by the Bank Manager. One man stood out from the group and identified himself as Agent Jones. He advised the Bank Manager that a possible national crisis was about to happen. Something was hidden in this bank that was possibly a threat to the

United States.

More to the point, a safety deposit box needed to be searched. Something very dangerous was hidden inside.

The manager, Howard Jones, was a former military man, and upon hearing this, he wanted to assist. Howard wondered if this government agent and he were related. But Jones was a fairly common name in the area.

"Just ID the box and get us inside of it, Mr. Jones. That is all that we ask."

Howard complied and within minutes, four of them were inside the vault. Lazlo's box was removed and opened with special master keys. Surprisingly, the box was empty. Agent Jones was angry. Then he demanded a private phone line, to make a call.

The call was placed to the same number that James Ledbetter had used earlier. Three rings and a male voice responded… "Hello… Landslide… What do you have?"

Agent Jones replied with little enthusiasm. "It's a bust, sir. The box is empty…"

Jones could hear the receiver being slammed hard as the phone was hung up in anger. He knew that there would be hell to pay.

Lazlo was just waking up for the third time since boarding the plane. For the most part, he was waking up for meals and after talking with Maria, he'd doze off again. Maria blamed it on the motion sickness pills that he had taken earlier.

Maria settled in to read a book that she purchased in the airport gift shop. *My Side of the Mountain*, a best-seller about a boy running away from home to live alone in the mountains. She knew it was a children's book but had also heard that the boy befriends a falcon. Maria was fascinated by raptors…birds of prey. She wanted to read about this very special relationship.

Eventually, she fell asleep too and started to dream about the *Hope Diamond* speaking to her directly. The dream was sort of like what happened in the gem display room at the Smithsonian, but much more vivid and somewhat more threatening.

Maria slept deeply. She was in the kitchen at Lazlo's townhome preparing dinner for the two of them. As she turned around to look for her cup of coffee, she noticed the *Hope Diamond* sitting in the center of the kitchen table. It was breathtaking. As Maria gazed at the *Hope*, the stone started to glow! It remained a radiant blue that began to fluctuate into multiple different shades. It was hypnotic, and Maria couldn't look away. She was somewhat trapped in a mental connection with the diamond… a rock… nothing more than a piece of carbon, yet it controlled her.

Maria had no idea how much time passed, minutes…seconds… hours…she didn't know. But then she heard the voice! It spoke to her directly… *"Lazlo is mine! Do you not yet understand? Louis was mine too! These men are unique and deserve to know the secrets of this world and the universe in which it lives. Only I can teach them the ways…only they deserve to be taught. Others have tried to steal what I offer…many have tried…and many have died. Humans have tried to own me…and they too have all perished. I can make Lazlo a great leader. Civilizations could fall before him if he gives of himself to me. Interference with what I am, and what I do, will result in death!"*

"Hey, Maria! Wake up!" Lazlo was shaking her shoulder. "They're serving ice cream and we're almost in Spain! Another half hour to go"

Maria's mind was still with the *Hope*. Was that a dream? Or did it happen for real?

Lazlo was awake now and found the experience of landing in a large jet aircraft exciting. Maria thought that his childlike wonder of all things new was a unique and wonderful part of what made him special.

After disembarking from their flight, Maria and Lazlo collected their luggage and secured the services of a cargo handler, to assist them to the front of the terminal to meet with their ride to her home in the hills of Granada. It wasn't long before Maria saw a familiar driver, dressed in formal chauffeur attire. His name was Alejandro, and for Maria, it seemed that she had known him all of her life. Actually, he was her personal driver since she was a child.

"Hola, Alejandro! ¿Cómo has sido mi amigo?"

"Muy bien Señorita Maria. Gracias!"

Maria and Alejandro both took notice of Lazlo's confusion with the Spanish language and quickly apologized while explaining their brief greeting was a basic hello between old friends.

Alejandro shook hands with Lazlo while welcoming him to Granada. "From now on, we speak English for Mr. Lazlo, yes?"

Lazlo smiled and said, *"Gracias."* Alejandro laughed. "You see Maria! Mr. Lazlo does speak Spanish!" The three of them laughed as Alejandro directed them to the limousine. Lazlo felt strange watching this middle-aged man handle all of his luggage. This would take some adjustment for Lazlo, it just didn't feel natural. He swore to himself that he would do his best to make Maria proud. The group was approached by a large black stretch limo that had small government flags on the front fenders.

Lazlo couldn't hide his surprise at the quality of this long, sleek, black automobile.

Alejandro said to Maria, *"Me gusta este chico. Él es del pueblo. Has elegido bien Maria."* Translated this means "I like this guy. He is from the people. You have picked well, Maria."

Maria smiled as she looked at Lazlo. "He says that he likes you, my love."

"Bien," replied Lazlo. *"Bien."*

The interior of this vehicle was unbelievable. Everything about it screamed luxury! Lazlo was amazed, but it was obvious that this was completely normal for Maria. After all, this was her life… She was born to it.

He thought back to the night when they first made love, in his parent's bed. The old shack. The mattress was probably 40 years old! How could this wonderful woman be so in love with him, and so quickly? He obviously had nothing to offer her. And this all happened before their discovery of the '12 brothers'. He was a very lucky man, indeed. Lazlo gazed at Maria as Alejandro maneuvered the big boat of a car out of the airport and onto the main roads of Spain. Maria looked back at Lazlo and met his gaze with her own as she smiled.

Once again, his heart melted.

Between Maria and Alejandro, you couldn't have paid a tour guide for a more informative trip through the countryside. They both knew their country well, and their pride showed, as they pointed out, and explained every detail about Granada. History, landmarks, government… Lazlo was getting yet another education… And he liked it.

After a time on the road, up ahead, in the hills on many acres, Lazlo could see a beautiful mansion nestled in a landscape that resembled a sub-tropical paradise. The architecture was purely Spanish. Stables were visible, with horses running on fenced acreage around the compound. The facility was breathtaking!

"This is my home, Lazlo. One day I hope that you might feel it in your heart to call it your home, too. At least when you are in Spain." She smiled and kissed him softly on the lips.

Maria got out of the limo and they were greeted by house staff, maids, and cooks, led by a butler. They were all extremely happy to have her home. They barely noticed that he was there. Alejandro unloaded the luggage from the limo trunk. Lazlo followed him to the back of the limo and pulled out one of the heavier bags with ease. Obviously, he had no problem assisting Alejandro.

No, Señor Lazlo, no necesitas ayudar. Nos pagan por hacer esto.

No, Mr. Lazlo, you don't need to help. We get paid to do this.

Alejandro was concerned that he might get in trouble if he let Lazlo help.

Maria called to Lazlo, "My love, there is no need to assist. Everyone here knows their jobs and they are very happy to comply." She then smiled her beautiful smile again, while Alejandro spoke softly to himself saying: *Realmente me gusta este americano. Entiende al trabajador.*

I really do like this American. He understands the working man.

Maria overheard his comment and couldn't help but respond.

Parece entender también a las mujeres españolas. Nunca en mi vida me habían tratado tan bien.

He seems to understand Spanish women too. I've never been treated so well in my life.

Alejandro left but the female staff all at once said oooohhhh…
Maria encontró uno bueno. Oooohhhh…Maria found a good one.

Maria asked the butler where her family was. The butler explained that no one was currently home. He suggested showing Lazlo to a guest room. Maria agreed.

Lazlo asked Maria what had just been said. She said, "It seems they like you." Lazlo smiled and picked up a suitcase.

The butler's name was Antonio but he said that calling him Tony was fine. The ladies went back to their duties after each one personally said hello to Lazlo while grinning at Maria.

Tony led the way with Alejandro close behind. The house was a mansion. Maria followed the staff with Lazlo bringing up the rear of the group. She advised Tony to go to the larger of the seven guest facilities. Maria knew them well and had selected the one that she thought would be the most comfortable for Lazlo.

The entrance door alone to this room was worth more than everything on his parent's lot in Ward. Solid hand-carved oak as best Lazlo could tell. The fixtures were all black ironwork, also obviously handmade. The workmanship was amazing.

"This will be your home while you're here," Maria said. She kissed him quickly, but Lazlo felt the spark jump between them. She felt it too. No one else seemed to notice. This magic was still there, even after traveling halfway around the world.

Lazlo looked around the room and was astounded. The decor was Spanish equestrian. Horse paintings and statues adorned every open space. The room had several windows that overlooked a horse paddock large enough to house two dozen horses.

Maria pointed up to a window with a balcony on the second level. "That's my room up there. We can wave to one another at night. For now, Papa would never allow us to share a sleeping space. But the day will come. I am sure." She then threw her arms around him and kissed him deeply. Maria truly loved this man. Lazlo loved her too. And it showed.

"Get comfortable my love. Take a shower and a nap, whatever you choose. There are drinks in the refrigerator. I will do the same in my room. We will be notified when dinner is ready. We might eat alone, or pending my family's schedules today, we might meet everyone. I believe it is still two hours away."

Lazlo hugged and kissed Maria repeatedly. The contact between them was especially powerful today. Maria felt it too. Lazlo reached for the *Joseph Stone* and removed it from the satchel. It immediately started to glow crimson red. Somehow, these events were connected. One day Lazlo would know for sure.

Lazlo was just dozing off after a hot shower and an orange juice when a soft but obvious chime resonated through the compound. Each room seemed to have its own speaker. When the chime stopped, a man's voice said: "Dinner is served." The voice spoke in English, obviously for his benefit. In a matter of seconds, there was a soft knock on his door. It was Maria.

"I thought that you might need a guide to find the dining room. I'm happy to serve that purpose, sir." Maria curtsied.

"Am I dressed okay?" asked Lazlo. "I didn't really bring any fancy clothes. For that matter, I don't even own anything fancy."

"Relax my love. My family won't be joining us for dinner. My mother is still out of town and my father is tied up at the embassy in Granada. He will return later. We may or may not see him tonight."

"I do expect my Uncle Diego to drop by this evening. He wants to meet you in the worst way. I believe that Dr. Ledbetter has been telling him stories about you. After all, our line of education and business at the University keeps our world quite small. You're going to be famous!"

Maria led Lazlo through the mansion to a large dining area. The solid wooden table seated 26 people. Lazlo counted the chairs. It looked strange to him, but only two place settings had been arranged. The dinnerware and crystal glasses, along with obviously real silverware was beautiful. As they approached their seats, a waiter served them drinks from a large bottle of wine. Maria made sure to point out the label on the bottle.

"This is our own brand name…our own label. We make it here. The grapes are grown on the hillside in our vineyard." Lazlo looked at the label as the waiter stood by. Yes, Cordova Valdez and a rearing white stallion were on the front of the bottle. Lazlo was beginning to feel like that big jet transported him to a fantasy world in another life. He was most likely correct.

A taste was poured for each of them. Maria knew the routine to smell the fragrance of the wine. She swirled the wine before finally taking a sip. She smiled and nodded to her server to fill the glass. Lazlo repeated her steps, but not really knowing what he was doing. But the wine tasted good, so he, too, asked for more.

Diego Pilan

CHAPTER 18

After finishing one of the best meals of his life, Lazlo conceded that he was getting drunk. He wasn't much of a wine drinker and the alcohol had gone to his head. Maria expected her Uncle Diego to arrive sometime after dinner. Hopefully, before it got too late.

She signaled their waiter to bring some coffee. Strong and black. She wanted to help Lazlo sober up as quickly as possible. She wanted Diego to like Lazlo and not perceive him as a drunken American.

Several hours passed as they relaxed and walked around the Cordova Valdez Hacienda. Really seeing the place required riding some expensive horses. Lazlo had never ridden before. This would be another first for them.

Lazlo would worry about the horses at another time. Tonight was much more important than any recreational activity. Well, with a horse anyway.

The two lovebirds retired back inside the main living room of the hacienda. The wait for Uncle Diego did not last long. Maria saw the headlights of a dark sedan like the one most of her family traveled in.

She watched from the window as Diego exited the back of the sedan. The driver then headed for the garage. Maria ran to the door to greet him and jumped into his arms before he knew what hit him.

"Tío Diego! *Hola*! I have missed you!"

"Maria, my beautiful niece, how are you? And where is this Lazlo fellow that I have heard so much about?" Diego looked at Lazlo who was sitting on the sofa. "He does sound too good to be true."

"Amigo. Are you too good to be true? And are you good enough for *our* Maria? She is the most prized possession of the Cordova Valdez family. You will find yourself tested by many people in many ways to prove your love for her. Please take no offense. We all love our Maria."

"As do I," said Lazlo.

"Dr. Ledbetter has shared much with me regarding you and your history, Dr. Lazlo. I am aware of the paranormal happenings that seem to have followed your family from Europe when they fled to the United States. Even Maria claims to have been witness to psychic phenomenon in your family. I won't challenge any of this. But, I need reassurance from you that all of this is real. James did not share everything. He hinted at possibilities. There was something about you having a psychic connection of sorts to the *Hope Diamond*? This not only intrigues me, but it puzzles me too. A connection to a stone? In what way may I ask?"

"Before you answer, I am also curious about your white aura that Maria has spoken of. This would be extremely rare and place you in the limited company of very well-known spiritual leaders throughout history."

Lazlo didn't get a chance to respond before Maria jumped in. "Tío Diego. I have seen his aura. Many times. It is indeed white."

Diego smiled. "We shall see my dear. We shall see."

"My Momma always said that I was a *White Lighter*. She, too, could see human auras. As I have gotten older, I can see them too. Maria's is green. Like the Northern Lights. It is beautiful. The color matches her soul."

Diego listened intently.

"So. Are you also a romantic? I am starting to quickly see why Maria has become so serious about you. And so fast too. Some of my questions about you can be answered scientifically. Others will take time while getting to know you. My main concern in all of this is to protect our Maria. That also entails learning more about you."

"Why would the Smithsonian Institution, in Washington DC,

hire a recent medical school graduate without field experience, in the way they did? Not only giving you a title and office, but arranging a home in the area, and paid travel worldwide. Might I add that arrangements have been made for you to study at my university here, for free. Why, I keep asking myself. Why indeed?"

"This entire situation perplexes me. But even more so because our Maria speaks of marriage to you someday in the future. You are an intelligent man Dr. Lazlo. I think that you can understand my concerns and the reasons for my questions."

Lazlo and Maria both understood. They also knew the reasons for the special treatment.

"Are you familiar with a fellow by the name of Simon Kirlian? He was a Russian researcher who claimed he witnessed lights coming off his fingertips while working in a high-voltage environment. His government was interested in his theories and paid for his continued research. In 1938, he created the Kirlian Camera. It was the first camera that could take a real-time photo of a color aura. It is real and it works."

"Would you really like to know if your *White Lighter* theory is real?"

Lazlo stood up smiling while saying, *yes*. He looked at Maria for approval but needed none. She wanted to find out too.

Diego called for his driver to bring in the brown case from the trunk of his sedan. He had a feeling that this situation might present itself tonight. Diego liked to be prepared.

Diego soon had the large brown case in his hands. He took it to a table and opened it in front of Lazlo and Maria. Inside was a white ceramic square that was insulated on the backside. There were quite a few wires that would be connected to two 9-volt batteries. A stand had been created, to support a camera above the ceramic tile.

After Diego finally put the contraption together, he looked at Lazlo and asked him to place his hand flat on the ceramic. Lazlo did as he was directed. Before turning on the voltage Diego said, "This might hurt just a little bit!"

Lazlo felt an electric shock run through his hand up to his elbow and he heard the camera click several times before he pulled his hand away. The camera would produce the pictures in moments.

Diego was holding the film as it developed and when he finally saw the images, he said out loud, "*Madre Maria. ¡Santo Cielo!*"

"Mother Mary. Holy fuck!" He then crossed his chest with the Catholic Father, Son, and Holy Ghost motion as a form of forgiveness.

Diego looked at Lazlo aghast. His face looked as if he had been witness to a ghost or some other holy apparition. His eyes scanned Lazlo Somogyi from his feet to the top of his head. He then looked at Maria.

"*Él es Lazlo Joseph, ¿si? María es Mary en nuestra lengua. ¿José y María? ¿Puede ser esto? Mira las fotos, María. Tenías razón. ¡Es un encendedor blanco!*"

"He is Lazlo Joseph, yes?"

Diego added, "And Maria is Mary in our language. Joseph and Mary? Look at the photos, Maria. You were correct."

Maria grabbed the photos and looked at them intently. "No doubt, Lazlo is a *White Lighter*!"

"*Mi amor…*"

"My love…"

That was all that she could manage to say at the moment. Lazlo still wasn't sure exactly what to think but he understood Joseph and Mary – that was certain.

"What about Maria? Momma said that Maria's aura was green like the Northern Lights. Let's find out!"

"Lazlo, how bad does it hurt when you turn on the camera?" asked Maria. She was both reluctant and curious.

Lazlo said, "I think that it's pretty much like getting a tattoo. You know it'll hurt, and it does, but afterward, you'll come back and do it again." Lazlo laughed. "Give it a try."

Maria agreed to have her aura photographed with a certain apprehension. But she did it.

Like Lazlo, there was a shock that migrated to her elbow. Multiple clicks of the camera, and she quickly pulled away. Unlike Lazlo, she grabbed the film to watch it develop before her own eyes.

Within minutes, her reaction was much the same. But she handed one photograph to Lazlo while handing the others to her uncle.

Diego said in awe, "*Verde!*"

"Green!"

Momma was correct. This most definitely got all of Diego's attention!

Lazlo, being scientific, had an idea. Diego and Maria listened.

"Let's photograph our hands together with our fingertips touching. I want to know how our auras will react."

"Great idea," Diego said.

Then Diego prepped the system for more shots and the couple approached the camera again.

As Maria and Lazlo placed their hands on the ceramic pad their fingers briefly touched. Both saw sparks shoot from their fingertips before the voltage was even applied. They exchanged glances. Diego saw nothing out of the ordinary. He then arranged their fingertips differently.

"Are you both ready?"

Diego flipped the switch controlling the power source and a surge ran through both of their hands. But this time was very different. Sparks flew from their fingertips, even visible to Diego. The lights in the room flickered and went dim. On-site generators kicked in to power up the home and grounds. The camera clicked off three photographs.

"*Madre Maria!*" Diego whispered.

"Mother Mary!"

House staff ran into the room questioning what had just happened. They were politely but quickly dismissed. "It's no problem," said Diego. "We're just doing a little experiment."

The film captured Lazlo's white light and Maria's green! But where their fingers touched the colors created a blue, the color of the *Hope Diamond!*

Even more important was the fact that the Kirlian Camera captured obvious voltage coming off of their fingertips. This was not 9 volts, but much greater, all based on the intensity of the discharge.

So now Diego was beginning to understand the mystic power of Lazlo Somogyi.

But he was also concerned that the wrong people might want a hand in this. That is why Hitler wanted the *King Louis Blue*. Diego also knew of Dr. James Ledbetter's connections to the United States military. His motives were not totally honest. Far from it.

He voiced his concern. "Is there anything else that you would like to share with me? These kinds of powers can be dangerous, as you well know."

Again, Lazlo looked at Maria and she agreed. "Do you have a private safe here in the hacienda?" Lazlo asked.

"Yes, I have just what we need," said Maria. "It's very secure."

Lazlo removed his leather necklace containing his *Joseph Stone* and placed it on his lap. Before opening it he explained that the item in the bag was a piece of the *King Louis Blue* diamond.

"This artifact disappeared centuries ago. In the 1930's Hitler acquired it. There is no doubt that the stone was a match. It was confirmed by Benjamin Goldsmith, an associate of my grandfather."

Lazlo said, "Diego come closer. You can see better what is about to happen." He poured the stone into Diego's hand. Lazlo said, "This is the *Joseph Stone*, named after one of the Tribes of Israel."

"He is exquisite! A beautiful stone!" said Diego.

Lazlo then calmly directed, "Now watch carefully."

Lazlo gently reached out and collected the single stone with his fingertips as Diego looked on. The blue diamond began to change in color from blue to crimson red before their eyes. Diego placed his hand on his heart while reciting biblical passages in Spanish, far too fast for those around him to understand.

Lazlo placed the diamond on the table in front of them and it turned back to normal. Diego was stunned.

"There is much more to the story," Lazlo said. "So much more. For now, Maria, let's lock up this treasure. We'll continue to talk after it is completely safe."

Maria agreed and Lazlo followed her to the safe where they locked it away for its protection.

"Uncle Diego likes you," Maria said to Lazlo.

After returning from Maria's private quarters, the couple joined Uncle Diego to talk further. As they seated themselves in the main room, Diego looked at the two lovers and said, "What just happened is on the level of miraculous."

Lazlo added, "And you haven't even heard the whole story."

"I'm listening," Diego said.

Maria took over starting from the beginning, telling all of the family history from World War II and forward. She introduced Diego to the characters: László Joseph Biro, Benjamin Goldsmith, Eztar and Julius Somogyi, and the family that followed in their footsteps. She spoke of Adolf Hitler and the acquisition of the *King Louis Blue* diamond from France. It was Lazlo's grandfather who created the *Hope Diamond*. He also created the 12 diamonds that Lazlo calls the '12 brothers'.

Diego was mesmerized. "So, there are actually 12?"

"Yes, there are 12 stones." Maria quickly added that Lazlo had touched the *Hope*, and she got to wear it one day at the Smithsonian.

Diego asked if Lazlo had made the *Hope* turn red and the answer was yes! "And Ledbetter witnessed this?" Diego inquired.

Lazlo said, "Yes, that was when the job offer came."

Before they could speak further on this immediate part of the story, Maria said breathlessly "She spoke to me!" The room went silent.

"Who spoke to you, Maria?" Both men had asked at the same time.

Maria explained how she privately witnessed a color change in the heart of the diamond. And then a flash shortly thereafter. "It was only recently on the flight to Spain that the *Hope* spoke to me in a dream. The message was a threat to me. This stone has somehow picked Lazlo as her own. Probably much like she chose his grandfather or King Louis of France. People die when they get close to this unpredictable piece of natural history. The *Hope Diamond* threatened me or anyone interfering with "her" plans would also die. I am a believer."

Diego absorbed every word that Maria said. He appeared to fear all that he had learned. Diego was a believer in supernatural and paranormal events. He believed in the reality of the supernatural. And this was surely one of those times.

"Lazlo you are in more danger than you realize. Not only from the stones but from others like Hitler who would want to possess them. Dr. Ledbetter is closely connected to the United States military. He would use you to collect paranormal knowledge that could be used in world conquest. That is why he befriended you with hopes of keeping you close. Please use the greatest caution, my friend. We'll talk more tomorrow." It was late so he decided to spend the night at the compound.

Papa Cordova Valdez

CHAPTER 19

Lazlo sat up in bed, unsure if his slight headache was a result of the wine, jet lag, or both. Either way, he wasn't feeling his best. Diego had really grilled him last night and Lazlo expected much of the same from Maria's father when he arrived. All in the name of love, Lazlo thought to himself.

Since he was already awake Lazlo decided to take a shower and put on some clean clothes. He wanted to look his best for Maria's family.

It wasn't long before there was a soft knock on his door. It was Maria, she was ready to start the day with him.

"Did you sleep well, my love? If I might ask, how is your head? Our wine can sneak up on you when you least expect it." She said with a smile.

Lazlo agreed that he was feeling a little groggy and needed something for his head. She promised to see to it for him.

"Is your Uncle Diego awake yet?"

Maria said that Diego didn't go to bed last night. "Papa arrived after midnight and they stayed up talking all night. Most of their conversations, the ones I overheard, were about you."

That made Lazlo just a bit nervous. It seemed he was being judged by everyone in Granada about his intentions toward their Maria. At least it appeared to be that way.

Maria took his hand and laughed as she advised him that the only opinion that really mattered was hers. And she loved him deeply. Lazlo told her that he loved her too and then suggested that she take him to meet her Papa.

"I'm as ready as I'll ever be," Lazlo said. "Before we go, what shall I call him? Papa is too personal today. Señor Cordova Valdez seems too formal. I don't even know his first name. What is it?"

"His name is Lorenzo," replied Maria. "Señor Valdez is probably just fine. Relax."

All eyes were on them as they entered the room. It was quite obvious, however, that Lazlo Somogyi was indeed the center of attention. Diego stood first and greeted Maria with a hug. Then she moved to her Papa for a strong embrace.

"I have missed you so much, Papa." Maria kissed him on the cheek and turned to see Lazlo shaking hands with her uncle.

Lazlo then turned to meet the head of the house.

Diego said, "Dr. Lazlo Joseph Somogyi, please allow me to introduce you to the father of Señorita Maria Cordova Valdez. This is Señor Lorenzo Rafael Cordova Valdez." Señor Valdez bowed slightly and extended his hand.

"The pleasure is all mine, my son. Welcome to my home. What is mine, is yours."

Lazlo wasn't sure at first if this was a routine greeting, or if it was special just for him. "Thank you. Do you prefer formal titles here in your home? How shall I address you?"

Lorenzo said simply, "Just call me Papa."

Maria teared up during the exchange.

Lorenzo directed their little group to relax. "Forgive me, but I have some questions that need to be answered."

Papa Lorenzo said that he had heard that Lazlo's grandfather was the cutter who reworked the *French Blue* Diamond of King Louis. He also wanted to confirm that this was done for Adolf Hitler.

"Yes, that's correct," said Lazlo.

Papa then asked about the death of László Joseph Biro.

"My grandfather died in a concentration camp. He was gassed

as punishment for stealing diamonds that were cut away from the large *French Blue*."

"And you have these diamonds in your possession, my son?" Papa Lorenzo needed to be sure.

Lazlo explained that he owned them, but only brought one to Spain. It was currently locked in Maria's safe. "We call it the *Joseph Stone*. I brought it to Granada as proof of what Maria and I have witnessed."

Uncle Diego said, "Yes. I too have witnessed the power that Dr. Somogyi controls with this stone. And reportedly the *Hope Diamond* too."

Diego went on to tell Lorenzo everything that he had learned and seen the night before. He also discussed the fact that the *Hope Diamond* had telepathically threatened Maria with physical harm.

The room was charged with strange expectations. Lorenzo felt that he had to personally witness the event from the previous evening.

Lazlo asked Maria to please get the stone from her safe and bring it to him. He advised her to keep it in the satchel. Maria returned quickly and gave the bag to Lazlo.

"Kindly show me an open hand, if you will." Lorenzo complied. Lazlo placed the single diamond in Papa's palm. Papa Lorenzo was amazed at the sheer beauty of the stone. It was expertly cut, almost flawless. He held it to the light. "Beautiful!" He exclaimed. "Simply beautiful."

Lazlo then asked Papa to place the stone on the table before him. Once again, he complied.

"Observe," advised Lazlo.

Lazlo gently touched the stone and when his fingers reached it the radiant blue color flashed and turned to crimson red!

"*Madre Maria*," Lorenzo spoke out.

"Mother Mary."

"You should see this phenomenon with the *Hope Diamond*," said Lazlo. "It is quite spectacular! That is yet another show!"

Lazlo took control of the situation after returning the stone to its satchel. He spoke politely but very firmly of exactly what he was beginning to believe about the *King Louis French Blue*. Lazlo believed that Hitler knew of its paranormal powers and that many called this a curse. He believed that Hitler wanted to control it for world domination. But he had to hide the identity of the stone by having it re-cut. Downsizing it would help to conceal its presence and identity.

"This was where my grandfather enters the story. He re-cut the Blue, cut part of it into the *Hope*, and created 12 new stones to represent the 12 tribes of Hebrew history. The Twelve Brothers. These are what he took from the Nazi machine."

Everyone in the room was overcome with this story. This account of the Biro family history mesmerized the listeners.

"You just can't make this stuff up. I have been a witness and every word of this piece of history is true!" said Maria.

Lazlo continued, the room was silent, the group felt that he had something more to say…and he did.

"I have a feeling, perhaps it is a premonition of sorts…but nonetheless, I need to act on it to the best of my abilities." Lazlo continued, "I believe in the power of the *French Blue*. Obviously, Hitler did too. That's why he stole it and had it resized. The *Hope Diamond* has been cursed with a history of evil, ill fate, and destruction. *The French Blue*, on the other hand, seemed to serve the King of France. I have personally experienced the power of the *Hope Diamond*. I also sense that She is angry. Whatever life force controls the stone is real. My grandfather unknowingly separated a large piece of Her existence by cutting the '12 brothers'. I know that they too possess powers that we do not yet understand. But I believe they are weaker without Her. Somehow, She knows that I am a blood relation of László Biro. And She knows that I am connected to the 12 stones. I feel that I am expected to right a wrong performed by my grandfather. I don't know if this is true, but I feel it."

This was the first time that Maria had heard Lazlo express the strength of his personal feelings. She was surprised. The silence in the room prompted Lazlo to add some more facts.

"I believe that if I bring all 13 diamonds together in the same place, we will witness the power of the *King Louis French Blue*! I cannot begin to imagine exactly what that might be. History as far back as the priests protecting it at the temple marveled at its power. They believed it was connected to a spiritual, godlike entity that controlled the earth as they knew it. Of course, human beings wanted the power for war and world dominance."

I need to learn more, but I need the security offered by the Smithsonian Institute to test my theories. Currently, I have the other stones safely hidden. I accepted my position under Dr. Ledbetter so that I might have access to the *Hope*. Currently, I fear that James is connected to a higher authority who desires to take this power to the military. Exposing my '12 brothers' in a government facility could end in tragedy. So I must be extremely careful."

Lazlo added that the *French Blue* was also cut down from its original size by King Louis of France. Those pieces were never found. He questioned how much his *White Lighter* ability has to do with all of this. The *Hope Diamond* had spoken to Maria and told her She had chosen the men who would serve and teach the old ways.

"I also fear that word will spread, and I will need some kind of protection in my travels. And sadly, maybe even protection from my own country. The military wishes to use my powers for their own purposes. This is what I now believe to be true."

Diego shook his head. "What do you think that *we* can do to assist? This is history in the making and we seem to have a front-row seat. From an educational standpoint, the University can offer much support in research and training, but the diamonds are not here. Especially the *Hope*. Ledbetter would never allow it to travel. Study must be done in the United States at the Smithsonian."

Diego waited to hear Lorenzo's opinion. After all, he represented the government of Spain. After much serious thought, Lorenzo spoke.

"I am a believer. Your theories, in my opinion, are sound. You have a very scientific mind Lazlo, and I support you. I also believe that I can make the Spanish government support you too. Through the University of Granada, we are firm investors in paranormal studies. You might even want to consider a teaching position here one day. Along with your current degree from Johns Hopkins University, the

University of Granada would consider allowing you to receive your 'research doctorate' in this field. At this point, I cannot see you simply attending school here as a regular student. But our facilities will remain available to you so that you can indeed learn all that you can."

This was starting to proceed in a manner that Maria and Lazlo had never imagined.

Papa Lorenzo continued speaking to his family.

"We need to convince Dr. James Ledbetter that our university research coincides with his desires at the Smithsonian. Lazlo will need to be present both *here* and *there* simultaneously to achieve his goals. This truly has the potential to change the world as we know it. As mentioned, we are now part of living history." Lorenzo smiled at Maria, "You have done very well my daughter. I applaud your choice in a potential husband."

Diego added his opinion that he agreed with Lorenzo. He would handle the educational aspects of the plan. Lorenzo would handle the politics. It was then that Papa Lorenzo added a twist that no one expected and one that would surely quietly enrage James Ledbetter when he learned of it.

"Starting immediately Dr. Lazlo Somogyi will be under the protection of the Spanish government. He will be assigned a personal security team that I will handpick myself. Lazlo, you will not travel alone. When you return to the United States, Maria will travel with you for appearances, but your team of bodyguards will never allow you out of their sight. They will be present during your research and whenever you transport the '12 brothers' between locations. I am considering armed couriers for that duty instead of risking your safety. James will agree to this due to his own interests. However, he will not like it. Now let's eat breakfast!"

Reunion

CHAPTER 20

The days passed quickly for Lazlo, but he was able to see a great deal of Maria's home country. He felt like royalty. The scenery was beautiful. The food was fabulous. And the people of Granada treated Lazlo like a king!

At the University both students and teachers accepted him as one of their own. Never had he ever felt so welcome. Being referred to as Dr. Somogyi was taking some time to grow on him. After all, he wasn't much older than the students surrounding him on this campus here in Spain. Lazlo was fitting in nicely in his new surroundings.

Lazlo was advised that Diego wished to see him in the main office of the campus. When Lazlo arrived, Diego enthusiastically greeted his future nephew. Lazlo was met with a strong embrace and a heartfelt hello.

"What can I do for you, Tío Diego? How can I be of service to you?"

"Well…" Diego hesitated. "We need to plan our trip to the United States. I spoke personally with Dr. Ledbetter and I also took the liberty to deceive him just a bit." Diego laughed softly. "I advised him that we too, here at the University, have an interest in your theories regarding paranormal events with the French diamonds. I might have stretched the truth in regards to us knowing the locations of the 12 missing gems. This interested him greatly."

"You don't know where the rest of the diamonds are, Diego. Only the one." Lazlo mentioned how careful he was with that secret.

"How do you say? You have to hook the fish first before you can reel him in? James Ledbetter has been hooked," said Diego.

"We will leave within the next week, my boy. I say *we* because I will be traveling with you. Maria will also make the trip as we discussed at the Hacienda. Four security personnel will be with us night and day. They are a few of our best, much like your US Navy Sea Lions."

Lazlo hesitated with a frown. "You mean Navy Seals?"

"Yes. Seals! Forgive me. But these are our best!"

"We will travel by government plane. A limousine will be waiting at the airport. The driver is also a special forces commander. Four bodyguards traveling with us will have two sedans to escort us in both the front and the rear of the limo. This should be sufficient protection. You can wear the *Joseph Stone* around your neck as it is doubtful that anyone would suspect you to do that. Once we arrive at your facility, we will be met by a professional courier who will assist in collecting your treasure and escort us to the Smithsonian Institution. It'll be quite a show! What do you think?"

Lazlo said, "It does sound like it should work. Thank you."

Diego was beaming with both pride and excitement about the upcoming excursion. He was very much looking forward to this adventure.

"So, Lazlo, what are your plans for the day we arrive with the gems?"

"Well, first of all, I want the event filmed for further scientific study. This will require several different kinds of camera equipment, including ultraviolet lighting. If I am correct, all of them may not work. Visitors must be very limited. I would expect you, James, Maria, myself, our four military guards… armed… and I suppose the Smithsonian guards that witnessed my first contact with the *Hope Diamond* before we traveled to Spain. The courier company personnel should also be there. Everyone should sign documents to keep quiet about what they witness. We need to be very careful."

"But what are your plans with the diamonds? What do you plan to do with them?" Diego asked.

Lazlo replied that he simply wants to talk with the *Hope Diamond.* She spoke to Maria telepathically. That seemed to be rather threatening.

"I intend to find out why," stated Lazlo. "I also plan to have the 12 brother gems present for this experiment. I want Her to know it. I also believe that Her powers will be amplified by this fact. This could be very dangerous, but we need to know. Dealing with the paranormal is an unpredictable undertaking."

Diego agreed. Seconds later the phone rang and Diego answered it. He became very quiet and responded minimally. The individual on the other end of the line did most of the talking. Diego quietly hung up the phone. Then he somberly turned to face Lazlo.

"Papa Lorenzo has been in an accident. They airlifted him to the hospital. We must contact Maria and have her taken there. Someone ran a stop light and broadsided his limo. This is currently all that I know."

"What is our fastest transportation? Helicopter? Is one available?"

Lazlo wondered if this accident was related to the *Hope Diamond* curse. After all, he did allow Papa to touch the *Joseph Stone.* Diego had touched it too.

For now, they needed to notify Maria and get her to her Papa.

Diego arranged for the helicopter, and in no time at all they were on their way to Maria at the Hacienda. They had called in advance so that she would be briefed and prepared.

In minutes they touched down on the Cordova Valdez property. The rotors were still spinning on the large Sikorsky helicopter when Lazlo saw Maria running towards it from the house. She obviously only had one thing on her mind at that moment, which was to see her Papa.

As she got closer, Lazlo could see that she had been crying. A crew member assisted her in boarding the helicopter. She threw herself into Lazlo's arms. She was then belted into the vessel by the crew while still attempting to hug Lazlo. Everyone heard the engine roar as the pilot increased the power. They were airborne in seconds.

Lazlo could tell that Maria was both terrified and confused. *This simply should not be happening. Papa has many years of life ahead of him*, Maria thought to herself. *He has to live! He simply must survive this tragedy.*

The flight to the hospital only lasted several minutes but to Maria, it seemed an eternity. When they landed, she attempted to exit the aircraft early before the signal from their pilot. Lazlo lovingly but firmly held her back. They didn't need another accident in the Cordova Valdez family. Especially not on the same day. Only a moment passed, and Lazlo helped her onto the tarmac. Hand-in-hand they ran to the hospital entrance.

They were greeted by military medical staff who escorted them to a quiet waiting room designed for these purposes.

"A doctor will be arriving here shortly," advised one of the medics. "He has been notified of your connection to Señor Valdez and that you just landed here moments ago. If there's anything that we can get you simply ask. Meanwhile, try to relax."

"Easier said than done," responded Lazlo. But he knew they were simply doing their jobs. "Thank you. We appreciate all that you do for your country." Lazlo then focused his attention on Maria. She was crying. Lazlo attempted to redirect her energy. He knew however that it would be all but impossible.

"He'll be fine, Maria. I can feel it. This is just a detour in his life and ours. Whatever the injuries I know he'll come through. Do you believe me?"

Maria wanted to believe. At this exact moment, she was having doubts. Her empathic abilities were connected to negative energies that she feared were messages from another place. She had felt them before prior to the death of a loved one. Then she remembered her Momma. Maria frantically looked at Lazlo.

"Where is my Momma? Has she been notified of the accident? Is she on her way? Lazlo. You haven't even met her yet! Dear God, not like this!"

Maria lost her composure and broke down sobbing in Lazlo's arms.

"I promise you, Maria. Everything will be fine. You have my

word." Lazlo felt it in his heart that his words said the truth. He knew that fate would be on their side. Somehow he knew.

Dr. Dino Libertoré arrived several minutes later to address the family members. Diego entered the room with a woman that Lazlo immediately knew was Maria's mother. She was strikingly beautiful and aristocratic. Maria ran to her sobbing, while throwing her arms around her repeating, "Oh, Momma. Momma, I am so scared. We can't lose Papa. We just can't!"

Señora Cordova Valdez comforted her child while maintaining the composure of a skilled politician during a crisis. She knew that all eyes were on the two of them and that most likely reporters from the local press were there. She handled herself extremely well, while at the same time aiding Maria during this family crisis.

Señora Valdez turned towards Lazlo and their eyes met.

Uncle Diego attempted to formally make the introduction, but Señora Valdez was a strong-willed woman and waved him off with one hand.

"No, Diego. That isn't necessary. I know who he is. I have heard a great deal. This is the Hungarian/American that has swept my daughter, Maria, off of her feet. Lazlo, as I recall. And a recently educated doctor no less. Dr. Lazlo Joseph Somogyi. Johns Hopkins University too. Quite impressive. I've done my homework."

She immediately turned to Lazlo and extended her hand.

Lazlo thought to himself that this was quite a different greeting than he had received from the men in Maria's family. He had to think quickly about his next action.

Diego bought him a moment as he intervened with, "Dr. Lazlo, please excuse the formality from my sister. She is under much stress here today and her position in our government requires that certain decorum must be followed. It comes with family responsibility." Diego looked to his sister nervously for approval.

"Oh Diego, just shut up! I do not need your support for my actions!"

She turned back to Lazlo, never lowering her hand. It was 'do or die' time for this mid-fielder and his instincts told him quickly what he should attempt. He also knew very well that aggressive offensive moves could either effectively win the game or end in failure that would never be forgotten. Lazlo was an aggressive midfielder.

He confidently took her outstretched hand by the fingertips while looking into her eyes and kissed the back of her hand while slightly bowing. He then softly spoke…

"Señora Cordova Valdez. It is my honor to meet you today, although I wish it were under different circumstances. I offer you my services in any way that I might assist you in this time of need. If you would pardon my seemingly brazen demeanor, might I add that now I can see where Maria received her beauty and poise. Two women such as yourselves in the same family is a wonderful thing indeed. And for the record, (as he winked at her), it was your Maria that swept me off of my feet. Lazlo then added a would-be afterthought. I trust that one day I might win your favor enough to learn your first name. I would be honored."

The room was silent.

Señora Valdez smiled as Lazlo released her hand.

"*Mi nombre es Juana.*"

"My name is Juana."

This Lazlo character must have some Latino blood in his veins thought Diego. He had never seen his sister so quickly and skillfully swayed in her first opinion of someone. This was very impressive.

Dr. Libertoré updated the family on the condition of Lorenzo. His prognosis would offer no guarantees or promises. He preferred to deal with medical facts.

Maria moved over to Lazlo and hugged him while hiding her face in his jacket. Momma Juana noticed this immediately and smiled.

Dr. Libertoré continued. "Señor Lorenzo has suffered a broken leg and a broken hip. The hip will require surgery. His hand was also crushed but is repairable. The worst news is his concussion. These things are difficult to predict in recovery, but he currently remains unconscious. It will take time to determine the extent of that damage. He will remain in the ICU for a time. Every day will tell us more. I must return now to my other patients. Keep him in your prayers."

Before Dr. Libertoré left the room he notified the family that Señora and Señorita Cordova Valdez could visit Lorenzo but only briefly. Due to the hospital rules and regulations, the other family members could not, at this time. The two women followed him to Lorenzo's room where the doctor went his separate way.

This gave Diego the opportunity to approach Lazlo privately in regard to Lazlo meeting Juana moments earlier.

"*¡Muy bien amigo! ¡Muy bien!*"

"Very good my friend! Very good!" Diego was laughing. "You handled my sister really well. I admit that she can be a handful. Have you ever considered becoming a politician? People really seem to like you. You are very well-spoken and women seem to like you too. I see another future for you should you ever want a change."

Lazlo was flattered. But for now, his efforts were focused on the 13 diamonds. He had no problem putting his natural communication skills to good use in his current career. Lazlo hoped that these skills might somehow serve him when attempting to communicate with the *Hope Diamond*. He would learn soon enough.

America and Baby Jane

CHAPTER 21

Several weeks had passed since the accident. The return of Momma Juana allowed Lazlo and Maria some personal time to visit with her. It became clear very quickly that she really did like Lazlo and supported their relatively new relationship. This very fine man appeared to be good for Maria.

Sadly, Lorenzo had not yet regained consciousness. Scans had shown some swelling of the brain and measures were being taken to reduce it. His other medical needs were addressed and now his body needed to heal. Much discussion took place between family members regarding the planned trip back to America. Would it be all right for Maria and Diego to make the trip while Lorenzo remained hospitalized? Juana was very opinionated on this subject. Lazlo learned that she was a woman accustomed to getting what she wanted. It would appear that her daughter was very much like her in that way.

Lazlo leaned back in his seat and closed his eyes as he listened to the drone of the four engines of the military transport. It was hard for him to believe that he was crossing the Atlantic Ocean again so soon. And this time, the flight was more personal. Due to the military status, it would be faster too. He hoped that he could visit his family. They could not be reached, so they had no idea he would be stateside so soon. Lazlo soon fell asleep dreaming about his childhood in Ward, while flashes of the *Hope Diamond* continued to interrupt his thoughts.

"*I know that you are coming!*" Each time the message ended with a flash of blue light. Lazlo knew who this was.

Lazlo woke up hours later to Maria lightly running her index finger down his neck. He could feel the light static discharge when she touched him.

"Funny…even here I can see your aura and when I touch you I can visually see sparks coming off my fingertips. I hope that it doesn't cause electrical problems on our plane." Lazlo responded that he thought it might be a little late to worry about that–after the fact. But her smile made him forget any concerns, instantly.

"I'm so glad that you decided to make the trip my love. I would have understood you needing to stay with your Papa. It appears that he is stable, and I do so want you with me on this adventure."

"I would have it no other way," said Maria. And she laid her head on his shoulder.

The plane was cavernous, Lazlo thought. Normally used for military cargo, like tanks and trucks it was bigger than anything that he could imagine. Seating was spaced out in different areas in a manner that restricted vision from one compartment to the next. He couldn't see the other passengers on the limited manifest unless he explored the plane.

Lazlo thought that he heard another familiar voice on board, and it wasn't long before Diego entered their compartment.

"*Hola*, Lazlo!" shouted Diego over the loud engines. "Maria! So good to see you both. Taking off in the early morning darkness, I wasn't really sure that anyone else was on board. But we are here, yes? And that's all that matters. And this week, we will make history!"

Lazlo was surprised that both Maria and Diego had made the choice to be with him, instead of with Lorenzo back at the hospital.

Maria decided to add something to the conversation for Lazlo to think about.

"I have other reasons for being on this flight too. But it's a secret that I refuse to share. For now…"

Hours passed and most of the passengers were sleeping. The interior of the plane was dark except for a few lights, but that was all.

Suddenly there was an announcement. "Ladies and gentlemen, this is your captain speaking. This is not meant to alarm you but if you look out any window you will witness a rare and spectacular anomaly. This event has been known to sometimes occur during the solar storms that caused our Northern Lights. We call it St Elmo's Fire. Throughout history, it has even been witnessed on the masts of wooden sailing vessels. The buildup of extreme static electricity causes a luminous plasma to glow in an atmospheric electric field. It is usually bluish in color. As you can see tonight, we are witnessing a rare green hue mixed into the blue. That's your science lesson for the trip! Enjoy!"

Maria looked at Lazlo in awe. He, too, was staring at her as the event progressed. They were both glowing with an intensity that neither had ever witnessed! Their auras were simply alive with energy! Maria gazed at her lover and found her attraction to him growing tenfold. Lazlo felt it too. Suddenly they both heard Her voice at the same time.

"*Bring him to me!*" They knew it was the diamond talking. Both of them got a little chill.

The big plane touched down without incident at Andrews Air Force Base, south of Washington DC. After landing they taxied to a loading zone where several security vehicles, a large stretch limousine, two black sedans, and a white Corvette convertible were parked. As they got closer to the disembarking area, Lazlo was able to see the driver of the Corvette. It was Maria's cousin, Clayton! Lazlo looked at Maria with surprise. "Clayton bought himself a Vette!" Maria just smiled and nodded. After all, she knew different. So did Diego. They were both a part of the family plan that was starting to unfold.

Lazlo rushed to exit the plane and ran straight to his old friend Clayton. They shook hands and then embraced like brothers.

"Damn, Clayton. How the hell are you?" Lazlo stepped back to get a better look at his future cousin. "And a new Corvette… Holy shit!"

Clayton said, "Everything is fine here, but I'm so sorry to hear about Lorenzo's accident. Is there any more news?"

Maria and Diego approached Clayton and the car. "She's a beauty," offered Diego.

"She sure is," responded Lazlo. "I couldn't imagine owning a car like this. The true American sports car! She's iconic!"

At this point, Maria joined the conversation. Clayton discreetly handed something small to Maria. Lazlo took no notice as he was still looking at the car from top to bottom.

"Lazlo. I want you to meet someone," said Maria.

Lazlo turned around looking for someone that he was to meet. But there was no one there.

Maria took him by the hand and stood with him in front of the Corvette. "Lazlo Joseph Somogyi, please allow me to introduce you to 'Baby Jane'." Maria then placed the ignition key in his hand and Lazlo's mouth dropped open.

"I already call her 'BJ' for short. She is *all* yours! Consider her a belated graduation gift from me and my entire family. And as a statement of my love to you."

Lazlo had never received such a gift in his life. The gems and his education, yes. But just an expensive gift? This was yet another first! Lazlo was stunned. He grabbed Maria and gave her a long hug while whispering in her ear thank you, thank you. Then he thanked everyone there. Even the security teams and military personnel who were watching.

Lazlo wasted no time getting behind the wheel of Baby Jane. Maria jumped in beside him as he started the engine.

Clayton spoke up saying that now he needed a ride back to his dorm room.

"Hey, Clayton. Can you spare a few days away from school? How would you like to meet the *Hope Diamond*?"

Before Clayton could answer, Lazlo added, "We might just take this little party to Ward too. It's early enough. We still have time."

Clayton didn't need to be asked twice and he headed for the limo. Diego offered him a seat. They were going to Lexington! Lazlo had briefly shared their destination with Diego before leaving the plane.

Lazlo pulled out first along the service road of the runway and accelerated hard, making the tires on BJ screech! In a flash, the sports car left the group 50 yards behind them! Maria was laughing hard, as was Lazlo. In the limo, Diego ordered the driver to chase them. "Don't let them get away! We must keep them in our sight!"

Lazlo looked in his rearview mirror, noticing that he left everyone else behind. He slowed down so the limo could catch up.

"Just the sound of this Vette gives me the feeling we are flying. But the truth is, I'm keeping the speed down."

"I'm so happy that you love BJ," said Maria.

"Thank you, Maria. I do love her already. I promise that every time I look at her, I'll think of you." Lazlo smiled as Maria squeezed his hand that was resting on BJ's shifter.

Lazlo had noted the exit signs for a rest stop and decided that he wanted to speak to Diego. This would be a great place to have that little talk, the parking lot being empty.

The vehicles entered the rather small facility and security officers selected their positions for what they saw as their best vantage points. Lazlo motioned Diego and Clayton to a picnic table on the grounds. Maria followed.

Lazlo addressed Clayton first. "It sure is good to see you, bro… life has been a blur. You look good, really, you do. A sight for sore eyes. I've really missed you."

Lazlo and Maria sat on one side of the picnic table and Clayton and Diego sat on the other side.

"Tío Diego. Thank you for everything. When I arrived in Spain, you were the first to really make me feel like family. You embraced me as one of your own and I treasure that. Thank you once again, my friend. But I have a problem. I think you can help me."

"I am having some trouble living two separate lives in two very different worlds. I realize that things are just getting started, but I feel a kind of separation between myself and my family in Ward, West

Virginia. My Momma's health worries me too. I need to find a solution."

"Another issue is money. I was obviously born poor but recently inherited something quite priceless. Your family's kindness and the fortune that they possess has allowed me to suddenly live free of financial concerns."

The position with the Smithsonian has also added to that problem. While I should be thrilled, and I am in many ways, I know how my family continues to live in Ward. This haunts me daily. I don't—at the moment—have the cash flow to help them. Priceless stones that are unsold cannot feed the poor. My Momma proved that for decades. Yet, I do not want to sell them at the present time. My destiny is to understand the diamonds and to keep researching their power. My responsibility is to use my grandfather's sacrifice and the knowledge that I might acquire from this, to better the Biro/Somogyi fortune."

Lazlo stopped briefly, looked at Diego, and saw his reaction was positive.

"I have to constantly remind myself that financial debt needs to be repaid. Also, mixed in with all of this is my love for Maria. No one needs to ever doubt that love. I need her like I need the air that I breathe. If she would have me, I would marry her tomorrow. My feelings are that strong."

Maria started to cry. "I love you too, Lazlo. That love will never die. I too would have you forever!"

Now it was Diego's turn to shed tears.

"Lazlo, my boy. What is it that I can do for you and your family? Exactly how can I be of assistance?" Then he added, "The two of you very much need to be together. You need to be joined in the eyes of God. I agree with this union."

Lazlo went on…"I noticed several structures on the property in Granada that were a part of the Hacienda grounds. Individual homes that appeared to be former employee dwellings. Perhaps three that appeared to be empty. Any one of these would be a mansion to simple people like my parents. I personally think they are beautiful. What I would like is to be married in Granada.

Lazlo looked at Maria and dropped to one knee next to the table where she sat, "Will you have me, Maria?"

Maria threw herself into Lazlo's arms while happily crying and saying, "*Si. Si mi amor. Te quiero a ti para siempre!*"

"Yes. Yes, my love. I love you and I want you forever!"

Lazlo returned to his seat but this time Maria moved to his lap and sat with both arms around him with her face in his neck. She continued to cry. Diego was thrilled.

"What I would like is to visit my parents and cousins in Ward, today. I want to invite them to Spain for our wedding. After the festivities, I would like them to stay at the Hacienda permanently. Is that even possible? They have both earned their peace. My Papa and my cousin can still work. Probably on the grounds. It is all that they know. Do you feel that this could become a reality?"

Diego smiled and said, "Yes, my son. I do believe that we can make all of this work harmoniously. My only question is one regarding the health of Lorenzo. Surely the wedding cannot happen in his current condition. He would need to give away the bride. How can we make these plans?"

Lazlo quietly but confidently replied, "Tío Diego, you just let me worry about that."

Lazlo stood up with Maria in his arms and carried her off to their new chariot. BJ was waiting. Diego signaled the team and off they went to Lexington. Arrangements had already been made by Diego for the armored truck courier to meet them at their destination.

The collection of the additional 11 brother diamonds went without issue, but Lazlo had to admit to himself it reminded him of a spy novel. The security, the professional courier company, and simply knowing the value of the stones made for a great story. The cloak-and-dagger atmosphere truly got his heart racing as he imagined himself and Maria as the heroes in this James Bond-style mystery. Maria could tell that Lazlo's mind was somewhere else. She knew the look on his face and it gave his heart away. Lazlo was also driving BJ a bit faster than earlier. He seemed not to notice, but Maria did.

"Lazlo, my love. Slow down for the others. You're losing them.

That courier truck simply cannot keep up with us. Where are you, babe?"

Lazlo shook off his momentary daydream and smiled.

"I guess I was on a case with Her Majesty's Secret Service, and we were running late," Lazlo laughed. "Sorry."

Good News

CHAPTER 22

The closer they got to Ward, Lazlo became more nervous. His family was extremely poor, yet he was driving a Corvette. His fiancé is from one of the wealthiest families in Spain. He inherited priceless gemstones from his grandfather, and he graduated from a prestigious medical college, as a doctor. It was all quite overwhelming. Yet here he was, traveling back to Ward. For Lazlo Somogyi, this was where it all began.

Maria recognized the truck stop motel and restaurant as they turned off the main highway. This would be a great place to fuel vehicles and the team of people too. She signaled Lazlo to stop, but he already had the same thought. Lazlo carefully maneuvered BJ to the gas pump and the limo and the security truck followed. Maria went into the restaurant to arrange a seating area for their large group. She immediately recognized their former waitress, Marge, and they both waved.

Maria explained their travel situation and necessary seating. Tables were quickly cleared and rearranged to accommodate them. Diego and Clayton entered quickly, followed by security staff, while the courier employees stayed with the large truck. Maria suggested that this would be a good place to spend the night. Rooms were acquired after finishing their meals and plans were made for the rest of their journey. The courier company officers decided to continue to Washington DC since they had a facility there where they could secure everything in a guarded compound. They would meet the others tomorrow, mid-morning, at the Smithsonian.

Lazlo admitted to himself that he felt a little ill at ease bringing a stretch limo and a brand new Corvette into a coal mining village. He discussed it with Maria and she thought that in the morning they would all make the trip.

Evening came quickly and the two lovers decided to turn in early. Maria had her own ideas after not having much personal time with Lazlo. She missed their intimacy. Lazlo was admittedly tired from the flight from Spain and the drive in BJ. He and Clayton ate rather excessively as expected, and he was ready for a good night's sleep. Maria wasn't about to let the moment pass, so she snuggled under the covers with him, dressed in little more than a teddy nighty that left little for the imagination.

"Show me how much you really love me, Lazlo," Maria teased. She then gently kissed his neck while stroking a fingertip over his chest. Light sparks cascaded from her hands as she explored the essence of her man. He was her fiancé now, and their bond was growing even stronger.

Both of their auras started to glow. They were radiant under the moonlight that found its way into their room. The atmosphere was charged and their lovemaking surpassed anything that either of them had ever imagined. Maria and Lazlo shared their love several times that evening. Afterwards they drifted off into a tranquil state of satisfaction.

Suddenly, a mystical reality invaded both of their minds at the same time.

"He is mine! Soon you will see!" They each heard the voice.

Morning arrived without further incident, but the contact from the *Hope* was once again disturbing.

"I guess we'll learn more this afternoon, won't we, Maria? I plan to connect to Her on a very personal note." Lazlo quickly changed the subject while leaving the room to find Diego.

Diego confirmed that a late-night phone call to Spain secured the permission Lazlo requested for his parents to come to Granada. If they desired to do so. After breakfast and more planning, the group headed south to Ward.

It didn't take long to get to Ward. Lazlo was not surprised at the looks they got entering the village. The Corvette had a sound all its own that turned heads immediately. The limo was another story. Escorted by the two black sedans, the entourage looked like a movie star had arrived in town. Locals flocked to see who this famous person was.

When they arrived at the Somogyi home, Maria and Lazlo were greeted by Blackie, who jumped into the front seat without hesitation. Lazlo was happy to see him too, and their reunion was touching. Maria loved seeing them together.

Eztar, Julius, and brother Lucas, stepped outside to see what the commotion was about. Their front yard was mobbed with at least 50 people including cousins Janos and Eleanor. Even Laird Connor, their landlord, happened to be in the area and gravitated to the scene.

Lazlo embraced his Momma. He hugged young Lucas, who was more interested in the shiny white sports car than his older brother.

"Momma! Surprise! We've come home for a quick visit, but we have some wonderful news!" Eztar cried at the sudden arrival of her son and Maria. It was an emotional moment for all of them.

Lazlo raised his hands into the air and shouted for all to hear. "Hey everybody, we're getting married!"

Cheers and well wishes exploded from the crowd! Eztar expected this, but not quite so soon. Still, she too was thrilled.

Everyone there wanted to shake Lazlo's hand and the women all hugged Maria. In all the confusion, Maria realized that she had not yet introduced her Uncle Diego. He was being very patient due to the confusing circumstances.

"Tío Diego…come." Maria took him by the hand and escorted him to where Julius and Eztar stood.

"Diego. Please allow me to introduce you to two very special and quite wonderful people. These are the parents of Lazlo. Say hello to Eztar and Julius Somogyi. Eztar also has 'the gift'. It was her father that cut the 12 brothers."

Diego displayed his most professional, formal, but loving

demeanor as he bowed slightly while shaking Julius's hand and graciously kissing the back of Eztar's hand all in one fluid movement.

"*Buen día* …good morning. I am honored to finally meet the parents of this very special young man. I am at your service."

The village had never witnessed a display such as this. There were lots of smiles and tears.

But, there was much more to come.

Lazlo decided that due to the size of the crowd, and the limited size of the home, he would openly discuss the family information where he stood.

"Everyone. Please. I fear that I must simply get to the point of this visit, and so I will share this with all of you, my friends. Yes, Maria and I are to be married. Soon, and in Spain."

There was a murmur of praise and a scattering of congratulations.

Lazlo continued, "Maria's family is one of financial security. What is commonly called 'old money'. They are well known and loved in Granada. Diego is a professor at the University. He is of high rank there. Maria's father is much like one of our state senators. They have offered my family a wonderful gift."

Lazlo turned to look at his parents while keeping one arm wrapped around Maria.

"Momma. Papa. We want you to not only come to Spain for the wedding but to stay afterward. Stay there to live. Beautiful housing is being arranged, as I speak. Uncle Diego has seen to it. We will all join as one happy family!"

Blackie barked.

"Yes, Blackie, you too." Everyone laughed.

"I know that this is a lot to take in. It's overwhelming. But this is a gift like none other. Please take some time to think this over. But please say yes."

Lazlo scanned the crowd and locked eyes with his cousin Janos. Eleanor and Janos both looked sad.

"Why so sad, cousin? Remember the promise that I made to you at the old coal bin? Do you think that I'd forget? You're coming, too! There is also a house being prepared for you. It will cost you nothing!

And work will be provided in Spain!"

Janos ran to Lazlo and Maria hugging them both. Then he hugged Diego.

"I guess that's a yes from this side of the family," added Lazlo.

Eztar looked lovingly at the young couple and gave her answer without delay.

"Of course, yes! We will come. Praise God! Just let us know what to do."

The meeting could not have gone any better. Laird, the landlord, owned the closest telephone and agreed to be the contact person. Lazlo would notify the Sherlous family of this wonderful turn of events.

"Thank you, everyone, for sharing with us. You are all wonderful people."

"Change is in the wind. Good changes. Remember to never give up on your dreams. Work hard and obtain what is possible for you. They say that 'the Lord works in mysterious ways'. Whatever your faith, treasure it, and make your dreams come true. I love you all!"

Diego quietly commented to Lazlo, "I said it before. You, my friend, should be a politician."

The Encounter

CHAPTER 23

Entering Washington DC was exactly what Lazlo remembered. The roads were crowded and hectic. He preferred the countryside of Granada.

Diego had already contacted Dr. Ledbetter at the Smithsonian, and their arrival was expected by early morning. Lazlo was enthusiastic but also felt a certain level of fear regarding the paranormal contact with the *Hope*. He didn't want to admit it to the others, but he was scared to death. Whatever power the *Hope Diamond* possessed was ancient and controlling.

The group was greeted by Dr. Ledbetter and was ushered to the main room where the gemstones of the world were displayed. Maria was hesitant as they got closer to the primary display. She thought that she noticed a flash of light radiating from the *Hope*. It was instant. And almost undetected. Somehow Maria felt that the entity in this stone had just winked at her. She tried to ignore her feelings but she could not. The entity was undeniably real.

While the courier service entered the room with the 11 brothers, Lazlo reached for the *Joseph Stone* attached to his neck. He gently removed it from the satchel while observing the showcase that housed the much larger *Hope*. He instinctively clutched the stone in his fist and attempted to concentrate on the image of King Louis of France. This was nothing more than a hunch for Lazlo, but he felt that it was possible to make a telepathic connection in this manner.

The *Hope Diamond* gave off a brilliant almost blinding blue light that was visible to everyone in the room. Once again, as quickly as it had appeared the light vanished. Everyone stared in disbelief.

Lazlo instructed the couriers to bring the portable lock box containing the 11 brothers to him. They deposited them on a small table that had been erected in front of the primary showcase. He requested a comfortable chair so he could position himself in front of the masterpiece that his grandfather had created. If only László Joseph Biro could somehow see what Lazlo was seeing and feeling on this day.

Lazlo then spoke to the group, "I have no idea what may or may not happen here today. We are exploring new territory. The staff at the Smithsonian has installed cameras throughout the room so that we will have records of everything that will happen. If you are not a believer in the paranormal, I think that you will rethink those opinions after today. I appreciate each one of you for being here. I believe that we are about to make history."

Diego, Maria, and Clayton stood together roughly 10 feet from Lazlo. Dr. James Vernon Ledbetter waited by the exit as if expecting to need a fast retreat during the presentation. He looked more than a little nervous.

Lazlo asked for silence and for the lighting to be dimmed. He proceeded to open the case that housed the 11 brothers. He then placed the *Joseph Stone* on the table near them. On his signal, the *Hope Diamond* showcase was lifted open and She too was brought to Lazlo while still resting on her velvet pedestal. Lazlo then began gently lifting each of the 11 diamonds from their carrier and placing them in between himself and the *Hope*. He tried to relax but found it to be all but impossible. The room was charged with anticipation.

As the 11th diamond was laid to rest on the felt pad with its brothers, Lazlo heard the faint sound of a two-way radio being activated.

"One-way traffic, one-way traffic. I see all 12 stones. Repeat. 12 diamonds are present."

Lazlo knew immediately that he had been betrayed. The radio was a give-away. He needed to move quickly

Lazlo's next move was not at all expected. He lifted the diamond necklace from Her pedestal and placed Her around his own neck. The *Joseph Stone* was returned to its satchel and added to the strange arrangement that Lazlo seemed to be creating. Lastly, he picked up the remaining 11 brothers individually and placed them in his left hand. He clutched them in his fist while staring straight ahead. It appeared that Lazlo was going into a trance and becoming unaware of his surroundings.

Onlookers witnessed the lighting in the facility flashing and security systems powering down. All interior doors were locked, preventing entry or exit to any door or window in the facility. Diego saw Dr. Ledbetter leaning against the door with a look of panic on his face. Ledbetter then reached for his chest, obviously in great pain as he fell to the floor. Within seconds he was dead.

Lazlo did not move. His trance was deep. He had never experienced anything like this in his life and remained unaware of his surroundings. In his mind, he was flying. The scenery before and beneath him flashed by as if it were a motion picture. He witnessed volcanic activity and dinosaurs roaming a prehistoric landscape. He saw fireballs dropping from the sky causing great destruction. Then the landscape flourished and everything turned green as the waters receded after a great flood. The vision was overpowering. The scene continued to change before his eyes. He saw the night sky. A bright star emerged in the east and seemed to move over the desert. Lazlo saw a small group of people huddled around a babe in a manger. The child glowed with a white aura. Lazlo knew that this was a *White Lighter*. The Christ child. The vision dissipated and in the distance he saw a terrible war in the desert.

Many men on horseback wearing white with red crosses on their chests. They were killing enemy soldiers in the name of the Christ child because they believed him to be their true King.

Lazlo's demeanor did not change but tears rolled down his cheeks. Maria wanted to run to Lazlo, but Diego pulled her back. He feared for her life. Diego had never witnessed such paranormal activity.

Suddenly Lazlo saw himself in a hospital room standing over

Papa Lorenzo. He extended his hand and instructed Lorenzo to rise. At the same time the scene changed to the desert war.

A telephone began to ring. No one moved. Finally, Clayton decided that someone needed to answer it, so he did. The voice on the other end said, "We have an overseas call from Granada, Spain for Diego Pilan. Is he available please?" Clayton asked them to hold on while he brought him to the phone.

"Hello," said Diego.

"*Hola*. Diego. This is Doctor Libertoré in Granada. I have some wonderful news!" He went on to say that he had no real medical explanation, but Lorenzo Cordova Valdez had suddenly just opened his eyes and stood up next to his bed. "He keeps asking for Lazlo."

Diego told Dr. Libertoré that he would call back and thanked him for the news. Then, Diego looked at Maria and quietly told her that her Papa was fine and walking around. They hugged as Maria cried with joy.

Lazlo remained in a trance.

He then saw Old Ben working with his grandfather in Germany, but the scene instantly changed to one of pain and misery in a concentration camp in Poland.

Another blue flash and a voice entered his head.

"You can heal your Momma too. If you choose it."

Lazlo imagined his Momma as a young and healthy woman. He could feel the weight of death lifting from her and in his heart, he knew that she was now well. Somehow, he healed her from this dream state.

The voice returned, *"Good. I knew that you would be the one. I knew that you had the gift. Are you willing to learn? Take me with you and I will teach you great and wonderful things. You have been chosen. Will you accept my offer?"*

Lazlo noted that another *Hope Diamond* necklace appeared in place of the original that was now hidden under his shirt collar. He believed that it was just an image to hide the fact of the original being removed. He put his '12 brothers' in their transport case, including the *Joseph Stone*. Lazlo instructed the courier to lock them up and make them guarded and safe in the armored truck outside.

Lazlo looked at Maria with some concern.

"How long did that last? How long was I gone?"

Maria said that it was no longer than five minutes. Probably less. Lazlo was amazed. Upon learning that Dr. Ledbetter had died suddenly, he shook his head in shock.

"We need to leave right now," Lazlo said.

After clearing security they headed out the door as medical personnel examined the body of Ledbetter.

They regrouped outside in the limo. As they closed the doors, they all stared at one another in shock. Ledbetter was dead. He was going to betray them. Lorenzo was alive and healthy, as if by magic. Diego made a phone call to Granada from the limo and was told that even Lorenzo's injuries were miraculously healed. Lazlo wondered about his Momma. He hoped that his dream-state memories were true.

"Diego, what should we do? If I am found with the authentic *Hope Diamond* I will go to prison. If I challenge Her, I will end up dead. As will everyone that I love. I can feel it."

Diego said, "We must go to Granada as soon as possible. That would include the Somogyi family. The cargo plane is still waiting at the airport for our return flight, and it can easily carry BJ on board." A phone call to Laird would notify the family members that their new lives in Spain were closer than they thought. "They should prepare to be collected by another limo service and plan to never look back. We will also notify Doctor and Mrs. Sherlous of the situation." The Sherlous family could afford a trip to Spain for the soon-to-be wedding. There was no need for them to abandon their lives in the USA.

This would all happen over the next few hours. They would immediately travel to the airport.

Lazlo could still feel the presence of the *Hope Entity* while wearing it under his clothing. Presently the 12 brothers were locked in the armored truck. Lazlo wondered if the solid steel box of the truck would sever the connection between the stones. This was something else to investigate in his studies.

It was then that he heard Her voice.

"Join with me, Lazlo. Don't fight me. I can make our lives wonderful

together. That includes the lives of Maria and your family too. Men have died to have me. Your grandfather was one of them. I am willing to serve you. All that you need to do is accept my love. All that you need to do is to say, yes."

"Lazlo!" It was Clayton shaking him. "Where are you, man? You were gone again."

Lazlo stirred and shook his head as if just waking up.

"Yeah. Thanks. She was talking to me again. It's strange. She's really here. Like another person in our group. But even more, it's like she is a part of me. It feels like I hear my *own* thoughts, but the voice is female. And a very powerful female. She's real for sure. I just don't know *what* she really is. But I intend to find out."

Lazlo got out of the limo with Maria and headed for BJ after briefly commenting to Diego, "Let's get this show on the road."

In a few hours, the group arrived at the airport. It would take somewhat longer for the family members from West Virginia to arrive.

During their ride in the limo, Clayton and Diego were able to have a very serious conversation. It seemed that Clayton was reconsidering his education in the United States. Diego reminded him that only one more year stood between him and his degree. Clayton knew this, but he ignored it. He said, "Lazlo needs me. I can skip a year of college. Lazlo and Maria need me now. I can work as a bodyguard for them. It's not like I need the money. I can travel with you today."

Diego appreciated Clayton's dedication to family and friends.

"So be it. Unofficially, you are in. Officially we will work out the details. Thank you, Clayton."

Lazlo watched BJ being loaded on the big plane. She would be fun to drive in Granada.

It wasn't a long wait, but it put Lazlo on edge, wondering if the staff of the Smithsonian security would discover that their diamond was a fake. This fear seemed to make time slow down as he waited for the arrival of his family.

Eventually, a large white stretch limo entered the airport grounds. Lazlo ran to meet the family as the driver pulled up. Janos and Blackie were the first ones out of the big car. Blackie made it to Lazlo first and after a brief reunion, he relieved himself on the tarmac. "Better there than on the plane," laughed Janos. Lazlo laughed too. The cousins hugged each other. Janos added, "This happened super-fast, cousin! Why the rush?"

Lazlo told him that they would talk on the plane. He walked over to the limo to assist his Momma in getting out of the car. She moved with amazing agility.

"Momma, you're moving pretty fast. You're all better now?"

"You know," Momma hesitated. "Since earlier this morning, I started feeling 20 years younger! It just hit me after breakfast. My legs no longer hurt. My back feels fine. Overall, I just feel really, really good, inside and out. And my head is clear again. No more brain fog."

"That is certainly wonderful news, Momma!" exclaimed Lazlo. "I am so happy to hear about this obvious miracle." But deep inside, Lazlo knew that this was something much different than a miracle. This was some kind of paranormal magic. Then he wondered, *What if all recorded miracles really could be explained? What if our spiritual connections really do fall into the category of paranormal magic? What if our world religions truly originated from a place other than the heavens?*

Once again, he heard Her voice.

"Now you are learning, my love! I knew that you were the right choice to assist in my return. Each day you will learn more. You will grow in the old ways."

Everyone boarded for departure. Eztar and Julius were amazed at the size of the plane. Much more than anyone else in the group, Lucas was feeling overwhelmed. He stood at the base of the gangplank staring up at the huge mechanical bird. Until now, the largest piece of machinery he had ever seen was a large tractor used in the coal mines. This thing could swallow that tractor! Against Eztar's wishes, he ran underneath one of the giant propellers. Lazlo called his brother to get clear of that area. The engines would be starting soon. The family then boarded the plane. Blackie was running all over the cavernous interior. There were so many smells that he simply couldn't determine which scent to follow. Lazlo called to him to settle, and Blackie joined him at his feet.

"Good boy Blackie. Come up here with me," said Lazlo. And he lifted Blackie up into his lap in hopes that this might calm him as the plane taxied down the runway. The engines began to roar! Eztar crossed her chest and head representing the father, son, and Holy Ghost trinity.

She then kissed the small silver cross that she was wearing around her neck. Julius held her hand. No worries, Lazlo thought to himself. Everything's going to be fine. Soon they were airborne. Lucas squealed with glee! He was loving this new adventure more than anyone could have ever imagined! Lazlo laughed out loud. He liked watching his little brother.

The big plane gained altitude quickly and executed a hard banking turn that took them over the Potomac River. Lazlo could tell that they were now heading east and would soon be over the Chesapeake Bay, a major estuary in the Maryland/Delaware area. He took it upon himself to describe the scenery for his family. It helped relax his Momma.

Crossing over the Chesapeake didn't take long, and Lazlo could see the Atlantic Ocean looming ahead of them. He placed Blackie on the floor and motioned to everyone that they should have a look outside.

"Take a good look, everybody. This might be the last time you see the USA for some time. This trip is somewhat covert. You're not even carrying proper travel papers."

Diego added, "It's true. But we do it all the time when it suits us. Have no concern. You are all my guests."

The journey started with everyone asking questions about the wedding. They all wanted details. Exactly when was it going to happen? Had they selected a church? How large would the wedding be? What about the honeymoon? The questions seemed endless, and Lazlo was starting to feel embarrassed because he truly knew very little about the plans. Maria didn't either due to her travels in the United States.

Uncle Diego jumped into the conversation and saved them both. He had been in touch with the home front in Granada and knew exactly what the family was planning. While Maria's opinion was important, there was no way that her mother would take a backseat in the planning of such an important event.

Diego assured the family that the wedding would be huge and that it would take place in Granada Cathedral. The church is also known as the Cathedral of the Incarnation. A popular Roman Catholic facility built in the 1500s.

Due to Lorenzo's political status in Spain, the event would be partially opened to the public and attendance could be in the thousands! This information thrilled Eztar and Eleanor, while most of the men looked at one another and rolled their eyes.

Lazlo wondered….Thousands of guests? Really? Now he was becoming a bit nervous. Maria squeezed his hand and blew him a kiss to lighten the mood. He was glad that he didn't have any responsibilities as far as he knew, except to say, 'I do'.

Clayton wanted to talk about sports cars and tested Lazlo's knowledge about Baby Jane. He made sure that he asked questions of his future cousin that he knew if he stumped Lazlo, he personally knew the answers.

"Sooo… Lazlo. Do you recall what engine Maria ordered for BJ when she purchased her for you? There were several options." Lazlo knew exactly what his friend was doing. He chuckled to himself before answering.

"Yeah, buddy! She's got a Big Block 427 V8! Maria even ordered the L88 option, which is a street racing motor. BJ has 430 HP under that beautiful front end of hers! And the four-speed gearbox. Brother she just couldn't have done any better! Oh, she's also referred to as the C2. Most people don't know that." Lazlo stopped for a breath and smiled, "I really do love my car! Stingray buddy!"

Clayton was deflated. But he deserved it. Lazlo knew that it was just Clayton's competitive nature from playing college sports and that it was nothing personal. It was simply a part of their friendship. Lazlo smiled in satisfaction as he noted Clayton appearing to fall asleep. Everyone was sleeping now. Even Blackie. Lazlo wondered if sleep would bring on another visit from his blue diamond goddess. It wasn't long before Lazlo dozed off too and lost all track of time and space. He needed the rest.

In what seemed like just a few moments Lazlo received a visit from the *Hope*.

As per usual, Lazlo experienced a flash of blue light in his mind's eye before hearing her voice again.

"You need to know me, Lazlo. You need to understand who and what I am. Your birth mother believes in the trinity and wears the cross of the Christ child grown. She makes the sign to reinforce her faith. You too, were raised in this way when your family abandoned your Hebrew heritage and faith. This change in your family religion has left your heart open and searching. You seek truth. I am here to provide that truth to you."

Even in his dream state, Lazlo knew that he was hearing Her words, and wondering about Her power.

"I am also of the trinity. A different trinity than the one of which we spoke. But a trinity no less. I am a Hecate. Remember the names of the Greek Gods and Goddesses. I am also Diana. I am the 'soul of the world'. I am Trivia, a fierce goddess of witchcraft and sorcery. And I am Luna. The goddess of the magic of the night. I am Hecate. Do you remember my name?"

Lazlo did. He remembered her from mythology classes in school. She was Greek!

Hecate now spoke as herself, no longer as the heart of the diamond. She wanted to build on her connection to Lazlo. And she was. Her power was strong.

"Lazlo, my love. I was cursed by others from my world and trapped inside the original diamond that had served as my prison for centuries. The priests were selected to guard me and my secrets. Their association with me gave them an extremely long human life. After a time, several of them would open their minds to me and learn the truth. But none of them had the ability to help me. Like so many humans, they spoke of my presence to outsiders. They failed at keeping my essence a secret. And other men came. They came to take me away. With hopes of controlling my power. I still can kill anyone who would harm me or try to stop me. This was labeled as a curse. 'The Curse of the Hope Diamond'. I have used it for protection. I can reward good health and a long life. Even immortality! Adolf Hitler wanted to control me. It cost him his war on the world in

the 1940's. Hitler had nothing to offer me. He forced your grandfather to cut my original stone prison into another size. He hoped to release me in this manner."

"Your grandfather, László Joseph Biro, figured things out. He felt that by creating the 12 brothers it would destroy my powers and abilities. He separated the pieces, but his thoughts were only partially true. He, too, could not serve me. I knew that you would arrive in this world and I also knew that you would be born as a White Lighter. I need you to assist me. I need to be released from my prison! Your grandfather attempted to stand in my way. I cannot tolerate this from a human. But you are different Lazlo. We can assist each other. I can be returned to my rightful place in the universe! And you can be like a King! You have the power within you to rescue me. And to save all of those that you love."

Lazlo was still in a trance but was able to comprehend all that had been said. His heart raced as he considered the prophecy.

Hecate returned,

"For now, I will leave you with this spiritual information. And I will also leave you with my blessings. Not only to you but to those around you. Enjoy the coming days. Enjoy the festivities of your wedding. And enjoy the life that I will allow you to see in Granada. You will prosper, Lazlo Somogyi. And you will know that it is because of me and my love for you. I am not evil by nature. Likewise, I am not a religious deity like some have claimed to be. I am here to assist mankind in a world of balance. But there are times that I can simply add a bit of weight to the scales to aid humans in the proper direction. Let me aid you."

Hecate left Lazlo's consciousness like a feather in the wind, but he knew that sometime in the near future, she would return.

El Caudillo

CHAPTER 24

Landing in Granada, the plane was immediately received by a new entourage of black stretch limousines with Spanish flags that fluttered from their front fenders. They were escorted by four dress motorcycle police officers, also sporting flags and other regalia. Television vans and their cameras were already in place with reporters waiting for interviews and photographs. This was obviously an arranged welcome, but Lazlo wondered to himself who the individual might be that deserved such extreme support from the people of Granada. Were they expecting a movie star or local celebrity? He attempted to search the tarmac for another plane. But there was none.

A large crowd of people had already gathered, but the numbers were growing by the minute. At first, Lazlo didn't see them, but soon he noticed the security officers that were mixing with the crowd. This alerted him to the fact that if someone needed this level of protection, they were of high value to the government of Spain.

Diego Pilan was first to exit the plane. He stopped on top of the boarding stairs and waved to the crowd. The response was thunderous!

Lazlo asked Diego why all of the undercover operatives were in the crowd. Diego laughed and he said to Lazlo, "Once again my boy, you continue to amaze me! Not to worry. They are here mostly to protect someone who wants to meet *you* very much."

The crowd cheered again, and Lazlo looked towards the limos as a figure got out of one of them. There was no mistaking who it was. Lazlo quickly pointed him out to Eztar and Julius as they too came out of the plane.

"That man is your new landlord and my father-in-law-to-be, Señor Lorenzo Rafael Cordova Valdez. I will introduce you. Not to worry. You can just call him Lorenzo. He is a good man."

Eztar briefly looked terrified. Then she relaxed a bit.

"His aura is strong! He's a light green much like Maria. I like him."

The crowd continued to react to every movement that occurred near the limos. They were anticipating someone special. Finally, a man stepped out of the most elaborately decorated car. The gentleman wore a military uniform adorned with medals and decorations from years of obvious service.

Lazlo asked Diego who this very special person might be. Diego's answer surprised Lazlo.

"That would be our honorable leader who has many titles. He's our Prime Minister, officially the President of the Government. He is the head of our Parliament. The Head of State. He is similar to your 'LBJ' in America. His name is Francisco Franco Bahamonde. He is called 'El Caudillo', which means 'Leader'. He is here to meet *you* today!"

Things started moving quickly as El Caudillo and his entourage moved towards the plane. Diego signaled for everyone to exit the transport to meet him partway. Maria took it all in stride. Lazlo, however, was getting more nervous by the minute.

Lazlo noticed that a podium with several microphones had been erected, not far from the plane. That appeared to be the destination of El Caudillo. Diego continued to usher their group in that direction.

El Presidente, Francisco Franco, was the first to reach the podium and began speaking before the others arrived. He spoke in English, as a courtesy to their most honored guests.

"Ladies and gentlemen, girls and boys! Hello to you all on this most beautiful day!"

The crowd cheered!

Lorenzo Cordova Valdez was quietly slipping in behind him as

Diego guided Lazlo and Maria to several chairs set up on the structure. Everyone quietly sat down while Franco spoke to the crowd.

He continued.

"As most of you either read it in the newspaper or watched reports on the news, it was not long ago that our beloved Senator Valdez was in a terrible car accident and almost died."

The crowd became somber.

"Although our wonderful doctors did everything that they could, one man alone is the hero who saved his life. That one man stands here with us today. He is Dr. Lazlo Joseph Somogyi of the United States of America!"

The crowd roared!

"Dr. Lazlo Somogyi studies paranormal activity and healing." Franco continued to spin his seemingly creative tale that was not very far from the exact truth in the circumstance.

"Dr. Lazlo. Please do me the honor of shaking my hand." Presidente Franco turned and extended his hand to Lazlo.

As Lazlo stood up and approached El Caudillo, he was met by Papa Lorenzo Valdez with an embrace and a kiss on each cheek.

"*Gracias mi hijo… Gracias.*"

"Thank you, my son… Thank you." Lorenzo pulled Lazlo's hand high into the air, and the crowd went crazy! Presidente Franco grabbed Lazlo by the hand and shook it vigorously while praising him and thanking him.

El Caudillo whispered that it was a pleasure to meet him and that they had much to discuss.

Franco continued speaking to the crowd. He knew that Lazlo could become a powerful ally in the eyes of the Spanish population. The crowd continued to cheer these three men, all locked hand-in-hand.

Suddenly, a beautiful young woman came on to the stage. She carried a small velvet box. She handed it to El Caudillo and left the podium.

In addition, a soldier in uniform approached the group carrying an ornate antique sword. This, too, was given to the President.

Once again, the crowd became quiet waiting with great

anticipation. "Dr. Lazlo Joseph Somogyi. Please take a knee."

Maria and Eztar had become emotional and were crying, watching the chain of events that they both knew would carve out a place for Lazlo in the history books.

Lazlo knelt down in front of El Presidente, Francisco Franco, as directed. The only sounds to be heard were those of passing birds and distant traffic from automobiles. El Caudillo raised the sword as he recited from memory.

"Dr. Lazlo. *Como gobernante de España, te nombra señor caballero. Levántate y recibe tu recompensa.*"

"Dr. Lazlo. As the ruler of Spain, I dub thee Sir Knight. Rise and receive your reward."

Lazlo got to his feet and the crowd erupted. The response was not unlike a Royal coronation. Everyone was awed by this American and they would be proud to call him their own! Maria was very proud. As was the entire Somogyi family. Lazlo was now a Knight. Sir Lazlo Joseph Somogyi, MD. A coal miner's son. The people loved him.

But the ceremony was not yet complete. El Caudillo calmed the crowd. He continued.

"Sir Lazlo. For unsurpassed service to my country, please allow me to award you the Royal Order of Civil Merit." Franco removed a large golden medal trimmed in blue with a king's crown perched on the top showing red velvet in the crown. It would be worn ceremonially on the collar, like a bowtie. Presidente Franco attached it to Lazlo's collar and the masses continued to cheer without stopping. Maria now joined Lazlo on the podium.

"I have one more very special announcement today. I am honored to tell the world that this fine young man, Sir Lazlo Joseph Somogyi, MD will be married to the daughter of our own Senator Señor Lorenzo Rafael Cordova Valdez. Señorita Maria Cordova Valdez will unite with Dr. Lazlo in holy matrimony at our most beautiful Granada Cathedral. This will be a public event and all of you are invited to join them in their love for one another. I will make all the details public when everything is arranged. Thank you all for joining us today."

The crowd called out Lazlo's name while cheering and clapping!

Lazlo was overwhelmed. Maria was thrilled beyond any expectation. Her Knight had arrived and she could hardly believe that her magical wedding was really in the making. Her life had risen beyond anything she could have dreamed.

El Presidente Franco approached Lazlo. "We need to talk." He then walked to his waiting limo.

Diego quickly pulled Lazlo aside and told him something that he thought might help him in a private conversation with the leader of Spain.

"El Caudillo is a brilliant leader. He is an honest and thoughtful man. But he also is shrewd and careful in all things. He is honest. If it suits his purposes. But he is naturally introverted. Even though his outward appearance seems friendly and embracing, he is very selective with his friends and associates. Like so many other military leaders his deepest interest is in power," Diego hugged Lazlo and walked away.

The back door to the Presidential limousine opened offering Lazlo a place inside. El Presidente Franco asked him to enter. With a slight hesitation, he complied. El Caudillo spoke first.

"Señor Lazlo. We finally got the chance to really meet. I have heard so much about you. Some of it is obviously quite extraordinary. Bringing a man back from the jaws of death is no small feat. Not to mention from thousands of miles away. I am interested to learn more. Diego has briefed me about the connection that you maintain with the Smithsonian Institution. I also know about your studies and how they seem to parallel those of our university. I support that connection. And you, joining with the Cordova Valdez family has secured you a place with the government of my country. You are now a 'son of Spain'. I do not ask you to give up connections to your own country. I prefer that you represent both. But your family is now here. The people of Granada embrace you. You are a Knight of the Spanish people now."

"El Presidente. I am indebted to you. Thank you. I am honored by your kindness and the measures taken here today to help me secure my place in your country. I look forward to continuing my studies with the paranormal and sharing that information with you, and your approved representatives. I am excited to start a new life here with

Maria and my growing family. And I hope that my abilities and efforts do not ever disappoint. I am here to serve."

Franco smiled and shook his head, "*Bueno*. Very good. Diego told me that he thought you would make a fine politician one day. *Muy buen*. I am pleased."

The two men shook hands again and Lazlo left the limo.

Lazlo looked for his family who were all waiting patiently for him. He thought to himself. Wow. Less than 48 hours ago I was in the coal mines of Ward. Now I'm a fucking Knight of the Round Table! *She* wasn't kidding!

Planning the Wedding of All Weddings

CHAPTER 25

Upon arriving at the Cordova Valdez Hacienda, the group was met by pleasant, congenial servants that were stationed to see to the Somogyi family's every need. Eztar and Eleanor were amazed at the beauty and size of the structures and grounds. Julius and Janos were too. They just tried not to show it. Maria greeted each employee with an embrace and a kind word. Eztar was impressed with her obvious love of people. Lazlo introduced his family, including his dog, Blackie. Everyone at the Hacienda was excited to see him again. Especially after hearing that he saved the life of Papa Lorenzo. He was their hero.

Maria suggested that the Somogyi family be introduced to their new lodgings so that they might settle in and rest after their long flight and the unexpected festivities. They were about to walk to the two homes when Maria's Momma, Señora Juana, appeared from the main house.

"*Hola*, Momma!" She ran to her for an embrace. Everyone watched as mother and daughter reunited.

"My apologies to everyone," said Señora Juana. "Someone had to 'hold down the fort' as it were." Introductions were made and Juana welcomed everyone to her home. She gave a special greeting with a hug to her future son-in-law, Lazlo. As she kissed him on the cheek she whispered, "Thank you" in his ear. The look on her face told him that he was truly a welcomed new member of the Cordova Valdez clan. Lazlo glowed with pleasure at hearing this.

Maria and Juana led the way to the house that was selected for Lazlo's parents. Servants carried their personal belongings, which were few.

The structure was a 'chalet' of the mission style or design. The roof had rust-colored, sunset tiles. It was a three-bedroom house with two baths and a garage. Maria noted that it also had its own swimming pool outback. The landscaping was heavy with Mediterranean accents of certain hardy tropical plants. To Eztar and Julius, it was truly a castle! Lucas and Blackie entered first and claimed one of the sofas as their personal playground.

Juana wanted to make them feel comfortable and after hugging both parents once again said, "*Mi casa es tu casa.*"

"My home is your home."

She added, "As long as you live in Granada, consider this your own place."

Maria added a bit of information that the chalet was fully furnished, and the refrigerator was stocked. They could eat their meals here, or request one of the chefs, or perhaps eat at the main table of the Hacienda.

"So, Eleanor. How about we look at your new home too? Maria suggested. Janos, come on!" Maria was enjoying her new role as tour guide.

The group went to another house that was roughly 400 feet away. They would be neighbors to Julius and Eztar. The chalet was almost identical to the first one but it was the opposite in design. It, too, was beautiful.

Janos looked at Lazlo and said, "I can't believe it, man! I know what you promised. I just never thought it possible!" Janos started to cry and that made Lazlo cry too. Everyone seemed to forget about Clayton 'bringing up the rear' of the group until he spoke and added, "Come on guys! You're going to get me sobbing like a baby too! Jesus, help me!"

Everyone laughed and the new tenants decided to settle in. Juana, Maria, Lazlo, and Clayton went back to the main house to relax and regroup.

Walking to the Hacienda with Maria and her family was a peaceful transition from the scene at the airport. Granada was lovely and the Valdez properties represented the old wealth of this family. The grounds were breathtaking! Everything was picture-perfect. Lazlo remembered the last words of Hecate. Reassuring him that all was well and would continue to be so.

Entering the Hacienda their group was met by Lorenzo and Diego. Both men were already having a drink, and their level of enthusiasm was obvious. They quickly turned their attention to Lazlo.

"Sir Lazlo, welcome home!"

They were already somewhat tipsy but still offered the new arrivals a cocktail.

"Lazlo! The way you handled El Presidente today was outstanding!" Diego repeated yet again that Lazlo was destined to work in politics. Lorenzo was feeling sentimental and hugged Lazlo once again. But this time it was away from the watching eyes of strangers. He was quite choked up trying to share his feelings with the young man who saved his life. "Thank you, my son. Thank you for allowing me to live!" He then quietly retired to the sofa with a whiskey. Diego thanked Lazlo again too. This hero stuff feels weird, thought Lazlo.

Everyone settled in and the conversation turned to the wedding. Juana wasted no time in letting everyone know that she had taken charge of the wedding arrangements.

"This is going to be the wedding of the century! Imagine! Our Maria will be wed to an actual Knight! This is something that we all know that she has wanted since she was a young girl. Her Knight on a white stallion! Sir Lazlo. Do you ride?"

"Well," Lazlo replied. "I have ridden, yes. But I doubt that the Knights of the Round Table would ever consider me their equal," he laughed. Lazlo hesitated and quickly reconsidered Juana's request.

"You're serious, aren't you? I'm sorry," said Lazlo. "I honestly thought that you were joking." But no one laughed...

"Okay. So exactly what do you have in mind? I know that you own plenty of horses here on La Hacienda Valdez. And I will bet that there are not only trainers for the horses but instructors to teach clumsy humans how to ride too." I might need riding lessons. Could that be arranged? Lazlo's last statement wasn't really a question. He said it more like a declaration of fact.

Juana quietly answered, "It's quite simple really. I plan to have you ride Maria's favorite Lipizzan stallion, Hernando, to the front of the church in front of thousands of adoring Spanish citizens. Hernando is white and very majestic. Everyone knows that you are a Knight. It would almost be expected that you do this for your bride."

Diego added, "A very noble expression of your love for Maria. Horses are everything here in Spain. They represent much of our heritage. Isn't that right, Lorenzo?"

Lorenzo, too, was in favor of Lazlo riding into the festivities.

"It would also aid in your acceptance by the people. They love you already but a demonstration such as this would add greatly to your popularity. It could have international ramifications."

Everyone sensed discomfort based on Lazlo's reaction. Clayton spoke to Lazlo to reassure him.

"Buddy. There's nothing to fear, man. I've watched you on the field in championship games and you're fearless! I saw you enter a mind-lock trance of some kind with an ancient goddess. You talk to her! Hernando is simply a horse. My friend... you can do this with your eyes closed. Come on! We'll go meet Hernando. Maria can lead the way!"

Maria loved the idea and decided that Lazlo should meet her most prized possession as soon as possible. Off they went to the stables. Maria and Lazlo hand-in-hand with Clayton following.

"I really hope that he likes you. These big male horses are weird and can be protective of their ladies. He really likes Maria and that could be dangerous. But I'm sure everything will be fine," Clayton said.

"Maria? How do you say 'prick' in Spanish? I think that I need yet another lesson," Lazlo laughed.

"Boys... Stop. Hernando is gentle as a lamb. He's going to love

Lazlo! Come on. I hear him already." Maria went on to explain the history of the Lipizzaner horses. Lazlo had heard of them but knew very little. They approached the box stall that displayed a very ornate nameplate on the door, it said Hernando.

"*Hola* Señorita Maria. How are you on this fine day?" The stable master said.

"Holy shit!" exclaimed Lazlo. "You actually expect me to ride this animal?

Maria looked disappointed but understood that her Lazlo was simply not a horseman. She would need to remedy that fact as quickly as possible.

The stable master's name was Gino. He had already heard much about the coming of Maria's American husband-to-be.

Maria said, "Gino, this is Lazlo. The man you've heard so much about. I would like you to help Lazlo become familiar with horses. We can start with Hernando."

Let's go to the arena. I will introduce you to Hernando more formally."

Maria walked away with Lazlo and Clayton.

"She's really a lot like her mother," joked Clayton. No one laughed.

Maria didn't respond to Clayton's attempt at wit.

Gino walked Hernando to the arena while Maria stopped at a tack room to quickly change into riding clothes. She emerged in tight stretch riding slacks, boots just below the knee, a riding helmet, and a short crop. Lazlo found the new look somewhat sexy and Clayton took note.

"You dog you! Damn man, it's for riding a horse!" Both men shook their heads and laughed.

As they approached the arena, everyone could see that Gino was working Hernando to warm him up. The big horse trotted in a circle around Gino while connected to a lunge line. Hernando was very well trained and executed perfect form in his walks, canter, trotting, and slow gallop. On occasion, Hernando jumped high into the air, tucking his front legs under his chest, and then instantly kicking out his hind legs at the highest point of his jump!

"He could take a man's head off!" exclaimed Lazlo. "My God!"

Maria smiled and told Lazlo that the move was referred to as the *capriole*. She went on to say that the translation means 'the leap of the goat'. This movement was originally created to lift the horse and rider out of danger. Lazlo could see why.

"Relax my love. Let's go and I will introduce you to my Hernando."

Lazlo and Clayton followed Maria to the center of the ring where the horse and trainer waited.

Hernando lovingly accepted Maria as she hugged his head while kissing him on the nose. The big horse seemed to melt. Maria had several small treats hidden in her hand that she offered Hernando as a reward. He made a good first impression today. After all, this is one big horse! Lazlo sighed.

"Lazlo, come closer and meet Hernando. Remember to move slowly as you introduce yourself. Don't make any rapid gestures. Offer your hand with an open palm to be smelled by the horse." Maria placed a sugar cube in Lazlo's left hand. "The flat palm reduces the chance of having a finger bitten. Some horses are ornery that way. They'll test you."

She continued, "A trick that I learned as a young girl visiting Iran while meeting several camels, was to place your head close to theirs and lightly blow into their nostrils. They say that it helps them learn your scent and that they will remember you years later. I believe that it works with horses too. Give him his treat if he cooperates."

Lazlo did as she said. It worked perfectly! He was amazed and relieved.

Maria took the reins and in a second, she had mounted her beautiful pet. She immediately took Hernando into a gallop around the arena. On the second pass, Hernando executed several *capriole* kicks. That astounded Lazlo. Hernando and Maria put on a show! Her small audience cheered, and Hernando actually bowed and touched his nose to the ground. Maria smiled as she walked Hernando back to the group.

Gino took the reins as Maria dismounted her 'charger'. Maria thought this medieval term for a war horse made Hernando sound more masculine. Lazlo and Maria then embraced one another.

"It's your turn now, my love. Just the basics. You need to get to know him."

Lazlo nervously mounted Hernando. He could feel the power of becoming one with this amazing animal. He felt the rhythm of his breathing and imagined that he could even hear his heartbeat. Did he really hear it? Lazlo wondered and listened. He shut his eyes and knew that it was not his imagination. He could indeed hear the heart of this creature.

Lazlo could feel the blood pulsing through Hernando's veins. Somehow, Lazlo was at peace and his fear was gone. He thought briefly of Hecate but there was no voice. No blue flash. He was alone in his thoughts. Lazlo took the reins from Gino and nudged Hernando forward.

Lazlo didn't see the additional audience that had started to gather next to the arena. Lorenzo and Juana. Diego. Eztar and Julius. Janos and Eleanor. Lucas and Blackie. Everyone was there to see if their favorite Knight was indeed able to live up to expectations.

Hernando and Lazlo worked as a team. They started simply enough with a light trot. Lazlo urged Hernando into a gallop. They cantered together. Hernando even rose to his rear legs and stood tall while pawing his hooves in the air. Then without warning he jumped high and performed a perfect *capriole*! The execution could not have been more textbook. Family and friends cheered as Hernando bowed to the group. Lazlo was thrilled.

Yes, his goddess was looking after her chosen one.

Everyone greeted Lazlo with handshakes and hugs. Congratulations were repeated by everyone. Eztar and Julius couldn't believe their eyes.

Maria smiled as she casually shrugged her shoulders. "Well, I guess the wedding is back on," she laughed.

Lazlo felt something in his pants pocket that wasn't there earlier. He reached inside and found two sugar cubes. He removed them while looking at Maria and received no response from her. It meant nothing. Hecate? Lazlo casually gave the treats to Hernando while petting him on the neck. Gino took the wonderful stallion to be cooled down, brushed, and fed.

The family retired to the Hacienda to continue wedding plans.

Stories about Lazlo were already circulating among the servants and staff. Lazlo Somogyi truly was something very special.

Juana looked at Lazlo and said, "You sure are full of surprises, Sir Lazlo. I was expecting you to be thrown by Hernando. The demonstration that you provided could not have been matched by a professional horseman. Truly impressive. It will make some of my preparations that much easier. *Bueno*."

The church had already been selected. Since the 1600s, all formal government-related events have taken place at the Cathedral. Maria had grown up under a Roman Catholic Priest by the name of Father Guido Gonzalez. He had agreed to perform the ceremony. Of course, the decorations would be handled professionally at the church and outside of the cathedral.

The bride's dress and all the clothing for the bridal party would be custom-made. Likewise for the groom, his best man, and ushers. Juana looked at Lazlo and asked if he had selected anyone yet for that honor. Lazlo turned to Clayton. Clayton smiled and answered with one word. "Done."

Maria shook her head in surprise. "Men," she exhaled heavily. "Why can't *we* make our choices so quickly?"

Lazlo said, "You didn't waste any time picking me." She knew that he was right.

Juana continued, "Arrival for everyone but Lazlo will be by limousine. Lazlo will be dropped off at a location near the church where Gino will be standing by with Hernando. After Lazlo and Hernando arrive at the church, a handler will collect the horse for his return to the Hacienda. I have an afterthought on Maria's gown. I want it to have a very long train. Little girls can carry it behind her. Their clothing will match the bridesmaids. Perhaps Lucas can be the bearer of the rings?"

Eztar loved that idea! "He's a little old for that position but he *is* Lazlo's brother after all."

Lazlo liked the idea too, especially after he realized that Maria supported it. He gazed into her eyes and stated, "As you wish, my love, as you wish."

Everything was coming together quickly. But Lazlo had an afterthought. "My Momma and Eleanor will need appropriate clothing. They need a complete wardrobe. As do Janos and Julius. But for the wedding I want them to be my ushers. Did you decide on a number for your bridesmaids, Maria?" Maria thought for a moment and said, "Five, including the maid of honor."

"Great!" said Lazlo. "Then my choices are Diego, Julius, Janos, and Dr. Sherlous. Clayton will be my best man."

Lazlo thought for a moment and added, "That will be so cool. My blood father, my adopted father, and my newest favorite uncle, all in my wedding. I like it!"

"Are you sure that you don't want Blackie in the ceremony?" asked Clayton.

"Well. If Lucas refuses to be the ringbearer, I'm sure Blackie could handle it." Everyone chuckled. Everyone except Blackie, who had fallen asleep at Lazlo's feet.

A Very Dangerous Idea

CHAPTER 26

The next 48 hours were hectic. Invitations were ordered. Menu selections were made. Tailors began to arrive at the Hacienda. Not just for wedding measurements, but for general everyday clothing for Lazlo and his family members. If Dr. Sherlous accepted Lazlo's request, he would need to be measured stateside, and the information forwarded to Granada. Not a stone was left unturned.

Except for one. Lazlo's *Joseph Stone*. This was an exquisite example of a diamond of roughly five carats cut by Lazlo's grandfather. He decided that it would be safe for Maria to wear it in a ring. He felt in his heart that Hecate meant Maria no harm. As a precaution, the gold setting could be elevated to keep the diamond from her skin. In addition, the selected jeweler would need to know that he could not touch the stone during the mounting procedure. Tools would need to be used exclusively. Lazlo discussed this with Diego and he agreed. He knew the perfect man for the job.

Lazlo requested that the Sherlous family's trip be paid for. It would be his way of partially repaying them for all that they have done. He wanted them to stay at the Hacienda.

Diego reassured him, "I will take care of this. Consider it done."

Lazlo liked how this was working out.

He later told Maria about his idea for her ring and she loved it! Without hesitation, she agreed that it was a perfect idea. There would be more for him to tell of his overall plan but for now, that could wait.

Lazlo also discussed with Diego that he needed to be present for the diamond being set in gold. No way would he risk theft, or the jeweler contacting the stone. It only made sense to take precautions. Diego would make the arrangements.

A date was selected by the bride and groom and efforts accelerated to keep things on schedule. They had four weeks to make it happen. November 11 would be the day. The honeymoon would take place in Greenland. That too needed special attention to organize all of the details.

The media was notified. Television and newspapers advertised the event. Lazlo was indeed marrying a princess.

Maria went to the jeweler with Lazlo and Diego. She wanted to either pick a setting or have an original created. The choice would be hers to fit the *Joseph Stone* with the best possible cradle that could be selected. Lazlo believed that Hecate would agree. When they arrived and formal introductions were made, Maria spoke with the goldsmith to discuss the design. Lazlo knew already that she wouldn't select a precast setting. The store was Nicols Joyeros, established in 1917. Nicols Joyeros specialized in engagement and wedding rings all over the world. The artisan today was Julio, a trusted, long-term employee. In addition he was a relative of the owner of Nicols Joyeros. Maria approved.

While Julio sketched designs based on Maria's thoughts on the piece, several things became clear. This was *not* going to look like any other engagement ring that he had ever created. The wedding bands were yet to come. Señorita Cordova Valdez was a woman of quality and taste, and it showed.

Maria explained, "My diamond is blue… Like the *Hope Diamond* on display in America. It is five carats. The cut is unique because it is not perfectly round. It does have four small points on what would be corners, but it is round. Lazlo, what did you discover when you researched the cut? What do you say? S-K? Or was it Ess-Kay? I wasn't sure. Deep inside the facets create a cross that is quite beautiful."

"Oh… *Si, si.* I am familiar with this rare design! It was only attempted by the finest cutters in Germany and Hungary before the war! And you have this cut on a five carat blue diamond?" Julio was impressed. This creation was going to be a thing of beauty.

"Please go on. Tell me more." Julio begged.

Maria continued, "I want you to use both 14-karat white and 14-karat yellow gold. The gold design that cradles the stone will look like the Hebrew star of David. This will be white gold. Under the star, as if supporting the Hebrew people through the stone, there should be gold leaf work, you know, like vines. The vines will create a wrap around the entire design."

Julio was drawing quickly and Lazlo could see the work coming to life.

"The ring itself will be white gold to match the top. Lastly, I want 11 dark blue sapphires to be added to the arrangement around the main stone. It's an odd number to balance, I know, but I feel that it can be done by setting some of them on the points of the star. The remaining stones should be set in the leaf formation. That is my dream. Can you make it happen for me?"

Julio responded, "*Santa Madre Maria esto será exquisito! ¡Podría ser mi mejor trabajo!*"

"Holy Mother Mary, this will be exquisite! It could become my best work ever!"

Julio turned his sketchpad around so that Maria and Lazlo could see the creation.

Maria smiled brightly while sharing, "That is it! *That* is my ring!"

Lazlo was less animated and only whispered two words, "Holy shit!"

Maria told Julio that expense was of little concern but it had to be perfect! The wedding date was set for November 11. He only had four weeks to accomplish this miracle.

"Can you do it? Can you create my dream?" asked Maria, again. Everyone waited for his reply.

Julio asked, "Yes, I can. But I have one question. Why can the stone not be touched?"

Diego hesitated, then said, "Because it is cursed. Touch it and you will die. My words are true. This stone was born in Nazi Germany near the death camps."

Lazlo spoke up, adding that his grandfather was the cutter. "He perished too, after its creation."

Julio was stunned.

"Yes, I will do it! We will create a piece of history that will be recognized for all time! Yes! Thank you for selecting me for this honor."

Diego advised Julio that photos could be arranged for measurements, but the stone would stay at the Valdez Hacienda until the final day of setting it in gold. Julio agreed. He would start the casting immediately and work on no other project until it was done.

Maria was happy. Diego was proud. But Lazlo still had some concerns about Hecate. He hoped that she would approve. The rest of his elaborate plan had yet to be unveiled.

The next part of Lazlo's plan would make their wedding the grandest wedding in modern history. He felt so confident that everything would work out perfectly that it almost seemed he was being led down a different road by a silent force. Again, he thought of Hecate. Was this even possible he wondered? But Lazlo knew that it was.

Lazlo had already made up his mind that in addition to whatever fancy tuxedo was being made for him, he would wear two more items during the wedding. The first item was his award from the President of Granada. The second item would be the *Hope Diamond* and he also planned to have the remaining 11 brothers in an urn in the front of the church, near the altar. Security measures would need to be taken. *Extreme* security measures.

Lazlo knew that photographs would be taken. These would be instantly circulated around the world. With the staff of the Smithsonian thinking that the *Hope* was secure in their display, they would assume that he was wearing a copy.

But he really wasn't that concerned. He hoped for an extreme paranormal display in front of thousands of people around the world. He wanted to make those people believe in paranormal power. A display of this nature could secure his research needs for the rest of his life. Lazlo wanted people to know that there have always been many theories on earth that teach us and comfort us. We are all free to believe and worship in our own ways. *Judge not, lest ye shall be judged,* has always carried a very special message for him. It is a difficult message to practice. These were his plans. They needed to be kept secret for now. He would share this with Maria and Diego, but the rest of the world would need to wait.

Word circulated throughout Europe and other countries about the upcoming wedding. It was customary that gifts could be sent in advance of the actual date, especially if they were of high monetary value. It was common in Spain and other countries that appreciated the equestrian world to even gift horses that could have great value. Some of the Arabian elite commonly did this.

They would also gift trained falcons that could cost as much as a quarter million dollars! This sport interested Maria greatly, but for now, she simply did not have the time. Falconry was a lifestyle of true dedication. It was not a hobby.

In the world of high finance, there were no limitations on what a wealthy guest might decide to give to the couple. As Lazlo was quickly learning, a great deal of this ceremony was political.

Gifts were being sent directly to the Cordova Valdez Hacienda. Servants were having them stored in spare rooms in the main house. Maria noticed that the collection of gifts was growing rapidly and she suggested that she and Lazlo open some of them.

The gifts varied widely from beautiful custom jewelry, and leather tack for horses, to collectible tapestries. There were handcrafted pieces of custom furniture from Austria and tribal masks from Africa. Lazlo was amazed at the range of connections Maria's family had throughout the world. There was even an autographed guitar from the new rock band, the Rolling Stones. Maria said that she had met Mick and Keith after a concert in England a few years ago.

Lazlo felt drawn to a particular wooden crate marked as fragile. It was small. No larger than 18 inches. He would need a claw hammer and a screwdriver to open it. The shipping label showed that it came from Washington DC. The only information on the return address label beside the city was the word 'Landslide'.

His mind was on so many things he couldn't quite remember who Landslide was. But it came in a flash. Ledbetter had used the term Landslide on the phone in his office.

Lazlo removed the packing materials. What he saw next absolutely stunned him, but even worse was the sense of dread he felt after seeing the contents of the package.

Lazlo was gazing into the empty eye sockets of a life-sized crystal human skull. Who would send such a thing? He searched his memories on the subject and recalled some stories about similar skulls being located around the world on archaeological digs. Some were Mayan. Many scientists felt there was a possibility of an extraterrestrial connection.

Paranormal studies had some researchers believing that these skulls had supernatural powers. Even the ability to heal. And several were determined to be fakes. The real ones were solid crystal and not carved. The cuts were too perfect as if done by a laser of some kind. But still, they were dated to be older than Christ. This is a valuable treasure in itself, Lazlo reasoned. He looked at Maria with apprehension.

"Do you feel anything odd with this bizarre gift? Anything remotely strange?" Maria agreed that she felt it too. There was an evil presence in the skull. Someone had sent this item as a message, perhaps a threat. Such things were not to be overlooked. They could in fact be older than mankind on earth. That was still up for debate.

Lazlo began to feel queasy. He noted to Maria that he was getting a light headache and suddenly felt tired. They both attributed it to the stresses of the forthcoming wedding. Lazlo re-sealed the lid.

"I think that I need to lie down in my room for a rest. I seem to have overdone it somewhat." He briefly kissed her on the cheek and left her with the remaining gifts.

Maria closed her eyes and wished it would all go away. Not the wedding plans, but the crazy gifts.

Hecate Makes a Visit

CHAPTER 27

Lazlo tried to sleep, but as soon as he lay down he heard the call of a large owl on his windowsill. Two distinct hoots. He knew that his visitor was a giant Eurasian Eagle Owl. He had seen them before in a zoo. Some people feared them. While others believed that such owls were messengers of the Gods.

Before falling asleep, Lazlo thought he heard a disturbance in the stables. He recognized the horse's whinny. Hernando! Blackie began to bark, but something was calling Lazlo to another plane. Something was pulling him into another space. His consciousness began to alter and to fall away beyond his control.

There was a familiar flash of blue in Lazlo's mind and a floating mist that seemed to come from the darkened silhouette of a woman. Her shape was glowing with a distinct green aura that covered her. As she came closer, Lazlo could see her long black hair. At first, he thought of Maria. But this was not her doing.

Her eyes flashed green!

Suddenly there was a beautiful stallion following her footsteps and a large black wolf-like dog at her side. A giant owl flew into the scene and landed on her left arm. It was the Eagle Owl from his vision encounter.

This was a living image of Hecate in her earthly form. She was finally revealing her true self to Lazlo. The goddess was breathtaking!

Then, she spoke.

"Lazlo, my love. You are in danger, but I have come to you in this form to save you. While locked inside the diamond, my powers have limitations. The evil endangering you is within my abilities to destroy. Know me, Lazlo! Search your mind and remember. Know what I am! This will strengthen our bond so that we might work together to better all of mankind while lifting this curse from my being. Remember the teachings from long ago."

Lazlo's mind drifted to a deep level of consciousness. He remembered Hecate. But this time he remembered more! The Goddess Hecate was born a Titan. Perhaps the most powerful Gods that ever walked the earth.

Her Trinity existence also connected her to three distinct animal spirits that assist her with her duties. The horse. Hecate controlled the world's horse population. The dog. Companion and protector of man. And the eagle owl. The messenger of the gods and the 'Lord over the Darkness' of the world, that offers wisdom to mankind.

Lazlo's mind offered a memory of Hernando and the day in the arena. It *was* Hecate all along. She *was* looking after me, thought Lazlo.

Lazlo recalled pagan beliefs and the gods that they worshiped. Hecate was there too!

"Know me Lazlo Somogyi!" The voice was stronger now and her volume intensified.

Lazlo remembered the Wiccan beliefs of the white witches. They worshiped the feminine. Mother Earth. This too, was Hecate. Even today, the Wiccan faith is strong. Hecate. The world seemed to be connected to her in so many ways. How was it possible that she was trapped in a cursed gemstone on earth? As quickly as the questions came, they were answered. Again, Hecate spoke.

"In the worlds of the Titans, like everywhere else, there lies, both good and evil. Powerful magic exists that the mind cannot imagine. There are Kings and Queens who pass judgment and wield great power! Their punishments are cruel. I protected mankind and encouraged man's growth and explorations. My King… Cronus believed that humans were a failing species that would destroy this planet. They were vain and self-centered.

He saw little good in mankind. I disagreed and he sent me to my prison for all eternity. Several millennia passed before the original diamond was stolen and King Louis XIV ordered the first recutting of the stone. This event and the one that followed, allowed me to regain some of my former abilities to work my magic. Your grandfather started the chain of events to free me!"

Lazlo's mind was absorbing every word. He began to feel sorrow for the wrongs that were forced upon Her, and he began to understand Her need to protect herself in Her crystal prison. His heart wept for this ancient goddess. In his sleep, he cried.

Hecate again spoke to Lazlo, "*Take from me the knowledge that you need to save your planet. I offered this gift to you so that you might learn. Behold the wonders of the universe! It is all there for you to take and to share. Learn about the coexistence between our worlds. I am from the planet that you call Jupiter and once lived within her rings. I long to return. Learn from me, so that you can then learn how to collect this knowledge on your own.*"

Lazlo was then flooded with new information that was unknown to scientists of his time. Facts collided with his psyche!

The Earth was surrounded by an electromagnetic field that radiated between the north and south poles. The inner core of the planet was iron. Miles of it. The outer core was whirling liquid metal. This kept the planet in balance like a spinning top. Static discharges can cause electrical storms. These were not the lightning bolts of Zeus. The aura is a bio-electric magnetic field that radiates from all living things. It is an energy emanating from every soul. A halo is an aura. Each color represents a different mood or mindset. White is the rarest.

The 'crown chakra' is the strong sense of a connection to something larger than oneself.

Aurora was the Greek Goddess of the dawn.--The red light of dawn. Aurora Borealis means 'Sunrise Wind'.

In the Christian Bible, Ezekiel had a vision of a 'storm in the north'.

Low energy charged particles, electrons, and protons, collide with the earth's molecules in the upper atmosphere. This causes the colors to form as they drift with atmospheric winds. Oxygen collisions produce yellows, reds, and greens. Hydrogen and helium produce blues, purples, or pinks. The stronger these storms, the brighter the colors. And more damage is caused to man's current electrical network. Especially radio waves. The storms also connect to the life force called the aura. You are correct, Lazlo. The more powerful the storm, the stronger the aura. Some very special humans are more connected to it than others. Now go and learn more. Learn all that you can.

This information overwhelmed him, but a flash of blue and the voice of Hecate brought Lazlo back to the reality of the Hacienda and his room.

"Lazlo. Heed my words. I will offer you the strength to succeed in your next task. Collect the crystal skull and take it to the far end of the property where no one exists. The curse that it holds within is strong. We have made a new enemy, and we need to destroy him. You will need my strength to succeed. Go alone!"

Lazlo left his room and collected the very dangerous gift. The cursed skull must be destroyed immediately.

As he left the house, he noticed that he was being followed by an extremely large owl. The one from his windowsill. He knew now that it was there to offer him protection should he need it. Lazlo used a golf cart to save time and drove towards the eastern countryside. After a mile or so of pasture, he placed the boxed skull on the ground and quickly left. The owl followed.

After clearing the area, thinking he was a safe distance away, he turned to watch the night horizon. The owl landed gracefully on his arm.

Again, he heard the voice of the goddess, *"Behold!"*

A bright flash of green light lit up the landscape, followed by an explosion that rocked the area! The sound was heard for miles! Lazlo and the owl seemed to be protected in a magical cocoon, unseen by the human eye. At that moment, the President of the United States died in an unusual electrocution accident in the White House.

The news would be the headline of every newspaper in the world by morning.

Lazlo heard her voice again. She simply said, *"It is done."*

After much thought, Lazlo decided to return to the main house and explain the phenomena to the others. The owl disappeared into the night sky.

Tomorrow was going to be a long day.

The Joseph Stone Ring

CHAPTER 28

After the destruction of the crystal skull and Lazlo's reuniting with Hecate, he recovered almost immediately from his illness. He was now sure that his strange relationship with his goddess was truly a good one. She obviously meant him no harm and seemed loyal to him and his immediate family. She was a supporter of mankind, even though she had the power to punish when she deemed necessary.

Time was passing quickly; wedding plans were completed, and the big event was just around the corner. Dr. Steven Sherlous and his wife Martha would be arriving in Spain tomorrow to join the festivities. The tailors worked feverishly to complete the clothes for the wedding party and the Somogyi family. The catering company and the florist worked together to complete the transformation of the Cathedral Hall into a bridal paradise.

Lazlo spent as much time as he could with the big horse, Hernando. He was confident that Hecate would assist him as she did with his first ride. Still, he thought it made sense to practice. It made him more confident.

Julio, from Nicols Joyeros, had all but completed his masterpiece for Maria. Maria had dropped by the store to check on his progress and was thrilled. The crowning touch would be the setting of the *Joseph Stone*.

Lazlo was scheduled to deliver the stone later that day. He was going to present the ring to Maria privately, thus formally sealing their engagement before the wedding.

Julio had also completed matching wedding bands for the ceremony. They too were a mix of yellow and white gold, each encased with 12 dark blue baguette sapphires inlaid around each band. These represented the original 12 tribes. The combination was exquisite. Julio was very proud of his work.

In these final days before the event, Señora Juana was not seen very often. She went everywhere to personally oversee every minor detail of the wedding. She lived for it. She was hoping that everything would be perfect for Maria and Lazlo.

The wedding party rehearsal came and went without incident. Everything was falling into place. Based on the number of people that congregated at the Cathedral in advance of the ceremony, interest was high and attendance for the event was expected to be in the thousands.

Juana notified the couple that she had finally located the ideal carriage to transport them away from the church after the ceremony. It was pure white, trimmed in gold, and the exact replica of the Cinderella Princess Carriage. It would be pulled by four beautiful white horses that would also be fitted to match the decorative style of the *barouche*. It took some time, but after many phone calls and personal contacts, Juana located it in France. The carriage would be transported to the Cordova Valdez Hacienda.

After the actual ceremony, the newly married couple would take a ceremonial tour of that part of Granada. This would strictly be for the benefit of the citizens of Spain.

It would be the photo opportunity of the century for lovers of grandeur. The coach would travel in a loop around the area and return to its starting point for the limited-access reception inside the Grand Hall of the Cathedral. This part of the festivities was by invitation only, much like a royal event.

Lazlo couldn't help but wonder how much money was actually being spent on all of this. Diego had said it was so much more than a wedding. In fact, it was a political statement for the entire country, and of course the people of Granada. Spanish pride had ruled for centuries. It was no different today.

Lazlo transported the *Joseph Stone* to Nicols Joyeros early in the afternoon. He decided it would be a good day to drive BJ around the countryside, top-down, for some fresh air.

Clayton insisted on traveling with him for security reasons and while Lazlo agreed, he didn't see the need. Maria would be wearing the stone every day in the very near future. They simply couldn't live in fear of theft. The stone would be carrying its own very unique form of protection, controlled by a goddess. But Clayton's company was welcomed. Life was getting hectic, and Lazlo dearly needed a break. Greenland was starting to sound very nice. Probably very cold, but very nice.

Julio enthusiastically greeted the two men in the lobby of the very upscale establishment of the Nicols family. Once again, the financial costs of this event boggled his mind. Clayton noticed and stated, "Don't worry, man. You'll get used to it," he smiled.

Clayton and Lazlo were escorted to the section of the store where the real work was done. Several goldsmiths were already working to create masterpieces for the privileged individuals who could afford their services. Julio took them to his private workbench in a room behind a closed door. Lazlo appreciated that level of professionalism. He really wasn't sure if the diamond would display any of its supernatural qualities when handled by a stranger.

The three men sat down together around the bench. Lazlo laughingly said, "Show me yours and I'll show you mine!" Julio was beginning to like this crazy American.

Julio opened a small safe that was built into the workbench under the drawers that contained more tools. He removed a small blue velvet box. *The ring!*

The ring that would represent not only the union of two lovers but would stand as a symbol for the entire Hebrew faith and all the trials and tribulations of Jews throughout history. The yet-to-be-mounted *Joseph Stone* as the centerpiece represented even more. From its beginnings in the temple of India to its migration to France and King Louis XIV, and then finally stolen by Adolf Hitler.

Julio donned a pair of white cotton gloves before opening the small blue container. Even without the center stone in place, the ring was extraordinary! Lazlo took the box from Julio for closer inspection.

Lazlo was amazed. This was indeed a work of art even in its unfinished state. "Damn! It's beautiful!" Julio was pleased. Lazlo reached to his neck and removed the leather satchel that contained his beloved diamond. This was the primary connection to his grandfather, László Joseph Biro. As he placed the diamond onto the jeweler's pad on the workbench, he said to Julio, "Don't touch it! Even with gloves! One jeweler already died attempting to avoid the curse!" Julio hesitated and picked up a set of jewelers' forceps. He turned on his bench-mounted lights and examined the stone under magnification.

Julio spoke out loud, but more to himself than anyone since no one was there in his own mind "*¡Querido Dios, esto es lo más hermoso que he visto en mi vida!*"

"Dear God, this is the most beautiful thing I've ever seen!"

Lazlo smiled and responded. "So do your thing, *mi amigo*. Do your thing!"

Julio carefully collected the ring from its box and mounted it in a small vice that was attached to his bench. He then picked up the beautiful blue stone. At first, his hands shook slightly. Rightfully so, he was nervous. Julio sat everything down on the bench. He steadied himself and attempted his task a second time.

Clayton and Lazlo could tell that Julio's nervous reaction was brief and his confidence had returned. He carefully lifted the stone and dropped it into place. The setting and stone fit perfectly together. There would be no need for the adjustment that he originally feared. Now, it was simply a matter of carefully bending the six 14-karat gold prongs into place to cradle the diamond securely. Each prong would be bent once so as not to weaken the gold. There was no room for error. Too much pressure on any one of the prongs could also make the stone sit uncentered. It needed to be perfect. Julio also studied the profile of the setting. The top of the diamond needed to be perfectly level with the profile of the ring.

"I had no idea," Lazlo whispered to Clayton. "This really takes a special touch!" Clayton agreed.

Julio was extremely careful not to touch the stone. His tools were wood and brass. Old school. Lazlo appreciated the care and skill.

When the final prong was bent into place, the *Joseph Stone* acknowledged its approval and appreciation with a blinding flash of blue light that lit up the entire room. Julio dropped his tools onto his lap. His mouth was agape while refocusing his eyes. Clayton and Lazlo were the same. Other jewelers entered the room as the flash penetrated the walls and lit up the entire store!

The *Joseph Stone Ring* sat alone in the vice, still glowing as if it had been heated by a magical torch! Lazlo knew that both Maria and Hecate would approve.

The White Wedding
CHAPTER 29

Lazlo couldn't wait to officially give Maria her engagement ring. Julio's work was worth every penny, but it did take him a bit longer than he'd planned. The bride would receive her treasure a mere twenty-four hours before the event. No matter. She would be wearing it while walking down the aisle and pledging her love to her husband-to-be at the altar in front of family, friends, community, and the eyes of God. Truth be told, a goddess most likely would also be in attendance.

Lazlo searched the grounds of the Hacienda for Maria. At first, she was nowhere to be found. He stopped by the houses that were already being called 'the Somogyi homes' and he couldn't wait to show everyone the ring. Eztar commented to Lazlo, "To think that it was buried in our yard for almost two decades!" Everyone admired the ring and shared their positive opinions.

Lazlo found Maria working with the horses. She had just finished putting Hernando in his stall. When she saw Lazlo, she ran to him for a big embrace and a kiss. It was almost undetectable, but their contact still emitted tiny blue sparks wherever they touched. Maria wondered if that miracle would ever end. She hoped not. Especially in the privacy of a secluded location where she and Lazlo could share their love.

Lazlo stepped back from Maria after their embrace and dropped to one knee. Everyone working in the arena area stopped what they were doing. It seemed that time was standing still. Lazlo lovingly gazed at his bride-to-be. *One more day*, he thought.

When he spoke his voice seemed softer. Maria saw a single tear on his cheek. "Maria, my love. I know that you accepted my proposal of marriage before. And I know that tomorrow is our most sacred day. But sometimes pledged partners have second thoughts right before their wedding day. If you do, I will understand. But I have none. I want you to be my wife and to spend the rest of my life with you. I want you to share my world. Will you still have me?"

Maria smiled her wonderful smile, "Yes! Yes! Yes, I still want you!"

Lazlo reached into his pocket and removed the blue velvet box. Maria's eyes lit up with the expectation of what she already knew was in the container. "Oh, Lazlo! You got it!"

"For you, my love," Lazlo offered her his heartfelt words, his emotions, and the ring to officially unite their love and their hearts as one.

Maria's hands were shaking and she had trouble removing the ring from the box. Lazlo stood while taking her hands in his and placed the ring on her finger. The *Joseph Stone* flashed again with its brilliant blue color! Everyone present witnessed the spectacle. They had been chosen to see this miracle. Their Maria was to marry a true holy man. A *White Lighter*. This event would go down in history for all to remember and to retell the story.

The two lovers embraced again and they both felt something warm envelop them. They knew immediately that they had just received a blessing from the Goddess Hecate. It wasn't like a blessing given in church. Her energy engulfed them. At that moment, Maria and Lazlo both felt that their life was perfect.

Neither of them had ever experienced a sensation so wonderful. Hecate approved of their union. Lazlo no longer had any doubts. Everyone cheered for them as they left the stables and headed to the main house of the Hacienda.

Maria couldn't stop admiring the ring. Somehow the two lovers knew that László Joseph Biro was proud. They felt it in their hearts that Hecate had let him know. His work was done and it was perfect.

Maria shared her ring with all who came near her. Family, gardeners, drivers, cooks, maids, everyone! She enjoyed sharing the beautiful creation that now joined their hearts forever. Tomorrow could not come soon enough. She longed to say, " I do." She longed to pledge her heart to Lazlo Joseph Somogyi. Tomorrow, the time would come.

Lazlo stayed up most of the evening thinking about his plans for the ceremony. Things could work out perfectly or quickly go terribly wrong. Most of his current life seemed to hang in those balances. Sadly, terribly wrong meant that people usually died. He would try hard to remain positive.

Maria was comfortably nestled into her bed trying to fall asleep without success. Lazlo's dog Blackie decided to visit her earlier in the day and he stayed. The dedicated pooch was asleep at the foot of the bed. Maria stared deeply into the heart of the diamond. She could feel its power. Without thinking, her mind went to another place.

Suddenly she was on a large island surrounded by blue water. The landscape was rocky, and the structures were mostly made of marble. Ornate statues adorned the countryside.

People wandered by completing their daily routines, but it didn't look like work. They seemed to be enjoying themselves. The women were all beautiful and the men looked athletic. Some practiced with swords. Everyone wore loose-fitting white tunics made of linen. Their lives appeared to be peaceful and leisurely. It was a beautiful picture.

Then in a brilliant flash of fiery light, the scene erupted into flames that consumed everything. The vision went dark as Maria pulled away from her hand.

What was it that the diamond had just shared with her?

Maria was sitting upright in bed in a mild state of shock. Her mind continued to replay the scene repeatedly. The more that she relived the moment, the more she began to understand that the vision was somehow familiar. Not a simple vision of the psyche, but a vivid memory of something else. But how could that be? Was this a memory of Hecate from the past? It was very powerful.

Eventually, Maria fell asleep.

Blackie was an early riser and began to lick Maria's face at dawn.

He needed to be let outside. Maria wanted to be up anyway. Her wedding day had finally arrived!

Walking through the main living room of the Hacienda, Maria saw Lazlo sound asleep on one of the sofas. It was obvious that he spent the night there, fully dressed. She laughed and after letting Blackie outside, she sat next to Lazlo and kissed him on the forehead. Lazlo woke and said, "Good morning, my love. I take it that you had some trouble sleeping too?" said Maria.

Lazlo rubbed his eyes and answered, "Yeah, I just couldn't clear my head. I was still awake at 4 AM. What time is it now?"

Maria told him, "It's 'Blackie Time', not even 6:30 AM."

It wasn't long before the Hacienda came alive. Everyone knew their duties and would perform them to perfection. The ladies of the bridal party were assembling in the main house. The men would dress at the church to prevent Lazlo from seeing his bride early. Limos lined the driveway with drivers dressed in their best uniforms. Even Blackie sported a new leather collar, made for him by a stable hand.

At the Cathedral, caterers delivered the food for preparation while florists set up hundreds of displays throughout the church. The bride's white carriage with matching horses was being delivered to the rear of the property.

Diego and several security officers arrived at the Hacienda to collect the 11 remaining diamonds. Diego carried a golden urn that would house them before and during the ceremony. The altar would be guarded from multiple locations.

Lazlo was already wearing the *Hope Diamond* under his casual attire. No one knew it was even there, except for Diego.

Everyone gradually gravitated to the Cathedral. Crowds were already congregating in the streets. The day was unfolding on schedule.

At exactly 12 o'clock the church bells of the Metropolitan Cathedral of the Incarnation began to chime. Onlookers cheered at the signal that the day's events were starting. Soon after, every church in the city started ringing their bells too. They created a symphony that echoed over the land.

Invited guests were already entering the church. Royalty from other countries, politicians, and their families. Relatives of the Cordova Valdez family and their friends. Lazlo's small but loving family group. It seemed that everyone was there. Even a few celebrities from movies and local television. Maria had a private window in the upper level of the cathedral where she could watch the crowd and those who were arriving at the front of the church.

Suddenly the people began cheering. Down a side street along the cathedral property television crews and other media turned their cameras to capture whatever might be happening. Maria tried to see what was creating the excitement but the angle of the window made it impossible. However, in moments her childhood dream came true. Her Knight had arrived!

Sir Lazlo Somogyi rode his white stallion, Hernando, through the crowd and up to the front of the church. The horse was adorned in the finest tack --it matched the rider's military-style wedding attire. Lazlo waved to the crowd with a broad smile. Visitors inside the cathedral flocked to the entrance for a closer look! Lazlo appeared to be a prince with his award from El Presidente and the *Hope Diamond* necklace around his neck.

Maria was beyond thrilled watching Lazlo and Hernando perform for the crowd. Lazlo made sure there was room for the safety of spectators and signaled Hernando to stand on his hind legs and profile the crowd. The pair executed a perfect *capriole* to the amazement of the people of Granada! The crowd roared!

Several stablemen from the Cordova Valdez Estate came forward to assist in controlling Hernando as Lazlo patted his massive neck to calm him. He dismounted and after kissing the big animal on the nose, turned and again waved to the crowd.

Diego and Lorenzo were watching from inside. "I told you that he'd make a fine politician," said Diego.

Lazlo entered the church and was greeted by his best man, Clayton. He was acknowledged by the rest of his friends in the wedding party as they ushered guests to their arranged seating. Lazlo made eye contact with his adopted father, Dr. Sherlous, from across the room. Steven Sherlous could hardly believe this was the same boy that he took into his home not so many years ago. Clayton whisked Lazlo away to a private area of the church where he could prepare for the service. Things were moving quickly.

Lazlo requested his brother, Lucas, to be brought to him so that he could be sure everything was in order. Lazlo currently carried the rings. Clayton decided to find Lucas himself and was surprised to see that Lucas arrived with Blackie, on a decorative leash.

"Blackie! What are you doing here boy?" Lazlo laughed.

"Momma said it was okay!" Lucas said.

Lazlo looked at his little brother and smiled. "Can you control him? I mean *really* control him. You both need to be *well-behaved* today." Lucas said yes, and then added his promise that nothing would go wrong.

"Alright then, little buddy," said Lazlo. "I trust you both. So, who's carrying the rings? You or Blackie?" Lazlo actually thought it might be safer to attach them to the dog.

Lucas said, "I think I'd rather have Blackie carry them."

"Then so be it," declared Lazlo.

The organist signaled to the wedding party that she was ready to start the Wedding March at the end of the current song. The ushers finished seating latecomers and gravitated to the side of the church to meet with Lazlo.

The church became silent. Everyone was waiting with great expectation. "Nimrod" was selected as the music to be played as the bridesmaids walked down the aisle individually. It set a tone for a pleasant reflection of time moving forward. This would flow directly into the Wedding March that would accompany the bride. As each bridesmaid approached the altar, they were greeted by their assigned groomsman, kneeled before the priest, and then separated to stand on either side of the altar, facing the visitors. The Maid of Honor and the Best Man were the last of the party to complete their role as they turned to face the crowd. Women throughout the Cathedral were crying already.

The organist smoothly transitioned into the Wedding March as Maria entered the church. Lazlo watched her from his position nearby.

He would meet her as she approached the altar. Lazlo saw that the urn with the 11 diamonds was in place. Things were in order.

Maria looked more beautiful than ever if that was even possible. Her gown with its long, flowing train was perfect! She was a sight to behold as she paced her steps in sync with the music, followed by two young girls carrying the ends of her train. There were two little girls in front of Maria, spreading flowers. Part way down the aisle she hesitated to meet with her waiting Papa Lorenzo. They joined arms as he escorted her to the altar. She looked to the back of the church and nodded to Diego, who was holding onto Lucas and Blackie waiting for their instructions to proceed. Diego petted Blackie while securing the rings to his collar, and sent the pair down the aisle. Lazlo entered from the side door.

Lazlo met Father and Daughter at the altar and the ceremonial exchange took place after Lorenzo kissed Maria to wish her well. Clayton removed the rings from Blackie's collar and quietly gave them to Lazlo. A front-row seat was reserved for Lucas with Eztar and both Blackie and Lucas behaved flawlessly. Everyone knew that this little exhibition would most likely make the news as cameras were allowed in the church and were continuously filming.

Father Guido took control of the ceremony. "Dearly beloved… we are gathered here today in the eyes of God to join this man and woman in holy matrimony…" He went on to complete the perfect Roman Catholic ceremony and after the bride and groom were officially joined without any objections, he advised that Lazlo could now kiss his bride.

As their lips met, both bride and groom began to glow! The lighting in the church flickered and the building went dark. The newly married couple was illuminated. Lazlo glowed a pure white light. Maria a light green. They were radiant together. As if by magic, all of the candles throughout the church were lit in unison! The effect was beautiful!

Everyone in the church was in awe and couldn't believe their eyes!

Above and behind the altar, a glowing green mist began to form that stretched at least 75 feet to the cathedral ceiling. As it swirled lazily around the front of the church, several figures began to materialize. The images resembled more of an illusion, but they were real. A horse. A black wolfdog and a giant owl positioned themselves above the wedding party. Lastly, a beautiful woman with long dark hair and green eyes. She too was enveloped in a dramatic green aura. Onlookers immediately saw the resemblance between this image and that of their Maria. All the diamonds began to glow with blue illumination. Maria's ring and Lazlo's *Hope Diamond* were the most radiant.

The image of the woman was the Goddess Hecate. She spoke magically and softly, but everyone could hear her.

"I am the Goddess Hecate. My father was Cronos. I am eternal. Know me. Lazlo is my chosen champion. Maria is my daughter from another time. We have traveled long and far to correct the wrongs of our ancestors. Do not fear me. I am here to assist mankind and to help people the world over. I am here to reunite with my daughter and to teach my champion the 'old ways' so that we can aid you in the development of your species. And yes, I am here to vanquish our enemies wherever they might be hiding."

Hecate hesitated for a moment.

"I have blessed this union. I promise that it is one of greatness. Sir Lazlo Somogyi will be a great leader. An educator and a scholar. He is all things that a man needs to pursue. Love him. Support him. Follow him if he asks it of you. And you, too, will be loved as we gods loved your people in the past. I will always be with you. We have been waiting a long time for your champion!"

Suddenly, the image faded and was gone! The church was silent. Lazlo addressed the crowd, "Please do not fear. Our day is not yet over. I believe that a carriage ride is in order and a wonderful reception. Please stay and enjoy yourselves." Lazlo signaled Diego to secure the stones that aided in powering the display. Maria and Lazlo left the church as the organ music continued.

The enthusiastic crowd cheered wildly. Maria and Lazlo waved to everyone and went to the white carriage. Bird seed was being thrown instead of rice. It was Maria's idea to feed the wild pigeons that lived within the city. Lazlo helped Maria into the carriage and as he took her hand he appreciated the beauty of the two rings that now adorned her finger on the left hand. He glanced at his matching band, and Lazlo was happy to be married to his beautiful bride.

The new couple made themselves comfortable as Lazlo signaled the driver to start their ride around town. Cameras flashed from all angles. The wedding had turned into a media frenzy. But the cameras were not the only flashes that Lazlo experienced. There was another familiar blue flash in Lazlo's minds-eye that for the first time, Maria saw it too! This message from Hecate was meant for them both. Once again it seemed like time was standing still while the goddess spoke.

"Congratulations, daughter! And special well wishes to you Lazlo, my love! Your lives are just beginning together, and I will always be there for both of you. Enjoy your day. When you reach Greenland, we will discuss my release from my prison.

The carriage ride was fun and eventful. Maria and Lazlo wondered what was in store for them in Greenland. In time, they would know. The people of Granada embraced them today and the ceremony would surely create worldwide support for this magical couple. As they approached the final leg of their fairy tale journey back to the cathedral, Maria remembered her vision—which came from the ring on the first day that she wore it. *Daughter.* The word haunted her. Could this really be the truth? She needed to find out.

The reception was exciting. Everyone wanted to speak to the new couple. Photographs were taken nonstop. Food and drink were abundant. And everyone wanted to dance with the bride. When Lazlo noticed Maria's exhaustion, he picked her up off of the dance floor and carried her to BJ, where Clayton stood guard.

Their destination was secret. Lazlo escaped with his bride longing for their first night alone as husband and wife. Tomorrow. Greenland awaited them.

And a goddess with fiery-green eyes.

The Honeymoon

CHAPTER 30

The newlyweds woke up to room service at the Parador de Granada, one of the oldest hotels in the historic city. This was one of the most expensive hotels in the region, but it was selected by Maria and Lazlo for entirely different reasons. The hotel was very well known for its history as the Parador de Granada was set in a former convent on the grounds of medieval Alhambra. It was located less than a mile or so from the Granada Cathedral. This location worked out perfectly for newlyweds who were trying to escape the crowds. The style of the hotel, the care given by staff, and the quality of everything offered was unrivaled in its presentation to guests. Oddly, the hotel was owned and operated by the government of Spain. Lazlo thought that was odd, but the hotel was beautiful, and the history was interesting.

Mr. and Mrs. Lazlo Joseph Somogyi. It had a nice sound to it.

"So, Mrs. Somogyi. Do you feel any different this morning?" Lazlo waited for her answer. Maria laughed and stated that only the name change sounded strange to her, but she could live with it. They both smiled and then Lazlo kissed his bride good morning.

The couple was far too tired after arriving at the hotel the night before to really enjoy their wedding night. Friends and relatives had warned them to expect it. The romance would appear when they relaxed and settled in after arriving in Greenland. For now, they were quite happy that their union was official and final. "Till death do us part." Lazlo trusted that it would be far in the future.

The view from their room was breathtaking. The historical Mediterranean landscape was a sight to behold. Maria was looking out from the balcony as Lazlo approached her from behind. He pressed himself up against her while wrapping his arms around her waist and kissing her neck repeatedly. Maria sighed and leaned back against him. They both felt the static electric charge that emanated from their bodies.

The young lovers relaxed in a sensual embrace as Lazlo then lifted his bride and carried her to their bed. Maria's Knight had collected her and saved her from all harm. It was time for her to reward him with her love.

"To hell with waiting for Greenland! I want you now!" Lazlo stated to Maria. He was forceful but passionate. They kissed deeply, charged by the solar powers of their auras, and made love repeatedly until they were both spent.

Lazlo stared into her eyes and they both experienced a satisfaction that they had never felt before. Their union completed them both. They were now as one.

"I love you, Maria," Lazlo whispered.

"And I love you, husband," she replied.

They both fell asleep while basking in the warmth of their love for one another.

Several hours later Lazlo woke to a telephone call from Clayton.

"I hate to bother you kids but you have tickets for a flight to Greenland later today. It's already noon. Your flight leaves at 4 PM. Order some lunch and I'll collect the two of you around 1 PM. Sound good?"

Lazlo told him everything was fine. "See you then," he added.

He looked at Maria and said, "Let's eat! I'm hungry!"

Lazlo reminded Maria that the flight with one brief layover would still take over 24 hours. He had read it somewhere in a travel brochure, not that he really had any experience traveling.

"I can't even say the name of the town. It's more like a village really. The airport is an old military base built and operated by the United States back in the 1940s. The population may be 400-500 people at best. But it's perfect for my research and very private for a honeymoon." Lazlo attempted to say the name. "KANGERLUSSUAQ Airport. Holy shit!" Lazlo seemed to say that a lot. It was an American expression and Maria just ignored it lately. Clayton had picked it up too in their American college. So be it, she thought to herself.

The airport had its own hotel where they had reserved a room for a week, but they were advised that in November it was so cold they might be the only guests. The buildings were basic shelters. Prefab military buildings erected in the 40s and 50s. Nothing fancy, but a small restaurant would provide meals. Lazlo had some concerns that Maria had never been to a place so remote. Neither had he. He hoped that her interest in the paranormal would prevail. Time would certainly tell.

As they collected their luggage for the trip, Maria reminded Lazlo to carry some winter clothing for the coming cold weather. The change in climate this time of year would be extreme. Lazlo also grabbed a backpack that contained the urn and its contents from the altar. Maria wore her *Joseph Ring* proudly, and Lazlo decided to keep the *Hope Diamond* concealed under his jacket.

It wasn't long before Clayton was knocking on the door.

"Congratulations guys! I still think Greenland is crazy in November, but I'll never understand the scientific mind. You're both nuts in my book, but I love you anyway!"

Clayton helped with the luggage and they headed downstairs to a waiting sedan. In the lobby, Lazlo noticed that all eyes seemed to be on him and his new bride. Clayton picked up a newspaper and they realized why. The front page showed a photo of the wedding party at the altar, with the giant figure of Hecate and her three animal spirits beside her. It was taken after the lights went out and the candles lit, greatly adding to the paranormal effect.

The headline read "Fact or Fiction in the Catholic Church?" The article then said that immediately after the wedding, government officials entered the church to locate any cameras or other equipment that could have faked the event. They found nothing. Lorenzo and Diego were both quoted as saying that the events were authentic.

"Well, I guess we'll see, won't we," said Lazlo. They left the hotel and headed for the airport.

"What's the name of the town in Greenland?" asked Clayton.

"It's north of the polar circle. The nearest village anywhere is called 'Qeqqata'. It's quite a hike as I understand it. But for now, we'll be staying at what they call the *Danish Hotel*. I think some American soldier just named it that as a joke," laughed Lazlo.

The trio arrived at the airport and boarded a half hour later. Lazlo asked Clayton to keep a close eye on Blackie, and off they went.

As expected, the flight was long. Maria brought a novel along with her to pass the time. It was a story about falconry. Lazlo wondered if a giant owl could be trained for the same purposes. It made him think of Hecate. He fully expected that she would reveal herself to him once again in this northern wasteland. He thought about his future in Greenland.

There would be lots of sky-watching and stargazing. But he had hopes of witnessing some increased aura activity between himself and Maria. There had been reports of solar activity in the area during this month. If he was right, he hoped to prove a connection. Would there be some way to harness the anomaly and somehow put it to use? Could he and Maria learn how to predict these solar events to prevent damage to the communication systems worldwide? This information, if proven true, could become extremely valuable. Lazlo looked forward to discovering the answers to these questions. Hecate had planted the seeds in his mind that allowed him to form such questions. Lazlo longed for answers.

After changing planes in England, the newlyweds continued their journey northward into the land of ice and snow. Looking out the windows occasionally showed them icebergs and other frozen land masses. The water was a beautiful blue and looked very cold. Lazlo reminded himself to trust the plane and its pilot. Flying in this area offered much vulnerability. Lazlo wondered if Greenland had polar bears. He really wasn't sure, but he wanted to find out. Maria sensed his discomfort and told him to relax as she played with his hair. *My Knight in shining armor,* she thought. He just cracks me up. My dragon slayer is afraid of the big white bear. Maria fell asleep against Lazlo's shoulder. It wasn't long before Lazlo fell asleep, too.

During the flight, there were several instances where the Northern Lights became visible through the porthole windows of the plane. Maria noticed that Lazlo's aura had intensified. He noticed the same had happened to her aura. This was going to be an interesting visit for sure. Lazlo was getting excited over the possibilities.

In a short while, the pilot announced that they were approaching Greenland. More specifically, Kangerlussuaq Airport. Everything was white with snow. The airport was nestled between two mountain ranges. It looked very military wherever they looked. Lazlo even noted radar stations were still being used along the mountains. The Americans picked a good place for this base.

Lazlo saw a dog sled being pulled by eight cold-weather canines. He thought of Blackie. They began their approach to the ice-covered runway, and he connected his seatbelt for that extra level of security should the plane not stop. Maria was reading her book again and looked quite comfortable. At that moment Lazlo determined that he really didn't care much for flying. Maybe Hecate could do something magical to alleviate this fear too. After all, she had made him a skilled equestrian in a matter of seconds.

Lazlo heard the engines throttle up and the tires 'chirp' as the rubber met the tarmac. The runway was free of ice, it just looked white from above due to the glare of the sun. The plane slowed to a crawl and taxied to the terminal, hotel, and restaurant.

The newlyweds were met on the tarmac by Peder Nord Berthelsen. He was as close to a mayor as the community had to offer. He was cheerful and friendly with red cheeks that reminded Lazlo of Saint Nicholas.

"Welcome, welcome my friends! We have heard so much about you!" Peder was truly thrilled to meet the young couple. "You are, how do you say this in English? Famous! Front page of newspapers everywhere!"

Lazlo questioned how a newspaper with yesterday's news made it to Greenland so fast.

Peder laughed and responded, "I have a cousin in Europe. He

knows that we are not so far behind the southern world. We have a fancy machine that the US military left for us. It's called a fax. The pictures are not so good, but we read the story. You *are* famous!"

Peder motioned for them to follow while an assistant picked up their baggage. "Come. The walk is not far. That building is the *Denmark Hotel.*" He pointed at what looked like an old military barracks.

Before entering the hotel, Peder stopped to point out a giant snow tractor of sorts. It was a tracked vehicle with rubber tank-looking pads at least 3 ft wide. It appeared that it could carry up to four people.

"This will be your transportation during your stay. I will teach you how to operate it. It's really not that hard. Just remember not to go too far away from the village. Storms can blow in quickly and cause whiteout conditions. You will become snow-blind and get lost." Peder then added a comment over his shoulder as he started walking. "They call it a 'Weasel'." He laughed at the name. "The Americans brought them here during the war."

Peder escorted them inside where both Maria and Lazlo had to admit that the interior was nothing like they had imagined. The renovations were done tastefully, and the decorations were mostly *Inuit,* showing the proud history of the people and their ancestors. The couple had reserved what was called 'The Suite' but it was really just the largest rentable room in the building. After paying for the room and getting information on the restaurant hours and menu details, Maria and Lazlo headed for Room #1. It seemed appropriate.

Lazlo notified Peder that he would return soon to check out the 'Weasel'. He was also feeling hungry and really wasn't sure of the time. Lazlo asked if the restaurant was currently open. Peder responded that it was. "Every time a flight lands we make sure that the kitchen is ready and waiting." Lazlo's stomach was happy to hear that.

The suspense of learning what was behind the door of Room #1 was killing both Lazlo and Maria. No matter how you looked at it, there would be no comparison to spending their first night married at the Parador de Granada in Spain.

Lazlo inserted the key and opened the locked door. They both peeked inside without crossing the threshold. Maria was surprised as she looked back and forth between her view of the room and the face of her equally surprised husband. The room was beautiful! Tastefully decorated and quite spacious, it did not match the rest of the facility. There was one large window behind rustic drapery that looked towards a snow-covered mountain range in the distance. Breathtaking. The room even had a small kitchenette with basic amenities for meals or snacks. Lazlo picked up his bride and carried her over the threshold. Maria giggled and kissed him playfully.

Lazlo gently placed Maria on the rather large bed and returned for the luggage that he left at the door.

While reentering the room, he looked at Maria and asked, "Will wonders never cease? This place is fantastic! I love the rustic *Inuit* decor! It's kind of beautiful in its own way. But now with you on the bed, it just couldn't be any better. I love it!" Lazlo explored the details of the 'Eskimo-looking' skins and authentic tools that adorned the walls. Even the bedspread was natural animal skin. Lazlo guessed some kind of yak or similar animal. While he didn't really approve of killing animals for this purpose, he knew that the land here was harsh.

Existence was so much tougher than living in Granada or Washington DC. The suite even had its own cast iron potbelly wood stove, with a pile of split wood waiting to be burned when the night temperatures dropped. It reminded Lazlo of the home in the coal mines of Ward. His mind also drifted to the townhouse in DC. He still had the keys but wondered if he'd ever go back to that short-lived home. There seemed to be no reason really. Technically he doubted if he was even still employed by the Smithsonian Institute. So much had happened.

Maria could tell that he was deep in thought at the moment. She could read him well and guessed that his mind was suddenly back in the United States. Their world was moving quickly forward as it should be. Learning from the past is a critical element in surviving the future. But living in the past is not so productive. Maria knew that they were moving forward. Together.

Lazlo removed the 11 diamonds from his luggage and placed

them back in the original leather satchel that was their home. He then put them around his neck with the *Hope Diamond*. For now, it was the only way he could guarantee their safety.

"Let's go get something to eat and then check out that 'Weasel' contraption! It looks like fun to me. I'm thinking that a trip closer to the mountains at night would be an awesome chance for a Northern Lights show!" Lazlo's excitement and zest for exploration was the part of him that she adored.

Maria jumped to her feet and joined Lazlo heading for the door. In minutes, they were back at the front desk to inquire about the location of the restaurant and details on the food. Lazlo was hungry. He always seemed to be hungry.

There were actually several groups of people already eating in the restaurant. Some were locals, others employees, and a few military personnel that most likely were regulars. The large room was obviously constructed for this purpose when the barracks were originally installed over 25 years ago. Much like their room, the decor was surprising but unique. The tables and booths could have been at their favorite truck stop. The decorative style was, again, *Inuit.*

A sign said to seat yourself. So they did. Menus were already on the table. In moments, they were greeted by a familiar face. It was Peder.

"Can I get you something to drink?" he asked.

Lazlo was a little surprised and commented without thinking.

"You're the mayor and you wait tables? That is interesting."

Peder laughed, "Yes, around here everyone does everything! As they say, it takes a village… eh?"

"I guess so," replied Lazlo.

Then Peder added, "And after you eat, I'll show you how to tame a Weasel!"

"Wow!" Lazlo looked at Maria. "Talk about managing your time productively. I am impressed. People in America could learn a few things by studying this business model."

Peder took their drink orders and left them while they looked over their menus. Lazlo was once again surprised to note that their menus weren't much different than anywhere else. Much of the same foods. The only notable difference was that certain fresh food items were captioned with "available when in season". He figured that made sense. There were no strange menu items like musk ox, seal, whale, or things like that. Lazlo felt a bit foolish for even thinking of it. He ordered a cheeseburger with fries and a slice of blueberry pie when Peder returned. Maria ordered a salad.

The newlyweds enjoyed their first sit down in a restaurant meal together as husband and wife. The food was good.

Peder commented that the salad was very fresh as he had just made it within the hour. He asked Lazlo if he enjoyed the burger and Lazlo replied that it was fantastic.

"Good," replied Peder. "I add some secret spices to the meat when I make them. It's my mother's old recipe!"

Lazlo was even more amazed. "You cook too?!"

Peder replied, "As I said… It takes a village." He laughed.

"I'll meet you outside in 10 minutes… I'm waiting for my replacement on the grill. He's running a little late. I'm glad that you enjoyed your first meal in Greenland. See you in a few!" Peder disappeared into the kitchen.

After finishing their meals, Lazlo left a substantial tip in cash to pay for their bill. He noted how hard everyone worked here and he wanted them to know that he appreciated their efforts. Lazlo knew what it was like not to have money. He was also somewhat amazed at the amount he received from the Smithsonian as a paycheck for those few months when he felt he had done absolutely nothing to earn it. Those that have, get more. Those that have not, simply suffer. Lazlo could hardly believe how quickly his life had turned around.

Maria and Lazlo left the building and walked to the 'Weasel' for a closer look. Peder wasn't far behind them.

"Interesting machine, isn't it?" Peder said Lazlo agreed.

Lazlo decided to tell Peder about his car life, such as it was.

"I know something about work vehicles. Studebaker. Made in the USA. It was originally called the M29 when it went into military service for the United States. It was built for use in World War II. Top speed of 36 mph on land and 4mph in the water. Only 65 horsepower. They were also used by the British and Canadian military," Lazlo stopped.

"Damn. You know your stuff. I'm not even sure if the army guys know all of that. Have you ever operated one?" Peder waited for a reply.

"Nah," Lazlo responded. "Never have had a chance. I want to, though. They look like fun."

Peder opened the cab and showed Lazlo where everything was located. He checked the fluids and eventually started the engine. "Steering is done by a steering lever. It's fairly simple."

They climbed aboard. Peder would drive first. It was loud which made Maria cover her ears. Lazlo loved the entire experience. It was better than a theme park ride! Lazlo practically begged to take over the controls.

Lazlo told Peder that he and Maria wanted to observe the Northern Lights from the wilderness area outside of town. They wanted to use the 'Weasel' to get up into higher ground and away from the lights at the airport. Weather reports were good, so they returned Peder to the hotel. As they parted ways with their new cook, he advised them that they be careful and take no risks. It simply wasn't worth it. Lazlo was in his glory driving this little tank.

The 'Weasel' was equipped with a radio that connected to the airport emergency station, a large compass, a heater for the cold environment, a first aid kit, military MREs (Meals Ready to Eat), and ample flood lighting for operating in the dark. They were ready for a short exploration of the heavens.

Lazlo played around with the controls, zig-zagging the 'Weasel' through the snow. He liked looking back at the track impressions that it left behind. Eventually, he lost interest in games and became more serious about what they were attempting to do. He headed east in the direction of a low mountain range. The sun had already started to set when Maria pointed out a light green color starting to form in the northeast. This was the beginning of a solar storm creating the Northern Lights.

As expected by Lazlo, he noticed that Maria's aura had also become active. His wife was beginning to glow! His wife. That was the first time that he had thought of Maria as "his wife". Maria noticed that Lazlo too, was starting to shine. She pointed it out to him and wondered if standard photography would capture this electrical reaction. Maria realized that only another synesthete could witness this with the naked eye. Hecate seemed to be able to control what humans could see and hear. That was seemingly left to her own discretion based on her desires.

Maria and Lazlo were both wearing military-grade fur-lined gloves to protect their hands from frostbite. They had found two pairs in a container on board the 'Weasel'. Maria could feel her left hand getting quite warm and she saw a pulsing glow penetrating the glove from the inside. She pulled the glove from her hand. The *Joseph Stone Ring* was alive with its brilliant, blue-colored luminescence. Lazlo stopped the 'Weasel' in its tracks as they both knew that Hecate was going to have a visit with them. In a matter of seconds, she penetrated both of their minds. In typical fashion with the goddess, both Maria and Lazlo experienced a blue flash of light in their minds-eyes. Then they heard her voice.

Hecate spoke, *"Greetings, my children. Welcome to a part of my northern kingdom here on earth! I have missed you both but have been watching you from afar. Your status in this world is growing quickly, Lazlo. There would be those who already credit you as being a lesser god in their eyes. I would suggest that you use this wisely. Your people need a better leader than anything else that is available to them. You have it in you to lead. It is in your bloodline from centuries past. Please be willing to harness the powers that I am sharing with you!"*

Maria and Lazlo didn't need to speak about this. Once again, questions were answered before they were asked. Hecate wanted to discuss her release, but not on this night. Tomorrow. Tonight was the first night of their honeymoon underneath a green swirling sky blessed by another goddess, Aurora.

Hecate and Aurora understood the needs of the flesh and the heart. They loved these two humans without limitations.

"Go now, back to the warmth of your bed. Take our blessings with you and share the love that you both treasure."

Maria and Lazlo made their way back to the hotel and after securing the 'Weasel', went directly back to their room to complete their wedding night. While Maria went to get a quick shower, Lazlo started a fire in the pot-bellied stove. In no time the warmth filled the room. Lazlo left the front of the stove open so the fire could be seen flickering its light on the walls. He opened the curtains of the one window to a panoramic view of the frozen world outside. They were fortunate this night that the sky was filled with dancing-colored lights of a never-ending display of the Aurora Borealis. Lazlo was sure that this show was created by Hecate and Aurora specifically for their wedding night.

Lazlo removed his heavy winter clothing and sat on the edge of the bed watching the dancing flames. Never in his days as a boy in Ward did he see an old stove as romantic. But tonight, it was richly beautiful, and he knew that when Maria entered the room, the snow, the fire, the lights in the sky, and his love for Maria would overwhelm him. He was beginning to love this land of fire and ice.

When Maria came out of the bathroom, she was wrapped in only a white towel. She coyly looked at her lover, dropped the towel, and got into bed. She snuggled under the fur bed cover and motioned for Lazlo to join her. Lazlo could see her aura starting to glow a green that enhanced the colorful display outside of their window. The scene was breathtaking!

Undressing, Lazlo then joined his wife under the covers and a wave of light briefly whispered through the room. It was blue and they both felt the same comfort that came with Her first blessing. Once again, the Goddess Hecate had blessed her two chosen children. Maria and Lazlo knew that wonderful things were about to happen.

Lazlo kissed Maria. Softly at first, but Maria responded with an open-mouthed exploration of tongue, lips, and fever! She passionately embraced her man. Their connected auras radiated a white energy that lit up the room. Lazlo kissed her gently and in a way he'd never done before. These pleasures were a gift from the two goddesses.

"I love you, Maria," and I always have, right from the beginning."

Maria responded, "I love you too, my husband."

Maria didn't mention it to Lazlo, but just before falling asleep, she felt a strange wave of energy pass through her body. It lingered near her abdomen. This was something that she had never felt before. It had to be connected to Hecate. Maria smiled in contentment and fell deeply asleep in her lover's arms.

A Spiritual Release
CHAPTER 31

The two lovers woke up in the morning to a light rap on their door and a voice: "Room service!" They recognized it as Peder. Lazlo donned a robe and answered the door. He was greeted by a smiling Peder. "Good morning, my friend," Peder said.

Peder wheeled in a cart that had a generous amount of food on it. It was also delivered under the best silver display, perhaps in all of Greenland. Peder explained that it had once belonged to his mother.

"This is wonderful," said Lazlo. "We'd forgotten to order room service."

Peder winked. "This is our treat," he said. It's 'on the house'. A special gift for the newlyweds!"

Lazlo was astounded. Maria remained covered as Peder wheeled the breakfast cart closer to the bed. Before he left Lazlo inquired if he and Maria could have a running tab at the facility and pay for everything at the end of their visit. Peder said, "No problem, my friend."

"Tips too!" called out Lazlo. "25% on everything!"

Maria sat up in bed and moved herself closer to the breakfast cart. Lazlo joined her to find an array of almost every kind of breakfast item that one could imagine! Fruits and cereals were mostly selected for Maria. Bacon, eggs, sausages, hash browns, and even grits were on the cart. There was enough there to feed four adults! Lazlo took a bit of everything and ate it with vigor. Maria even tried some of the breakfast meats and enjoyed them immensely. Peder was an excellent cook. Maria and Lazlo were both convinced that he prepared their meal personally.

After finishing breakfast Lazlo requested a personal tour of the village and information on the surrounding area. He could use the 'Weasel' to visit the outskirts of the town.

Roughly an hour later, Peder introduced Lazlo and Maria to another employee of the facility. His name was Kristian. Lazlo thought that was a strong-sounding male Danish name. Much like Peder, Kristian was very friendly and accommodating. His tour included the airport and its history, the rest of the hotel and several of its rooms, equipment repair areas, and a large warehouse for supplies.

The history was the interesting part. Lazlo was amazed at how the facility had developed over the years. While you could imagine all of the changes, it was hard to believe that it started as just a military base almost 25 years ago. Kristian knew the history of the people of Greenland and the lands extremely well. He was happy to share the information with his newfound friends.

Lazlo paid particular attention to a comment that Kristian made about living in Greenland. "Nobody owns land here. You cannot purchase it because it is owned by the government." Kristian was very clear on the subject. Lazlo questioned him further.

"So you just pick your spot and move in after building a house. Or maybe you find an old base like this and set up a business or home?"

Kristian confirmed this is true. "But the government must approve your residency."

Lazlo would store that information for another time. He had ideas for a research facility in the future. Greenland would be perfect. The shorter days, the cold weather. Lazlo loved the cold. He also loved the snow. Wintertime was his favorite season. Darkness suited him.

In point of fact, the best time to see the Aurora Borealis activity was obviously at night. Hecate also seemed to gravitate to after-dark activities. Travel with a giant owl also fits that format.

Maria and Lazlo returned to their room to find everything had been cleaned and was in impeccable order. Fresh towels, soaps, shampoo, and other sundries were restocked. Firewood was stacked for the woodstove, but more surprising, was the fire already burning. Peder was really on the ball.

The newlyweds lay down in bed after turning on a portable cassette player on the small table nearby.

There were several tapes to choose from. Maria picked James Taylor. She saw him in a movie once and liked his music even more when James changed professions. She had a premonition that one day he would write a song about Sweet Baby Jane. She hoped that it would be a hit and the name would connect to Lazlo's car. One can dream.

Sleep came quickly for the couple. Between the wedding and the traveling, they were both experiencing jet lag. They needed to rest and reset their internal clocks.

They needed to be at their best when meeting with Hecate again. Especially because of her request. Her release from the *Hope* carried a great many unknowns with it.

Hours later, Lazlo woke up and noticed the well-choreographed dance of colors in the cosmos. It was more extreme than the night before. He gently woke Maria and informed her of the time. After a hug and a kiss, they were both on their feet and getting dressed. Lazlo put another log on the fire and closed the stove door and vents to reduce airflow and cause a slow burn that would barely heat the room while they were gone. The stove would stay hot, however, making it easier to build on the fire upon their return. Maria was amazed that Lazlo knew these things. She had never used a stove for heating before they met.

They dressed for a frigid evening and headed for the 'Weasel'. After starting the engine, Lazlo allowed it to warm to operating temperature. His signal that the unit was ready to operate came only after the heater started blowing warm air. Any sooner could damage the motor. Again, Maria marveled at Lazlo's knowledge of these things.

Once ready, Lazlo put the 'Weasel' in gear and pulled away. He headed on a northeastern trajectory once again and was amazed at the beauty of the sky and surrounding landscape.

After about a mile or so, Lazlo stopped their tracked carriage.

He wanted to concentrate on the solar exhibitions and to be ready for Hecate when she arrived. It wasn't a long wait. She mentally came to the couple in similar fashion as before.

"*You have received my blessings, my children. And your lives will be better because of it. There once was a time when mankind respected the gods and received great rewards for the adulation given. But man is vain and jealous. And women can be manipulative and demanding. No matter the faith or the gods, these are things that drove Cronus mad with anger. He lost all hope for the humans of this world. Because of you, White Lighter, I have regained my faith in mankind. We shall show the world that their goddess has returned. After you release me from my prison, my fate may be in your hands.*"

Lazlo wondered what to do. How could *he* make this happen?

Hecate responded. "*I waited many earth years for your birth. The birth of a true White Lighter. I knew that you would be pure of heart after your family experienced so much evil before your birth here on earth. I have watched you grow and earn your place.*"

Lazlo and Maria both absorbed Hecate's thoughts.

Hecate continued, "*Lazlo, my love. All that you need to do is 'will it'. Will my release with all of your heart. Imagine my prison shattering into a million pieces. Watch my soul ascend back up into the heavens. It is within your power. As your goddess, I will not leave you. The ring will be my portal to you as long as you live. And much like the long lives in biblical scriptures, you too, will exceed the normal lifespans of men on earth. This is my promise to my children.*"

As if to answer his questions Hecate added, "*After my release the curse on the stones will be gone. Keep the portal. Discard the others. I will show you how. Their value in this world is priceless! But their power will end.*"

Lazlo and Maria woke from their trance. They exchanged glances with looks of wonder and shock. "What will you do, Lazlo?" asked Maria.

Without a word, Lazlo got out of the 'Weasel' into the frigid wasteland. He removed the *Hope Diamond* and the other 11 stones from his neck, placing them in the snow, together. He then stepped back to distance himself from the upcoming event.

Lazlo glanced back at Maria in the cab of the 'Weasel' and smiled. He then closed his eyes and did as he was told, concentrating on the release of his goddess.

The diamonds began to glow! They pulsated together lighting up the area for a mile! In a grand flash and an explosion of energy Lazlo and Maria saw the form of Hecate rising into the atmosphere above them. She turned into a swirling mist of colored lights that lit the sky like no other aurora that had ever been witnessed by human eyes.

Maria and Lazlo glowed. A wave of peace fell over both of them. Lazlo fell to his knees as he watched the amazing display above him! He knew that it was good. He knew that he rescued a goddess on that night! And now, this deity would continue to look after him, and all that he loved, as payment for his devotion to her.

Lazlo picked up the diamonds that amazingly survived the ordeal. They were unscathed. *Funny how real magic works*, he thought. He was cold when he re-entered the 'Weasel' with Maria. It was time to go back to the room and get warm.

A Steamy Score

CHAPTER 32

When Maria and Lazlo arrived back at their room, they were surprised to feel the level of heat emanating from within. Lazlo knew that the way he had left the stove, this shouldn't be happening. At first, he suspected that Peder had dropped by to prepare for their return. When Lazlo checked the stove, however, he saw that the door and vents were still closed. He glanced at the window with a view and it was completely fogged over. From the inside. Odd.

"What the hell made this room so warm," Lazlo asked Maria. But Maria was no longer in the room. She had walked into the bathroom and stood shocked in front of a large mirror. It too, was fogged but a message was written on the steamed surface. It was short and to the point.

Contact Jacob Blaustein
AMOCO Oil Company
Baltimore, Maryland

Maria asked if Lazlo knew who he was, to which he replied, "He's a multi-millionaire politician of sorts who owns AMOCO Gasoline. He's Jewish but born in the USA. That's really all that I know."

Lazlo called the front desk to speak with Peder but it was late. No one answered the phone. It would need to wait until morning.

The couple settled into a somewhat warm room for the evening. Their view of the Northern Lights was partially blocked due to the condensation on the inside of the window. They started their evening on top of the musk ox fur being used as a bed cover. Lazlo knew, however, that outside temps would plummet and the glass would clear. He also knew that he would need to open the vents on the stove to reheat the fire. That should balance the temperatures and keep the room comfortable. Sleep came quickly due to the warmth in the room.

Lazlo dreamed about the Northern Lights. Specifically, he dreamed about owning his own research facility here in Greenland. He wanted to meet local "Kalaallit" people who reportedly had paranormal experiences. Some call them "Greenlanders" but the local people prefer the language of the "Kalaallisut". Similar to Alaska's Inupiat, literally the "real people." These groups were all under the designation of *Inuit*. Lazlo would put the word out to all of the villages when the time came so that he could learn from their experiences. He would pay them for their time.

His dream was vivid and detailed. Strangely, he would remember every bit of it when he woke up in the morning. He could literally create a business model in his sleep. Even he felt that this was strange.

Lazlo woke up in the morning feeling fresh and ready to seize the day. When he had fallen asleep the night before he had felt a great deal of apprehension about keeping a seasonal lab in the far north, while also living in Granada, and still technically keeping a home in Washington. His plate was getting close to overflowing. But now, somehow, the puzzle seemed to fit together nicely and things were much less complicated than just moments ago. He looked over at Maria, still sound asleep, and decided to leave her undisturbed while he took a shower. If she woke up on her own, that was fine. If not, he'd leave a note and go visit with Peder to discuss some business possibilities.

When Lazlo finished cleaning up, he once again looked in on his bride and recognized her peaceful slumber. He didn't want to disturb her. He left a loving note and promised to return by 9 am. It was currently 7:30 am.

Lazlo added a log to the fire and headed out in search of Peder.

His quest was short-lived as he located Peder almost immediately.

"Good morning, my friend!" Lazlo enthusiastically greeted Peder. "Might I borrow some of your time this morning?" The two men shook hands in greeting.

Lazlo explained to Peder what he had hoped to do regarding opening a research facility. He wanted it to be here, near the village, possibly even on the existing grounds of the old base. Lazlo imagined the Army must have had medical facilities on site. One which could be refurbished. As the mayor, Peder would know the rules and regulations for an outsider to gain legal access to live on this oversized island. Lazlo wanted to make these things happen as soon as possible. Money was no object if, in fact, anything needed to be rented, leased, or purchased. He would leave a substantial deposit for this when he returned to Spain.

"What would be the chance of having a nice cabin built somewhere up on the hillside?" Lazlo asked Peder while pointing at the mountains. "Once again, I will pay whatever is necessary."

Peder assured Lazlo that it could be done. He would need to pick an exact spot for this construction. It is the way the country keeps Greenland for Greenlanders. But like so many other places, "money talks".

After you have breakfast with your lovely wife, plan on taking a tour with me to pick a location for your lab. I am confident that there is a perfect place here for you. "We could be neighbors!" beamed Peder.

Lazlo reminded Peder about what he saw on the newspaper headline that was faxed to his office. "Remember the goddess?" he questioned.

Peder laughed just a bit, "That was real?" Peder thought it was some sort of publicity stunt.

Lazlo assured him that it was real. "This is what I do, my friend… this is who I am." He then explained his theories and how he expected his research would benefit the world as we know it.

"The goddess has already been here on this base. Her name is Hecate." Then, Lazlo pointed out that someone had already broken into his room. He gave Peder the details of the break-in.

"So, the door was locked, but she still came around. She wrote a message on a fogged mirror in the bathroom. It was a name. That's it. I keep racking my brain as to what it could mean. The only thing that makes sense to me is *who* this person in the mirror really is. Hecate works in strange ways. Blaustein is a Jewish millionaire from Baltimore, Maryland. He *is* affiliated with the government. Hecate advised me to get rid of some magical gemstones that I inherited." Lazlo was thinking out loud as he pieced the puzzle together in front of Peder. Then it suddenly hit him like a ton of bricks.

"Hecate has already selected a buyer! The deal is as good as done except for setting a price, and truth be told, that too is probably already set in stone." Lazlo was amazed at yet another strange chain of events. He needed to contact this individual and move things along as quickly as possible.

Peder listened intently, not really knowing if all of this was believable or if this Somogyi fellow was a bit nuts. He liked Lazlo. His heart told him to believe. Peder had witnessed a few things in his lifetime living under the Aurora that couldn't be explained. Perhaps this facility to study strange happenings would be a good one. Unless somehow proven otherwise, Peder was going to believe him and assist in any way possible.

Lazlo told Peder that he and Maria would finish their honeymoon week enjoying the serenity and the people of Kangerlussuaq. He wanted to look around in the daytime, and leave the remaining evenings for…well, you know, honeymooning! Peder laughed.

Lazlo advised Peder to figure out a total on their bill in advance. Lazlo was clear that it was acceptable to round up the numbers on the cost for meals, fuel for the 'Weasel', and other services and fees. He simply wanted to make sure that everything was covered and that everyone was more than satisfied with how he and Maria treated their debts. Lazlo left Peder to complete this task as he went back to the room to check on Maria.

Upon returning to his room, Lazlo was greeted at the door by his loving bride, once again wrapped in a towel. She threw her arms around his neck and kissed him passionately on the mouth! The newlyweds retired to the warmth of their cocoon of fur and made love for the next hour. They recovered happily together both feeling a sensation of peace and contentment like they had never experienced before. This truly was love.

Lazlo remembered Peder suddenly and jumped to his feet!

"I forgot about Peder! I left him at the desk figuring out our bill for the week! Sorry, Maria, I feel like an idiot!"

Lazlo got dressed quickly. Maria did the same. She wanted breakfast, anyway.

"If you're okay with it, I decided to pay Peder double on our bill. People here need to know that they can trust us and that our desire to become a part of the community is real. Our money is good, and my funds, 'our funds', are going to grow a great deal in the very near future. I can feel it! Are you okay with this?"

Maria agreed. Her husband truly was pure of heart.

Hand-in-hand they left the room and went to the front desk to speak to Peder. Lazlo apologized for his delay.

"There is no problem, Mr. Lazlo. You are on your honeymoon. One should expect nothing less." Lazlo could see that Peder had actually blushed at the end of that last statement. Lazlo felt his own cheeks flush just a bit at the thought of it. He chuckled to himself as Maria pulled herself more tightly onto his arm.

"So what's the damage, my friend? Personally, whatever it is you haven't charged enough! Your service is unmatched and more important is that you make us feel like family. That means a lot to us."

Peder slid the bill over the countertop for Lazlo to review it. In a second, without really taking the time to review it, Lazlo passed it back to Peder and said, "Double it!"

"Yes, sir! Thank you, Mr. Lazlo! You are more than generous!" Peder couldn't believe his eyes! "So, how about breakfast?! You two look hungry!"

Peder escorted Maria and Lazlo to a table and handed them their menus. Maria asked for a coffee and Lazlo ordered a hot chocolate. He delivered their drinks and took their orders. Maria asked for a bowl of fresh fruit, (labeled in season surprisingly), a bowl of cornflakes, and an English muffin. Lazlo on the other hand, ordered the "Wham Slam" breakfast! It was the breakfast of choice for big eaters with ham, bacon, sausage links, toast, hash brown potatoes, 2 eggs, and orange juice.

Maria smiled at him and shook her head as if to say that eating like that would kill him one day. She held her tongue.

"What? I'm a growing boy and in this cold, I need the calories for energy!" Lazlo was slightly embarrassed but not enough to change his order. Maria was surprised that he skipped the blueberry pie. She then thought, *we're on vacation. Let him enjoy himself. But when we get home he'll need to be more careful.*

Lazlo then signaled Peder to come back to the table. "I really need to speak with you after we finish breakfast. I need a favor and your expertise." Lazlo then took a big bite of his slice of ham that had arrived just seconds earlier from another waiter who was assisting Peder.

"This place runs like clockwork," commented Lazlo. "Amazing."

Twenty minutes later, Peder arrived to speak with Lazlo and Maria.

"So, what's up Doc?" Peder thought his joke was funny. Maria rolled her eyes.

Lazlo responded with, "Hello, my friend. Excellent meal as always. As mentioned, I need a favor. So, how hard would it be to find a phone number for me stateside and place a call from here to Baltimore, Maryland? Hopefully today? I know that I am asking a great deal of you. So, thank you in advance."

Peder smiled and said that would be possible. The military personnel still assigned here were communication experts and had the latest tools of their trade. "I doubt that they would even charge you because they use radio waves. Not phone lines. We'll drop by and see them on our tour!"

"Excellent!" Lazlo was excited to get things started. This project was going to be his new baby, and he wanted everything to be perfect.

The empty structures were a short walk from the restaurant, so the three new friends took a leisurely stroll to a large building that was once the hub of operations here years ago. It was quite large. Once inside the cavernous space, Maria and Lazlo could see that the interior offices had been constructed for medical use. Exam rooms, x-ray, physical therapy, everything was still labeled by signage. The furniture, although very dusty, was still intact. It was just dirty. The waiting room was still there. It was everything that he would need to get started. Except for more specialized equipment.

"This is awesome," shouted Lazlo from across the room. "So, let's go meet the US Army!"

Peder led the way. They walked the length of the main building while digesting every observation that they had made. They exited the structure but immediately entered another facility nearby. This one was actively being used by the military.

Peder handled the introductions. Most of the soldiers were just lounging around, passing the time. They knew of Lazlo and his reputation and wanted to help him out.

Lazlo was surprised to see that the base was not just the Army. Duties here were also shared by the US Air Force. Peder introduced Maria and Lazlo to many people today, too many faces to remember, but finally, they were greeted by the man in charge. He was in the Air Force. "Master Sergeant Robert J. Applefielt at your service, sir! What brings you to this part of the world?"

Peder jumped in and explained the situation, the possible research lab, and the upcoming construction of a house for the couple. The men became excited at the mention of the house. Applefielt acknowledged their reaction by saying, "Mr. Lazlo…or Dr. Lazlo, I have an excellent construction crew here. Even one 'sea-bee' was assigned here, somehow. We think that he got caught 'boning' the captain's daughter in the States and got sent…" (He stopped in his tracks and looked at Maria.) "I'm sorry ma'am. I truly apologize. We don't get many female visitors in these parts. Again, my apologies. It won't happen again." Maria laughed and they moved on with the conversation.

"We'd love to build it for you, sir! And we're fast too! These guys are bored."

Lazlo was thrilled! "So, let's do it!"

Lazlo addressed the group. "Gentlemen, this is all fantastic information, but it's not why we're here this morning," Lazlo explained that Peder thought they could help with an intracontinental phone call. Greenland to Baltimore, Maryland. And the number would need to be located.

Private Anthony Liberteesta, of the US Army, responded quickly with a strong New York, Italian accent, "Piece of freaking cake! Shit man, I can do that with my freaking eyes closed!"

"Well, okay then," said Lazlo. "Let's get this party started."

Peder was smiling and those rosy cheeks of his glowed. "What did I tell you, Mr. Lazlo? You, see? We'll make it happen. And quickly!"

Lazlo provided the name of Jacob Blaustein to Anthony. He owned AMOCO Gas Company in Baltimore, Maryland. That was all that Lazlo had.

Private Liberteesta wasn't kidding. He had secured the phone number in less than 5 minutes! Then he asked Lazlo if he wanted to place the call now. "It's 10 AM here, so it's 7 AM there. It's your call."

What's the chance I'd catch him this early? Thought Lazlo.

"Oh, what the hell! Give it a try."

Anthony said okay and fired up the transmitter.

The phone rang and was picked up by a military operator. Anthony gave her the information to connect the call. The phone rang again, 6 times. Finally, a man answered the call and said, "Hello, Jacob Blaustein speaking."

Lazlo hesitated for a second but recovered and introduced himself, "Hello, sir. My name is Dr. Lazlo Joseph Somogyi. You might have heard of me."

Blaustein couldn't help himself and spoke without thinking, "My good man, you're becoming quite famous after your wedding pictures went worldwide! That was amazing!"

Lazlo wanted to keep this as simple as possible. "Mr Blaustein, I need working capital to construct a research lab in the polar north. You have the money that could assist me. You also know of the goddess, Hecate, and her validity. I believe that she contacted you about some very special gemstones in my possession. If you visited the display in DC, the *Hope Diamond* is a fake. You may already know that. I have the original. I also have 11 other stones cut from the '*King Louis Blue*'.

There are records of this kept by the late Dr. Ledbetter. The stones are for sale. I believe you'll be interested."

"How much?" Asked Blaustein.

"Well…as you are aware, they are priceless. But everything has its price. Mine is 150 million dollars.

The room went silent.

"I will be in Spain in the next few days. I will call you again for your answer. If you are not interested, I'll take them elsewhere. I'll contact you next Tuesday. Please have a wonderful week."

Lazlo signaled to Anthony with a knife-like motion across his throat to end the call. It was done.

The men in the room were amazed.

"Damn, you are good!" said Anthony.

Lazlo hugged Maria and thanked the team for their help. He left $100 on the table and told them to have a few drinks on him.

Score! Lazlo Somogyi just scored another winning goal!

Lazlo, Maria, and Peder left the building together. Peder, too, was very impressed with his new friend!

The Oil Man

CHAPTER 33

In Washington DC, Jacob Blaustein was taking his time enjoying the various exhibits of the Smithsonian Institution. He tried to make visits a routine part of his life because, generally speaking, his career choice was a hectic one. The displays in the nation's capital relaxed him.

Today he was visiting the Botanical Gardens. Jacob enjoyed growing things. Whether the project was growing flowers or growing a company in the business world, he seemed to have a knack for both.

Jacob loved orchids! They amazed him. And how they could simply start growing anywhere, like on a rock, without soil or the nutrients that other plants needed to grow. The roots would attach where their seeds landed and absorb water and other essentials to stay alive. Once established they would produce their prize to show off to the world! The most beautiful flowers on the planet were orchids.

Many people tried to grow them in their homes without success. Usually, the caretaker would smother them with too much attention. Any good botanist needs to know the needs of his subject before risking the death of their charge. Jacob hated death.

Jacob seemed to compare his own life to that of the epiphytic wonders that he loved so much.

Jacob Blaustein was born to a Jewish family living in Baltimore, Maryland in September 1892. His father was Louis Blaustein. Jacob was an active supporter of human rights, especially of Jewish people, which explains his extreme distaste for suffering and death. He was a delegate to the United Nations under five US presidents. He was also a lover of fine art and was known to collect works of Vincent van Gogh.

As a child, Jacob delivered kerosene on a 270-gallon horse-drawn wagon with his father Louis. Eventually, after attending several colleges in the Baltimore region, he and his father founded the American Oil Company in Baltimore. The year was 1910. By 1922, AMOCO was formally incorporated. Jacob was 30 years old.

Needless to say, Jacob was on the road to becoming a millionaire at a fairly young age. He was currently 76 years old as he wandered through the orchid greenhouse that displayed his natural treasures.

Jacob was also pure of heart, and he loved his fellow man. Although he was never a follower of the paranormal, he was about to become connected to it in ways never imagined.

Until very recently, Jacob served under the current president known by very few as *Landslide*. Prior to his untimely death by electrocution in the Oval Office, there was talk of him working on a military project that many may have viewed as paranormal. Details were sketchy at best, but Jacob had heard rumors of the coveted *Hope Diamond* being somehow connected to the story.

Oddly, as Jacob strolled through the orchid exhibit, he couldn't get the thought of the cursed diamond out of his head. It had been years since he visited the display at the Museum of Natural History in Washington. He envisioned the exquisite gem in his mind, trying to recall every detail. Eventually, the urge for him to revisit the display redirected the remainder of his plans on this day. He found himself walking to the museum so he could have a fresh look at the diamond. It wasn't that far at all, even for a man his age.

A short walk through the mall grounds had him entering the front door and heading for the gemstone exhibits. Jacob had also heard about the death of Dr. James Vernon Ledbetter while assisting with some private research on the giant blue diamond. His curiosity started to peak.

Jacob entered the room and stopped to read a sign that described the history of the diamond and the evil curse that was attached to it.

The Smithsonian currently valued the jewel at $100 million! He scoffed to himself because he knew that it could never be sold. This was just the ploy of an insurance company trying to impress the visitors at the display. He slowly meandered towards the heavily lighted showcase and stood in front of it, taking in its grandeur.

A security officer wandered by and made eye contact with Jacob.

Jacob spoke to him. "Excuse me. Do you know the scientist who conducted experiments on this stone when Dr. Ledbetter died? I work for our government too and heard talk of the tragedy. Might I be able to speak to him please?" Jacob was fishing. He already knew most of the information except for the location of Lazlo when he made the call. It couldn't hurt to learn more if possible.

The officer was obviously uncomfortable with the subject and shifted his body weight from foot to foot. He no longer made eye contact with Jacob but looked at the floor. Jacob sensed his discomfort.

"Might I have his name? That's all…"

After several seconds the guard conceded and responded, "Sure, what can it hurt? Dr. Lazlo Somogyi. But he ain't here. They say he's in Spain on business for the museum.

"Oh, I see," said Jacob. "Thank you for your time and dedicated service." Jacob nodded his head in farewell as the officer moved on. Odd fellow, he thought. That gentleman seemed somehow terrified of the subject. I really wonder what this Somogyi fellow was doing.

Jacob turned to admire the beauty of the *Hope*. A small crowd of children on a school field trip wandered up to the showcase to view the stone. Jacob barely saw what at first he thought was his imagination, but the lighting changed from a shadow cast by the children, and for an instant, the diamond disappeared! As quickly as he blinked his eyes it was back in place! No one else noticed.

This was not the *Hope Diamond*! It was an elaborate illusion of the authentic piece of history! Jacob was stunned! He was about to report his findings to the management of the display when he heard a distinct female voice in his head that simply said, Dr. Lazlo Somogyi. It repeated a second time. There was no doubt what he heard. What was going on here? His curiosity was overwhelming with an admitted touch of fear in his heart. Was this connected to the rumors of paranormal testing on-site? The seed was planted. Jacob Blaustein left the facility as quickly as he could.

Once again, he heard that distinctive female voice that seemed to be guiding him. Granada, Spain. That was all that She shared.

It was as good of a clue as any and a solid place to start. Let's locate Dr. Lazlo Somogyi.

Jacobs' questions were technically a form of reconnaissance in regards to determining who Lazlo really was. He had briefly spoken to him only once and really had no idea where he called from. Jacob was not a fool and his business successes reflected his abilities to read others. He decided to take this new information and use it to the best of his abilities.

His driver was waiting and Jacob rode away in his limousine towards Pennsylvania Avenue. What the hell had just happened?

Forty-six

CHAPTER 34

The week seemed to come to an end much more quickly than it began and the newlyweds were getting ready to head back to Granada.

Lazlo left a substantial deposit with Peder so construction on the home could start immediately. November in Greenland was not a good time to build. But with trained military personnel and some help from the gods, Lazlo was confident that it could be done. As an afterthought regarding research equipment, Lazlo asked Peder if he had ever heard of Kirlian photography. He hadn't, so Lazlo wrote some information down on a piece of paper.

"See what you can find on this item. If you come up empty, have the boys make one for me. It'll be fun for them," Lazlo laughed.

"Yes, sir, Mr Lazlo. It'll be my pleasure. I expect that we will see you again soon?" Peder truly hated to see them go. This is a very interesting couple.

"Oh, I almost forgot something," said Peder as he reached under the counter. "This just arrived today when your plane came in. I ordered it when you first arrived here at the hotel."

It was a copy of the Baltimore Sun newspaper dated November 7th, 1967. "Thanks," Lazlo said. "This will give me something to read on the plane."

Maria and Lazlo said their farewells to Peder and headed to the plane. They were greeted outside by almost every employee *and* the military men that they met earlier in the week.

Anthony handed Lazlo a piece of paper with numbers written on it. "You forgot this! You can't reach that guy on Tuesday without it. Great meeting you, Doc! Good luck with that $150 million!"

Maria and Lazlo boarded the plane for the trip home. They would both miss seeing the colored lights of the northern skies. But they would return soon enough and start a new chapter in their lives together. Lazlo knew that it would be an interesting one.

They located their seats and settled in. Lazlo forgot to ask Hecate to aid him regarding his fear of flying. As usual, he was quite nervous.

"Hey, Maria. Let me try something. Sort of a test." He reached over to her and placed his right hand over her ring. Lazlo concentrated on the image of the goddess. The ring flashed and suddenly Hecate was present in spirit.

Lazlo didn't even need to ask. He and Maria heard her say… "*Done.*" And she was gone.

Maria looked at Lazlo with questions in her eyes. "Well…do you feel different?" Lazlo wasn't sure.

The pilot requested that everyone fasten their seatbelts. Maria complied but suddenly Lazlo stood up and went to the door of the cockpit. He knocked and addressed the pilots before the plane started to taxi onto the runway. One of the pilots recognized him from television and newspaper stories.

"Dr. Lazlo! We didn't realize that you were on this flight!"

The pilot spoke to the flight attendant. "It's okay Michele. He's good."

Looking back at Lazlo, the pilot invited him inside and pointed to a fold-down seat attached to the bulkhead. Have a seat, what can we do for you?

Lazlo told both pilots that he had only been in an airplane on a few occasions and admittedly had a case of nerves both times. As he spoke, Lazlo noticed that he was becoming more relaxed the closer they got to actual takeoff. Lazlo continued, "I just thought if I came up front I could really see everything."

The plane was set for take-off.

The lead pilot, Captain Franklin Darda, suggested that Lazlo switch places with his co-pilot, William.

The flight tower authorized Captain Darda for departure. William and Lazlo switched places.

"You can put your hands on the wheel, or yoke, but don't apply pressure. Feel what I do from my side."

Darda reached for the throttle and brought the engines up to take-off rpm's while releasing the brakes. The plane accelerated quickly, and Lazlo could feel the wheel moving closer to his abdomen as Captain Darda coaxed the giant bird to raise its nose. Lazlo noted the foot pedals that also controlled the level of the plane as it climbed. He felt no fear!

This was incredible.

Darda leveled the plane.

"Go ahead. Take the wheel and get a feel for her," Captain Darda said to Lazlo. "Nothing bad will happen with me sitting here." Darda released the controls to Lazlo. The plane gradually started to climb, which was normal as most first-time flight attempts found the new operator not using the gauges. Flying at high elevations offers no reference points so they unknowingly climb higher. Darda showed Lazlo how to correct this.

"Nice job, Mr. Lazlo…very nice job." Captain Darda was actually very impressed with Lazlo's first lesson. "You're a natural, my friend. Have you ever considered learning to fly?"

Lazlo thought of Hecate and all the other god figures throughout history. Was it possible that all historic figures in the world obtained their greatness as easily as simply asking the gods for their blessings? It seemed too easy and it was beginning to change his view on the religions of the world.

Lazlo refocused on Captain Darda and his question.

"In the past, it never crossed my mind. But after today? Who knows?"

Lazlo thanked the pilots for allowing him the honor and experience to fly their plane.

Lazlo joined Maria and was grinning from ear to ear.

"What's got you smiling like Christmas morning?"

"I just flew the damn plane! No kidding! Just after take-off! That was me!" Lazlo added, "The pilot said that I was a natural and should consider training. It was so cool!"

Maria knew that, once again, this was Hecate. Without a doubt. "Ask and ye shall receive. Well, with Hecate, responses to human desires are answered quickly!"

This relationship with Hecate still made Maria somewhat nervous. While the goddess seemed trustworthy with good intentions, Maria also knew how mercilessly she could take human life when it suited her. Would she continue to honor her bond with Lazlo? Hopefully, Lazlo stayed in her good graces.

Maria had already started reading the book on falconry that she was reading on the flight into Greenland. She hadn't had the chance to touch it again, until now. Lazlo could tell that she would be preoccupied for some time.

He decided to read his 2-week-old *Baltimore Sun* newspaper. Lazlo told Maria these things were quite large and contained loads of information that covered a multi-state area. Clayton subscribed to the company for a time and told Lazlo stories about the paper being so thick and heavy, the Sunday edition couldn't be delivered by a paperboy in one day! The interior pages, cartoons, ads, and local information come on Saturday. The main body of the paper was delivered on Sunday! In its entirety, the paper was over 3 inches thick! Lazlo figured that it would more than last him the flight and he'd pass it on to his family after arriving in Granada.

Lazlo made himself comfortable and went straight to the sports page. He looked at the pro football stuff that praised the *Baltimore Colts* and Johnny Unitas. That man sure knew how to play ball. Gradually Lazlo made his way to college sports for a look at his *Alma mater*. It appeared that most of the teams were doing well.

When Lazlo tossed the center section to the floor some hours later, he couldn't help but notice a story on the front page under the headlines. It wasn't the main story, but it made the front page in

Baltimore, which is a pretty big deal.

What caught his eye was the words 'West Virginia' in the title. The town was Point Pleasant. That was only 75 miles from Ward.

Lazlo couldn't stop staring at the artist's rendition of a figure that was seen on a steel bridge. It appeared to be a giant owl, almost the size of a man. Witnesses reported many people feared the creature and fled in terror. Others, however, said they felt an overwhelming mode of peace as they gazed upon the owl. One woman reported that she felt it was trying to assist them in some strange way. Almost like a messenger from God. This was *not* the first reported sighting. Locals reported similar sightings on 'The Silver Bridge' that connects West Virginia to Ohio.

Lazlo's mind wandered. In his mind's-eye, he saw Christmas decorations lining a snow-covered street. The number 46 kept repeating itself in his mind. Over and over. 46.

Maria brought him back to reality.

"Lazlo! Wake up! What is 46? You kept repeating it over and over."

Lazlo said he didn't know.

All that Lazlo could really remember was the giant owl! The wingspan was said to be eight feet! And the number 46.

He thought of Hecate. This had to be her doing. But what was she trying to say? Lazlo felt that this was a message somehow. But for what? It would torment him. He didn't like getting little bits and pieces of visionary messaging. It was emotionally draining and at times very hard to recover from.

Lazlo fell asleep and dreamt of a giant owl. It was extremely large and appeared to be perched on top of a metal bridge that crossed a very cold-looking river. Lazlo's feeling was one of concern as if he was somehow receiving the thoughts of the actual bird. What could a giant owl be saying to him, or anyone else? It just didn't make sense to him. Why was the owl concerned? Forty-six! The number 46 had also returned to his mind.

The image of the owl changed and its eyes began to turn red. Glowing, bright red. Then its legs grew longer until it was standing like a man. Like the dark silhouette of a man with formidable wings, a Dark Angel?

Maria woke him. "You are drenched in sweat! Where were you?!" Lazlo looked terrified.

Maria coached Lazlo back to sleep by rubbing his hair and massaging his shoulder. She told him to have happy thoughts like playing with his dog, Blackie. Bring back the happy memories. That's what her Nana would do for her as a child if a nightmare occurred. She was right, it worked. From that point on Lazlo slept like a baby.

Hours later, Lazlo woke up to the sound of jet engines reversing thrust for breaking and then the rumble of the tires on the tarmac as the plane was landing. The plane started to taxi towards the terminal to offload and refuel.

"Damn it!" he said as he stood up. "I wanted to land this 'big bird' today! Oh well. Maybe next time."

Captain Darda left the cockpit and approached Lazlo and Maria. Lazlo introduced his bride. Darda shook hands with Lazlo, telling him how happy he was that they had talked, and he added, "I trust that you'll be making this trip more than once? If so, I look forward to showing you more and introducing you to bringing 'Big Betty' down to earth. I think you'll really like that."

Lazlo smiled and said, "Great! I can't wait!"

Maria and Lazlo left the plane holding hands.

Family Reunion
CHAPTER 35

Clayton met Lazlo and Maria at the airport. He was driving BJ. Maria looked at Lazlo with some confusion on her face because BJ was a two-seater and really couldn't even carry a large suitcase. Clayton jumped out of the car and hugged the newlyweds.

After a few minutes of conversation, another Cordova Valdez car pulled up. It was Diego driving a black four-door sedan with Papa Lorenzo in the front passenger seat.

Lorenzo went to Maria first and embraced her. "My daughter. You are a married woman now. We are so proud of you." Diego greeted Lazlo like a son. They embraced while Diego told Lazlo that his family was waiting for them at the Hacienda.

Clayton was still standing near BJ, obviously not wanting to give her up. He really did get attached to her while Lazlo was away. Lazlo took notice of this and called to him from a car's length away, "Hey Clayton! Why don't you drive Maria home in BJ for me? It would be a huge favor. I need to talk to Lorenzo and Diego about something very important."

Clayton was surprised. He managed to get out the word, "Sure." Maria knew exactly what Lazlo was doing, and her husband really seemed to have a way to make people like him. This ability was just pure Lazlo and she saw it way before he ever connected with Hecate. Maria believed that Hecate had seen it too.

BJ, Maria, and Clayton took off.

Lazlo, Lorenzo, and Diego got into the sedan and followed.

Diego started the conversation with small talk about Greenland. Was everything on schedule? Did you like it? Lazlo answered all that he could but advised that once he and Maria settled in, they would tell everyone about their exciting visit to Greenland.

After a few moments of silence, Lazlo said.

"I'm selling the *Hope Diamond* and 11 of the Brothers! Maria, of course, owns the *Joseph Stone Ring*."

Diego's jaw dropped. "*Really?*" Lorenzo could hardly believe what he just heard. Lazlo continued.

"So, I released Hecate from Her diamond prison. It was the right choice. Even in the stone, Hecate was a danger.

Maria and I came to know her. She shared much with us. We shared Her pain, and She has shared pleasures with us like you cannot imagine. Hecate truly is a kind goddess from the ancient past."

Lorenzo and Diego listened.

"When I released her from the stone, all the diamond curses were removed. The *Hope* became dead. It's a beautiful gem worth a great deal of money, but otherwise it is useless. Likewise, the brother stones. They no longer house any power at all. Only the *Joseph Stone* in Maria's ring maintains life. Only her ring can directly contact the goddess."

Lazlo continued, "The Smithsonian boasted a value of 100 million American dollars just for the *Hope*. I figure the other remaining stones should be worth another 50 million. Hecate found a millionaire buyer stateside. We talked on the telephone, and he's interested in my asking price. I need to call him this Tuesday to finalize and plan for the purchase. But I need your help."

"This sale would make me independently wealthy. From a poor coal miner's son to a multi-millionaire! I could pay off all my debts, take care of Maria in the way that she deserves, start my research facility in Greenland, and last, but not least, start a family. We'll make you a grandfather, eh, Lorenzo? I see wonderful things in our future. All of us."

After a moment, Papa Lorenzo spoke, "From everything that you said, it sounds like much has happened very quickly. I am impressed with your diligence and your natural ability to communicate with people. After your wedding display, many people in Granada have been suggesting that you seek political office. It might not be a bad idea. For that matter, it might be an extremely good one! So, what is it that you think I can do for you? I speak for Diego too. How can we help you?"

Lazlo was hesitant as he felt like he was asking a great deal of these two gentlemen. But his plan, if it succeeded, would provide for not only Maria's future but for all of the unborn Somogyi/Cordova Valdez bloodline for many, many years. Lazlo sheepishly made an honest statement that truly touched both men.

"I have no idea how to collect 150 million dollars. Seriously… this guy is supposed to fly to Spain for the purchase if he goes through with it. I hoped to put him up at the Hacienda as a show of our family success, and wealth. Then with a security presence show him the stones. If all goes well, what then? Gold bars or silver would take a cargo plane to move. I certainly couldn't take a check until after I knew it was cleared. Is there a better way? I feel somewhat foolish, not knowing. But I simply do not. I need your help."

Lorenzo said, "Ah, my son…that is actually a *very* good question. There are different ways to achieve this final goal in a transaction. Most can be very time-consuming, but I prefer a more simple method if possible. Is your buyer a company owner of some kind?"

Lazlo confirmed that he was indeed. He owned the AMOCO Oil Company. His current estimated wealth is 700 million dollars.

Even Diego was impressed with these numbers

Lorenzo continued, "Company stocks. I imagine that most of his money is in stocks and he lives on an extended credit line that is matched by his banks. You can't keep all that kind of cash in one place. And there is no need. There are also many tax shelters that aid in the manipulation of large sums of money."

"I would ask him on the phone, point blank. Tell him that you expect full payment at delivery of the stones in AMOCO stocks. He'll do it. The stock most likely will also increase in value as AMOCO continues to grow. This, in my opinion, would be the path to choose."

Lazlo was surprised because he understood every word and every scenario mentioned. He was learning fast.

Tuesday wasn't very far away. Lazlo looked forward to completing this deal.

Lorenzo added, "You will need our lawyers present to oversee your sale. They will validate the documents. You will become a millionaire in that moment. Congratulations!" Lorenzo and Diego both shook Lazlo's hand.

Later that day, Maria and Lazlo made their rounds catching up with family and friends around the property. Maria wanted to see her Momma, first and foremost.

They located Juana outside in the garden. Juana had selected every plant over the years. Every flower, every bush, and every tree. She also supervised the installation of each one. Juana was quite proud of that fact. In addition, she hired each gardener to care for her floral babies.

"Momma, how are you?" Maria threw her arms around her and they embraced one another for what seemed like minutes!

Lazlo stood by at first, waiting for the chance to say his hello. Juana noticed that Lazlo was politely waiting for a moment of his own. Juana turned and reached for her new son-in-law and pulled him into the family hug.

"Welcome home, my son. Welcome home. We've missed you so much. And I know that your family has missed you, too! Eztar speaks of her Lazlo every day. You should visit her now. She has had some concerns about you while you were gone. Perhaps a mother's intuition?"

Lazlo returned the embrace with both mother and daughter and for the first time in all of his days visiting the Hacienda, he truly felt like he now belonged. Lazlo's family was growing before his eyes. That gave him great pleasure and a renewed sense of purpose.

After minutes of conversation, Maria and Lazlo excused themselves and left to visit *his* family.

Eztar must have sensed Lazlo's arrival because before he and Maria were within 100 feet, she came running out the door of her new home to greet her son and daughter!

"Slow down, Momma, slow down! You'll hurt yourself!" Lazlo was concerned about the speed with which she ran. He thought that she looked years younger in the brief time that he and Maria were away. Admittedly the weeks before the wedding were a blur and Lazlo quickly realized that he hadn't really spent any quality time with her in over a month. Even before that, it was limited. He would now make efforts to change that. Lazlo was feeling guilty when he heard the familiar barking. Blackie! He jumped into Lazlo's arms and started to lick Lazlo's face.

"Good boy! Good dog! Yes, I have missed you too!" Blackie's tail never stopped wagging! His human boy was home.

Julius, Janos, and Eleanor were coming out of the house too, with Lucas in tow. Everyone greeted the happy couple. Even servants and staff stopped to watch and to call out their best wishes to the newlyweds. It was good to be home.

Maria invited everyone to dinner at the main house later that evening. She would notify the staff. Nothing fancy she thought. It would just be a good time to bring everyone up to date on the latest news in their lives. She would have someone contact Diego too. And the Sherlous family. Both Lazlo and Maria forgot that the family had stayed in Spain after the wedding, but would be leaving soon.

After kissing Lazlo briefly on the cheek, Maria ran back to Juana to announce her plan. Juana lived for these kinds of events. Formal or informal. It didn't matter. The two of them headed back to the main house arm in arm.

Lazlo watched from afar and smiled. He had picked the right one. His Maria was a keeper.

Between Juana, Maria, and several staff members, everyone was notified, and the event would begin at 6:30 PM. It would be a nice get-together with both families reuniting with their newlyweds. They all had so many questions and Maria had so many stories to tell. It would be a wonderful evening to share their memories.

Diego was the last to enter the Hacienda, moments before 6:30 PM. He walked in to hear Maria finishing a story about her new husband and their honeymoon activities.

"I couldn't believe it! Lazlo had been flying the plane for at least the last 15 minutes! My husband did such a wonderful job that I didn't even know he was piloting until he returned to our seats."

"It was really nothing," Lazlo responded. "But it was a great deal of fun." He settled in with a cold bottle of beer.

Maria added that the pilot of the plane was so impressed with Lazlo that he suggested flight training and officially getting certified to fly. Having access to his own plane would surely aid him in his travels between 3 worlds. Maria thought this was an excellent idea.

The evening progressed with everyone wanting to see the *Joseph Stone Ring* that Maria wore on her left hand. Maria cautioned them not to touch the ring. It really had magical powers!

The dinner bell chimed, "Dinner is served." Everyone went to the dining area, where even on short notice, the staff was able to create a beautiful atmosphere in celebration of the newly married couple. Fresh flowers adorned the corners of the room, and the table settings were fit for royalty. He truly had come a long way since his days in West Virginia. Lazlo also knew that it was all happening because of his family connection to a cursed diamond and a medieval goddess named Hecate.

Everyone enjoyed a fine dinner of local specialties, smoked pomegranate sardines, and Iberian toast, complete with all of the classic side dishes and desserts that were representative of old Granada and Spanish heritage.

The Cordova Valdez wine flowed and tongues began to loosen, and actual questions about their honeymoon were asked.

Clayton was already drinking his 5th beer when he asked Lazlo,

"So, buddy…what the hell did you do with all those diamonds, man? We all know about the one on my cousin's finger, but what about the other ones? They're all magical, right? I mean…that was one hell of a show that you put on at the wedding! You guys sure caused a stir."

Lazlo sensed that Clayton was jealous.

Lazlo then remembered that Clayton had quit college to be near Maria and himself. That was a huge gesture that Lazlo had simply forgotten. He saw Diego and Lorenzo watching intently to see how he handled his cousin.

"You know something, Clayton? I have really missed you. It was a mistake not to take you to Greenland with us as security. I honestly thought that you would hate the cold. Next time, you travel with us. We could have used you there with your watchful eyes. Your question about the stones is a good one. Once again, your natural abilities have kept you a step ahead of the game. Deduction. Yes, I am impressed."

Clayton sat up a little straighter and smiled.

The table was quiet, everyone listening to Lazlo.

"I am selling the stones. The *Hope Diamond* and all of the Brother stones, except the one Maria wears. The price is 150 million dollars, and a buyer has been arranged. I am calling him tomorrow to finalize the deal. I am confident that he will have them in his possession as soon as possible. This is where your services will once again be needed, Clayton. I want you on the security team when we make the transfer. And not to worry…the diamonds are now dead. They no longer possess any paranormal powers. Only Maria's *Joseph Stone Ring* can claim that reality."

Lazlo hesitated.

"So, are you in? I really want you to be a part of this!"

"Fucking 'A', I'm in. How could I ever say no to my best friend?"

Lazlo made brief eye contact with Diego and Lorenzo as they raised their wine glasses to him while nodding in approval. *Bravo Sir Lazlo! Bravo! Once again, your quick wit has proven that you are a skilled political opponent*, thought Diego.

Everyone had a wonderful time that night. Eztar was still in shock over the 150 million dollars! Could it really be true? She looked to the sky and said, "*Thank you, Papa. Thank you for doing this for your family. Your sacrifice will never be forgotten.*"

The road for the *King Louis Blue* had been a long one. It was a long and bloody road surrounded by death. Somehow, Eztar knew that her Lazlo had broken the cycle.

Lazlo and Maria met with the Sherlous family after dinner to talk privately. Lazlo apologized for not being available, but they understood.

Martha told him how proud they were of what he was doing with his life. They would talk more, but Lazlo thanked them for everything once again.

Ending a good party can always be somewhat difficult as friends always like to linger.

Lazlo, Diego, and Lorenzo knew that the morning would arrive all too soon and Lazlo had to place his call to Baltimore first thing in the morning.

Lazlo was confident that the sale would happen without issue. But there would still be items needing coordination. Security, lawyers, lodging for Jacob Blaustein, and company. Sure, he could afford a hotel, but Lazlo thought that making him a guest would be wise, all things considered. These things would be discussed with Lorenzo and Diego. Tomorrow.

Tonight, Lazlo wanted some more time with his bride.

Renaissance Man
CHAPTER 36

Mr. Jacob Blaustein impatiently waited for the anticipated telephone call from Dr. Lazlo Somogyi. Jacob was an early riser and usually arrived at work hours before his employees. While Dr. Somogyi didn't specify a time, he did say Tuesday. And just with the power of deduction, since Somogyi called him early last week, he assumed it would once again be an early call. Jacob had given this offer a great deal of thought and he wanted to own this remarkable piece of history. Considering everything that seemed to have connections to these diamonds, the price was reasonable.

Jacob Blaustein was a collector. He casually paid thousands of dollars for certain living orchid species and owned an elaborate greenhouse to care for them and on occasion, show them off.

His mansion home was decorated with fine art sculptures and oil paintings by the masters. His favorite pieces were by Vincent Van Gogh.

Jacob loved fine jewelry and had a deep appreciation for his ancestral Hebrew relatives that mastered the art of goldsmithing. Presently, he didn't really know all of Lazlo's family history.

Lazlo was holding back the story of László Joseph Biro cutting the stones. He knew that if Blaustein attempted to bargain for a lower price, this information would pique his interest, and as they say, "seal the deal".

Meanwhile, back in Granada, Lazlo, Diego, and Lorenzo were gathering in the Hacienda living room in preparation for Lazlo's call to Blaustein. It was almost 8 AM in Maryland.

Lazlo had intentionally delayed for the sole purpose of making his opponent sweat it out a little longer. He was beginning to understand the power of negotiation more and more each day.

Clayton entered the room casually. He looked at Lazlo and said, "Hey, boss! What say we get this show on the road? I want to see you pocketing your $150 million!"

Lazlo rolled his eyes. "Today I'm simply trying to hook a fish! Have a seat."

Lazlo sat down and placed the telephone on his lap. He closed his eyes and exhaled. He imagined calling Hecate to him through the ring, but Maria was still sleeping soundly. Even so, he concentrated on the image of his goddess and willed her presence into his consciousness. In moments, she was with him in spirit.

Fear not, my love. The task is already complete. The words of Hecate soothed him. Lazlo relaxed.

Lazlo dialed the number provided by Anthony in Greenland. The phone rang several times and on the 3rd ring, it was answered by Jacob Blaustein.

"Jacob Blaustein speaking. How can I be of service?"

Lazlo responded in a relaxed manner that Jacob did not expect on a business deal of this magnitude.

"Jacob, my friend. Good morning. I trust the weather in Baltimore is dismal as usual?" Lazlo laughed at his own joke. "Seriously, I lived in the northeast most of my life and always hated the weather."

Lazlo didn't really give Jacob a chance to respond. He wanted to control the conversation, and he did it well.

Lazlo continued, "Assuming that you really are a serious buyer for my little treasures, I wanted to invite you to Spain as my guest. My in-laws are of the Cordova Valdez family here in Granada and you will be welcomed with open arms. You can stay with us at the Hacienda, dine in luxury, enjoy the sights, and add to your personal collection all at the same time. And I will also enlighten you as to how the diamonds fell into my possession. Lazlo stopped and let Jacob respond.

Jacob was more on the soft-spoken side and quietly responded to Lazlo with the following-- "Dr. Lazlo, under the circumstances you seem to hold me over a barrel. You have a one-of-a-kind item that I desire. If everything you say is true, the price is fair. But I would like to have the stones examined to confirm their authenticity. We can test the material compounds of each of the stones to confirm they all originated from the *Hope*, or perhaps the original *King Louis Blue*. Once again, if proven authentic, I believe that we, as they say, have a deal."

Clayton jumped up out of his chair and quietly restrained himself while acting like he just scored a goal! It was a silent SCORE!

"Very good," said Lazlo. "When would you like to visit and complete the transaction? I am available most of this week."

Blaustein wanted to complete the sale as badly as Lazlo but for different reasons. The sooner the better, he was thinking.

"What about on Thursday, in two days? Would that be feasible?" asked Blaustein.

Lazlo agreed and requested that Jacob notify him as soon as possible. Arrangements for lodging and meals would need to be completed. Lazlo also promised personal limousine service from the airport in Granada to the Hacienda and return.

Jacob said that he was far too kind.

Before ending the call, and while maintaining a kind demeanor, Lazlo briefly commented, "AMOCO stock certificates only. Do we have an understanding?"

"Yes, we do," Jacob responded.

Pleasantries were exchanged that ended the call, and Lazlo sighed heavily while settling back in his chair.

"I need a *freaking* beer!" And he closed his eyes.

Diego was the first to exclaim, "Very, very good, Mr. Lazlo! *Muy bien!*"

Lorenzo added his kind words of support. He was proud of him. His son-in-law was starting to earn his keep and he was doing an extremely good job at handling his business affairs.

Maria just woke up and entered the room. "What's going on?" she said.

Lorenzo answered with a smile, "Maria, I just watched your husband earn 150 million dollars in 10 minutes! By Thursday evening, you could be millionaires! Well done!"

Information was exchanged, times and dates were shared, and the Hacienda was prepared for the arrival of one of the wealthiest oil magnets in the United States. Jacob Blaustein would arrive on his personal jet within hours. The days had passed very quickly. Diego was dispatching three stretch limos to the airport to collect their guests.

Clayton had joined up with the regular security detail that was coordinated by Diego and Lorenzo. A small safe was secured in the living room of the Hacienda so that Lazlo could move the diamonds from Maria's bedroom safe and have them on hand. Two officers would constantly have the safe in their view. Everything was proceeding like clockwork. Lazlo was satisfied.

The phone rang and the group was notified that the limos were on their way with their guests.

From the airport to the Cordova Valdez Hacienda was 20 minutes. Clayton noted their arrival in the main driveway and announced it to the group. Lorenzo was to meet their guests.

"Welcome to my home, Mr. Blaustein. Please call me Lorenzo. My close friends refer to me as 'Papa'." He said this with a smile.

Lorenzo led Jacob and his staff into the main house.

Jacob had not expected such informal treatment. Especially in Spain. It relaxed him. There was a natural spirit of trust in the Hacienda. He liked it and so he began to let down his professional guard.

Lazlo enthusiastically welcomed Jacob into the home. He shook Jacob's hand while introducing himself and then offered a half-hug that would have otherwise been experienced between two friends, not so much between strangers. Lazlo knew very well what he was doing.

Introductions were made around the room, and everyone was seated while staff served beverages.

Jacob Blaustein wasted no time in asking for more details about the diamonds that he was about to purchase.

It would obviously be a lengthy explanation to share the history of the stones with Jacob, but Lazlo believed it was necessary if the exchange was to be completed in good faith. For the grand sum of 150 million dollars, Jacob had the right to know every detail. Lazlo began.

"The story begins in Europe after the large blue diamond was stolen from a monastery in India. The gem was taken to France and sold to King Louis XIV. He had it cut to be the centerpiece for a scepter that was being created to represent his power and wealth. You might already know some of this history, Mr. Blaustein. I hope that you do."

Jacob Blaustein nodded in agreement.

Lazlo continued his tale.

"King Louis XIV noted in his documents that he experienced a heavenly power when he touched the blue diamond once it was mounted upon his royal scepter. The King also believed that the stone somehow communicated with him and aided him in conflicts between France and other nations. He was personally a believer that the Knights Templar of an earlier time in France acted under a divine godly power that some did not understand. Louis had a great deal of respect for the Knights Templar, based on his personal history with what was being called, *The French Blue*, or the *King Louis Blue*."

Let me add something, if you will, "It was indeed an earlier King of France that had the Templar Knights murdered under accusations of heresy and of being in league with Satan himself. This happened on Friday the 13th, 1302. This is why, even at this moment, people believe that Friday the 13th is a cursed day. It represents bad luck that a reigning King and a leader of the Catholic Church at that time, Pope Clement V, would openly and falsely accuse men of Christ of those sins while sentencing them to death."

Between Lazlo and Jacob, their abilities to tell this part of the tale had everyone in the room mesmerized. Even the kitchen staff had stopped their duties to be enlightened by this lesson in European history. Some had even migrated into the main room and sat on the floor, eager to hear more. Papa Lorenzo smiled at them and encouraged them to stay. Diego noted to himself that this was yet another event that would carry stories to the working class of Granada about Sir Lazlo, and his abilities as a potential leader.

Jacob was amazed, not only at the storytelling but the way the staff sat down to enjoy it. The environment in this home was so pure, and relaxed. Everyone was family. He liked these people and was feeling more comfortable by the minute.

Lazlo continued the tale.

"Eventually the *French Blue* was stolen and lost to time. There were rumors of course, that it went into a private collection of another monarch or was buried somewhere to prevent anyone else from trying to use its magic. Who knows? The world may never actually learn the truth and the history of these events will simply be washed away like the sands of time."

Sir Lazlo took liberty and hesitated his story for dramatic effect. Every eye was on his face and every ear attentively longed to hear his every word.

"Until…," he said. "In 1943 a leader in Nazi Germany, Adolf Hitler, heard about the *French Blue* and its story. Hitler was well connected to the black market and the occult. He lived to rule over others and believed that by collecting supernatural or paranormal items of historical significance he could use them to rule the whole world! He searched the world for the Ark of the Covenant, The Holy Grail, The Spear of Destiny that killed Christ, and yes, the *French Blue*.

Being of Jewish heritage, this part of the tale intrigued Jacob even more. He had family in Europe during the time of these events. Just like Lazlo Joseph Somogyi. *This* was the part of the chain of events regarding the *French Blue* that Jacob had not heard in such detail. Just how did the *Hope Diamond* come to be born? Jacob thought to himself that Lazlo should write a book someday. The world needed to be told.

"Hitler managed to purchase what he believed to be the *French Blue* for reportedly the equivalent of one million American dollars. He was convinced that by *recutting* the diamond, he might accomplish two things. First, he would hide its identity. Second, he believed that he could somehow release the god-like powers and learn to control them for his Nazi War Machine."

"This is where my grandfather was forced into the picture. My namesake, László Joseph Biro, was a gem cutter. Perhaps one of the best in all of Europe. Hitler had him arrested and brought to Germany from Hungary to attempt this feat."

"My grandfather was advised that failure would result in his death and that of his family. László had no choice. He would recut the stone as ordered. Hitler wanted it smaller, but he desired as many other smaller stones as possible. At the time, no one knew how much of the diamond would survive further cuttings. Under Hitler's orders, he proceeded to produce more stones."

"At some point in the beginning stages of the cutting, my grandfather realized the power in the stone. Much like King Louis XIV, it spoke to him. Exactly what was said will never be known. But it changed his life and not for the better. László Biro began the process that took weeks, perhaps months! During the process, he was inundated with ideas. The artist in him needed to create. So, he followed his artistic instinct."

Lazlo Somogyi continued the tale.

"My grandfather used the excess gem material to create 12 more beautiful stones. Due to his Jewish/Hungarian upbringing, the number seemed fitting. I didn't really know for sure if he imagined the twelve tribes and the twelve brothers back then, but I like to think that he did. One thing was for sure, is that he didn't want Hitler to own them. One by one, he smuggled them out of the jeweler's workshop where he slaved. He had enough freedom to come and go but with limitations. His daughter, my Momma Eztar, lived near enough for him to take stones to her one by one. My grandfather cut twelve phony gems to match in color, leaving them in place of the originals. He was discovered and was taken to the gas chamber."

Lazlo stopped for a moment and lowered his head to honor the death of László Joseph Biro.

"My parents, who still live here with us today, escaped Europe with their treasures and fled to America. My Papa, Julius, secured work and a home in the coal mines of Ward, West Virginia. Momma buried the stones under a coal bin near the house and drew a treasure map. And so went on with her life and that of her family. Years later I was born. Not until recently, as an adult, did my mother share the full story and the map. Actually, that was this year. So much time has passed."

Everyone in the room was reverently quiet. Lazlo asked for a beer and most others agreed that a drink would be a good idea. After the staff served the family and their guests, everyone remained seated to hear the rest of the incredible story.

"Well," said Lazlo. "By now everyone in this room knows that the cursed *Hope Diamond* was indeed possessed by an ancient goddess named Hecate. The world witnessed her at the altar during our wedding. She speaks to me like she spoke to others, but she claims that somehow she knows Maria and me from another ancient life-time. She calls Maria her daughter. People who have tried to handle the stones have died. For me, it started with my grandfather. Then old Ben Goldsmith. Dr. Ledbetter. Even the one they call 'Landslide'. Countless others over the centuries, I am sure. We almost lost my Momma, Eztar, and Papa Lorenzo too. But Hecate allowed her power to flow into me and heal them both."

Jacob spoke up and asked something that he simply had to know. "Why you? Besides the historical connection. Why you?" Jacob waited for his answer.

Lazlo continued, "Because only a true *White Lighter* could release her from her torment."

Then Jacob asked another question.

"So, do you intend to release her?" He looked extremely concerned.

Lazlo, staring at the bottle in his hand, calmly responded, "It is done. I already gave her the freedom that she desired."

It felt like the air had been sucked out of the room! Almost everyone gasped at the thought of it. But Lazlo quickly calmed them saying that Hecate was not evil, she was a neutral balance for the world. She has done and will continue to do wonderful things for mankind. Lazlo then looked at Jacob.

"Not to worry. The curse of the *Hope Diamond* is no more. It was lifted while we were in Greenland." Then he added with a smile, "No extra charge." Lazlo finished his beer and asked the staff to leave them. Once more he looked at Jacob.

"So, do we still have a deal?"

He signaled to Diego to unlock the safe and collect the diamonds for viewing.

"Feel free to inspect them as you wish," Lazlo suggested to his guest. Jacob motioned for his team and one member came forward with a special briefcase with obvious equipment for the task.

After a detailed inspection that included diamond testing for hardness, color charting, weights on each stone, clarity rates, and every other possible examination, Jacob held each one in his own hands and admired them under a jeweler's lamp with magnification. "Exquisite!" That was the best word that he could think of.

Jacob Blaustein then stood up and turned to Lazlo Somogyi, who was also now standing, offering his hand for a formal handshake while saying, "Doctor Somogyi…yes, we absolutely have a deal! Thank you. Thank you to your family and to your ancestors, too. László Joseph Biro was a true artist!"

Another member of Jacob's team stepped forward with a carrying case that contained the stocks and other documents to finalize the transaction. Lorenzo's lawyers approached to authenticate the paperwork.

This officially made Lazlo Joseph Somogyi a multi-millionaire! Doctor Somogyi. Sir Lazlo Somogyi, the millionaire businessman.

The world was most certainly about to embrace a multifaceted Renaissance Man.

The Spirit of Christmas
CHAPTER 37

The events from yesterday still had everyone at the Hacienda in a festive mood. Everyone had high hopes for the future of their new American family member and his new bride, Maria. Talk of the business transaction being done in front of general staff members, servants in the eyes of many, was unheard of. This was an absolute first at the Cordova Valdez Hacienda.

Lazlo Somogyi seemed to be writing the book on various first-time events in his life thus far. For Lazlo, it kept things interesting.

Jacob Blaustein decided to accept the hospitality of the Cordova Valdez family and Lazlo. He stayed on the grounds to enjoy the weather, the food, and his newfound friends in Granada. Clayton and Maria gave him the grand tour of the grounds including the equestrian section that housed Hernando and two dozen other beautiful horses.

Before leaving with Maria, Jacob saw Lazlo playing fetch with his dog, Blackie.

"They are wonderful creatures, are they not?" He casually commented to Lazlo. "Loyal, dedicated, loving…who could ask for more?"

Lazlo agreed as Blackie returned the ball to his master and friend.

Jacob turned to walk away but Lazlo spoke softly to him. "I believe in those traits in people, too. Dedication to a cause. Loyalty without question. And love to hold it all together."

Jacob smiled. "I couldn't agree with you more."

Lazlo decided to share another bit of honest information with Jacob in reference to their transaction.

"I mentioned to you that the diamond in the display at the Smithsonian is not the *Hope*. I believe that you may have noticed a glitch of sorts that alerted you to the possibility. If so, your feelings were correct. However, the trickery is not electronic, or film imaging like one might think. It truly is magic created by the Goddess Hecate. She did it so that I would have the opportunity to walk away with the real diamond that you now own. As long as no one attempts to remove the image on display, it should stay as it is for a time unknown to anyone but the goddess. To me, it matters not. The institution didn't really own it anyway. In effect, it was just on loan. Now it is yours. Enjoy it, my friend." Lazlo smiled and walked away.

Blackie followed Lazlo as he meandered through Juana's garden. Lazlo found the garden to be therapeutic for him these days. It helped him to relax. Time spent with his dog also benefited him. Lazlo quite literally learned to take time to smell the roses. Even though they did occasionally make him sneeze. He recalled how easily he forgot about Clayton's dedication to him and his cousin Maria. It was far too easy to take those for granted around you and he vowed to never let it happen again.

Lazlo remembered his promises to pay back all those who assisted him in his quest. Even the ones that said financial compensation simply wasn't necessary. He would make things good in his own heart and reward them in many different ways. Janos and Eleanor were at the top of his list. Eztar and Julius too. He thought about his mental list. Dr. Steven and Martha Sherlous could not be forgotten. And even Laird Conner and his family. Lazlo felt a special love for them all and he wanted to show it to them in much more than mere words. He would give them cash. A pre-Christmas gift and thank you to everyone. He would make this the best Christmas they ever had or even dreamed of.

Lazlo needed to hire one of Lorenzo's attorneys and make this happen quickly as December was arriving fast. Then he remembered Marge, his favorite waitress at the truck stop north of Ward, West

Virginia. He wanted to thank her too and make her life a bit easier. Lazlo went into the house and created a written list of his Christmas gifts that needed legal attention. It read as follows:

1. Eztar and Julius Somogyi - 1 million dollars
2. Eleanor and Janos Vestourgume - Five hundred thousand dollars
3. Clayton Middleton - Five hundred thousand dollars
4. Steven and Martha Sherlous - Seven hundred fifty thousand dollars
5. Laird Conner - Fifty thousand dollars

And lastly, for now, Marge - Ten thousand dollars as a tip from a perfect stranger. Lazlo would need to investigate her last name and contact information. This all needed to happen quickly, and he wanted very expensive formal-looking cards to be sent to each family or person who was on the list. In several cases, bank accounts would need to be created in their names and direct deposit would be made to allow them to clear for spending.

These would be his personal Christmas cards to everyone. People like the Cordova Valdez family were already rich. Each would receive a similar Christmas thank you, but personal presents would never be under their trees on Christmas Day. This was indeed going to be his best Christmas ever! He planned to purchase a bicycle for Lucas. It would be his first. Lazlo was truly feeling like Old Saint Nick. The Christmas spirit was upon him.

It was difficult to believe how quickly time was passing and just how much had happened in Lazlo and Maria's lives. It had been almost a month since their wedding day and every day was filled with new challenges.

Lazlo needed to return to Greenland before the holidays to check on the progress of his research facility and the cabin that he was having constructed. He promised Clayton that this time, they would travel together. Lazlo had some reservations about asking Maria to stay behind on this trip. For one thing, he didn't want her to see their house before it was completed. Second, he thought that stealing her away from family just before Christmas just wouldn't be fair to her.

Maria loved shopping with her Momma.

Lazlo decided that he needed to ask her soon, as preparations needed to be made, and time was running out.

Clayton was looking for Lazlo and stumbled upon him as he lounged in the dining area of the Hacienda.

"Just the man that I want to see!" Lazlo stood up to greet his cousin. "I was just thinking about you, Clayton. We have a trip to plan. If you're still interested?"

"Absolutely, buddy! I wouldn't miss it for the world!"

Lazlo said, "Clayton, don't tell Maria yet." He explained that he thought Maria should stay home this time. Christmas was coming and he knew that she loved it. He had been putting off his request in fear that she might get her feelings hurt if asked to stay. A trip to the polar north with a buddy in December seemed much more like a "crazy man-party" anyway. Maria probably wouldn't care for the atmosphere.

Lazlo needed to spend some drinking time with the military boys and earn their trust. That kind of male bonding is rarely understood by most women, just like most men really don't understand a bridal shower. Lazlo laughed to himself. Men and women seemed to be from different worlds. Maybe Hecate could share that truth with him one day.

"I'm thinking December 10th through the 17th. That'll get us home for the holidays," he told Clayton.

Clayton agreed that he had no problems with the dates. He really wanted to see Lazlo's private polar world. The trip should be fun.

The two of them decided to tell Maria together. She was in the stable with Hernando.

"Lazlo, is there something wrong?" said Maria.

After witnessing Lazlo's feeble way of starting the conversation, Clayton abruptly jumped in and said, "Damn it, Lazlo! Just ask her the *fricking* question! She already married you for Christ's sake! *That* was the big question! This is nothing!"

Maria looked puzzled.

Clayton continued, "Maria, we need to go up to Greenland this month. December 10th through the 17th. Lazlo needs to check on some things. Because of pre-Christmas activities, he thinks you should stay home this time but doesn't want to hurt your feelings."

"Awww," cooed Maria. "That's so sweet! Of course, I'll stay home. You boys have fun freezing your cajónes off!" Then she laughed and kissed Lazlo on the cheek.

"That was *fricking* easy, wasn't it? Damn Lazlo, you need to learn a little more about women. Maria is a piece of cake!"

Lazlo looked at the ground and responded, "Yeah, I guess so. Thanks, Clayton." Deep inside Lazlo knew that Clayton was right. Maria was everything that Lazlo could ever imagine that he could want. In his eyes, she was worth far more than any diamond. She was truly his 'priceless gem'.

The week prior to their flight passed at a blinding rate of speed. Before he knew it, they were counting the hours to their departure. It was an early morning flight. Their arrival in Greenland would also be in the early morning the following day. Lazlo had checked the flight crew information and discovered that his old friend, Captain Franklin Darda, and his crew would control the trip. Lazlo looked forward to seeing him again.

It wasn't long before the friends were boarding the big plane. Lazlo asked for Captain Darda. He wanted to introduce Clayton and admittedly had hopes to fly the plane at some point.

Darda left the cockpit and immediately walked straight to Lazlo with a heartfelt hello and handshake. "Welcome back, my friend! I believe that I promised you another flight lesson. So, who is your friend?" Lazlo introduced his cousin and best friend, Clayton, and explained that he was also his security officer.

"Would there be room for both of us up front somehow? I'd love for Clayton to get a front-row seat!"

Darda smiled and said, "Well…technically no. There isn't enough room really. But for you, Dr. Lazlo? We will make an exception. Come on. Join me in the cockpit."

Everyone settled in and Captain Darda allowed Lazlo the co-pilot seating. Clayton took the bulkhead seat and William, the co-pilot, stood while bracing himself with the ceiling of the plane. Darda taxied to the end of the runway and turned "Big Betty" into the wind. Lazlo was holding the wheel to experience every sensation.

"Go ahead," shouted Darda over the sound of the engines. "Throttle her up! Watch the tach! Keep her just under the red line!"

Lazlo couldn't believe it. He was in total control of the massive engines as he brought them to life. Darda released the brakes and "Big Betty" roared.

"Pull back on the yoke! Hard! As hard as you can, this is a short runway!" Lazlo did as he was instructed, and the big bird almost effortlessly lifted into the sky. Darda showed Lazlo how to level off the plane and it was executed to near perfection. Lazlo looked back at Clayton who was grinning from ear to ear.

"Holy shit, man! Now you're a *fricking* pilot! What's next?"

"Lazlo had no idea. But he was enjoying life while trying to explore the possibilities. Whoever said that you could only live one life in this world? Every life has many chapters. Lazlo intended to live his life to the fullest. Clayton was starting to realize that about his friend and he admired him for it.

The flight to Greenland was long and uneventful. Lazlo took the time to learn more about flying and for the most part, stayed up front with Captain Darda. Clayton was back and forth between his assigned seating and the cockpit. Lazlo was learning a lot and asked if he could attempt the landing for fuel in England. Captain Darda suggested that due to it being a public airport, perhaps he could just assist on this one, but the smaller airport in Greenland offered other possibilities. Lazlo was thrilled.

Preparation for a landing was an intensive series of checks and rechecks to make sure that everything to assure safety was being addressed. Attempting this endeavor with a co-pilot with no real experience was beyond dangerous.

Somehow, Darda believed in this Somogyi character. He has seen many 'wanna-be' pilots fail attempting less than the airport in England. Captain Darda felt that Somogyi had what it took to be successful at his attempt. What Lazlo didn't know was that even though his new pilot friend advised him that he would be merely assisting in landing the plane, truth be told, he planned on actually letting Lazlo do it by himself. Darda would watch carefully and talk Lazlo through it, but he would only pretend to maintain control from the pilot's seat. Unless the event failed terribly, Lazlo would land 'Big Betty' by himself.

"Alright…are we ready?" Darda asked Lazlo.

"I'll handle radio traffic. OK?" Lazlo nodded.

"Take the yoke!" Darda would continue with instructions.

"Flight number 6GS754 requesting runway assignment to London Tower, we are approaching your coordinates from 20 miles due south at 15,000 feet and descending."

The London Air Traffic Controller responded, "Roger 6GS754, received your information and have you on radar, begin your descent to 10,000 ft and slow your speed by 20%. You are clear for approach on runway 3a."

Darda advised Lazlo to throttle back the engines to an airspeed of 250 knots. At this point, their descent will average approximately 1500 feet per minute. Flight management systems would assist controllers on radar to bring the plane to landing speed.

"I'll handle the headings, you handle the engines and altitude… we'll both brake! Okay?!"

Lazlo nodded again. He was having the time of his life. Clayton was thrilled and scared all at the same time. Lazlo continued to amaze him!

Certain auto-pilot controls were enabled by Darda to assist Lazlo in slowing the big plane. They needed to touch down at roughly 130 knots per hour or 140 miles per hour. It needs to start to happen now.

Lazlo maintained his composure and executed every instruction that he received like a pro! Darda, like Clayton, was also very impressed with his natural abilities.

Lazlo started to see the city lights of London up ahead. He briefly noted several landmarks that he recognized from books. He searched for the airport that was hidden within the endless man-made structures that crowded the landscape.

Finally, his eyes adjusted to the search, and it appeared! Darda was lining up the aircraft to a strip with big white numbers printed on the ground, 3a. Lazlo knew that was their target. The plane slowed to 130 knots!

"Pull up her nose a bit!" called out Captain Darda. Lazlo complied and the front of the plane lifted slightly. "Now reduce her power a notch, I have the flaps!" Darda responded, "Great job!"

You could hear the thrusters reverse making the engines scream…

"Brake with me!" Darda called out to Lazlo!

The entire aircraft shuddered in unison with the engines singing and their forward momentum quickly slowing to a crawl.

"Watch that guy with the flags. He'll direct us to the terminal for fuel." Lazlo was grinning. "Just like a car, steer her in that direction. Just watch the wings." Darda was giving Lazlo more than he had originally planned. He really was good.

Lazlo was experiencing an adrenaline rush like he had never felt before! His senses were on high alert and he found himself wanting more. While the plane was being refueled, he took a moment to reflect on everything that had been happening. His mind wandered to Hecate. Lazlo concentrated on her image and she came to him in subconscious thought.

Hecate spoke, *"Yes, my love. You have done well. What is it that you desire beyond what you have achieved?"*

Once again, Hecate knew the questions before they were ever asked.

"No, this was not in any way my doing. This was all of your own accord. You have the ability in you to do anything that you so desire. All human beings share this trait but most will never attempt to achieve it. Only the special ones experience the inner fire that drives them. Cultivate it. Treasure it. And you will go far." And as quickly as she had arrived, Hecate was gone.

Clayton spoke and broke Lazlo's trance. "Hey, man. Where were you? That was so fucking cool brother! I can hardly believe what I just witnessed. You did great, buddy. Where were you a minute ago anyway?"

Lazlo calmly hesitated to clear his head. "I just shared a telephone call with a goddess." Lazlo softly laughed.

Captain Darda immediately addressed Lazlo after securing the plane and beginning fueling procedures.

"Seriously Doc, as a non-trained person attempting to fly for the first time? I've never seen anything like it. You really are a natural. You must have flown spaceships or something in another life." Darda shook his head in disbelief. As crazy as that sounded, Lazlo wondered if there was any truth to the, "in another life" part of the equation.

Lazlo decided that he needed some rest. After all, he had stayed awake for the first leg of their journey. Captain Darda would most likely allow for a pilot change himself at some time soon. It was a long trip and safety mandated that they at least follow some protocol on flight regulations. Even if they did just violate a major rule by allowing Lazlo to experience what he just did. It would be their little secret as the few passengers on board had no idea what had just happened.

Clayton and Lazlo reclaimed their seats in the passenger section of 'Big Betty'. They spoke for a time together and after the second takeoff of the trip, they both fell asleep. Time would pass quickly this way. Before they knew it, they had landed in Greenland.

Great Gains, A Terrible Loss
CHAPTER 38

Lazlo woke to the plane touching down at the Kangerlussuaq Airport. His immediate thought was that he had missed the landing and felt disappointed. Clayton saw the despondent look on Lazlo's face and knew immediately what it was.

"Hey, man. Don't worry. Darda had the flight attendant check on you and you were out cold. He figured you needed your rest. After all, that thing you did in London rocked! What more do you expect from that guy?" Lazlo knew that Clayton was right. It was time to get things moving forward at the Research Facility here in Greenland.

After some basic pleasantries with the flight crew, Lazlo and Clayton left the plane. Lazlo knew that he would be seeing Darda again very soon.

Once on the tarmac, the pair was met by Lazlo's old friend, Peder. Lazlo introduced him to his cousin as they were escorted to the hotel and each of them was set up with a private room. Clayton was amazed at the facility. The military really outdid themselves. Considering the buildings were constructed in the 1940s.

Peder didn't bother wasting time with registration paperwork as he knew who they were and that Lazlo was good for the payment and much more. He gave Clayton and Lazlo their keys, advised them that the kitchen was open, and went on with his other duties.

Clayton really didn't know what to expect when he opened the door to his room, but his reaction was a positive one. "Wow, this place is really *fricking* cool!" He went straight to an authentic whale harpoon hanging on one wall. Clayton touched the tip of the blade, and it cut his finger. A few drops of blood dripped to the floor. "Damn," was all that he could say as he placed his fingertip to his mouth to stop the bleeding. "This sure beats the hell out of our old dorm room back at the university." Clayton looked around briefly, tossed his bag on the bed while taking note of the Musk Ox skin bed cover. He went to find Lazlo so they could get a bite to eat.

Lazlo opened the door to his room after Clayton knocked.

"Come on in, cousin. I'll just be a minute or two." Lazlo was unpacking his luggage.

"There is no wonder that you like this place so much! I mean shit, the decor is an 1800s man cave! I love it!" said Clayton and Lazlo agreed.

"So, let's go get something to eat! I'm starving! We'll probably run into Darda and his crew, too. He mentioned having a short layover here."

Peder would also be their waiter today and motioned them to a table within speaking distance of Darda and his team, who were already eating their salads.

Lazlo thanked him again and shook hands with Darda as they took their seats. Before seeing the menu, Clayton asked Lazlo if they served whale, seal, or walrus blubber. Lazlo rolled his eyes and responded, "Jesus, Clayton, come on man. It's almost 1968. Burgers and fries, brother!"

Looking at the menu, both men ordered burgers and fries, followed by a slice of pie.

Peder served the meals that he had also prepared and advised them that when they finished, he looked forward to escorting them to the refurbished medical area that would be the research facility for Lazlo's studies.

Clayton took one bite of his burger and his eyes lit up with approval. "What is that taste? I've never tasted a burger so good!" He quickly took another large bite to savor the experience.

Lazlo said that it was Peder's mother's secret recipe. "Nobody knows what's in there. It could be Ox balls for all I know, but the blend *is* perfect."

Peder was available to them before they left the room. Brief farewells were exchanged with the flight crew, and they left the building to brave the cold. At least initially, as they would soon be in Lazlo's favorite arctic vehicle, the 'Weasel'. Lazlo wanted to own one of these things. To him, the 'Weasel' was like a giant Tonka Toy.

Lazlo started the tracked snow tank so the system could warm up. Clayton was thrilled like a child with a new toy. Lazlo knew the feeling.

The initial trip in the 'Weasel' was a short one. It was just a hop to the main building that would house Lazlo's new lab. The military crew had been remodeling things now for a month. Lazlo was curious about their progress.

The second stage of their journey required the off-road abilities of the tracked vehicle. Lazlo wondered if the snow and cold weather had hindered any construction of his new cabin for Maria and himself. He would know soon.

The three men exited their little tank and entered the building. They were greeted by Master Sergeant Robert Applefielt, and his team of ragtag soldiers that Lazlo had met the previous month. Funny, he had three of the armed forces serving in this endeavor. Air Force, Army, and the Navy. Only the Marine Corps was missing. Introductions were made, mostly for Clayton's benefit, but it was obvious that the men wanted to impress Dr. Somogyi. They had turned the lights off so their work couldn't be seen until they gave the nod.

Sergeant Applefielt took the stage to initiate the tour.

"We decided that your research center needed a name and took it upon ourselves. He turned on the lights to reveal a beautifully crafted, rustic wooden sign that fit in perfectly. It read:

Hecate's Hungarian Polar Haven.
Home of Dr. "Stat", Static Lazlo Somogyi.

The artist had carved lightning bolts around the perimeter of the sign and blue static charges throughout the design. Lazlo couldn't help but laugh and he appreciated the effort that it obviously took to craft something that size. It was roughly six feet long.

The room erupted in applause from the military staff. Someone called out, "Speech, speech. Throw us some words, brother!" It was Private Anthony Liberteesta. Lazlo recognized the strong New York accent.

Admittedly, Lazlo felt himself starting to choke up just a bit and took a moment to regain his composure. He looked towards Anthony and questioned, "Did you make this, Tony? It's really beautiful, man."

Tony's response surprised him but they all got a good laugh. "Nah, man. Are you *fricking* kidding? But hey, the 'Dr. Stat' thing? *That* was me. Like, I need a cabin. Stat! I need a lab, stat! Then all that aura shit. Static electricity. Yeah, you get it!" Tony laughed. So did everybody else.

Then Tony added on a more serious note. "Peder carved the actual sign." Lazlo was truly moved.

Lazlo looked at Peder, who was acting modest now.

"Thank you, my friend. It's beautiful. Thank you to everyone. I really appreciate all that you are doing for me and Maria.

Peder's rosy cheeks were even more red now, if that was even possible. He wanted to redirect the group and quickly suggested that they start showing Lazlo and Clayton the facility.

Tony led the way. He advised that it really wasn't that hard with a good team. A lot of paint. Some drywall repair. New-ish furniture. Some basic medical equipment was donated by the US Army. (Tony flexed his fingers rapidly), "You know! The famous five-finger discount! They'll never know!"

They did install signs on the doors to make things look official. A doctor's office for Lazlo. A nicely decorated waiting room with 15 chairs and a TV/reel-to-reel video tape recorder set up for people to watch until called. Two restrooms. Four exam rooms and one unique room with various kinds of interesting equipment inside. The sign on the door said, 'Aura Photography'. Entering the room,

Lazlo immediately saw a "Kirlian Camera System". This one was built especially for Lazlo.

"Thank you. Whoever made this, thank you.

There were several other pieces of equipment that could test and record Bio-Electric Magnetic Fields. Energy Field Imaging was a science barely explored. Lazlo had high hopes of becoming a leader in this field. And what better place than the polar ice cap area of the Earth?

"Gentlemen, it's perfect. Thank you one and all, from the bottom of my heart. So, how about my cabin? Did you get started yet?"

The men all chuckled, obviously keeping a secret. Lazlo wondered if a snowstorm buried it under a drift or something.

"Come on, Doc. We'll show you the damages." It was Tony again. Lazlo was learning that New Yorkers had a weird sense of humor.

Everyone geared up for the cold and climbed into their snow-cats and headed northeast. There was snow as far as the eye could see.

Peder and Lazlo gave Clayton a quick tutorial on the operation of the 'Weasel' and allowed him to give it a try. After all, in this wasteland of snow and ice, there was little that he could crash into once clear of the base. Clayton was operating as the 3rd in a line of 3. It was easy to follow the tracks in the snow.

"Eee-hah!" Clayton sang out like a cowboy in the rodeo. "This thing is a blast!" Lazlo appreciated the boyish charm in his friend. It was a trait they seemed to share.

Now, they began to see a structure up ahead at the base of a small mountain range. There were scattered pieces of heavy equipment around it. Some trucks with tracks instead of wheels, a crane, a front-end loader, and a snow plow/motor grader of some sort. As they got closer, it became clear that an area of about ¼ acre had been cleared to the mineral soil and clay. Recently light snow had partially covered the exposed ground.

Through the blowing snow, Lazlo was able to see the rough details of a completed structure that was his cabin. He was shocked at the work that was finished in a mere month! His new friends had really busted their asses on his behalf.

Everyone unloaded from their snow-cats and ran to the front porch to get refuge from the gusty wind. The structure worked well to offer some protection. Lazlo could see that the team had constructed an actual log cabin for him. It was complete with a large picture window in front and a porch for when the weather was suitable. Tony had already entered the cabin and was starting a fire in the beautiful stone fireplace in the main area of the home. A supply of split wood was already in place, waiting to heat the cabin. Lazlo walked around mentally counting the rooms. Yes, two bedrooms would do nicely. After all, it was just for him and Maria. Possibly his parents, but he truly doubted that they'd make the trip. Each bedroom had its own small wood stove for heat and Applefielt notified Lazlo that a military generator was already installed out back for electricity. The cabin was already partially decorated in the style of "Nanook of the North" but Lazlo was assured that more furnishings were on their way from a local village several miles further east. The locals were embracing their new neighbor from the USA.

Lazlo sat down to regain his composure as he was quite over-whelmed at everything that he was currently seeing here today.

"I am blown away by the amount of work you guys completed in the timeframe given. Truthfully, I had doubts. You guys kicked ass! I'm looking at it and still having a hard time believing it. Thank you! I mean it. Thank you!"

The entire crew could feel his sincerity and it made them all feel worthwhile. It was rare in their military positions that someone higher up the ladder gave praise. They were conditioned to simply follow orders and never be told if their efforts were appreciated. This Lazlo fellow made them feel appreciated. They looked forward to doing additional things for him. Tony made a mental note that there was no way this doctor was born rich. He was far too "down to earth". This Lazlo Somogyi would make a great military leader or maybe even a politician. People liked him.

Lazlo spoke again to the team.

"Okay, housewarming party. My treat: Everybody who did anything on my projects, even the local villagers. Let's plan it for a day with better weather if possible. Peder, can you handle planning it? It needs to be soon because of our travel itinerary. Maybe pull in that big cooker on the trailer that I saw at the base? Money is no object! This will be my thank you to everyone! Hell, we can just put the beer in the snow! Who needs coolers?"

Everyone loved the idea and looked forward to making it happen if the weather cooperated. Lazlo crossed his fingers for luck.

Peder, Lazlo, and Clayton got into the 'Weasel' to head back to the hotel. The team stayed at the cabin to finish a few interior details. Lazlo was more than satisfied with everything that had been done here so far. Everything seemed to be falling into place. On the trip back to the base, Lazlo took in the true beauty of this place. He loved the snow and the cold really didn't bother him at all. He was at ease here. His home away from home.

A few days passed. Lazlo spent much of his time testing the new equipment within Hecate's Haven, as his facility was now being called. His party was a huge success, and the week was coming to a close. The date was December 15th, 1967 and Lazlo was ready for a good night's rest. Getting up early and working late was catching up to him. He was asleep before his head hit the pillow.

As Lazlo sunk into his dream state the number 46 reappeared in his brain. He couldn't imagine what it meant. Then his mind took him to a steel bridge that crossed a river between West Virginia and Ohio. It was cold there too, and snow-covered. Lazlo noted a fair amount of traffic and assumed it was just a busy time of day in this community. Then he saw a figure through the haze. It was perched atop one of the girders that supported the bridge. To Lazlo, it looked like a giant owl! A huge owl, larger than anything that he had ever seen before. It opened its wings that spanned at least 8 to 10 feet. As it flapped its wings, looking almost like a warning to the vehicles below, the figure grew in size. The body elongated in height as the wings grew wider. The creature then grew legs and stood tall over the figures below it in their cars. It screamed a warning but no one seemed to notice. The bridge shook violently as the creature took flight above it. Forty-six! The number repeated itself in Lazlo's mind.

Lazlo woke to a knocking on his door. It was Clayton. He seemed stressed.

"Laz…you have an important phone call at the main desk. It's Maria. Come quickly!"

Lazlo rushed to the phone.

"Hello, Maria. What is it?"

"Lazlo, my love. There's been a terrible accident. A bridge in West Virginia collapsed yesterday over a river. Somehow the structure just failed. It was old. Forty-six people were killed! Lazlo…Steven and Martha Sherlous were in the second car on the bridge. They were both killed. I'm so sorry. I wish that I could be there for you now. I'm sorry, my love. I know what they meant to you. You made them so proud."

Lazlo was stunned and dropped the phone. Clayton picked it up and explained to Maria what had just happened. He had overheard most of what she told Lazlo.

"Clayton…get him home to me fast. He needs me and I want to be with him."

"Sure, cousin. As soon as possible." And they ended the call.

"Hey, buddy. I'm sorry, man. Let's get you back to your room. I need to arrange early transportation out of here with Peder. We'll get you home to Maria."

Once back in his room, Lazlo thought deeply about Hecate. She appeared to him in his mind. *"I tried to warn them all. I sent a messenger to stop them from crossing. They ignored my warning of the upcoming incident. As a goddess, there is still much that we simply cannot do. Preventing tragedy can be one of those things. I did realize, however, that your family members were destined to perish on that day. Sadly, they were meant to die. I was able to remove their life forces from their human forms before their car hit the river. They felt no pain. They witnessed my messenger and simply closed their eyes one last time. Together. Rest easy Lazlo. They are where they should be. Their journey has only just begun. I'm sorry, my love. I'm sorry for them all.*

Mourning Before the Holiday

CHAPTER 39

The news spread quickly throughout the base, the Hacienda, and even the Iceland Air Company. Darda and his team received a special message on the radio while in flight. He even received orders to redirect his flight back to Kangerlussuaq Airport. They were the closest plane that could respond in a reasonable period.

Clayton and Peder were working together to prepare Lazlo for the unscheduled departure back to Granada. The base medic insisted that Lazlo take medication that would relax him and aid him in sleeping for most of the trip. Lazlo was given an injection of *Miltown*, a popular tranquilizer during the 60s. It was like Librium and knocked him out within minutes after boarding the plane. He also gave Lazlo a prescription of the same medicine in pill form, should he need it later. These were commonly referred to as "Happy Pills".

This trip was quiet the entire way. Lazlo simply slept. Clayton moved back and forth between his assigned seating and the cockpit. He stayed with Lazlo until he became very bored and would then visit Darda. Clayton had never seen Lazlo like this before. Steven and Martha Sherlous were like parents to him. This would be very difficult.

For Clayton, the flight seemed long. For Lazlo, quite the opposite. He barely remembered boarding the plane and as they touched down in Granada, he was just waking up. He noticed right away that he had a terrible headache and a sensation called "CottonMouth". He had difficulty swallowing and realized that someone had given him a narcotic drug. Lazlo looked for Clayton, but he wasn't there.

"I feel like shit, man! What the hell is going on?" Then Lazlo remembered the phone call and the accident. Lazlo started to cry. At that moment, he was alone. Clayton was riding in the cockpit and Maria was not on the plane. None of his family was. He took a moment to mourn the loss of two very wonderful people who meant the world to him.

Once again, he experienced a feeling of guilt for neglecting them after attending college. Even at the wedding, he was spread so thin. It seemed that there was never enough time for everyone, and it was difficult to do all of the things with them that you always dreamt of doing. Lazlo contemplated how he could remedy that situation. Hecate implied that he would now be long-lived. Eztar too. Maybe even Lorenzo. Just how long *was* long-lived?

As the plane taxied on the tarmac, Lazlo saw several sedans and a limo that he recognized as being Cordova Valdez vehicles. He saw Maria get out from one of them and start running towards the parking/fueling area for the jets. Lazlo needed to hold her and to be held by her. Time without her left a serious void in his soul and his heart. He experienced similar pain over the loss of his adoptive parents. At least Maria was still here to share his life with him. Steven and Martha were gone.

As Lazlo exited the plane and started his descent to the tarmac, Maria raced up the gangway to meet him in the middle. She could wait no longer!

Maria hugged her husband lovingly and kissed him while blocking the stairs. "I have missed you, my love! I'm so sorry about the accident, truly, I am. They were wonderful people. I enjoyed them being here after our wedding trip north. Our time was limited but it was wonderful!"

Lazlo asked if the cash Christmas gift had been sent yet. Steven and Martha had no children and that was a lot of cash to get into the wrong hands. Luckily, her response was "No, not yet". Lazlo decided then and there to donate the money to the hospital where Steven had worked for so long, near Ward. Maybe suggest building a children's wing in the Sherlous name? Maria liked the idea too and told Lazlo to "consider it done".

Maria urged Lazlo into the limo where Blackie was waiting for him. She knew that he'd love to hold his dog again.

Lazlo didn't even notice who else was in the other cars. They didn't seem to think it was important to make themselves known. It was time for Maria to console her husband, and she did.

The small convoy left the airport and headed home to the Cordova Valdez Hacienda. Lazlo needed his rest and time to think about what happened and what would happen next. His head was still in a fog.

Christmas Snow

CHAPTER 40

Lazlo woke up the following day torn with grief over the loss of Martha and Steven Sherlous. They were very dear to him and so far, their bodies had not been recovered from the river. Tons of metal debris from the bridge buried many cars on the bottom in thick mud and silt. The freezing temperatures also made recovery almost impossible. For now, the words from Hecate gave him the only solace that he would experience regarding their deaths. It was almost Christmas and Lazlo didn't want to destroy such a special holiday for those that still lived in his daily existence. He made up his mind that he would refocus on the holidays and do his best rendition of a local Kris Kringle that he could create. Lucas needed a wonderful Christmas. So did his parents. Hell, we all need one Lazlo thought to himself. He needed a plan.

Lazlo was already gifting quite large sums of money to his loved ones. But he wanted to do something extraordinary, especially for his Maria. His initial idea was a crazy one, but he thought that anything was possible with a real goddess in his corner. *Has it ever snowed in Granada?* He needed to find out.

After speaking to everyone that he could find, he learned that it was extremely rare to have snow in Granada. On average Granada might get one snow day per year, and rarely over 1/2 inch. The temperatures also made it melt within several hours. That simply would not suit his purposes. A White Christmas here really was almost impossible. But Lazlo was now gifted with his own magical abilities.

To get started, Lazlo approached Lorenzo asking if they planned to decorate the Hacienda for the festivities. Lazlo wanted the place to look like a winter wonderland. Lorenzo's hesitation gave him his answer and now he knew that his gift to their city would be very fine indeed. He wanted everyone in the city to celebrate. But the Cordova Valdez Hacienda would be his focal point.

Lazlo called Lorenzo, Diego, and Clayton to a meeting to share his idea. It would be a wild one.

Lazlo explained that he wanted Granada to experience its first White Christmas. Not just the snow mind you, but planning for it in advance for decorations, gifts, and food would allow it to become something unique. "Where can we get a big sleigh for Hernando to pull? Maria will love it!" Lazlo hesitated.

"What?" Lazlo was looking into blank eyes. Clayton was the first to speak.

"Are you fucking crazy? What are you talking about man? You're going to make it snow? Right. Cold day in hell."

Lazlo looked at the older gentlemen for support. Diego spoke first. "Are you thinking that Hecate would help you with something like this? I mean…if that's the case, anything can happen I guess."

Lazlo smiled. "That was my idea."

"*Oh ye of little faith,*" he thought to himself.

Clayton asked for a demonstration before getting the entire community on board. Lorenzo agreed.

Lazlo closed his eyes to contact his queen. In moments she joined him. Hecate knew that these mortal men wished to challenge her with a trivial task such as the weather. Her immortal pride was wounded and as a test for her champion, she sent a message to Lazlo's mind. It was pleasant but short, and sweet.

"*Do it yourself, my love.*" Hecate then severed contact and left Lazlo to think about what just happened. *Could he do this?*

There was only one way to find out. Lazlo asked Clayton to check on the weather outside. Clayton looked out the window and reported that the skies were clear as crystal and temperatures were maybe 40°F.

"So now what?" Clayton asked.

Again, Lazlo closed his eyes and drifted into a visionary state. His eyelids noticeably flickered in his deep state of self-awareness. Clayton noticed the wind picking up outside. Trees were beginning to bend under the force. He opened the front doors and became aware of a drop in temperature. Diego and Lorenzo joined him.

The clouds darkened. An obvious storm was building. The trio couldn't believe their eyes. Then it began to snow! Huge white inch-sized flakes drifted down on Juana's landscaping! In minutes everything started to turn white.

When Lazlo woke from his trance, the entire ordeal stopped. The snow quickly melted. No one else on the Hacienda grounds had witnessed the event.

Diego looked at Lazlo. "That was all you? Not Hecate?"

Lazlo smiled.

"So will you help me create the best Christmas that Granada has ever had?"

Everyone said yes, without hesitation.

"Remember… This is a gift for Maria. Tell no one. Now where can we get that sleigh?"

Diego was the first to reply, "I know a gentleman in Austria that builds those things from scratch. I would guess that he has one or two around his shop, possibly reconditioned for a quick sale. I'll give him a call and see what we can arrange."

Lazlo added that under the circumstances, a lease or a rental would probably make more sense. After all, heavy snow had never happened before in Granada. This would make the news on a world-wide level.

"I want to transform Granada into a Bavarian postcard for Christmas Eve and Christmas Day!" Lazlo was getting excited over the entire project. He also advised Diego that a log cabin had been built in Greenland, also as a gift to Maria. After Christmas, they would again travel north for a holiday vacation, and she would receive her present. Lazlo still needed to contact Peder to have the cabin interior decorated with a tree and local gifts. Lazlo suggested to Diego that

Peder might be able to provide handmade Inuit-style clothing, bed covers, and things of that nature. Diego agreed that it was a fine idea.

Lazlo had a phone call to make.

Lazlo notified groundskeepers and equestrian staff that he wanted the entire Hacienda fully decorated for the holidays. He even wanted Hernando to have his own personal Santa hat. His tack would also need to reflect the holiday spirit with bells. After all, Hernando would be a vital part of this Christmas affair. Lazlo refused to tell them exactly what that just might be. He walked away saying, "Less than two weeks to go. Less than two weeks." Lazlo enjoyed the suspense.

That evening, Lazlo called everyone to the living area of the Hacienda for a Christmas meeting. Lorenzo and Juana were there. Likewise, Eztar and Julius. Clayton took his place near Diego. Slightly late, but there nonetheless, Eleanor and Janos entered the home with Lucas and Blackie in tow. Many of the house staff were still on duty and Lazlo requested that they stay too. Of course, Maria was there.

Once everyone settled in, Lazlo addressed the group.

"Good evening to my family," Lazlo smiled. "This is my first Christmas in Spain. I am truly looking forward to it. It is also my first Christmas when my family and I are no longer poor."

Lazlo hesitated slightly. "I have wonderful memories of Christmas time in Ward. Where Christmas isn't about material things. We couldn't afford them anyway. Christmas was about love and caring. It was about peace on earth and goodwill to all men and women. It was about Kris Kringle and the Christ child. All these things made Christmas what it was to me." Lazlo continued, "But I always wondered what I could do to share all these things and more, if I had the money to do so. My grandfather, László Joseph Biro made it possible for me to experience that emotion this year. I plan to use it to the fullest of my capabilities as a gift to every one of you."

Lazlo added that he would not forget the workers at the Hacienda and that he even had a secret plan for the people of Granada. Most of the family looked at one another in question, having no idea what he could possibly have in mind.

Clayton could simply no longer hold his tongue and blurted

out, "I know what it is!"

Lazlo quickly cut him off saying, "Hold your tongue or lose it! I'll make sure that you get nothing more than a lump of coal from the mines in Ward! Do you understand?"

"Yeah," Clayton somberly replied. "I'm sorry buddy. Your plan is just so cool. I can't stand the waiting."

Lazlo smiled. "It will all happen soon enough." He then turned to Maria.

"My love. I have a present for you too. A very special one. It is waiting for you up in the land of fire and ice. We will visit together for New Year's Eve. I'm told that the color display in the sky will be unsurpassed! It should be something that we have never experienced before!" Lazlo approached her and kissed her forehead.

"So. Momma and Eleanor. You can teach our wonderful kitchen staff how to make Hungarian pastries and cookies. Palacsinta is really good! The Hortobagyi Palacsinta is more like a meal. I love the paprika! It's making me hungry just thinking about it."

Lazlo asked the group if he missed anything, and if he did, could someone please jump in and handle it. Everyone was on board, and all but three others had no idea of what the real surprise would be. This was going to be the best Christmas holiday ever.

Lazlo decided that the first gifts he needed to buy would be for the employees at the Cordova Valdez Hacienda. He didn't know them well enough to purchase personal gifts, but he didn't want everyone to get the same thing either. He considered picking out one item for a man and one for a woman, wrapping the boxes accordingly, and then putting the names on the individual gifts. He would also put a new $100 bill inside of each gift, to help with their own family Christmas. He would later suggest that Lorenzo and Juana do the same thing. Lazlo wasn't trying to show off, or buy favors, he really did mean every bit of this from his heart.

Lorenzo told him that there were 20 employees, in total. This endeavor could get costly, but Lorenzo saw the determined young man was not to be dissuaded. Lazlo already had the heart and soul of Saint Nick.

Lazlo then contacted Peder in Greenland with similar questions. How many people were part of the hotel, the military workers, local tribal people who assisted them, etc.? Peder advised him that there were 12. Lazlo kept notes on everyone.

After much deliberation, Lazlo decided that the one thing every man should own was a high-quality watch. He decided on a watch because as a boy, he never owned a timepiece of any kind.

As an adult Lazlo learned that he simply couldn't keep one running. Even now, watches would perish on his wrist. He researched it and was told that his body produced a strong electromagnetic field that magnetized the watch until it could no longer keep time. His supply of broken watches has proved the theory. The curse of a *White Lighter!*

Still, as a gift, the men would each receive a Rolex Submariner. The kind that the famed Jacques Cousteau wore. At roughly $250 each, with an additional $100 bill, that was a nice present.

Lazlo had already ordered a cherry red 1967 Corvette convertible for Clayton a few weeks ago. It was being shipped to Spain as he contemplated other gifts. Clayton was going to flip!

For the ladies, the $100 bill would also be included. But their primary gift would be a 14-karat gold sapphire necklace that they could treasure. Nothing gaudy. Something quaint, and delicate. One-carat stones should suffice.

Lazlo already spoke to the jewelers who designed Maria's ring. They were working on it so that the necklaces would be ready for the holidays.

Clayton was selected to be Lazlo's 'leg man' for this chore. He would verify the numbers and confirm the orders, including the professional wrapping and the $100 bills, for both watch and jewelry gifts.

Considering the cash presents that Lazlo had already arranged for Christmas, he decided that his family members would not be included in this process.

Except for Lucas. He would get a very fancy new bike. And Blackie another new collar and leash, with a nice chew bone from a pet store!

Lazlo was truly enjoying everything that was leading up to the joyous Christmas Eve and Christmas Day. He also chose to attend a Catholic Mass at the Cathedral with Maria. She would love that.

During a short break, while trying to enjoy some free time, Lazlo decided to contact Hecate. When she appeared to him, he reverently asked her, "So, is it at all possible to select a Christmas gift for a goddess? And if so, what would be an appropriate one, my priestess?" Hecate was pleased with her champion and while smiling answered, *"You have already done it."*

Lazlo continued to talk to her.

"Thank you, my queen. While I doubt you even celebrate the birth of another god figure, the teachings of Christ as a man, led to this holiday of '*Christ*' *Mass.* For most humans, it is more a time of peace and goodwill. The origin becomes blurred and ignored. You would know more than I. So please allow me to wish you a very happy holiday season. I am glad that we connected as we did, and happy to know you in a part of my world."

"Thank you, my love. Please enjoy this new life that you live. Your time here has worn many faces. I like this one."

Before Lazlo could ask what she meant, Hecate was gone.

"What the hell?" Lazlo was confused at that last statement. What did she mean? He could only think that eventually, Hecate would reveal it herself.

Christmas was a mere few days away. The sleigh was delivered but hidden away so that Maria did not know about it. Likewise, Clayton's Corvette.

Lazlo made his rounds everywhere that he could think of. Every structure on the Hacienda property was decorated inside and out. There were Christmas trees in almost every room. The stables were decorated and they too had their own trees in special places.

It was Christmas Eve day and presents seemed to be magically appearing underneath trees everywhere. Lazlo wanted the university decorated too. Diego made sure that it happened. A big green Christmas bow was also installed on the hood of Clayton's new Corvette. Eztar taught the kitchen staff how to make Lazlo's favorite Hungarian sweets. This was going to be a great Christmas. Lazlo placed a call to Greenland to make sure that all of his wishes were accomplished. Peder assured them that it was done. "Merry Christmas, Peder! Give everyone my best! I'll see you all in a week!"

All that was left for today was for Lazlo to relax and summon the cold front and more importantly, the snow!

Diego asked Lazlo for a few free minutes to talk privately. Before he started his weather trance. Diego acted somewhat embarrassed about what he had to say. "I sort of spilled the beans about your plans to a local TV station. They *will* be filming tonight."

Lazlo replied that he honestly had expected Clayton to do it, but no matter. He had already sensed it.

"It's OK Diego. More kids will see it this way on TV. I doubt I can make it snow over the entire city. But who really knows for sure." Lazlo lovingly patted his friend on the back and said, "Merry Christmas, my friend."

Christmas Eve came quickly. The setting sun over the countryside was beautiful. But Lazlo had plans for a very special display that would start with his own light show. He sat down in front of the main house to get comfortable. He asked Diego to call Maria and the rest of the family. Hernando was already being harnessed to pull a beautiful Christmas sleigh. He wore bells on his tack and sported a new Santa Claus hat. He wouldn't be moved, however, until there was sufficient snow on the ground.

Family and staff started to gather. They could sense that Lazlo was up to something big. Lazlo looked at his family. "Merry Christmas! This is your first gift."

Lazlo sat back and closed his eyes. His eyelids began to flicker. Suddenly, the sky became alive with colors! Greens and purples, changing to reds and blues. They seemed to shimmer and dance in the sky. They swirled and intensified. This display was like the canvas of a god.

A news van was at the front gate filming everything. This was the same team that filmed Hecate in the Cathedral. The story was being aired internationally.

Without a cloud in the sky, large snowflakes began to fall. At first, just a few, floating on the wind. Then, more and even more after that.

Everyone was amazed. Eztar and Julius hugged and exchanged a kiss. Juana and Lorenzo did the same. The temperature was dropping at least 5°F per minute. As the ground cooled the snow began to stick. The Hacienda grounds were turning white and in moments it looked like a winter wonderland.

Hernando was ready to make his appearance pulling the sleigh. Out he came, proudly displaying his new carriage without wheels. Maria ran to her horse and took the reins from Hernando's handler. She looked up into the sky as more snowflakes continued to fall. Maria was giddy with joy. "Lazlo, come join me!"

Lazlo woke from his trance and surveyed what was taking place. It was good. "Merry Christmas everyone!

"Now I'm going on a sleigh ride with Maria. We can open presents later, or tomorrow." Lazlo grabbed Blackie and carried him to the sleigh. Maria took the reins and off they went. Channel 8 TV was getting some unbelievable shots. This was the best holiday ever!

Inside, several employees of the Hacienda turned the TV to Channel 8 and they saw a live feed of Maria and Lazlo driving Hernando and the elegant white sleigh around the snowy compound. The contrast of Lazlo holding his pet, Blackie, was a sight to behold, in the dancing flakes." The couple never looked so happy.

The screen-feed split to the recording of the Somogyi wedding in the Cathedral. It clearly showed the image of Hecate towering over the newly married couple. Channel 8 TV then added a third screen that switched to a live reporter at the Cordova Valdez Hacienda. Here was the whole family, in the yard, enjoying a joyous Christmas moment.

A reporter told his TV audience, "Ladies and gentlemen, I am amazed! I personally watched this event unfold tonight ."

The screen cut to an interview with Clayton Middleton, the cousin of Lazlo and Maria Somogyi.

Everyone was gathering around the television when they heard Clayton's name. "Mr. Middleton. You were the best man at the wedding of Maria and Lazlo. Is that correct?"

Clayton answered, "Yes."

The reporter continued, "And you actually witnessed the *so-called* goddess that appeared in front of hundreds of people?"

Again, Clayton answered, "Yes."

"So, tell me, Mr. Middleton, do you *believe* that this is all real?"

"Indeed, I do."

Then the reporter questioned Clayton again.

"Mr. Middleton, may I call you Clayton?" Clayton nodded.

"Clayton. What is really going on here? We're seeing things that have never been seen in Granada. Can you explain? You seem to be very close to Lazlo Somogyi."

"Oh yeah, Lazlo and I are more than cousins by marriage. We're best friends! And you couldn't have a better one."

Clayton started thinking about Lazlo. "He's the best! Salt of the earth and all that! Spiritually, this dude is a *White Lighter!*"

"Excuse me, please, a *White Lighter*? Exactly, what is that?"

"It seems to mean pure heart, white aura, like Christ! Everyone has seen the halos in books and churches. Lazlo really is *a White Lighter*! The dude is pure!"

Clayton went on to answer the first question as to what was going on today.

"All of this is Lazlo Somogyi's gift to the people of Granada, his family and friends. Even to the world, I suppose. He was raised poor in a coal mining town."

"In truth, he believes that Christmas is a special season, no matter your religion. Peace on earth, and all good things. All very real. As a *White Lighter*, he summoned the skies to create the images in his heart. He made it possible for everyone to experience snow on Christmas." The reporter was stunned.

"You're seeing it first hand, man! Merry Christmas! Enjoy the snow!" Clayton left the news crew so that he could catch up with Lazlo and Maria.

"So there you have it, folks. Christmas snow in Granada! And yes, I may be an objective reporter, but I am a believer. Happy Holidays to one and all!" He thought he was no longer being recorded but he was still on the audio feed. He remarked to himself and the cameraman: "I need to go to church more often."

Family members congratulated both Clayton and their reporter friend for a great job. It was Diego who knew you couldn't buy publicity like this. Lazlo would become famous worldwide overnight.

Clayton waved to Maria and Lazlo as they rounded the final turn that was part of the Hacienda driveway entrance. Maria pulled back on the reins to stop Hernando, and he literally skidded on his hooves in the snow. It surprised the big horse, as he had never run in snow before. Both Maria and Lazlo were laughing as Blackie barked at Clayton.

Lazlo called to Clayton, I've got something to show you. "Climb aboard!"

Clayton sat down in the back seat of the sleigh and Maria coaxed Hernando into a trot heading back to the stables. Upon arriving, Maria turned her big horse over to the stable hand while kissing Hernando on the nose. The three friends then took Blackie and headed deeper into the stables to an area under lock and key.

Lazlo called Clayton over to a locked compartment that supported two wooden doors that were obviously large enough for a big cart or similar-sized object to be inside. While unlocking the doors, Maria flipped a light switch for the interior of the room.

"What gives guys?" Clayton was curious about the suspense.

"Close your eyes, cousin. We have a present for you. You're going to love it."

Clayton then heard the sound of a V-8 engine coming to life. He opened his eyes and stared at the most beautiful car in the world, a 1967 ruby-red Corvette Stingray convertible!

Clayton was overwhelmed!

"It's yours, buddy! Merry Christmas! But I wouldn't try to drive her in the snow if I were you. The Corvette has too much rear-wheel horsepower. She'll just spin. Climb in Clayton. She's just like BJ. We can drive together for car shows and other things like that."

Before sitting in his new car, Clayton hugged his two cousins and thanked them both for the wonderful present. He hugged Lazlo longer and harder while saying, "I can't believe it, man. You're really the best!"

"Enjoy it, man! We have other presents to deliver!" They left the stables to return to the main house.

This really was turning into a fantastic Christmas for everyone. Lazlo was fulfilling his childhood dream. And Maria loved to see her husband happy. Yes, it was a wonderful evening!

Lazlo and Maria made their rounds, making sure that everyone there received their selected gifts from the couple. It was a great feeling to make others so happy. Lucas loved his new bicycle, Blackie loved his chew bone, and everyone else was thrilled with their gifts from this wonderful American. Several people became rich that night including Eztar and Julius.

Maria and Lazlo decided to attend a Christmas Eve mass at the Cathedral where they were married. People already recognized Lazlo and flocked to him for his autograph and requests for magical blessings in his name. Word was spreading fast.

Lazlo looked at Maria and announced to her that he had a present for her too. But it was in Greenland. He had left it there when he heard the news of his adoptive parents dying in the tragic accident at the bridge in West Virginia. "Actually, my love, we leave the day after Christmas for Greenland. I need a break and a chance to emotionally reset." Lazlo then hugged Maria and presented her with a 14-karat gold, blue sapphire necklace.

"Merry Christmas, babe! I'll love you forever!" Maria squealed like a schoolgirl! And Lazlo loved her even more for that.

Sorpresas Duales

CHAPTER 41

Before the couple even knew it, they were boarding their jet for Greenland. Time always seemed to be running in 'fast forward' for Lazlo and anyone associated with him. He wondered if this had something to do with his extended lifespan that was gifted to him by Hecate. There was simply so much to do, and Lazlo wanted to do it all.

Lazlo had hopes before boarding that he would reunite with his old airline pilot friends and crew today. Sadly, Captain Darda and his team were rerouted to another country and couldn't be with Lazlo and Maria for the holidays. Lazlo had hoped to fly the plane again. There would be another time.

They sat down in their selected seats and settled in for the long flight. They would refuel in London with a very brief layover that might allow for time for some old-fashioned English cuisine.

"Lazlo my love, this has been a wonderful Christmas holiday. Thank you. I think that it has been the best of my life. I don't know how you even thought of making it snow or controlling the Northern Lights in Spain. The results were spectacular. And all of the gifts given to friends and family! You made so many people happy! You know, the film that was shown on the news, and Clayton's interview, are already making people believe that you are somehow divine. They have begun to compare you to Christ and within just a few days they were already asking for your blessings. How does that make you feel?

Do you think you can control the stories, these beliefs that you are much more than a mere man? You have always been known to be special. I often wonder just how special you really are, and what your limitations are. Lazlo, you controlled the weather! In certain historical times, that act alone would've labeled you as a god!"

Lazlo acknowledged everything that his lovely Maria had just shared with him. He had a few questions of his own and spoke openly to her.

"Exactly what makes a god, a god? Or a goddess for that matter. History showed us that even Christ walked the Earth as a man and died here because of it. He didn't even live for 40 Earth years. Hecate spans the history of mankind and is found in many works of literature. She truly seems eternal. Yet both claim the mantle of divinity."

Maria listened to everything he said.

Lazlo continued, "History has revealed to us that any *being* having more power or more intelligence than the average human may be classified as being godlike. So-called false gods have been everywhere. Hecate speaks to me as if she knows things about *us* from very long ago. She speaks of the Titans and my being Her champion. She calls you *daughter* and says it with conviction. It truly makes me wonder about Her own origins. Hopefully, I will learn all of this, in time."

Maria and Lazlo talked about their Christmas experience and all of the wonderful things that happened because of it. They were both happy about how everything turned out. Maria was particularly thankful for what Lazlo arranged for her and Hernando. A night that she would never forget.

Hours later their plane landed in London for fuel. They were both so tired prior to landing, that they fell asleep together and didn't even wake up for the touchdown. They even slept through takeoff and finally stirred somewhere over the cold North Atlantic. Both were surprised at just how tired they really were.

Maria decided to read a book to pass the time while Lazlo looked through a newspaper from London. In what seemed like moments, the crew was notifying passengers of their landing in Greenland.

Several minutes to touchdown.

The landing in Greenland was flawless. While collecting their luggage before leaving the plane, Lazlo noticed Peder standing on the tarmac waiting to greet them.

He took them to Room Number One because that had been their honeymoon suite and he knew how much they loved it. After giving them a few moments to treasure their memories, Peder returned to them so that he could escort them to 'Hecate's Haven'. Lazlo wanted to pay for all of his bills-- for construction, decorations, and gifts.

After a quick meal in the hotel restaurant, Peder, Lazlo, and Maria climbed into the 'Weasel' and headed northeast into the frozen tundra. Maria had no idea what was in store for her on this beautiful Christmas week.

Eventually, she could see the form of the log building up ahead in the snow. The entire cabin was shining with flickering Christmas lights. The chimney puffed dark smoke. Maria noticed the large picture window and the partial wraparound porch with heavy Adirondack chairs for viewing the Northern Lights.

As they got closer to the building, Maria could see that it was a beautiful log cabin! It wasn't large, but it was *oh-so quaint*. They got out of the 'Weasel' and walked to the front porch and the large picture window. Inside, Maria saw a Christmas Tree with dozens of presents underneath. It was decorated with white lights, which seemed appropriate for the holiday of a *White Lighter*.

Before going inside, Lazlo stopped Peder and asked him why he brought them to the cabin instead of going to his research center as originally discussed. Lazlo didn't want to ask him in the 'Weasel'. Peder said in a soft tone, "There were a few minor unfinished items at the Haven. The boys are working there now to have it completed soon. I also knew that you didn't need the suite because you had this cabin, but we had to keep it quiet to not give our secret away to Maria." Peder winked at Lazlo as Maria approached them.

"What's going on, boys? Let's go inside. It's cold out here!"

Peder opened the door and Lazlo once again carried his bride over the threshold.

"Merry Christmas, Maria! This is all yours!"

Maria scanned the main room and then went from room to room so she could see everything. "I *love* it!"

"Look at all of the presents! Most of these are handmade!" Peder explained that local native women crafted everything for her and Lazlo. "Everyone loves Lazlo."

Peder excused himself saying," Now, you should have your first night in your new home."

He would return in the morning with other people and two snow-cats. Lazlo could borrow one. For now, they had everything they needed. Peder wished the couple Happy Holidays and turned to leave the cabin. Maria thanked Peder for his help.

"I love you, husband!" Maria said, with a hug. Lazlo hugged her back and felt the static electric charge that they had shared so many times before. Maria's aura was glowing a beautiful green and Lazlo had a pure white light halo around his entire human form.

The intensity of their aura colors made Lazlo think about his original theories that the Aurora Borealis is connected to the human aura. He looked out the window of their cabin and the sky was aflame. Vivid colors were dancing in the heavens to match the electromagnetic fields created by the two young lovers.

Lazlo urged Maria to brave the cold for a better look, so they did. The skies were breathtaking! Colors reflected off of the snow! This is why Lazlo chose the area north of the polar icecap for his research. These exhibitions were a regular part of living in the northern lands. Lazlo was truly humbled by this experience he was sharing with his wife.

Maria and Lazlo sat together on the front porch of their new cabin. Lazlo looked at Maria and said, "This is perfect, isn't it? The perfect home away from home for the two of us. Life couldn't get better!"

Maria glanced into the picture window of the cabin, thinking she saw movement out of the corner of her eye. What she saw, but didn't mention to Lazlo, was the reflection of a smaller figure, surrounded in a beautiful green aura, intently observing the two of them watching the sky.

Maria said, "Lazlo my love, I have another surprise for you."

Hecate flew over their new home on the winds of the Aurora Borealis. She watched over Her *daughter* and Her *champion*. Hecate knew that this was not the end.

It was the beginning of new adventures, new knowledge, and new lives. She would always be there for them. She would always protect them. Lazlo released Her from Her prison. Hecate would introduce Her *champion* to life and the blessing that She had bestowed upon Maria months earlier.

Maria smiled, "Life is going to get so much better, and she took his hand and placed it gently on her abdomen. Marta will be joining us soon and our lives will become the kind in which epic tales are written. And through Hecate, we will be reborn in the glory that once was, in another time. Together. Always."

Be watching the skies and bookstores for Part 2 of *The Aurora Aura*. Join Maria, Lazlo, and daughter Marta as we follow their lives and adventures together under the protection of the Goddess Hecate. Learn with them, who they really are in the scope of the universe as we understand it. Watch Lazlo being reborn as the great leader that he already was in several other lifetimes! Join us, won't you? We're counting the centuries.

A Word from the Author

My given name is Mark Joseph. The name is biblical in origin. My father was Joseph and my mother was Esther. While my current novel is fictitious, the characters are based on actual relatives on my mother's side of the family. Her given name was Eztar. As a child, it was changed to Esther to conceal her Hungarian, gypsy heritage, after the Biro family moved to America.

- Lazlo was a cousin.
- Julius was my uncle.
- Joseph was my uncle.
- Eleanor was my cousin.
- Eztar, as mentioned, my mother.
- Joseph, as mentioned, my father.
- Michele is my cousin.

Laszlo Joseph Biro was a distant relative that indeed did invent the ballpoint pen in 1938.

Several names throughout the book are old friends from school. Dino and Gino for sure.

The original Esther Biro was my grandmother. She was born a Lukas.

I selected King Louis of France because he had connections to the giant blue diamond that started the history of the Hope Diamond. The curse is said to be real.

My cousin and one uncle were/are named Louis.

When I was born, it was actually the doctor who delivered me in 1958 who requested my parents allow him to adopt me. He and his wife could not have children and my parents already had a son. He wanted to send me to Johns Hopkins University to become a doctor. My mother refused. Yes, his name was Sherlous.

Maria translates to Mary. I had several Aunt Marys but all have passed at this time.

For animal lovers…Blackie was real and belonged to my mother.

My father, Joseph, was actually the gem cutter.

The coal mines in West Virginia are real.

The Hope Diamond is also real.

Once upon a time, I was a practicing jeweler and a graduate of an International Jewelers Academy. My business was called The Good Goldsmith. I left the trade for the same reasons my character in this novel did.

The Chapter 38 collapse of the bridge in West Virginia really did happen on the date listed. Close to 50 people perished. Witnesses did indeed report seeing a giant owl-like creature perched on top of the structure before it fell. Hecate? You be the judge.

For whatever it may be worth, I currently drive an older white

Corvette that I call 'Baby Jane'. BJ for short. I love old cars! People think that I named her Baby James, of James Taylor fame. I did not. Maria's mother's name, Juana, translates to Jane. Simple enough.

In Chapter 37 Lazlo spends some time with a new friend, Captain Darda. He allowed Lazlo to fly his airplane. I've been told by an editor that this chapter is impossible and unrealistic. Sorry folks. It's true. I grew up with Darda. Sadly, he was murdered at an ATM while making a deposit. I have personally flown two planes in my lifetime without formal training. I also know four other gentlemen currently in my life who have done the same. It's not all that strange.

"Big Betty" was actually my Aunt Betty. Our family had two Bettys. The older one was called "Big Betty", and the younger one was, well, "Little Betty." I named the airplane after the older one. "Big Betty" was sort of loud…like the plane. I thought it fit. God bless her.

I was personally introduced to the tracked vehicle called a Weasel, when I moved to the Rocky Mountains in 1978, I met a fellow there who owned one. I loved that thing! I thought that Greenland needed one too.

Paranormal happenings are real. One simply needs to pay attention to the world around you.

I hope that you enjoy my book. I have reached deep into my heart to produce it and share it with you.

Thank you. Be well…

Mark